POLARIS

POLARIS

MINDEE ARNETT

Balzer + Bray
An Imprint of HarperCollinsPublishers

Library of Congress Cataloging-in-Publication Data
Arnett, Mindee.
    Polaris / Mindee Arnett. — First edition.
        pages   cm
    Summary: "Jeth Seagrave and his crew of mercenaries are pulled into
one last high-stakes mission"—Provided by publisher.
    ISBN 978-0-06-223563-3
    [1. Mercenary troops—Fiction.   2. Space ships—Fiction.   3. Brothers
and sisters—Fiction.   4. Life on other planets—Fiction.   5. Freedom—
Fiction.   6. Science fiction.]   I. Title.
PZ7.A7343Pol   2015   2014022111
[Fic]—dc23   CIP
                                                                   AC

Typography by Ray Shappell
15 16 17 18 19   PC/RRDH   10 9 8 7 6 5 4 3 2 1
❖

First paperback edition, 2016

To Jay, for believing every time

CHAPTER

01

THE SPACEPORT'S CASINO WAS THE PERFECT SPOT FOR THE deal to go down.

Jeth Seagrave knew it the moment he stepped inside. The place seemed to envelop him, the lights so bright they made it almost impossible to see and the noise a constant vibration, everything from the hum of the slot machines to the shouts of dealers calling for bets. Some kind of mild, hypnotic music played in the background, blending the sounds together in a reassuring soundtrack—*time does not exist here,* it seemed to intone. *Here you are safe. Here you belong.*

Jeth knew better. There was nothing safe here. Everything was suspect, and that was all right. His shady dealing would be one among dozens.

He made a casual scan of the room, getting his bearings in the maze of tables, gaming booths, and gamblers. Then he turned to the right and headed for the casino cage, which held more than a dozen cashier windows. Even though Jeth had seen his share of casinos, he couldn't help but be impressed by the size of this place. Of the few Independent spaceports in the galaxy, Nuvali was the biggest and the hardest to get to, which gave it the dubious honor of being the favored hub for drifters, criminals, and expatriates seeking refuge from the tyrannical reach of the Interstellar Transport Authority.

A sardonic smile crossed Jeth's face as he realized he could be described by all three. But any humor he might've felt at the notion dissolved at once. For the last eight months the ITA had been hunting him and his crew. Life on the run was wearisome and fraught with sacrifice. Even now his belly felt like a pinched, hollow ball. He hadn't eaten since yesterday, and that meal had hardly been enough to take the edge off his hunger, let alone assuage it.

The smells in this place weren't helping. The sweet, sharp aroma of steak frying in garlic butter, the salty tang of roasting peanuts, and half a dozen other scents, wafted out of the kitchen entrance a few meters down from the cage. Jeth sucked back saliva and fought off the almost overwhelming urge to forget the deal and just enjoy his first full meal in weeks.

Except he wouldn't. There were cheaper ways to eat, and despite his protesting stomach, he hadn't yet reached the limit of his endurance.

Jeth stopped in front of the first open cashier and pulled a roll of unis out of his left pocket. "Two thousand, with a sixty-twenty-twenty split, hundred high," he said. This was the last of the reserve money. He didn't want to gamble with it, but he had to play the part until Wainwright arrived. He had a couple hundred in his boot, just in case, but that was it. *It won't matter if I lose some,* he reassured himself. *Just so long as the deal goes down the way it's supposed to.*

"There you are, luv," the woman behind the counter said as she finished loading the carrier with his requested breakdown of tokens. She smiled broadly at him, her teeth artificially bright in the lights overhead.

Jeth cracked the knuckles of his left hand and schooled his expression to something close to eager. Time to play the part. He picked up the carrier and turned back to the action on the floor. He did another sweep, this time searching for a game to join.

His gaze slowed when he spotted two of his crew standing side by side in front of one of the retro slot machines. Sierra and Celeste had arrived some ten minutes before, part of the backup plan in case the deal went sideways. Old habits died hard. Before they'd become fugitives, Jeth and the original members of his crew, the Malleus Shades, had been professional thieves for one of the most powerful crime lords in the galaxy. Tonight they would deal with another criminal organization, and Jeth wasn't leaving anything to chance.

Jeth's breath caught as he watched Sierra raise one slender, bare arm and pull the lever down, setting the digital reels to spinning. He'd never seen her dressed like this, in a glittery, fitted thing that made her look all curves and nakedness. There wasn't any reason for her to dress that way aboard *Avalon*. Spaceships made for cold homes.

Jeth knew that both she and a similarly dressed Celeste were armed, but he couldn't imagine how or where. Well, he *could* imagine it, but this wasn't the time or place for that sort of distraction. Especially when he was carrying two thousand unis' worth of tokens around a roughneck space-port casino without a firearm of any sort. Wainwright's men would surely pat him down before they entered the final stage of negotiations.

As if she sensed him staring, Sierra glanced over her shoulder, her eyes meeting his at once. Celeste caught Sierra looking at him, and she stepped in close to whisper something in Sierra's ear that made a blush blossom over her fair skin and set her to grinning. To an outsider they were just two girls flirting with a stranger.

Grateful for Celeste's ruse, Jeth started to look away, but then he saw her gaze flick past him, her smirk deepening into her own grin. Jeth followed the direction of her eyes and spotted Vince sitting at the bar, his eyes fixed on the video screen overhead while he idly sipped a beer. The personal comm unit hanging from his belt was the backup for the backup plan.

More like the doomsday plan, Jeth thought, noting Vince's position. He doubted Celeste had meant to point Vince out to him. She just couldn't help herself. *No more than you can,* he mused, stealing another peek at Sierra.

Finally moving on, Jeth spotted an open seat at a poker table toward the back, not far from the private rooms where he would join Wainwright later. Exactly how much later, he wasn't sure. Wainwright had been sketchy on the details.

Jeth raised his right hand to his head and pretended to scratch behind his ear, activating the comm patch fixed to his skin. The touch of his cybernetic fingers always brought on a surreal feeling of detachment, as if the hand belonged to someone else. He'd had the prosthesis for more than six months now, but he didn't think he would ever get used to it.

Ignoring the feeling, and the shimmer of painful memories it brought to the surface, he said through the comm, "What's the buy-in three rows from the back, two over?"

"Hang on," Lizzie's voice answered a second later from her position aboard *Avalon*. The ship was moored in one of the short-term docks several floors below, the closest spot they could get to the casino. Not that location mattered so much. Jeth's genius of a little sister could have hacked into the spaceport's security and surveillance systems from anywhere.

"Okay, looks like that table's . . . ouch, a thousand." She paused. "But two down is only five hundred and the guy with the blue hair is just leaving."

"Right," Jeth said, disguising the word as an exhale. He kept his voice low and hardly moved his lips at all. It was a trick he did well, from years of practice. "But give me some help with that omniscient vantage point of yours."

"That's cheating, you know."

"Consider it a tactical advantage, unless you like skipping meals." They might be preparing to make a gold mine of a deal, but they wouldn't be able to access the money right away. It would take time and caution, a transaction like that liable to draw attention. They would need every uni they could hold on to for food, supplies, and fuel.

"Good point." Lizzie fell silent again, but Jeth had heard the hint of something more in her voice and he braced for what was coming next. "Are you sure we want to go through with this?"

Jeth drew a deep breath and let it out slowly. Lizzie had sprung this argument on him yesterday, just moments after they'd finalized the deal to hand over the Mirage Cipher to Wainwright for a three million payoff. The amount wasn't the source of her protest, though it should've been: the cipher would give Wainwright the ability to decrypt all transmissions sent by the Mirage Corporation, including flight path information on shipments. Mirage was the leading weapons manufacturer in the galaxy, making the cipher the proverbial golden goose for a crime lord in the arms business. It was worth double what Wainwright was offering. But criminal beggars couldn't be choosers, and Wainwright's deal was the best they were going to get.

Lizzie's protest, however, was more sentimental.

"I'm sorry," she continued, "but it just doesn't feel right, not knowing what he'll use it for."

"You mean supplying criminals and terrorists with military-grade weapons?" Jeth said as he headed farther into the casino toward the five hundred table.

"To put it *not* mildly—yes."

He sighed. "This is what we do. It never bothered you before, when we were working for Hammer."

"That was different. We didn't have a choice, and it felt less . . . personal."

Jeth didn't respond. He knew exactly what she meant. When they worked for Hammer, it had been like a game. They never had to witness the consequences of their crimes, the impact it had on real lives—people caught in the crossfire of warring gangs, workers laid off when a targeted company chose to cut their losses from the bottom rather than the top. They had just been following Hammer's orders.

Now, the blood would be on *their* hands. Jeth swallowed, the memory of what they'd gone through to get the cipher threatening to upset his cool.

He pushed it away. Yes, the decision to steal the Mirage Cipher and then hand it over to a man like Wainwright hadn't sat well with him either. But there was nothing for it. *The story of my life.*

Wanting to end the argument once and for all, Jeth said, "Do you want to free Mom, or not?"

"I . . ." Lizzie's voice caught. "You know I do."

"Then drop this." He didn't mean to be cruel, but they had to make the deal. They needed a big score like this to buy a stealth drive for *Avalon*. It was the only way to complete their next—and last—job: rescuing their mother, held captive these past eight years by the ITA. Not only was the ITA the most powerful entity in the universe, but they were keeping her in a fortified lab on First-Earth, the most congested and heavily monitored planet in all the systems. Getting her out of there would be tougher than anything they'd ever faced with Hammer, damn near impossible.

Like trying to steal a piece of raw meat from a school of sharks.

He'd seen something like that when they had been working for Hammer, back in the aquarium at Peltraz Spaceport. A man who had crossed Jeth's old boss had been sliced open from nose to navel and dropped inside the tank.

With Lizzie silent once more, Jeth approached the table and set the token carrier on the empty space. "Mind if I join?"

The five players looked up in near unison. Their expressions as they assessed him were dubious, but Jeth knew what they saw: a young man, still a boy really, with plenty of tokens to burn. Even more, the prosthetic pieces he wore on his face to disguise his identity made him look faintly aristocratic. He appeared an easy mark.

He flashed an arrogant smile, encouraging the belief.

The dealer, a pretty brunette in a black tuxedo dress, gestured for him to sit. Jeth did so and pulled out five hundred worth of tokens, setting them in front of him. The dealer dealt the cards and, moments later, Jeth was down three hundred unis. Lizzie offered a few tips but he let them slide, afraid of drawing attention with too much good luck too soon. He had to blend in until Wainwright arrived.

With his thoughts on the meeting, Jeth slid his hand into the pocket of his flight jacket, his fingers closing around a false token. He waited to make sure no one was paying any attention, then slid it from his pocket and placed it on the table near the small pile he'd made with some of his real tokens. The new token looked exactly the same as the others except for a tiny deviation in the anchor emblem imprinted on the top. It was so small no one would notice unless they were looking for it.

"Remember not to bid with that," Lizzie said.

Jeth grunted at the reminder. He reached out and snagged one of the real tokens, a matching blue one. He waited a second, once again making sure no one was watching, and then slid the normal token into his pocket before returning his full attention to the game.

Sometime later, with his patience beginning to wane in direct correlation to the growing strength of his hunger pains, Jeth made another scan of the room. The arrival of four newcomers drew his eye. There was nothing conspicuous about the men, stopped a few feet inside the doorway, other than their complete lack of conspicuousness. They wore plain suits of varying shades of drab. They were neither large nor small, their expressions neither eager nor guarded.

"I think those are Wainwright's men," Lizzie spoke into his ear.

"I know," he whispered, and turned back to the game.

The player directly across from Jeth, a man with dusty-colored hair and an indistinguishable accent, slid forward a tidy stack of black tokens, raising the bet. The man to the left shifted in his seat slightly, although his eyes did not move off the cards in his hand.

Jeth tapped his finger twice on the table, the sign Lizzie had given him to use when he decided he was finally ready to employ her tactical advantage.

"Call or raise," she said a few seconds later. "They got nothing."

Jeth called, keeping his gaze focused on the cards in front of him, even when he saw Wainwright's men moving toward the hall of private rooms out of the corner of his eye. He wondered if Wainwright was already inside. *Probably,* he decided.

"Incoming," Lizzie said, and a moment later, Jeth felt a tap on his shoulder. He looked up to see one of the men staring down at him. The man handed him a card that bore an invitation to a private game in the Ruby Room. Jeth pocketed it without a word and the man walked away.

Once all bets were in, Jeth showed his two pair, winning the hand just like Lizzie had predicted. This time his grin was genuine while he gathered the tokens in the pot.

"That's it for me. Seems I've got another engagement." He tapped his jacket pocket, then returned the tokens to the tray, making sure the false one was on top of the smallest stack, within easy reach.

He headed for the Ruby Room. Two of Wainwright's men stood guard just inside the door, but neither moved to stop him when he entered. The door slid shut behind him automatically, but he didn't hear the click of the lock. In a casino like this one, he doubted the doors could be locked by patrons.

It was darker in here, the air murky with pipe smoke. Jeth breathed in, managing not to cough thanks to years of living with his uncle Milton, who favored the same noxious pastime.

"Come in, Jeth, come in," Wainwright called from where he sat at the single round table in the room. His wide, welcoming smile emphasized the narrowness of his face. The warmth in that smile did not extend to his eyes, which remained locked on Jeth as he stepped forward and set the token carrier on the table next to a tray of food. The sight of the food—fruit, cheese, vegetables—set his mouth to watering.

With an effort, he swallowed and forced his gaze away, making a quick scan of the room. It had earned its name. The walls were a uniform red, broken only by a couple of gold-trimmed paintings and the four vid screens hung in each corner. Red glass shaped like teardrop rubies decorated the chandelier centered over the table.

More noticeable than the decor were the two men standing behind the crime lord. Jeth couldn't see any weapons, but he knew they were armed. He cocked an eyebrow at Wainwright. "I thought this was supposed to be a private game? Looks more like an interrogation."

"I find life itself enough of a gamble." Wainwright waved to the man to his right. "Check him, Albert."

The man came around the table at once and began to pat Jeth down. As Jeth had hoped, Albert checked his pockets, soon pulling out the token. He tossed it onto the table.

Wainwright scooped it up with one small, feminine hand and examined it. "Is this what I think it is?"

Jeth adjusted his jacket and sat down. "We are here about the cipher, yeah?" He grabbed a grape off the tray and popped it into his mouth, doing his best to stifle a moan of pleasure as the taste burst over his tongue.

Wainwright cleared his throat. "I'd prefer to think of the cipher as just the opener."

Jeth's hand stilled midreach for another grape.

"What does he mean?" Lizzie's voice whispered in his ear.

Jeth recovered quickly, but instead of a grape he picked up a die from beside the tray, its gold and silver surface glittering even in the murky light as he rolled it between his fingers. "I don't recall any talk about further business. The deal was for the cipher."

"It *was*." Wainwright picked up the pipe resting in the stand next to his elbow and took a long drag, filling his cheeks with smoke that he let out slowly a moment later. "But from what I hear you have something much more valuable to offer than the Mirage Cipher."

Jeth slid the die into his pocket for safekeeping then leaned back in his chair as if bored. Beneath his cool surface, his heartbeat began to quicken, sweat stinging his armpits. "Hate to contradict you, but you heard wrong."

Wainwright set the pipe down and brushed off ash from the sleeve of his pinstriped suit. "I have it from a reliable source that you possess something of great importance to the ITA, something to do with the failing metatech."

Jeth didn't move, didn't breathe, not until he managed to corral the thoughts stampeding through his mind. *He knows about the Aether Project*. Word was bound to get out sooner or later that Jeth possessed a data crystal that contained all of the ITA's secrets about space travel and the metatech that made it possible. But the timing couldn't have been worse.

He composed himself. How much did Wainwright know? If all he knew about was the data, things would be okay. But if he knew about Cora . . .

With a deep inhale Jeth let a slow, cocky smile stretch across his lips. "No offense, but if I had something that valuable, I wouldn't be wasting time on a deal as small as this one."

Wainwright rubbed his thumb and forefinger over his dark mustache, his expression inscrutable. "Perhaps. But my source was quite reliable. An undercover ITA special operative one of my captains found tracking an unknown target, one he later revealed to be you. He was a tough one, didn't want to tell me what he was after, but it's amazing how forthcoming a man can become when you start to remove his skin."

Jeth was too familiar with crime lords and their methods to react. He widened his grin, baring teeth. "Oh, I'm sure he talked a right storm, but you should know better than to believe he was telling the truth. ITA special ops don't break so easily. He fed you a story. An easy one to swallow, given my reputation, but that doesn't make it any more true."

Wainwright let out an exaggerated sigh. "I sincerely hope not. If you don't have the information I'm after, there's no point in our talking further."

Trying to ignore the flush spreading up his neck, Jeth shrugged. "If that's how you feel. I'm sure the cipher will be worth something to someone else."

Wainwright tented his fingers in front of him. "Wrong. The cipher *might* have been worth something if you hadn't left all those witnesses alive. Witnesses tend to talk, and it's only matter of time before word of the theft gets back to Mirage."

Jeth clenched his teeth. Not all of them were still alive. *Not that stupid woman. Why did she have to—* He stopped the thought and forced his jaw to relax. "Mirage won't be able to modify their encryption software overnight. There's plenty of time to gather flight intel and to intercept enough shipments to make it worthwhile."

Wainwright shook his head. "Mirage will double the security on all flights and give their pilots authority to fly unrecorded routes. No, the cipher is practically worthless already." He sat back in his chair, crossing one leg over the other. "This metatech information on the other hand, that would be worth a great deal. Rumor has it that the ITA has no idea why so many metadrives are failing. If things keep on the way they are, there won't be any shipments for my people to intercept at all. Travel in the universe will come to a complete halt. But if you have the key to changing that . . ."

Jeth racked his brain for a response. It was all true. The metatech was failing, and he did have the key to stopping it. But he wouldn't hand it over. Not for all the money in the worlds.

He opened his mouth to deny it once again, but before he could, the vid screens in the corners flickered to life, flashing a uniform red. For a second, he thought it was some part of the room's design, but then the star and eagle emblem of the ITA appeared across the screen. Gooseflesh broke out over his skin at the sight of it.

"What is this?" Wainwright said, turning.

No one answered as the banal background music cut off and a message began to play. For a second, Jeth couldn't make sense of it. This was an Independent spaceport; they had no obligation to broadcast ITA special bulletins. But then with a sickening wrench in his gut, understanding clicked. The bulletin was an announcement of a newly posted ten-million-uni reward for the capture of an ITA fugitive. Nuvali was Independent, but it knew its clientele well.

Too well, it seemed, as Jeth watched his own face and name flash across the screen.

CHAPTER

02

HIS FIRST THOUGHT WAS, HELL, FOR THAT SORT OF MONEY, I should turn myself in.

His second was that the image looked nothing like him. The dark brown hair was the same and the green of his irises, but the boy in that picture was too young, the eyes too soft. And Jeth was certain an honest smile as carefree and cocksure as that one hadn't graced his lips in a long time.

Nevertheless, it was indeed him. He recognized the photo as one Hammer had taken two years ago for a fake ID Jeth needed for a job. He couldn't remember which; there had been so many. The next second, panic blossomed in Jeth's chest as a hot, thrashing spasm ready to explode out from him in a bellow.

He held it back, his body absolutely still in his desperation to stay calm.

Wainwright glanced at him, smirking. "Heard wrong, did I?"

Jeth didn't reply as Wainwright returned his attention to the screen. Jeth looked too, overtaken by the same curiosity. So far none of his crew had been mentioned. Instead, the bulletin had gone on to detail Jeth's crimes that ranged from extortion (*true*) to acts of terrorism (*what the hell?*). This last, they claimed, was for the destruction of a C-93 Strata cruise ship carrying more than four thousand civilians—an act supported by video footage.

Jeth watched transfixed as the massive, cumbersome ship appeared on the screen, a giant innocuous whale in a tranquil sea of stars. A moment later, a brilliant burst of light exploded out from it. One second fire and chaos filled the screen, and the next there was nothing but space.

The footage was chilling, but the idea that he could be responsible was laughable. Jeth Seagrave: Super Villain. In truth, Jeth had been lucky to make it off that Strata with his life—his resulting cyborg hand proof enough of the close call. And the Strata hadn't been carrying innocent civilians but renegade soldiers, scientists, and mercenaries. Jeth hadn't even known the ship had been destroyed—the footage could have been real or doctored. Either was possible when it came to the ITA.

"Oh my God," Lizzie's voice filled his ear. "What are they doing?"

Flushing us out, Jeth thought. It had been inevitable. The ITA had been pursuing them for months, growing more and more desperate in their attempts to recover what he'd stolen from them—both the Aether Project data file and his little sister Cora. First it was ITA soldiers and special operatives, then covert mercenaries. But this was their most desperate move yet: enlisting the public.

There's still a way out of this, Jeth said to himself. *There's still a way out of this.*

But then the bulletin reached its final segment, guidelines

for catching and approaching the armed and deadly Jethro Seagrave.

Capture his ship, the bulletin said and flashed a picture of *Avalon.*

Jeth's heart tumbled into his knees, and he choked on a sudden intake of breath. He might be able to get away from Wainwright, but there was no protecting his ship, no way to keep her hidden. Black and streamlined into a fierce, predatory shape, *Avalon* was unmistakable. Unforgettable.

And parked within firing distance of every bounty hunter, crime lord, and wannabe criminal in the entire Nuvali spaceport.

"So," Wainwright said, turning back to him. "Shall we try this negotiation again?"

Jeth swallowed, reading Wainwright's gaze. The man had no intention of negotiating anything. Why should he, with Jeth in easy reach? He could have the Mirage Cipher, the ITA reward, and the Aether Project if he played it right.

To hell with that. Jeth placed a hand on the table, ready to give the signal that would have Vince, Sierra, and Celeste bursting through the door.

Lizzie's panicked voice buzzed in his ear. "They know we're here! They're locking us down. Security's on the way."

Jeth didn't think, just moved. He jumped to his feet, grabbing the tray of food and flinging it across the table at Wainwright's head. Wainwright ducked, colliding with Albert, who was moving to protect him. Spinning away from them, Jeth grabbed his chair, hoisted it into the air, and hurled it at two more men moving to intercept him. The chair struck the first man in the knees, and he went down, tripping the other on the way. Jeth hesitated long enough to grab the token carrier from the table and leaped over them both, charging through the door.

"Get us prepped to fly and get everybody back to the ship," Jeth said through the comm.

"Already on it."

Back on the main floor, Jeth spotted Celeste, Sierra, and Vince moving toward him, and he waved them away. They turned at once and headed for the door. He hurried after them, walking as quickly as he could. There might be holes in Nuvali's security when it came to weapons, but there weren't when it came to the guards. Any sign of some-one trying to make a break for it, and they would close in, suspecting a thief. It was a fact Jeth remembered, but Wain-wright's men did not. They charged after him, making it just a few steps before Nuvali guards converged on them.

Jeth pressed on, his breath coming in rapid pants as adren-aline charged through his system. His friends exited just as he was passing the casino cage. He glanced at the empty cashier window, wishing he could stop and change out the tokens. But he couldn't, not now. They would have to find a way to come back and change them out later.

"You there," one of the Nuvali guards called as he reached the exit. "Where do you think you're going? You can't remove tokens from the floor."

Jeth halted, eyeing the gun at the man's side. Instinctively, he pulled the false token out of the carrier, keeping it hidden in the palm of his hand, as the guard looked him up and down.

"Why are you in such a hurry?" the man asked, his gaze narrowing.

Trying not to think about how much he would regret this, Jeth threw the token carrier at the man's face then bolted through the door.

All that money gone. He gritted his teeth against the thought as he ran down the deserted corridor beyond to the elevator that would take him to the mid-level decks. The money didn't matter. Not when his ship was in danger. His ship and all the precious cargo she was carrying. His crew. His uncle. And both his sisters.

He made it inside the elevator before the guard could catch him.

Panting, Jeth said through the comm, "Talk to me." When Lizzie didn't immediately answer, fear made his head spin. He leaned against the back rail to steady himself. He'd been in dozens of fights and close calls, but nothing like this. Everyone in the galaxy must've seen his face by now. And all of them would know his ship.

Lizzie finally answered, her voice calmer than before, though still with a note of breathlessness. "I'm trying to get us unhooked from the dock, but they've turned on the automatic override. It'll take time for my hack to complete."

"What about the others?"

"Shady and Flynn were already back before the bulletin

aired," Lizzie said, forgetting to use their call signs. The lapse made Jeth's fear spike again, and he took a deep breath. The elevator had almost reached K Deck, and he needed to be calm and focused before the door opened.

"The rest of you are trapped outside," Lizzie went on. "There's a bunch of dock security goons blocking the dock on both sides. They're trying to get into *Avalon*, but that ain't happening without explosives."

Jeth licked his lips and stepped toward the front of the elevator as it came to a stop. He had no doubt that the guards wouldn't get through the security on *Avalon*'s door—Lizzie had designed the code herself—but with ten million unis on the line, he didn't think explosives were out of the question.

"Can you shut down all the elevators to K Deck and close off the corridors to the dock?" Jeth said, a plan forming in his mind.

"Sure. Elevators are no problem, and I can trigger the bulkhead doors to seal the corridor."

"Do it then, but far enough away none of the guards outside *Avalon* notice."

Jeth turned right out of the elevator and moments later came across Sierra, Celeste, and Vince holed up in one of the observation nooks in between the various docks. He slipped into it, joining them. *Avalon* was moored several docks down, blocked from sight by the nearest ship. He scanned all he could see of the open space beyond the window, looking for incoming patrols, but so far the area remained clear, nothing but black dotted with starlight.

"Did you stop for some sightseeing?" Sierra said, stepping close to him automatically, their shoulders touching. A relieved smile crossed her lips, and he leaned into her, drawing comfort from her nearness.

"Ran into trouble with a casino guard." Jeth inclined his head toward *Avalon*'s dock. "What's it look like?"

"Five on each side, give or take," said Vince from where he stood next to Celeste. "Didn't get much of a look before they turned us back. But I think it's all local security."

Jeth nodded, processing the scene in his mind. Local security was better than mercenaries. They would move and react as a team, making them easier to manipulate.

"Elevators shut down and bulkhead doors closed," Lizzie announced through the comm.

"Good," Jeth said, then returned his attention to Vince. "How far apart are the guards standing?"

Vince rubbed his chin. "Fifteen meters, probably. What are you thinking? Little Felix?"

"Yep, unless one of you has a clever way out of this." Jeth eyed the others, some of the pressure easing now that he knew that all the ways into the dock were locked down.

Sierra frowned up at him. "How are you going to get close enough to set it off?"

"Easy." Jeth pulled one of the prostheses off his nose and tucked it into his pocket before moving on to the next. "Vince will pretend he just captured the ITA's most wanted. That should put us in range for Felix."

Celeste's mouth opened in a grimace. "That plan takes

first prize for dumbest ever. Those security guards can't possibly be that stupid."

Jeth hid a wince. "I didn't say it was brilliant, but it'll work."

"Yeah, it will," said Vince, crossing his muscular arms over an equally muscular chest. "Even if they don't believe us, it's not like they'll shoot us on sight."

Celeste pinned Vince with her dark-eyed gaze, a look capable of rendering most people temporarily awestruck with its ferocity. "You can't be sure of that."

A wide grin spread over Vince's lips and he winked. "Sure we can. With looks like mine, they'll know at once I'm too pretty for deception."

Celeste's face contorted as she fought back a smile. "Whoever said you were pretty?"

"What? You don't think so?"

To Jeth's astonishment, Celeste blushed. In the years he'd known her, he could count on less than three fingers how many times such a thing had happened. But then, Celeste and Vince had been circling one another for weeks now, the flirtation getting more and more obvious. Jeth couldn't understand what was taking so long. Normally, once Celeste set her eye on someone it was a done deal. Boyfriends were her hobby, a way of unwinding and passing time. She'd always been the type to go after what she wanted. But with Vince she'd been holding back, as if afraid. Of what, Jeth didn't know. She certainly liked him, that much was clear.

Jeth shook his head and snapped his fingers. "Can we

focus, please? Besides, if the guards try to turn us away or if they suspect something, we can just toss Felix at them." It wasn't a great plan B, considering how hard it was to be accurate with something as inconveniently shaped as a personal comm, but it would work, nonetheless.

"That's right," Vince added. "And there's no way they could guess we have a Little Felix anyway."

Jeth nodded. The nerve bomb alone was hard to come by, and the antidotes needed to be immune to it were even harder. Jeth's uncle and a little bit of money had made it possible. Once upon a time Milton had been a doctor and scientist for the ITA, a background that gave him the know-how on unusual things like nerve bomb antidotes.

Sierra laid a hand on Jeth's arm, drawing his attention. "They might not fire on you at first, but if you don't take all of them out with Felix then they definitely will."

"I know." Jeth placed his right hand on top of hers. And for once, touching her, the hand felt like his and not some stranger's. "That's why I'll need your gun. Vince and I will take care of any stragglers."

Sierra's mouth closed, the tight line of her lips signifying her disapproval. She might be quieter in her protest than Celeste, but to him that just meant it went deeper, mattered more. Most times Sierra was the lull before the storm, exaggerated calm and silence. That was, until she became the storm itself. He loved her both ways.

Jeth tightened his fingers around hers, careful not to hurt her with his artificial hand. "I'll be okay," he said. "I won't miss."

"I know." A nameless emotion crossed her face. Or perhaps it was a memory, the same one that appeared in his mind—of her surrogate father lying dead in a shock of blood. So much destruction from a single bullet, one shot from Jeth's gun. Wainwright might've been right when he said leaving witnesses alive was a mistake, but Jeth didn't regret it. He didn't want to add to the blood already on his hands. He wished he could've left all of them alive.

Sierra pulled away from him and then slid her hand behind her back, emerging again with a gun clenched in her fingers. The M.U.L.E. .32 was small enough that the bulge it created in her dress had been hidden by her long blond hair, but it was big enough to take down the Nuvali guard easily.

"Okay," Jeth said, as he loaded the mag then tucked the .32 into the front of his pants, hidden beneath his flight jacket. "You two stay here until Vince and I have cleared the road."

Celeste glowered, that ferocious look back in her eyes. "Next time I get to play Capture the Most Wanted."

"I certainly hope so," said Jeth.

Vince touched Celeste's arm, his playful manner from a moment ago turning serious. "See you soon."

She started to nod, thought better of it, and took hold of his face with both hands, drawing him down for a kiss. Vince recovered quickly from his momentary surprise and began to kiss her back in earnest. Celeste seemed to melt into him, her fingers sliding through the disheveled lengths of his hair, as black as her own.

Jeth scoffed. "Now? You pick now to finally do this?"

They broke apart, both a little red in the face, but not

from embarrassment, he could tell.

He shot them a halfhearted scowl before exchanging his own good-luck kiss with Sierra.

He stepped out into the corridor and said through the comm, "We're heading in."

"I've got eyes on you," Lizzie replied. "And I've almost got *Avalon* free."

Vince joined Jeth in the corridor, and Jeth put his hands behind his back, letting Vince grab hold of his wrists with one hand while the other pressed the barrel of his gun against Jeth's back.

"You want me to wait for your signal?" asked Vince.

Jeth shook his head. "I trust your judgment." Before joining the Shades, Vince had been an ITA soldier, part of an elite combat unit.

"Right. Let's go." Vince nudged him forward hard, getting into character.

Moments later they came within sight of the Nuvali security guards. To Jeth's momentary panic they were indeed fixing explosives to *Avalon*'s door. He tamped down his alarm and looked away, assessing the rest of the situation.

Most of the guards stood in a wide semicircle around those laying the explosives, but three of them were a couple of meters down on the other side of the dock, confronting a man whose long brown robe marked him as some kind of priest or holy man. He had the hood pulled over his head, but Jeth could see enough of his face to tell he was old, his cheeks sunken and face skeletal.

"We told you already," one of the guards was saying, "if you need to get to your ship you have to go around. We can't let you through."

Whether or not the old man listened, Jeth didn't see as one of the nearer guards finally noticed their approach.

"Stop right there."

"It's okay," Vince said, pressing Jeth forward. "I've got who you're looking for, but I could use a little help."

The guard appeared dubious for a moment, and then excited when his gaze alighted on Jeth's face. "Captain Carson," the man called.

Another of the guards, one in the center of the action in front of the door, turned and faced them. He wore the same navy blue, gold-trimmed uniform as the rest. The only thing distinguishing him as captain was a little extra gold on the sleeves and a dual-star insignia on the breast pocket.

Jeth drew a deep breath as the captain approached them. By his guess all the security guards were in range, minus the three with the old man, who hadn't retreated but was still arguing with the guards in that belligerent way old people sometimes did. Three was doable, Jeth decided, and the old man didn't present much of a threat. Now all he had to do was wait for Vince to come to the same conclusion and set their plan in motion. Jeth focused on the press of the .32 against his side, fixing its position in his mind and visualizing how he would grab for it when the time came.

Vince held still until Captain Carson was close enough they could count his nose hairs while he scrutinized Jeth.

Waiting was a good decision; the guards farther out pulled closer, both to back up their captain and to satisfy their curiosity. To them, Jeth must have looked like a walking, talking paycheck.

"Thank you for turning him over to us," Carson began. "We'll take it—" The captain never finished speaking. Jeth felt Vince's grip on him release, and there was a faint pop, followed by the chemical hiss of the Little Felix. A moment later, Captain Carson and the nearest guard were falling to their knees, eyes rolled back in heads, bodies convulsing with mouths agape, foam covering their lips.

Jeth pulled the .32 free and took out one of the guards next to the old man with a shot aimed at his right shoulder. Vince dropped the other two, but neither of them had the heart to strike the priest who raised his trembling, rheumatic hands in surrender.

"Back up against the wall," Jeth said, aiming at the old man. "Stay put and you'll make it out of here just fine, I promise."

The old man nodded and backed up until he reached the wall. He slumped against it, looking tired and relieved. Keeping his gun fixed on the man, Jeth walked over to the three guards, making sure they were down for the count, and with his free hand, he relieved them of their weapons.

Satisfied the situation was secure, Jeth returned his attention to *Avalon*'s door, tucking the .32 into the waist of his pants again, within easy reach if he needed it.

"Come on out," Vince called, and Jeth heard Sierra and

Celeste running down the corridor toward them.

After a moment's examination, Jeth discovered that the Nuvali guard had been applying plasma charges, stable and relatively harmless until activated by the frequency device. He pulled the charges off and set them on the floor away from the door. Then he signaled Lizzie through the comm. "All clear. Open up."

"Your wish is my computer command."

Jeth grimaced. "We free of the locks yet?"

"Almost," said Lizzie as *Avalon*'s rear access door slid open.

He motioned to Sierra and Celeste. "You two head in. Vince and I need to scavenge what we can out here. Celeste, get us ready to fly."

"We don't have time for this," Sierra said, a question in her eyes as she looked at him. Those blue eyes were gorgeous but far too keen. He'd known the others would be able to guess he'd had to leave the tokens behind, but he'd hoped the pressure of the situation would've let him avoid the reality for a little bit. He thought he might be sick.

"We'll be quick. Trust me." He inclined his head. "You should check on Cora."

The mention of his youngest sister did the job of distracting Sierra. If Cora sensed how much trouble they were in at present, things might get exponentially worse. And nothing mattered more than keeping her safe. Especially now that the ITA had gone public with their search.

Sierra disappeared into *Avalon* after Celeste, and Jeth turned to the nearest fallen guard. The man's convulsions had ended, and he had slipped into a coma. He, and the rest of them, would remain that way until their bodies were able to get rid of the poison, whether on their own or with medical aid. Jeth rummaged in the guy's pockets, pulling out cards, cash, anything of value, and stuffing it into his own pockets.

"You had to ditch the tokens, didn't you?" Vince asked as he searched the captain.

"Yes," Jeth said, his gut twisting. He could think of no curse word strong enough to express how screwed they were. "The damn casino guard wouldn't let me leave the floor with them."

Vince started to respond, but the sound of a throat clearing stopped him. Jeth turned his eyes toward the noise and saw that the priest had lowered his hood, exposing his skeletal face and a head of thinning steel-gray hair. The tentacles of a silver brain implant curled around the back of his skull, just behind the ears.

"You know," the man said in a crushed-gravel voice, "a wise man once said if you meet a thief, you may suspect him to be no true man."

Jeth stood from his hunched position, his mouth opening into an "O" of surprise, followed by anger as his brain translated the odd sentence. "What do you know of it, old man?"

Across from Jeth, Vince too had stood up, his gaze fixed on the priest and his hand prone before him as he debated whether or not to draw the gun holstered at his side.

"Oh, I know a lifetime of truths," the old man said. "I am the Storm that Rises."

Confusion furrowed Jeth's brow, the feeling made worse as Vince issued a strangled, panicked noise.

"Saar!" Terror filled Vince's voice. "Run!" he screamed, even as his fingers closed around the hilt of his gun.

Jeth reacted at once. In that moment, he was reduced to a herd animal, instinct rendering all thought meaningless, his own gun forgotten as he raced for cover.

Over his shoulder, Jeth saw Vince take aim, but he was too slow, and the old man impossibly quick, as if he stood in the faster stream of a different timeline. In slow motion, Jeth saw the man take aim with a gun that seemed to have appeared from nowhere.

He fired.

For a fraction of a second, a moment of cruel relief, Jeth thought the old man had missed. But then blood blossomed like red roses on Vince's shirt, over his heart.

Jeth drew his gun as his friend fell, the light in Vince's eyes winking out.

But before Jeth could pull the trigger, the old man took aim at him and fired. The gun in Jeth's hand exploded, shattered by the bullet. Hissing in pain and with no way to defend himself, Jeth ducked inside *Avalon* and slammed his hand against the door control.

He caught a final glimpse of the old man before it closed. He smiled at Jeth, a look of supreme confidence on his face. *This is only the beginning,* that look said.

For I am coming for you.

CHAPTER

03

SHOCK KEPT JETH STEADY AS HE RAN ACROSS *AVALON'S* cargo bay toward the ladder leading up.

"We're on," he said through the comm. "Get us out of here." The use of the plural didn't sting, not yet. What had happened couldn't possibly have happened. *Vince cannot be dead. He can't be. He can't.*

The denial reverberated through Jeth with every step as he made his way to the bridge, two decks above. He didn't want to go there, didn't want Celeste to see his face and ask him what was wrong, but he had to.

At least he didn't come across Sierra on his way to the bridge. Facing her would be worse. She and Vince had been raised together as brother and sister, a bond strengthened through years of suffering at the abusive hand of their guardian.

But when Jeth arrived on the bridge, all thoughts of Vince were driven out of his head by the view through the cockpit window. *Avalon* was only now coming free of the locks, and at least a dozen Nuvali patrols were waiting in attack formation just beyond the restricted area around the spaceport. Jeth knew they wouldn't shoot to destroy—the ITA's bulletin was clear that he must be taken alive—but they would do everything they could to disarm *Avalon*.

"Charge through them," Jeth said as he raced past Lizzie at the nav station and sat down in the copilot's seat.

Celeste didn't even glance at him from her position in the pilot's seat. Her hands were steady on the control column as she pushed it forward, *Avalon*'s engines roaring in response. The force of the acceleration pressed Jeth back in his chair. It was a risky move, but *Avalon* was a Black Devil, half the size of the Grenadiers that the Nuvali patrols flew. Jeth was betting they wouldn't fire at her directly during a forward advance. They would have to wait to get behind her and take out the engines and thrusters.

"Liz," Jeth said, glancing back at her, "turn nav control over to me and then get up to the crow guns."

"Okay," Lizzie said, her fingers flying over the nav station screen. "I've got the metadrive spooling up, but there's no way we can make a jump with all these ships around."

"Really? And here I thought we were hanging around just for kicks," Jeth shot back as he flipped on the main comm. "Everybody to stations. We've got heat." He realized too late that Vince's station would remain empty, and swallowing, he added, "Milton, I need you on the starboard guns."

Now Celeste did look over at him, only for a second, but it was enough for him to register her alarm.

"He's busy," said Jeth. "Don't worry." The lie hurt, the truth of Vince's death finally breaking through his shock. *I left him behind.*

Desperately, Jeth schooled his expression into a mask. His

shame deepened at how easily Celeste believed him, her focus returning to the scene before them as she banked hard to port, avoiding a crash with one of the patrols that had flown toward them on a collision course.

Jeth took hold of the copilot guns, aimed at the incoming patrol, and pulled the dual triggers. Gunfire lit up the space before them and slammed into the Grenadier's starboard thrusters. Jeth's aim was true, but it would take a lot more hits to penetrate the ship's shields.

Once past the first patrol, Celeste banked again, taking a risky path in between two more patrols flying almost on top of each other. *Avalon's* proximity alarms began to sound, filling the air with their shrill noise. Jeth would've liked to shut them off, but he was too busy with the copilot guns and trying to keep an eye on the metadrive system. As more gunfire burst out from *Avalon,* he knew the others were too busy, too.

A maelstrom of attacking ships enveloped them. *Avalon's* only advantage was her smaller size and greater maneuverability. Celeste flew them in and out, avoiding most of the incoming fire, but not all of it. Soon more alarms began to sound, and the screen in front of Jeth lit up with countless warnings.

"This is not going to work," Celeste said even as she sent them into a complicated spiral that was a Black Devil's signature move. "We're never going to get clear for the jump."

Jeth knew she was right, and all at once it was too much—Vince's death, the public manhunt, the hopelessness of their escape. Iron bands seemed to clamp around his chest, tightening into a vice that left him struggling to draw breath.

He closed his eyes, and with monumental effort, tried to force the feelings away. Hunger and exhaustion had robbed him of the resilience that had once been his mainstay, just as the consequences of the life they were leading had robbed him of the joy he used to take in the thrill of a close call.

Finally, too many seconds later, he regained control of his emotions and took a deep, full breath.

"Shit, oh shit," Celeste said. "Engines six and seven are down."

Jeth glanced at the screen, seeing the warnings. They either had to find a way to jump now or they'd be forced to surrender.

He reached up and turned on the main comm. "Flynn, see what you can do about those engines. Sierra, I need you on the bridge."

It seemed like no sooner had he called for her, than she was there.

He locked his eyes on the screen in front of him and asked, "Remember when we talked about turning off the proximity restrictor on a metadrive?"

"You mean when we *speculated* about turning it off?"

"Time to put the theory to the test."

"You want to jump right here?" She waved out the front window where even now they were surrounded by patrols that had tightened up the line. Celeste kept *Avalon* moving, but they kept gaining, pinning her in.

"Can you do it?"

When Sierra didn't respond, he risked a glance at her,

seeing the alarm on her face. It was true their speculation hadn't included the possibility of actually making the jump, only whether or not she could jailbreak the system successfully. Neither of them had heard of anyone making a jump with so much interference, at least not with a traditional metadrive, but . . .

"Sierra, can it be done?"

"Maybe," she said, a sharp edge to her voice. "But I have no idea what will happen. To us or them." She motioned out the window toward the ships.

Jeth met her gaze, unflinching. "We've got to try."

Sierra hesitated a moment longer, then swung around and darted for the nav station.

Seconds passed slowly. Jeth kept glancing behind him to see Sierra's intent gaze focused on the nav station screen. She'd said that she didn't think disconnecting the override would be difficult, but she might've been wrong.

Engine three went down in the continued onslaught, and now Jeth could feel the difference in thrust even though he wasn't piloting. They were moving slower. Maneuverability was down by thirty percent and shields by eighty, according to the warnings flashing in front of him.

One more hit and we're done. His hands were sweating on the gun controls. More sweat coated his brow and lined his back and arms, and yet he fought off the urge to shiver.

"It's done," Sierra said.

Jeth glanced back at her. "You sure?"

She nodded.

"Will the jump work?"

"If it doesn't, we'll be too dead to care."

"That's comforting," said Celeste.

Ignoring her, Jeth switched on the main comm again. "We're jumping. Get ready."

He motioned at Sierra, and she engaged the metadrive. Jeth braced for the jump as he felt the ship shudder around him. He sensed the light that always preceded the entry into metaspace, and even though he knew he should shut his eyes, he didn't. He clenched his muscles, waiting for the worst. With so much interference, the entry into metaspace could be affected. Part of the ship could be left behind or she could disintegrate entirely.

The light appeared, brilliant and burning against his eyes, and still he held them open. He watched as the light expanded out toward the four patrols directly in front of them. It reached the ships and then went through them, slicing the metal of their hulls open as easily as a bullet through skin.

When Jeth finally closed his eyes, that bodiless, lifeless feel of metaspace swallowing him, it was with the sight of those patrols drifting apart and then exploding burned into his mind. Each ship had a ten-man crew on board. All those people dead. Because of him.

Jeth Seagrave: Super Villain.

The idea wasn't funny anymore.

CHAPTER

AVALON MADE IT THROUGH THE JUMP CLEANLY, BUT NO ONE celebrated when they arrived on the other side, light years away from the chaos and destruction at Nuvali. They had disintegrated those patrol ships. And while the decision to make a jump in the midst of that chaos might've been Jeth's—his call, his guilt—he knew his crew too well to believe they weren't sharing in it.

Or maybe it was just some collective, psychic sense that something was horribly, desperately wrong.

How do I tell them he's dead?

It was a task Jeth had never performed before in all his time as head of the Shades. He'd lost crew members when they had aged out, back when Hammer had been running the show, and he'd even lost current members when his sisters had been kidnapped by a rogue ITA agent. But none of them had ever died.

What do I do? What do I say? He desperately wanted to hand off this burden to someone else. He considered Milton, the only real adult on board. Even now his uncle would be climbing out of the starboard gun station. Milton was a doctor. He'd seen death many times, likely even delivered news like this before.

Once again, he saw Vince falling. Once again the ache of leaving him behind filled his chest. *No.* Jeth steeled himself. Passing off the duty was the coward's way out, and he refused to take it. He just needed a moment to prepare himself.

"Talk to me, Flynn," Jeth said over the comm.

"We're limping," Flynn answered from the engineering deck. "I've got engine seven back up. But six and three are going to take longer, if I can get them running at all. It's not like I've been able to stock up on repair parts lately."

Jeth stifled a groan, remembering the lost money, both the reserve cash and the blown deal with Wainwright. *Please let it end,* he thought, teeth gritted. This wasn't just a string of bad luck. This was the universe declaring war.

He forced his jaw to relax, remembering this was Flynn he was talking to, the Prince of Doom. "Eight out of ten engines is enough to keep us moving, right?"

Flynn huffed, the sound like rushing wind against the comm speaker. "Like I said, *limping.*"

"Good enough for now." Jeth killed the connection.

"So where to, Boss?" Celeste said from the pilot's seat. The smile she turned on him cut him to the quick.

He stumbled over his answer. "Back to the Belgrave."

Celeste sighed. "I knew you would say that."

She sounded nothing more than annoyed, but he sensed something darker beneath. She hated that area of space known, among other names, as the Devil's Boneyard. The Belgrave was said to be haunted or cursed. There were hundreds of stories about disappearing ships and strange occurrences, some myth, and some truth, as Jeth and his crew knew firsthand. But scary or not, hated or not, the Belgrave had been their only safe haven these last few months.

"We won't be in there long," Jeth said, standing up. He switched on the main comm again. "I need everyone to meet me down in the common room in fifteen minutes. We've got . . . things . . . to discuss."

Wincing at his stutter, Jeth switched off the comm and reluctantly faced Sierra, his heart a hard, heavy fist thumping against his breastbone. *Her brother is dead.* Why had he been so stupid? How could he have so underestimated that old man? He ought to have known better. Anyone who wore a brain implant wasn't to be taken lightly. *But I didn't see it until it was too late.*

Jeth swallowed and somehow located his voice. "Cora doesn't need to listen to this. I'll stop in and ask her to stay in her cabin." Another lie. It wasn't that she didn't need to be there, but rather that he feared her reaction more than any other. Cora was dangerous when she became upset or angry or confused, capable of the same level of destruction as what they had just wrought on the Nuvali patrols. They would have to break the news to her carefully.

The blood leached from Sierra's face, and he knew she sensed his dread. Her mouth opened, and he raised a hand against the question rising to her lips. "I've got news, but it'll be easier for everybody to hear it at once."

Sierra nodded, but as Jeth turned to leave she said, "Cora isn't in her cabin."

He paused and looked over his shoulder. "Where is she?"

"The engine room."

"Again?" Jeth exhaled and turned away before Sierra could respond. He shouldn't be surprised. Cora had been spending more and more time on the engineering deck these days. He couldn't believe she'd been up there during the firefight with the Nuvali patrols rather than buckled into a seat, but it wasn't like there had been time to check on her. And Cora wasn't the most agreeable kid in the galaxy. If she didn't want to leave the engine room, there was no making her.

Jeth exited the bridge and headed up the stairs to the engineering deck. Part of him wondered if his decision not to tell Sierra in private what happened to Vince was a cowardly one. He'd never been good at dealing with emotions, not his nor others'. Emotions were tricky, impossible things, complex and contradictory. And when they were at their height, they couldn't be reasoned with or pacified. Emotions like that—rage, hatred, grief, love—were like wildfires. They blazed out of control, impossible to stop until they burned themselves out. Jeth would rather hide, or better yet, bury the emotions so deep inside that they withered and died.

But they never truly die.

Ignoring that inner voice, he stepped into the engine room. As usual, the place looked as if it had been ransacked by a pack of feral dogs. Loose cables were snaked over half of the floor in between the various equipment racks. At least four units in those racks were giving off sparks, and the whole place was as smoky as the Ruby Room had been. Jeth spotted Flynn standing a few paces down, in front of one of the more theatrically sparking units.

"Hey," Jeth said, stifling a cough. "It looks pretty bad up here."

Flynn glanced at him, his expression murderous on his ash-smeared face. "Isn't that what I said? Limping?"

Jeth grimaced. "Words didn't do it justice."

Flynn snorted. The food rationing they'd been under the last few weeks hadn't done his disposition any favors.

Returning his gaze to the equipment rack, Flynn said, "We were in the middle of a firefight five minutes ago. Please tell me you didn't come here to check on my progress."

"I came to see Cora."

"She's back there." Flynn motioned to the far end of the engine room.

Jeth walked past Flynn, finally spotting Cora where he'd known he'd find her—in close proximity to the metadrive compartment. Today she was sitting directly in front of it, several pillows strewn under her as a makeshift sofa. She looked up as he entered, a tired grin brightening her face. Her white-blond hair hung lank around her shoulders, and her unusually large eyes, as black as soot, looked larger still thanks to the dark circles rimmed beneath them.

Jeth's smile faltered at the sight of her. It wasn't the first time of late that he'd noticed her looking ill and rundown, but it had never been this pronounced. He swallowed, hoping it was nothing more than a need for natural sunlight and a few good meals.

Soon, baby girl, he thought. *Somehow.*

He stopped in front of her and offered a hand as she got to her feet. "Miss me?" he said, stooping over to plant a kiss on her forehead.

She bobbed her head and slid her arms around his waist, squeezing him. "Did you miss me?"

"A little bit, I suppose." He pulled away and reached into his pocket, withdrawing the golden die. "I picked this up for you."

Cora beamed up at him as she plucked it out of his hands. "Oh, it's so pretty."

"I knew you'd like it."

She rolled it across her palm, admiring the way it glittered in the light. "If you're back, does this mean we get to go get Mom now?"

"No, not yet," Jeth said, wincing. He regretted the day Cora had learned of the plan. Although she didn't know their mother the way Jeth did—the ITA had kept Cora apart from Marian the entire time she'd been their prisoner, before Sierra, an ITA agent herself at the time, had stolen her away from them—she was eager to be reunited, obsessing about it in the way only little children could, relentless and heart-breaking.

"Why not?" Cora asked, wrinkling her nose.

Jeth sighed. "Things didn't go exactly as planned. But don't worry. We'll get her soon."

Cora nodded and returned her gaze to the die, this time examining the dots imprinted on each side.

"Listen," Jeth said, running a hand through his hair. As always, he scraped a finger over the hole of the brain implant architecture in the back of his skull, checking to make sure his hair was still covering it. The gesture had become a nervous tic. He could let his hair grow two feet long and he still wouldn't be able to resist doing it. The architecture, the kind designed to hold a brain implant like the silver one Saar had been wearing, had been surgically inserted against Jeth's will.

He dropped his hand. "I need you to stay in your cabin for a little while. I've got some things to discuss with the rest of the crew."

Cora made a face. "Adult things?"

"Yeah, really adult." His voice broke on the words, tears choking his voice. *I left him behind.* He cut off the thought before it could go any farther. He had to get his emotions in check.

"What's wrong?" Cora poked him in the stomach.

Jeth forced a smile. "Nothing for you to worry about." *Not yet.* He drew a breath and let it out slowly. "But there might be some loud talk and shouting. I need you to just ignore it and stay in your room, okay?"

"Okay." Cora hesitated, glancing behind her where the door to the metadrive stood open. "But please can I stay up here?"

Jeth frowned, his gaze shifting from Cora to the metadrive, visible behind the glass shielding. Roughly cylindrical in shape, the outer shell of the drive was nothing extraordinary, mere metal and wires haloed around a strange object with a texture vaguely like ocean coral, colored in varying shades of red. That porous material was what made metaspace travel possible. Jeth, like the rest of the universe, used to believe that it was some kind of unknown tech or fuel cell, a secret invention of the ITA. That was, until he uncovered the secrets in the Aether Project.

In truth, that porous object was made up of living things, alien creatures called Pyreans. The Pyreans were a vast superorganism, one capable of accessing metaspace, the dimension beyond the perception of humans and human technology. The ITA had imprisoned them centuries ago, harvesting them to build the metatech and make faster-than-light travel possible. But now the Pyreans were dying off, their impending extinction the reason behind the metatech shortage Wainwright had been so worried about.

As he should be, Jeth thought, feeling the familiar wave of hopelessness at this truth. Soon the Pyreans would be no more and interstellar travel would come to a halt. The idea scared him, but all he had room to care about right then was rescuing his mother and keeping Cora safe from the ITA.

He returned his gaze to his sister, wondering—not for the first time—what she saw when she looked at the Pyreans, or more precisely what she *felt*. His little sister wasn't the ordinary human child she appeared to be, not entirely. Due to the unusual and mysterious circumstances of her conception and birth, her DNA was a mix of human and Pyrean. And like the Pyreans, she too could access metaspace, an ability the ITA was willing to kill to reclaim.

We're all going to end up dead. Just like Vince.

Stifling a shiver, Jeth forced a smile. "I suppose you can stay up here. . . . How come you want to?"

"Because," Cora said, as if this explained everything.

Jeth motioned to the metadrive. "Do you feel something when you're near that?"

Cora frowned. "What do you mean?"

Jeth searched for the words to explain it, but none came. At least not any that would make sense to a seven-year-old. *Avalon*'s metadrive should've been dying the same as the others, but for months he hadn't seen any signs of withering. More than once he and Sierra had speculated it might have something to do with its proximity to Cora, and her developing ability to manipulate metaspace.

"Never mind," he said at last.

Cora sat down on the pillows once more. "It makes me feel better. Less sleepy." She picked up a portable viewer that Jeth hadn't noticed before and switched it on. A cartoon of a singing cat and several dancing mice appeared on the screen. "Want to watch it with me?" Cora asked, casting a hopeful look up at him.

Not having the heart to tell her no, Jeth sat down beside her. "Only for a few minutes. I've got to get downstairs."

"Okay." Cora leaned toward him, snuggling into the crook of his arm. He hugged her to him, glad of the weight of her against him and the warmth of her tiny body. Resting his cheek against the top of her head, he fixed his gaze on the screen, willing his troubles away if only for a few precious minutes.

Cora laughed as one of the mice bit the cat's tail and a raucous chase ensued. The sound of her enjoyment seeped into Jeth, soothing the ache in his chest. Keeping her safe made the sacrifices worth it. He clung to that as hard as he could, wishing he didn't have to get up and face the others.

But finally, Jeth knew he couldn't delay any longer. He hugged Cora one last time and got to his feet. "Promise you'll stay here."

"Promise," she said, not looking up. She was idly rolling the die between her palms, her gaze fixed on the screen.

Satisfied she was thoroughly distracted for the time being, Jeth turned and headed for the exit. His heart thudded against his rib cage, the beat quickening with his each step like a crescendo building toward the moment when he would deliver his news—a blow that would crush them all.

CHAPTER

05

TO HIS SURPRISE, JETH FOUND THE COMMON ROOM EMPTY as he arrived. Even Flynn wasn't there yet, although he'd left the engine room before Jeth. Jeth supposed the girls were getting changed out of their casino outfits. The others were likewise cleaning up, probably.

He leaned against the gaming table in the center of the common room and was immediately aware of all the signs of lives-in-progress around him: a discarded sock poking out from beneath one of the reclining armchairs, a drinking glass crusted with some reddish stain sitting on an end table. Two gaming remotes lay on the threadbare sofa, left there by Shady, the first discarded when the charge ran out. Both were probably drained now.

A pair of punch mitts that they'd been using for hand-to-hand combat training had been left on another end table. The moment Jeth's eyes alighted on them, he glanced away, his throat constricting. The mitts belonged to Vince, a last-minute buy from the flea market in Moenia City. They *had* been Vince's, Jeth corrected himself. It was the first physical reminder of a life no more. He wondered how many more there would be.

One by one the crew filed in. Lizzie arrived first. Shadows rimmed her eyes, and her curly brown hair lay flat against her skull, the roots dark with grease. Shampoo cost money, and she'd been doing without as much as she could. She looked far older than fourteen, any baby fat long since burned off her by their current living conditions.

Shady came next, tall and shaggy-haired with crude tattoos covering his neck and forearms. The black ink looked dull in the soft light of the common room. He sat next to Lizzie on the sofa, picking up both of the gaming remotes and idly testing them for juice.

When Flynn arrived, he slumped down in the armchair nearest the sofa, He looked as irritable as before, but he'd washed the ash off his face and hands.

Milton showed up next and opted for an empty armchair, resting his head against the back. Age had painted him gray and wrinkled. Like Lizzie, he was too thin of late, although at least the usual redness in his nose and cheeks was less pronounced these days. Alcohol was a luxury he could no longer afford.

Finally, Celeste and Sierra arrived. Celeste, having donned snug black pants and a fitted red top, strolled in with her usual languid air and settled down on the sofa next to Shady.

Sierra hesitated just inside the door.

Here it comes. Jeth held his breath, blood roaring in his ears.

"Where's Vince?" She scanned the room but only for a second before turning her eyes on Jeth.

He felt himself shrivel beneath that gaze, and when

he spoke his voice was small, defeated. "He's . . . still at Nuvali."

"What?" Celeste's voice boomed in Jeth's ears, and she sat up straighter on the sofa, a cat ready to pounce. "Did he get caught?"

Jeth shook his head, his eyes dropping to the floor. "He's dead."

No one spoke for several seconds, paralyzed. Death was impossibly powerful, absolute, with no room for bargaining. One moment here, and the next gone. Forever.

"To hell with that," Celeste said, and now her voice cut the air instead of boomed. She leaped up from the sofa and swung toward the door, her straight black hair fanning out like dark wings. "We've got to go back for him."

Before Jeth could react, Shady was up and on the move. He grabbed Celeste by the wrist and hauled her to a stop. She swung back around, her face livid.

"Let me go." She threw a punch, but Shady caught it with his other hand.

Screaming, Celeste tried to fight him off, but Shady only pulled her close, pinning her arms to her sides.

"We can't go back. They'll kill us," Shady said, struggling to hold her. He was taller and had at least fifty pounds on her, but it didn't matter in the face of her heartbreak.

"We don't know he's dead! Jeth's not a doctor. Let me go!"

Each scream seemed to flay Jeth, and tears stung his eyes, some of grief and some of guilt. He gripped the edge of the table and said with as much strength as he could muster,

"He's dead, Celeste. The bullet went through his heart. It was instant."

Celeste ignored him, fighting harder. Jeth looked away, unable to bear the sight of her pain. But the others were hardly better. Milton's eyes were watery, his lips curved downward in a hideous expression of sorrow. Lizzie was openly crying, her hands covering her face as gentle sobs trembled through her body.

But the worst was Sierra. She stood frozen in place. She seemed beyond tears, beyond any reaction at all, and yet Jeth could feel her breaking. He wanted to go to her, to wrap her in his arms and gather the pieces, but he couldn't make his feet move. He couldn't be certain she would welcome the comfort. She should hate him.

Slowly, Celeste stopped struggling, and she sagged against Shady, her cries now wrecked and jagged. "You left him behind," Celeste said, not looking at Jeth. "We can't even say good-bye."

Jeth choked back guilt, fighting hard not to cry. *I didn't have a choice,* he thought, but couldn't bring himself to say it.

Celeste's words seemed to shatter the spell Sierra was under, and she staggered forward, heading for the nearest chair. She sank onto it, tears now flowing freely from her eyes.

"What happened?" she said.

Jeth swallowed. "It was that old man, the one in the priest's robes. I . . . I was stupid and didn't check him for weapons. I thought he was just a bystander, but then he said something that made Vince panic. Vince told me to run and I did. I only made it because he warned me."

"What did he say?" Lizzie asked, her voice thick. "The old man."

Jeth thought back, the memory blurred by emotions. He inhaled, expanding his chest as far as it would go, the sudden intake of oxygen making him momentarily dizzy. "He said 'I am the Storm that Rises.' Then Vince called him some name I didn't recognize."

Sierra sucked in a breath. "Saar."

Jeth frowned. "Yeah, that's right. Who is he?"

"Admiral David Saar," Sierra said, and now Jeth recognized the name.

"No, it can't be," said Milton, jerking upright. "It's not possible."

Sierra cut her eyes to him. "Why not? We know he's still alive."

Jeth crossed his arms over his chest. "Are we talking about the same Admiral Saar from the history books?"

Both Sierra and Milton looked up at him with alarmed expressions, as if in their mutual horror they were startled to find they weren't alone.

"The same." Milton sagged against the sofa again.

"But who is he?" asked Lizzie.

Jeth wasn't surprised that Lizzie didn't know. She'd spent less time than any of them in a classroom. But from their confused looks, Jeth guessed Flynn and Shady were in the dark, too. He couldn't tell with Celeste, who still had her face buried against Shady's chest.

"Admiral Saar," Milton said, "is a living legend. Not that any of you are old enough to fully understand what that means. I was your age when he was at the height of his glory. He's most famous for single-handedly ending the Emet Insurgence."

A shiver went down Jeth's spine as he remembered studying the Insurgence back at Metis Academy, the ITA-run boarding school he'd attended up until his father's death and his mother's imprisonment. He'd never been particularly interested in history, then or now, but he could recall with perfect clarity the videos and photos chronicling the conflict that his teacher had shown them. Most of the ones he remembered were of the aftermath—entire cities pulverized into an unknowable wasteland of twisted metal and ash; the murky water of poisoned rivers and streams; farmlands scorched into hellish landscapes; and piles upon piles of slaughtered livestock. And the dead of course. Millions of them.

Sierra nodded. "The ITA reveres Saar. All first-year agents are required to study his war tactics, whether we wanted to or not. Saar . . . liked to get his hands dirty, personally performing executions and whatnot. Sadistic. But there's no denying he was a genius."

Shady looked unimpressed. "What was this Insurgence?"

"The last time any planet ever attempted to secede from the Confederation."

This news didn't have any effect on Shady. In fact, he barely seemed to listen as he guided Celeste back to the sofa.

"Yes," said Milton, rubbing his eyes. "Saar's victory over

Emet secured the ITA's power over the aligned systems and it earned Saar the name Storm Scourge. Although if I remember correctly, he often referred to himself as the Storm that Rises."

"Yes, that's true," said Sierra.

Jeth didn't want to believe it, and yet he'd seen the man for himself. Saar had certainly looked old enough to have fought wars nearly fifty years ago. "If this is the same Saar, then why us? Why now?"

Flynn, who'd been silently following the conversation, added, "Yeah, if he's not dead by now then surely the guy's retired."

Milton shook his head. "Saar is not the type of man to retire. There hasn't been much need for his services since Emet fell, but he went on commanding smaller missions and excursions. The size never mattered to him. He went after little targets with the same relentless fervor that he did Emet. He is the ITA's greatest weapon."

Lizzie's tear-reddened eyes widened. "And now they've pointed him at us."

"So it would seem."

Jeth looked up at the ceiling, his thoughts turning to Cora. He wished the ITA would just give up their hunt for her, that they would realize she was just a child, with the same rights as anyone else, the right to live a normal life, not as some perpetual science experiment.

Only that was the crux, wasn't it? No matter what she appeared to be, she wasn't fully human. As long as the problem with the Pyreans went unresolved, they would never give up. They needed her too much. Her genetic makeup and ability to perceive metaspace was the key to finding the solution, the surest way to ensure their continued dominance of the galaxy.

Exhaling, Jeth lowered his gaze again. Movement across the way drew his attention to the door, and he saw Lizzie's yellow-haired cat stride into the common room, his bushy tail held high like a golden banner. In ironic contrast to the rest of them, Jeth realized how fat Viggo was looking these days, his belly a hairy satchel drooping between his legs.

Shaking his head, Jeth returned his focus to Sierra and Milton. "If Saar is so great, then how come I got away? He could've killed me but he didn't. He—" Jeth broke off as the truth broke the surface of his consciousness: *Saar let me go. On purpose.*

"If that's true then there's only one explanation," Sierra said, echoing Jeth's realization. "He let you go so he could track us. The bounty will force us into a corner and make us easier to catch. And he knows he must be careful approaching us, as he likely has orders to take Cora alive."

"Careful?" Celeste said. "Then why did he kill Vince? If the plan was to track us, why reveal himself at all?"

Sierra didn't look at Celeste as she answered, her quiet hurt the still waters to Celeste's raging river. "I don't know, except, killing . . . killing Vince seems to fit. Saar is an executioner, not an assassin. And Vince was an ITA deserter. A traitor, as far as Saar was concerned."

"Sierra's right," Milton said, slowly nodding. "Saar is the worst of enemies. He's a man with full faith in his own righteousness."

Flynn rapped his index finger against the end table. "So what you're saying is, we're screwed no matter what, and we should just turn ourselves in right now."

Jeth, well used to such an attitude from Flynn, straightened from his slumped position against the table, drawing all the energy and force of will he could muster. Things were bad, but he refused to give in or give up. And he wouldn't let any of the others do it either, not while they remained on his ship. "No, what they're saying is we need to search for the tracking device."

"Yes, that's the first place to start," said Sierra, sounding more like she did when she'd first entered the common room. Jeth supposed that having a purpose to focus on was a shield against grief.

Bolstered, if only by a degree, Jeth added, "And we need to figure out our next move. We're not beaten yet. The deal with Wainwright was a bust, but I still have the Mirage Cipher."

Lizzie stood up. "Once we find the tracker, I'll work on a list of other potential buyers."

"What?" said Shady, a lazy incongruous grin stretching across his face. "You think there's someone out there who'd rather have the cipher than the ten million bounty for turning us in?"

Lizzie scowled down at him, hands on hips. "It's always possible. We can go in disguised."

"Oh sure." Shady bobbed his shaggy blond head. Like Lizzie, his hair was in need of a wash. "Right."

"We *will* find someone," Jeth said, trying to head off the argument. "And we've got to do it quick." He hesitated, bracing for the next delivery of bad news. But it wasn't like he could keep it a secret from them. "I had to leave the casino tokens behind."

All five faces bore varying expressions of shock and horror. Celeste spoke first, venom in her voice. "You lost all our money?"

Jeth hardened. "I didn't have a choice. There wasn't time to exchange them, and I couldn't leave with them."

Shady swore, loudly and colorfully. "Choice or not, you screwed us hard on this one. Well, you better come up with a solution fast, Boss Man. Because I've no plan to starve out here in the middle of nowhere. Life was a helluva lot easier back when we were working for Hammer. If we get out of this, maybe I'll try my luck with Daxton."

Jeth felt the blood drain from his face and then rush back into it. Never in the four years they'd known each other had Shady ever talked to him like that. And it wasn't a hollow threat. Daxton Price was the man who had taken control of Hammer's criminal enterprise and by doing so helped Jeth and the crew evade capture by the ITA. Even Jeth had thought about how much easier it would be if they were under Dax's protection, as they had been under Hammer's for so long.

But then a familiar phantom ache blossomed in the back of Jeth's skull around the implant architecture. It was all the reminder he needed of why they couldn't go back to their former home. Hammer had forced the architecture on Jeth in the hope of making him a part of his organization, one controlled by the power of implants. Jeth had just barely escaped with his mind and free will intact. But Dax, already one of Hammer's elite Brethren soldiers, had claimed Hammer's master implant for himself—and it had changed him.

No, Dax couldn't be trusted. He was the new Hammer now, capable of anything—including selling them out to the ITA. It was a risk they couldn't take.

Jeth exhaled and kept his voice even as he said, "That's your choice, Shady. You're free to go and work for whoever you want. But my job is to keep Cora safe and find some way out of this situation. And I can guarantee you that does not include Daxton Price."

"What if there is no way out of this?" Shady said, unflinching.

"There is. I just haven't found it yet. But I will. I always do."

Shady snorted and got to his feet. "Yeah, right. You keep on trying, Boss. Who cares if the rest of us die for the cause?" And with that, Shady strode from the common room, his loud boot steps echoing behind him.

Jeth stood rooted in place, reeling from shock and outrage—and guilt. His determination from a moment before came crumbling down.

Celeste followed Shady's lead, her actions speaking far louder than any accusation she might have thrown at him.

Jeth held his breath, waiting to see who else would do the same. Not Lizzie, of course. And not Milton. They were family. But the idea of Sierra walking out on him made his blood feel like liquid nitrogen in his veins, freezing his heart.

When Sierra got up a moment later, he stiffened. But she came over to him and placed a kiss on his cheek, her lips wet from her tears. "We will find a way out of this," she whispered. "The ITA won't beat us. Vince didn't die in vain."

Her words made him feel better and worse at the same time, and he nodded, unable to speak. He was afraid if he did, she would hear the truth in his voice that they were beaten already, and it was only a matter of time before the fall.

CHAPTER

06

MOMENTS LATER, JETH RETURNED TO THE BRIDGE AND
brought *Avalon* to a halt, setting the anchor system to moor
them in place. They needed to get rid of the tracker before
they headed to the Belgrave. Their haven wasn't safe, but it
was certainly secret, the strange energy barrier around the
area making it difficult to triangulate positions. But there
was no guarantee the barrier would disrupt the tracker
enough to prevent Saar from locating them.

Finding the tracker proved easy. When it came down to
it, there weren't many places it could be. Lizzie had been
on *Avalon* the entire time they had been at Nuvali, and she
hadn't seen anyone attempt to approach the ship, not from
within the dock or on the outside. There had been a team
of repairmen in space suits working on the deck above, but
she'd kept a close eye on them and none had come near. No,
Saar must've planted the tracker right after killing Vince and
before *Avalon* had left the space dock.

Sierra and Jeth both donned space suits and then headed
outside the ship. Jeth found the device attached just to the
left of the rear access door, low, where it would be hard to
see. Small as it was, not quite as wide as the tip of a stylus,

he never would have noticed it if he hadn't known to look.

"Is that it?" he said to Sierra through the comm link.

She maneuvered closer, letting the light from her helmet shine on it. "Yeah, I think so."

"You don't sound certain."

"It's a really old model."

Jeth didn't say anything, his mind plagued with doubts. "Are you sure it is a tracker?"

"Quite sure. Just old. But I suppose that fits Saar's persona."

"Maybe." Jeth fell silent as Sierra pulled a tool from her belt and began to pry the device off the ship. He waited, body tensed, convinced that it would explode or simply vanish, proving it was nothing more than a wishful hallucination brought on by two minds deluded by failure and grief. Sierra had gotten her crying under control, but every once in a while she drew a broken, shaky breath, the sound painfully magnified by the comm.

The device came loose a moment later and began to float away. Jeth reached for it, but Sierra stopped him with one gloved hand.

"Leave it. They'll be forced to spend time looking for us in the wrong place."

"Right." They weren't near the Belgrave yet, and the chance of Saar guessing their destination was minimal. Still, the sooner they left the area, the better.

But as Sierra started making her way back to the ship Jeth said, "I'll be a minute."

She looked over her shoulder at him, her expression

difficult to read through the helmet visor. "Don't take too long." She paused, then added, "Would you like me to break the news to Cora?"

Jeth inhaled, his emotions rising up like a sudden flood. For a second he couldn't speak at all. On the one hand, he didn't want Sierra to face it alone, but on the other, Cora might handle the news better if it came from her. Jeth and Cora had grown close since she'd come into his life a few months ago, but it was nothing like the bond she shared with Sierra. Sierra always seemed to know how to calm her down and keep her from losing control of her ability to phase objects in and out of metaspace. Still . . .

"It's up to you," Jeth said at last. "Whatever you think is best."

"I'll tell her, then." She paused. "It'll be easier on everyone."

"Thank you," Jeth said, hating himself for feeling relieved.

Once Sierra was gone, he turned away from the ship's black, sleek side and faced the impossible expanse of open space surrounding him, a dark tapestry threaded with pulsating flecks of light. It was a sight that never failed to remind him of how small and unimportant he was. Even the weightlessness of zero-g was a reminder. He *was* nothing, just an empty, inconsequential thing, here for a fleeting moment before the cells and molecules that had come together to form his body disintegrated back into their smallest, immeasurable units.

And yet, despite how real his nothingness felt, he knew it wasn't. He did matter. His choices had consequences. This very day he'd made two that had cost Vince's life and those of so many nameless others. Soon he would have to make more decisions, face more consequences. The thought made him want to unlatch the hook on the safety line tethering him to the ship and float away.

But he couldn't do that either. Lizzie and Cora needed him. And so did their mother. Vince was dead, and there was no undoing that, but Marian Seagrave still lived. There was a chance for her.

Jeth allowed himself another few precious minutes of doubt and defeat, knowing he needed to get all the bad out now and leave it behind. He hung there, suspended in space, letting the cold seep in, wrapping around him like an icy cloak. He must be ready to decide his next move when he went inside. The rescue mission remained his goal, but he couldn't ignore what was happening with the crew. As much as he hated to admit it, Shady's anger was justified. Jeth was captain of the ship, but that didn't give him the right to take risks with the lives of its crew. They weren't soldiers dedicated to saving his mother and reuniting the Seagrave family.

The resolution came to him, hard and painful, and he inhaled frigid air into his lungs as he tried to make his peace with it. He had to give them the choice to stay or go—really give it to them, not just spout some rhetorical ultimatum. That meant heading somewhere planetside, a place where they had a chance of landing in secrecy. Benfold Minor would be the nearest. It seemed a decent enough planet. Besides, if Shady or whoever else wanted to go back to Dax, they could contact him from there. The idea of any of his crew leaving was like a knife to his heart, but Jeth steeled himself against it. He didn't want anyone on his ship who didn't want to be there.

Avalon was silent as Jeth reentered, the cargo bay a sad, abandoned place with its dim light and the water stains lining the walls and ceiling. He didn't mind the lonely feel. Anything was better than facing Shady or Celeste right now. He headed up the ladder to the bridge, passing no one. He spooled up the metadrive, calculated for the farthest possible jump toward the Belgrave Quadrant, and then gave the others a quick warning through the comm before initiating the jump.

When they came through the other side, he switched off the autopilot and flew the ship manually while he waited for the metadrive to respool. The sense of control the action gave him might've been false, but it made him feel better just the same.

Three hours and several jumps later, they arrived in the Belgrave. Jeth piloted them through the strange energy barrier, ignoring the familiar burst of white noise from the speakers. It was a phenomenon that would haunt them on a regular basis while inside this strange area of space, but they knew from experience that the noise was mostly harmless.

Finally, he brought the ship to a stop and switched on the anchor system. He stood and stretched, confident it was late enough that everyone would be in bed. No one had come to see him or checked in through the comm, which was fine by him. Facing them would be easier in the morning, after they'd slept and eaten. For once, the idea of food didn't make his stomach react, sadness and stress the best cure for hunger pangs.

Except, as he headed down the ladder to the passenger deck, he saw Sierra coming up the stairs, carrying Cora. The girl had her head resting against Sierra's shoulder, and for a moment, Jeth thought Cora was already asleep. But then she raised her head, revealing a swollen, tear-reddened face.

With his heart giving a wrench in his chest, Jeth held out his arms. Sierra came to a stop, and Cora reached out for him.

"How you doing, baby girl?" Jeth asked, hugging her tight.

"I'm sad," Cora said as Sierra brushed past them and slid open the door to Cora's cabin, one adjacent to Jeth's. "What happened to Vince is sad."

Jeth patted the back of her head with his free hand. "I know, but it'll get easier. I promise."

He wondered how well she actually understood what death meant, that Vince was gone and never coming back. He barely understood it himself. When you were a kid, the only permanence was the here and now, the things you could see and touch. Old toys, once out of sight, were so easily forgotten. Same with old friends and teachers, even pets. To Cora, Vince might've simply left on a long journey. Jeth supposed that sense of impermanence was a blessing.

He followed Sierra into the cabin and waited as she switched on the manual emergency light they'd been using in lieu of a night-light. Then he approached the bed and laid Cora onto it, her head against the pillow.

Stepping back, Jeth saw that, despite the evidence of shed tears lingering on her face, she was calm now. Almost too calm, he realized, taking in her unnaturally large pupils, so much black there was hardly any white at all. He guessed Milton had given her something, maybe even the last of the sedatives on board. Jeth swallowed. They didn't need to use them on Cora often, but it would only take one accident to destroy them all.

Pushing that worry from his mind before Cora sensed his fear, Jeth smiled down at her. "Are you ready to go to sleep?"

She shook her head. "Can I have more story first?"

Jeth hid a wince. The last thing he wanted was to read aloud to her. Fatigue lay heavy on his eyes and twisted his tongue. A cartoon video like the one from earlier would've been easier, but it wouldn't do the job of lulling her to sleep.

"All right." He picked up the electronic reader beside the bed and switched it on. The words blurred before his vision, and he squinted until he could see them clearly. He sat down beside Cora as Sierra settled herself in the chair opposite the bed.

Jeth searched for the right place on the page and then began to read, stumbling over the archaic words and sentence structures at first. They'd been reading *The Little Mermaid* for three nights now and were almost through. Jeth couldn't wait for it to end; the tale was long, boring, and like so many fairy tales, disturbingly cruel.

Ten minutes later, he read the final sentence then glanced up, hoping to see Cora was asleep. Her dark eyes stared back at him, as wide and alert as ever.

"Am I a daughter of the air?" Cora said.

Jeth blinked, surprised by the question. "Of course not. You're a little girl. Just like the princess."

Cora shook her head and said in a voice far too old for her years, "But I'm not human, and I'm not a mermaid. So I must be one of them."

Jeth didn't know what to say, whether to laugh or cry. For a moment he remembered what it had felt like when Cora had once transported him and the rest of the Shades through metaspace. When making the journey in a ship using ITA metatech, the experience was instantaneous, a moment so infinitesimal it didn't seem to exist at all. But when Cora had taken them through, Jeth had been aware of the passing. He'd even dreamed during it, of the Pyreans swirling around him like fish in the ocean, or perhaps like ethereal daughters of the air as in the story. Maybe it had been the same for Cora.

Jeth shifted his weight, contemplating an answer. A lie seemed easiest, but Sierra spared him the decision.

She came over to the bed and sat beside Cora, brushing the hair back from her forehead. "Firstly, the daughters of the air aren't real and you are. Secondly, what you are—human, mermaid, or anything else—doesn't matter. All that matters is the things you do. All right?"

Cora seemed to contemplate the wisdom of this statement. Finally, she nodded and then was overtaken by a huge yawn.

Sierra glanced at Jeth. "I'll stay with her."

Jeth set the reader back on the table. Then he stood up and bent over Cora long enough to brush his lips against her forehead. "Sleep well, munchkin."

"Good night," Cora said as she scooted back, giving Sierra room to lie beside her. Cora had no trouble falling asleep on her own, but lately she'd been plagued by terrible nightmares. For Cora, nightmares had the potential for physical manifestation in the form of shredded or missing furniture, even holes in the walls, like the one near the foot of the bed that Flynn had patched over with a piece of scrap metal. The nightmares happened less often when she fell asleep with someone beside her, as if the presence of another person kept her unconscious mind anchored to this reality and away from the dimension of metaspace.

As Jeth headed for the door, Sierra called for him to close it. He stopped and did as she asked, his heart an iron weight. Usually, she had him leave the door open so she could slip away more quietly. Jeth tried not to overthink her decision to stay the night with Cora. Knowing her, it was because Cora needed her more than he did. Or so he tried to tell himself.

He entered his own cabin at the head of the corridor, stripped off his clothes, and fell onto the bed, smothering his face in the pillows. He closed his eyes and willed sleep to overtake him. He couldn't remember ever being this tired, as if he'd been sucked dry and hollowed out, a dead battery disguised as human flesh.

But sleep remained just out of reach, blocked by the thoughts that refused to quiet. There were so many worries that they soon became a blur, and he slowly descended into a delirious half sleep in which his fears masqueraded as dreams.

Sometime later, the sound of his cabin door opening brought him fully awake. He didn't move, didn't breathe, as quiet footsteps crossed the room, followed by the soft swish of clothing meeting the floor. The mattress dipped at the foot of the bed and Sierra's familiar scent filled his nose. He slowly inhaled surprise then exhaled his relief, as quietly as he could, uncertain if he should let her know he was still awake or not.

But then her body curled around his, and he shifted to lay his hand against her side, drawing her deeper against him.

"Can't sleep?" she whispered against his ear.

"Not yet." He ran his fingers down her bare arm. "But soon, I think." It might've been his imagination, but he sensed a smile pass through her. She squeezed him once, and then her body relaxed toward sleep.

Although he knew he should let her be, he drew a breath and spoke into the darkness "I've decided to let them go. Shady and Celeste and whoever else wants to." He paused, hyperaware of Sierra's stillness. She might not be there at all except for the heat of her skin warming his. "I mean, I'm going to give them a real chance to leave." He let his voice trail off and then waited for her response. He wanted her to tell him it was stupid, that he was overreacting, but Sierra was not the kind of girl to appease his hurt with a lie.

"Where will we land?"

Jeth sighed. "I was thinking Benfold Minor." Sierra shifted against him, and when too many seconds passed without a response he asked, "You don't think that's a good idea?"

"No, it's fine." She paused. "I was just thinking about

how we're going to get our hands on a stealth drive now."

Jeth tensed at her words, resisting the urge to hug her tighter. He couldn't believe it. Even now, after losing her brother, she was still devoted to the plan to rescue his mother. She had more right than anyone else on board to want to walk away from all this, and yet here she was, worrying about the stealth drive.

He cleared his throat. "Any ideas?"

"One."

"Really?" He'd been kidding, but he should've known better than to be surprised that Sierra already had something in mind.

"Yes," she said, her voice solemn now. "I think we should consider selling the Aether Project."

"What?" Jeth rolled toward her, trying to read her expression in the darkness. The idea had crossed his mind before—of course it had—but he'd never voiced it out loud. There was too much risk involved. The Aether Project was full of information about Cora, Lizzie, and Jeth's mother. Like Cora, Marian Seagrave was no longer strictly human. Her DNA had been irreversibly altered when she discovered the Pyreans' home world, a mysterious planet known as Empyria. She'd been pregnant with Cora at the time, and something about the planet had changed them both. Sure, they could cleanse the data of anything to do with his family before handing it over, but there was no way to guarantee the path of information wouldn't eventually lead back to Cora again in the end.

"It's risky, I know," Sierra said. "But it's the most valuable object in our possession. It makes the ITA's bounty look like a drop of water in the ocean by comparison."

Jeth didn't say anything as he felt the walls pressing in on him. *The bounty will force us into a corner*, Sierra had said. As usual she was right. He adjusted his position on the bed, trying to get his mind comfortable with the new idea. It was better than giving up. "Do you have a buyer in mind?"

"When we were looking for jobs to get money for the stealth drive," Sierra said, "you mentioned an Enanti contact."

"Yeah, I did." Jeth shot her a puzzled look that she had no chance of seeing in the dark. "And you mentioned that you would rather saw off your own body parts and feed them to Viggo rather than deal with them."

Sierra made a disgusted noise. "I still would. But our situation has changed. With the ITA bounty, we can't trust any of your crime lord contacts not to turn us in. But the Enanti are fanatics. They won't be tempted by ITA money."

"No, they probably won't," Jeth said, mulling it over. The Enanti were a group of freedom fighters from the planet Tiglath. They'd been regular customers of Hammer's, spending millions to secure weapons and supplies to support their mission to overthrow the central government of Tiglath. The ruling regime was actively pursuing membership in the United Confederation of Planets, an act that would put the planet under the control of the ITA. The Enanti were determined to stop it by any means possible.

"You know they're terrorists, right?"

Sierra smacked his bare shoulder. "You are so tactless. Of course I know it, but do you have to remind me? I'm trying to get us out of this mess."

"Sorry," Jeth said, resisting the temptation to rub his stinging shoulder. "Does it help that I think you might be right? The Enanti would be a good choice. The safest."

"Less unsafe," Sierra corrected him. "We should probably discuss it with Milton first, but I really don't see any other option."

"Me either." A few seconds of silence passed between them. "What do you think the ITA will do when they learn we've sold the project?"

Sierra sighed. "They won't stop pursuing us, if that's what you're hoping."

"I wasn't." He knew better. The ITA still knew Cora existed, and would want her back with or without the Aether Project.

"I imagine they'll increase the security around the Harvesters for one thing."

Jeth considered the idea, supposing it made sense. The Aether Project contained the location of all the Harvesters, those places in metaspace where the Pyreans' dimension intersected with the one humans could perceive. Jeth struggled to wrap his mind around the strangeness of their state of being. The way Sierra described it to him, the Pyreans were like a giant tree that existed primarily within the dimension of metaspace—except for the Harvest sites. At those places, the very tips of the hidden tree branched out of metaspace into the human dimension. For years the ITA had drawn the material for their metadrives from these hidden places, and the Pyreans had continued to "grow back," so to speak. Until recently.

"Sure they will," Jeth said. "If they haven't already. With their impending extinction, what Pyreans they can still harvest are more valuable than ever." His stomach twisted at the thought.

"So the world turns," Sierra said, her tone bitter.

An idea sprouted in Jeth's mind, one that made his stomach twist even harder. What if they didn't sell the Aether Project to the Enanti alone? There was nothing to stop them from making dozens of copies of the data. Hundreds even. Once they rescued Marian from the ITA, they could sell the copies to all the ITA's enemies, or maybe just upload the data to the net. The Enanti alone stood no chance of using the data to dismantle the ITA, but if all the Independent Planets had access to the truth about the Pyreans and metatechnology that would be a different story.

War, he thought. *Intergalactic war.* War on a scale so large that the ITA would be too busy defending itself and its precious Harvest sites to worry about chasing Jeth. It could be the solution to everything, the ultimate play to get him all he'd ever wanted: freedom for him and his family. They could fly away and disappear among the chaos.

But then the images he'd recalled earlier from the Emet Insurgence came back to him. Did he really want to be responsible for something like that? For so much death and destruction?

"Anyway," Sierra said, derailing his thoughts. "Tiglath is as good a place to land as Benfold Minor. Sectors of Tiglath are safe enough that whoever wants to leave can do so without too much trouble."

Jeth slowly nodded, trying to ignore the sting of her words. For a few moments he'd almost forgotten about Shady's discontent. "Good point. I'll send out a feeler to my Enanti contact as soon as Flynn finishes the repair on the engines. Then we can figure out how to tell everyone."

Sierra's breath tickled his neck. "Okay." She fell silent again, and he almost let it go at that, but doubt refused to release its grip on him.

"Do you think letting them go is the right thing to do?"

She answered at once, her certainty absolute. "Yes. Everyone should get to choose to live how they want to live."

"Do you think they'll actually leave?"

Now she hesitated, and he could hear his heart beating in the intervening seconds. "I don't know, Jeth. But I'm staying. No matter what happens."

Feeling childish and stupid, and yet better, Jeth ran his hand down her arm once more, then went still. This time sleep came upon him at once.

HALF A DAY LATER, FLYNN FINISHED HIS REPAIRS ON THE engines. Jeth joined him in the engine room, wanting to see it for himself. The place wasn't much improved, but at least the smoke and sparking were gone.

"It's not perfect," Flynn said, casting a suspicious look at Jeth as he climbed out from behind one of the equipment racks. "But it's good enough to keep us going. I didn't have all the parts I needed, but I was able to use some of the fifteen-x plasinum-coated fiber-optic cable instead of the twelve-x by splicing it with—"

Jeth cut him off with a raised hand. "You worked your usual magic. I get it."

Flynn grinned. "Yeah, I suppose I did." He reached into his pocket and pulled out a piece of chocolate wrapped in shiny silver paper. From the crumpled look of it, Jeth guessed it might very well be his last piece. Flynn held it out to him.

Jeth stared back, wondering who this strange person was before him. Flynn part with his last piece of chocolate? That cold day in hell had arrived. "What's that for?"

Flynn shrugged. "Thought you could use some. But if you don't want it . . ."

"No, I do." Jeth took the candy, peeled off the wrapper, and slid the chocolate into his mouth. "This is poisoned, isn't it?" he said, biting into it.

A grin snaked across Flynn's face. "Not sure you warrant such a good death as one by chocolate."

Jeth didn't reply as the taste exploded over his tongue, making him gasp. All he'd had to eat today was half a protein stick. The flavor of the chocolate made his stomach burn. He'd never tasted anything so good.

"Like it?"

Jeth nodded and wiped saliva from his lips. "Think I understand why it's a death you would prefer."

"Yep. But don't expect any more. And be warned, I've got my stash well hidden."

Jeth didn't doubt it. "Don't worry. I'll be able to get my own here soon," he said. Then he filled Flynn in on the plan to head to Tiglath. He and Sierra had discussed things with Milton, and, as they expected, he'd agreed that selling the Aether Project was their only course of action. Jeth didn't mention to Flynn his plan to let anyone who wanted to get off for good once they landed. That was a speech he only wanted to give once, with everyone around to hear it.

If Flynn suspected that part of the plan, his face didn't show it. Instead he looked relieved at the prospect of a payday—and more chocolate, no doubt.

Jeth left the engine room a few minutes later and headed for the bridge. He needed to move them out of the Belgrave to send a clear transmission to his Enanti contact. But the sound of loud, angry music echoing up from the corridor below stopped him. *Uh-oh*, Jeth thought. Lizzie had always had an annoying habit of expressing her feelings through her music selection, but lately she'd begun emphasizing those feelings by the level of volume. Right now, the entire ship was vibrating with the sound of her unhappiness.

Jeth puffed out his cheeks and exhaled slowly as he headed down the ladder to the passenger deck. If he ignored her, it would only get worse. Lizzie's door was shut, but not locked, and he pulled it open and stepped inside. She was sitting behind the pullout desk on the opposite wall with her gaze fixed on the screen of one of the portable maintenance computers. She didn't look up as he entered. With the way his eardrums were about to start bleeding, it was no surprise she hadn't heard him come in.

He stomped over to the desk and turned down the volume on her music player with one swipe of his finger across the control screen. Silence descended like a bomb, and Lizzie jumped. She stared up at him, the surprise on her face quickly transforming into a glower.

"Do you mind?" She reached toward the player, and he slapped her hand away.

"Yes, I do mind. Don't you think things are tense enough around here without adding angry, kill-everybody-and-die music?"

"It's not angry, kill-everybody-and-die music."

"Oh really?" Jeth folded his arms across his chest.

"That's right. It's angry, let's-start-a-revolution-and-kick-some-ass music." She thrust a fist into the air.

Despite himself, Jeth felt his lips twitch as a smile

threatened. Lizzie had a way of getting to him like nobody else—one minute he was ready to strangle her, and the next he wanted to pick her up and tickle her until she cried like he used to do when they were little.

"What revolution are you hoping to start, exactly?"

"How about the let's-not-ditch-our-friends-on-some-random-planet one?"

Jeth closed his eyes and pinched the bridge of his nose. The smell of chocolate lingered on his fingertips, and he dropped his hand away, his stomach rumbling. He stared down at her. "Sierra told you the plan."

"Yes, and I think it's awful."

Jeth contemplated a dozen or so responses, but he couldn't muster the energy for the argument. He settled on the plain, harsh truth. "The Enanti are our best chance of getting the money we need for the stealth drive and not getting handed over to the ITA in the process. And I'm not ditching our friends. I'm letting them leave."

Lizzie clapped her hands. "That's my point. Don't *let* them."

"I can't make them stay. I never could." He shook his head. "They're only leaving now because they want something better than I can offer them here."

Lizzie bit her lip, her eyes flashing to the computer screen. "That's just it. What if . . . what if I have a way of making things better, for all of us?"

Frowning, Jeth shifted his gaze to the screen as well. He realized at once that she'd been examining the contents of the data crystal their mother had left hidden on *Avalon* shortly before she was captured by the ITA, nearly eight years before. The crystal was a log of the last trip she and Jeth's father had made into the Belgrave, the trip where they had finally found Empyria, the mysterious planet that was the origin of the Pyreans. If the Harvest sites were the tips of the tree branches, Empyria was the trunk and root. Marian and Robert Seagrave had worked as space explorers for the ITA, but for some unknown reason, they refused to disclose the location of Empyria. Robert had died protecting the information, and Marian had endured years of torture.

Jeth sighed. While the data crystal contained some photos and video streams of his parents, there wasn't much of concrete value to anyone other than them. "Why are you looking at this again? We've been through it hundreds of times. I thought you'd finally given it up as pointless."

"I had. But then something new occurred to me."

"Like what, Liz?" he said, not bothering to disguise his skepticism.

She scowled at him. "The file names. We always assumed they were gibberish, yeah?"

"Yeah." Jeth frowned, examining the screen again. The file names were the strangest aspect of the data crystal. The randomness of them went against everything Jeth knew about his mother. He remembered a woman who alphabetized the cans of food in the kitchen and who would create resource-loaded school schedules for him that detailed everything from what percentage of time he needed to spend on homework each night compared to time spent on sports and video games. The mother he'd known would never have used such a nonsensical naming system for her files. He and Lizzie had never come up with a good explanation for why she had.

"Well," Lizzie said, "I think we were wrong."

"How do you mean?" Jeth said, returning his gaze to her.

She ran a hand through her auburn hair, her fingers snagging on curls. "I think it's a code."

Jeth's breath caught, hope rising up in him despite himself. "A code to what?"

"I don't know for sure yet," Lizzie said. "I've only just started translating it. Took me forever to figure out the key. Mom hid it really well. But—" Lizzie paused, as if to draw out the suspense. Jeth resisted the urge to holler at her. "I think when I'm done it will reveal the location of Empyria."

Jeth blinked once, twice, the world seeming to slip into slow motion around him. "Empyria," he repeated, the word hardly more than vapor on his lips. That was where all the troubles that had plagued his family had started. "Empyria." He couldn't believe it.

"I know how you feel," Lizzie said, sticking out her tongue. "And if I am right, then this is the solution to everything." Her voice began to rise. "Finding Empyria is what the ITA wants more than anything, more than Cora and definitely more than more Mom, right?"

"Yes."

"So we offer them Empyria in exchange for Mom and a blank slate for the rest of us."

Jeth opened his mouth to respond, but Lizzie continued. "Picture it, Jeth. We could go anywhere we want without worrying about crime lords and bounty hunters. We could be free. And a family again. You know Mom will love the crew." Lizzie broke off, her face beaming with her mounting excitement.

For one brief, blissful moment Jeth almost allowed himself to hope that such a deal was possible. He shook his head. "I can't believe you, of all people, are saying this. Dad died to protect this information. Mom endured torture and imprisonment. And now you want to trade their secret?"

Lizzie looked crestfallen for a second, but then thrust out her chin. "Desperate times and all that. Besides, you've seen the video journals. Mom went a little crazy after she found Empyria. Maybe Dad did too. Do you think we can completely trust their judgment?"

Jeth frowned. He didn't disagree with her logic, but he hated hearing her say it, hated what it meant. Lizzie had always believed in the best of everyone. She was always hopeful, always willing to take the high road even if the low one was more practical, more useful. *Now she sounds like you.* Jeth gritted his teeth, searching for a response. "I don't know, Liz. I—"

A loud wail erupted around them, and Jeth flinched in surprise. For a second he thought it was her music player turning back on by itself, but then he recognized the proximity alarm.

Lizzie gaped up at him. "The ITA. They've found us."

Jeth pointed at the screen. "Hide that. Then get up to the bridge."

He spun and raced out the door and up the ladder, catching a glimpse of Flynn coming down from the Engineering deck. The bridge was empty as he ran inside, but the view beyond the main windows was filled with a sleek black spaceship, its shape as familiar to him as his own face. A Black Devil, same class as *Avalon*.

What the hell? Jeth hadn't seen another Black Devil in years. The model was out of production, but this ship looked brand new. Pushing the confusion away, he leaped into the pilot's chair. He double-checked that he'd left the shields activated, and some of his alarm dissipated when he saw that he had. No matter who was on that ship, a direct assault would be useless. He just needed to pilot them out of here.

Except, as he reached for the control column, a bright burst of blue light filled the window, obscuring the sight of the foreign ship. Jeth braced for impact, but none came. Instead when the beam reached the ship, Jeth felt an electrical charge pass through his body, like touching his finger to an open circuit, and then every system on *Avalon*—every light, every source of power—went dead.

Darkness wrapped around him, broken only by the view through the front window, where the blue light had gone and the Black Devil returned. Jeth gaped, his hair standing on end and his nerve endings tingling. His lifeless ship groaned around him, all the metal parts of her settling into permanent stop.

"What the hell was that?" Flynn said from his right.

"I don't know." Jeth pounded on the control column before him, desperate for a response, some sign of power.

There was none. *We're dead*, he thought, mind reeling. Already the air was turning cool and thin. It wouldn't be long before they suffocated. Whatever that beam had been, it had reduced *Avalon* to a lifeless metal shell. Their home had become their tomb.

Bile and rage clawed up Jeth's throat, and he swallowed it back, afraid of inducing panic. Already he could hear shouts and bangs from the rest of the crew as they struggled to find their way in the darkness.

"See if you can help them," Jeth said, turning to Flynn. He could just make out his shape next to the comm station.

"What would you like me to do? Use my superhero night vision to light the way?"

Jeth ignored him, and a second later Flynn moved toward the entrance and began shouting down the corridor for the others to follow the sound of his voice.

Despite knowing it was pointless, Jeth tried the buttons on the control column again. He pressed and pressed then pounded it with his fist.

He looked up at the other ship, hating its familiar shape. *Any way but this*. Who were these people to attack them without provocation? They hadn't even attempted to negotiate a surrender. It didn't make sense. The bounty was clear: Jeth and his crew were to be taken alive. They were completely worthless to the ITA dead.

A light flickered behind Jeth, and he turned to see Sierra and Lizzie coming onto the bridge, both carrying lit birthday candles in their hands, the tiny flames pathetic wards against the darkness. Sierra must've been near the galley when the power went out. Finding the candles and matches was some sort of miracle.

Cora was with them, her eyes wide with wonderment.

"Give me those and I'll go get the others," Flynn said, holding out his hand for the candles.

"What's happening?" Lizzie said as she guided Cora into a chair.

Jeth shook his head and turned back to the window. Beyond it, the Black Devil was swinging around, as if to leave. Jeth glimpsed the name painted on its side: *Polaris*. He didn't recognize it.

"What are they doing?" Sierra said, taking the copilot seat.

Polaris didn't fly away, but stopped rotating once its cargo bay door was aligned with *Avalon*'s prow. A moment later, the rear hatch slid open and two space-suit-clad figures emerged. They disconnected the towlines and then flew across the gap between the ships. Jeth watched them, stunned and helpless to stop the impending invasion.

"Are they going to tow our dead bodies back to the ITA?" Lizzie said.

"Dead bodies?" said Cora.

Sierra made a hissing noise. "Lizzie was joking, Cora," she said. "Nobody is going to die."

"Are they here to help us?" Cora stood up and came forward.

"Yes," Lizzie said, shooing her back to her seat. "Probably."

Jeth returned his attention to the window, not that he could see anything now that the two figures were out of view, attaching the towlines to *Avalon*'s prow. He wanted to hit something. Each second he sat here helpless was torture.

The others arrived, Flynn leading the way with his sad little candles. None of them spoke. The seconds passed like hours as they waited in the dark for something to happen.

Jeth was just about to ask Lizzie if she had any brilliant ideas brewing in her genius brain, when the ship's systems buzzed back into life. He blinked against the sudden light, breathless with shock and relief. *We're not dead,* Avalon's *not dead!*

"What was that weapon?" Sierra said, awe in her voice.

"Something like an EMP. But if there's one that can penetrate standard shielding like that, I've never seen it before." Jeth leaned forward and pressed the button to release the anchor. It didn't respond. He pressed it again and again, stabbing it with his finger.

"It's no use," Sierra said from the copilot's chair where she too had been trying buttons. "They've overridden all the systems."

Jeth glanced over his shoulder at Lizzie. "Think you can override the override?"

Lizzie bit her lip and sat down at the comm station. "I'll try."

Despising the doubt in her voice, Jeth turned back to the control panel and stabbed the buttons a few more times, a dissatisfying target for his frustration. He should've felt better knowing this was a capture and not an execution, but he didn't. Caught was caught.

"How did they find us out here?" Jeth said through gritted teeth.

The main viewer flicked into life and a woman's face appeared on the screen. No, not a woman, but a girl, one

Jeth's age. Recognition and disbelief collided inside him, and he stared stupidly at the screen, his jaw slackening. Of all the people who could've caught him.

"Hello there, Peacock," the girl said, her smirk filling the screen. "Still preening your feathers, I see."

Jeth cleared his throat, trying to gather his wits. "And you're still causing trouble, Trouble."

"Not as much as you," she replied. "Let's see. According to this Wanted bulletin, you're guilty of extortion, murder, acts of terrorism." She whistled. "And here I thought you were just a common criminal."

Jeth grunted. "Well, at least *you* haven't changed at all. Still trying to use me to score big. But if I remember correctly, that didn't work out so well for you last time. I ended up with the ruby and you ended up getting shot. By me."

She grinned. "True, but not before I left you trapped in a glass cage. And the way I heard it, you got lucky, getting out. Somehow, I don't think you'll be so lucky this time."

Jeth couldn't help the scowl that flashed across his face. It had been two years since the Grakkus job when he'd first collided with this beautiful terror in front of him, the leader of a rival gang. She looked the same as she had then—shiny brown hair, amber eyes that held a perpetual impish glint, and lips far too pretty for a girl he despised so much. She'd gone by the name Aileen back then, and he had no reason to suspect she'd changed it, but he preferred his chosen nickname for her.

Jeth twisted his lips into a smile. At least Trouble worked for a crime lord. Soleil Marcel was as ruthless as Hammer had been, but Jeth knew how to speak their language, and he knew how to get them to deal.

He cupped his hands behind his head and leaned back in the chair. "We'll see about that. I do have a way with women, after all. And from what I hear, Soleil likes her boys young and hard to handle."

Aileen laughed, the sound of it all kinds of wrong to Jeth's ears. It was far too certain and sure, even for her.

He waited, keeping his expression masked. Beside him, Sierra smoldered with hostility.

Aileen's laughter finally died away. "You silly boy. Whatever makes you think I still work for Soleil?"

A tremor of panic went through Jeth. *She's bluffing.* You didn't just quit on a crime lord.

"Who *do* you work for?" Sierra asked when Jeth failed to respond.

Aileen's gaze moved to Sierra for the first time, her eyes appraising, but the grin lingered on her face. "Oh, my employer is someone you all know well, to my understanding. He sent me to fetch you after he got the call you sent him yesterday. I must say the coordinates of where to find you were surprisingly accurate considering where we are. Then again, *Polaris* here is equipped with an exceptional navigation system."

Jeth's mouth slid open, blood pounding in his ears so hard that starbursts crossed his vision. "Who is your employer now?"

Aileen's grin widened. "Daxton Price, of course. Who else?"

DAXTON PRICE. DAXTON PRICE. DAXTON. PRICE. THE NAME seemed to reverberate throughout the bridge as loudly as the proximity alarm had moments before.

Understanding snapped inside Jeth's brain like the pull of a trigger. *He got your call,* Aileen had said. *The coordinates on where to find you . . .*

Jeth stood up from the pilot's chair, pivoted on one foot, and charged toward Shady, who was standing a few feet from the nav station.

He didn't slow down, but leaped forward, fist swinging. "You traitorous son of a bitch." The punch landed square against Shady's jaw with the distinctive hard, wet sound of meat striking meat. Shady stumbled backward and fell to the floor with a loud crash. Too late Jeth realized he'd used his right hand, the cybernetic one as hard as the plasinum used to construct spaceships. Shady never went down on the first punch.

Regret tried to battle its way to the front of Jeth's emotions, but his fury refused to give way. "Get up and fight, you coward."

"Stop it, Jeth," Sierra shouted from behind him.

Shady struggled into a sitting position and spat out blood and at least one shattered tooth, maybe more. "*I'm* the traitor? The coward? What about you? You promised us a better life, the freedom to do what the hell we wanted, and all we got was starvation and a dead friend." Shady lunged to his feet, fist swinging.

Jeth stepped back, just dodging the blow. Frantic hands grabbed his arms and shoulders, but none were strong enough to hold him. He reared back, ready to throw another punch even as Flynn stepped in between him and Shady.

"Don't do this," Flynn said. "You don't know that Shady gave Dax our position."

"The hell I don't," Jeth said, his breath coming in hard pants. He turned back to Shady. "What, you weren't man enough to come talk to me? You had to call Dax to come pick you up, like a little girl who got scared at a sleepover?"

As Shady tried to push past Flynn, Jeth swung again. Flynn managed to shove Jeth just enough that the punch went wild and his fist struck the nav station instead with a loud smack. The dent it left was a near perfect circle.

Jeth stumbled, then recovered. The hands grabbed him again, Milton and Lizzie helping Sierra to restrain him.

"Stop it, stop it, stop it!" Cora shrieked louder than the rest. Jeth felt her scream more than heard it. The sound struck him like a physical force, and the memory of what might follow broke through his fury. Body trembling, Jeth lowered his hands. The moment he did so, Shady swung, the punch connecting easily with Jeth's face. Pain lit up the side of his head and blood filled his mouth as teeth cut cheek.

"This is just you getting what's coming to you," Shady spat.

Jeth ran a hand over his throbbing face, somehow managing not to fight back. Anger vibrated in his voice as he said, "You're a traitor and a coward, and you're off my crew."

"Fine by me. Looks like I've got better prospects on the horizon." Shady glanced at the viewscreen, where Aileen was watching them with that infuriating, impish expression, utterly delighted by the free entertainment. Shady gave her a little salute and then strode off the bridge.

The silence this time was worse than any before. Jeth avoided the others' gazes as he headed back to the cockpit and faced the viewscreen. His outrage at Shady's betrayal throbbed like an open wound, but he ignored it. This wasn't over yet. Not while a pulse still beat inside him.

"So," he said, willing the breathlessness out of his voice. "You're working for Dax now. How did that happen?"

Aileen shrugged. "He's the new Hammer, yeah? I guess you could say me and my crew are the new Malleus Shades."

Jeth narrowed his gaze at her. "You took our place?"

"Don't look so surprised. Dax knows how useful you were to Hammer. I'm even more useful."

"Sure you are." Jeth pursed his lips. "You're taking us back to Peltraz then?" The spaceport had been his home for almost ten years, but the idea of returning to it filled him with dread. Hammer was gone now, but he doubted much had changed. Daxton might've been a good man once, but he'd been under Hammer's control for a long stretch of years, and now he had Hammer's power. Jeth didn't think there was any coming back from that.

"Yes," Aileen said, matter-of-factly. "Should take less than a day from here." Her eyes twinkled with mirth. "Might I suggest you make yourselves comfortable for the trip? And I do mean *really* comfortable."

Jeth's eyebrows inched up his face. "Why?"

"Oh, no reason." Aileen waved at the screen. "Just want to make sure you arrive rested and in good shape."

"Why wouldn't we be?" Sierra said, stepping up beside Jeth.

This time Aileen completely ignored her. "We'll be talking again soon. Bye-bye."

The screen went blank.

"Who *was* that girl?" demanded Sierra.

"Trouble," Jeth said, his unease building. "We ran afoul of her on a job we worked for Hammer about two years back. She's a liar and a leech."

"So I gathered. You say she used to work for Soleil Marcel?"

"Yeah," Jeth said, unable to keep the worry from his voice. Aileen was one of the best thieves he'd ever encountered, and she'd very nearly bested him back on Grakkus. Not that he would ever admit it.

"Then how is she working for Dax?"

"No idea. But I'd rather not find out." Jeth spun around and motioned at Lizzie who still stood by the nav station, not far from the new dent left by his fist. "See if you can get us some control back."

Lizzie nodded and returned to the comm station. Within

seconds her fingers began to do their dance across the screen. Jeth took a deep breath, expecting the best from his little sister. There was nothing she couldn't do with a computer.

But mere seconds later she began to curse.

"What is it?" Jeth crossed the bridge to her and stared down at the screen over her shoulder.

"I can't even get a connection."

"What does that *mean*?" he said, his temper inches from breaking the surface of his control.

Lizzie didn't raise her eyes from the screen. "It means that this is going to take a lot of time, if I can get through at all."

Jeth wrapped his fingers around the back of her chair, squeezing. "How much time?"

"I don't know." She didn't snap, but Jeth could tell she wanted to. He let go of the chair and ran his hands over his head, his fingers brushing against the hole of the implant architecture in the back of his skull. He barely felt it.

"It'll be okay, Jeth," Celeste said.

He wrenched his head around to look at her. She stood with her back to the comm station. Her expression was as strange as her tone had been, weirdly pacifying. Such behavior in Celeste was as out of place as Flynn sharing his secret chocolate stash or Shady committing such a betrayal. Shady. Loyal, steady, Shady. *How could he have done it?*

Celeste shifted her weight, uneasy beneath his glare. "Dax has helped us before. He might do it again."

Jeth turned away from her, unable to get the memory of how she'd stood by Shady out of his mind. But her words lingered as he returned to the pilot's chair and sat down. Dax had let them go after they'd helped him defeat Hammer. And he'd done it even knowing how much Cora was worth.

"I'm afraid it's unlikely his interests are in helping us this time," Milton said, easing himself down into the one of the empty chairs. "Not with this sort of welcome." He motioned toward *Polaris*.

Gritting his teeth Jeth said, "What's he after now, though?"

"It could still be the Aether Project," Sierra offered. "Hammer didn't have his own copy, I'm sure."

"Or it might be about the reward," said Flynn. "We've been hearing those rumors about how Dax is struggling to maintain Hammer's enterprise."

"Yes," said Milton, "and if there's truth to those rumors, capturing us might be as much about reasserting his power as anything."

A chill shot down Jeth's back, starting at the base of his neck and ending at the tip of his spine.

"Oh my God," Lizzie said.

Jeth spun in his chair to look at her. "What is it?"

She glanced up, her mouth open in a grimace of fear. "They're messing with the life support system. Pumping something into the oxygen supply."

Wordlessly, Sierra jumped up and rushed over to Lizzie. Jeth followed two steps behind her. Sierra's eyes moved over the screen, wide and panic-filled. "We're already breathing it in."

"What—" Jeth broke off as Aileen's words came back to him. *Make yourselves comfortable*, she had said, *really comfortable*.

The bitter taste of the gas filled his mouth and burned his nostrils. Jeth held his breath, but it was too late. A wave of dizziness went through him, and he felt his knees giving way.

This is going to be painful, he thought as his body met the floor.

Then he thought no more as black curtains closed over his eyes, plunging him into a sleep too deep for dreams. Or nightmares.

IN HINDSIGHT THAT DEEP SLEEP THROUGH THE JOURNEY back to Peltraz had been a blessing. Jeth didn't have time to speculate or worry about what Daxton would do when they arrived. He didn't have time to brace for the worst. He didn't even know the worst was coming until it was over.

He woke with a buzzing in his head. It was small and inconsistent at first, a spurting of sensation, not quite sound and not quite feeling but something in between. For those first few seconds as he regained consciousness, he was aware of nothing else but the buzzing.

Then slowly, his senses came back to him, and they began to translate the world around him into recognizable images and sounds. He was lying on his stomach in a small, gray-walled room that he recognized as one of the prison cells at Peltraz Spaceport. A thick crust of sleep rimmed his eyes, and as he shifted to get a better look at his surroundings, his muscles protested new and sudden movement after being immobile too long.

With the buzzing in his head growing louder and steadier, Jeth closed his eyes and forced the recollection of what had happened to the forefront of his mind. *Aileen. Sleeping gas in the life support system. And now here. At Peltraz.*

Jeth eased himself into a sitting position, his mind processing more information with each passing second. This cell was cleaner than the last one he'd been in at Peltraz. There was an almost sterile feel to it, like a hospital room, except the bench beneath him was cold metal.

He looked down and realized that someone had changed his clothes. Gone were his usual pants, shirt, and flight jacket. In their place was a pair of black pants and a black shirt, the cut and fit completely familiar to Jeth. This was the basic uniform worn by Hammer's soldiers. By Dax's soldiers now: the Malleus Brethren of the higher order and the Malleus Guard of the lower. Seeing those clothes on him could mean only one thing.

Hands trembling from a fear that ran deeper than any other he possessed, Jeth touched the back of his head. Something rubbery and slick met his fingertips, a tentacle wrapped around the base of his skull. He raised his hand higher, feeling another and another. All the air squeezed out of his lungs and black fog spread across his vision. He blinked it away, fighting to stay conscious. It couldn't be there. It couldn't. And yet it was. An implant.

Jeth wrapped his trembling fingers around the stem, instinct demanding he pull it out. But he froze, remembering Hammer's long-ago warning that only the Brethren implant, a black one, could be removed at will. The clearcolored Guard implant would self-destruct.

But which one was it? A chance of freedom or the end of

the line? The uniform told him nothing, not without a jacket and its distinguishing color of trim. Lowering his hand, Jeth got to his feet, swaying as much from fear as muscles weak from drugged sleep. He desperately scanned the room for a reflective surface, some way to determine the color of the implant. He had to get the thing out, its presence a violation of his mind, his soul.

He pictured what the implants looked like outside their hosts' bodies. Their stems were the length of his index finger at least. The idea of something so long inserted into his brain brought black clouds to his vision once more, and the buzzing grew suddenly louder as if to mock his delayed understanding of its cause.

With no reflective surface in the room, Jeth found his thoughts being drawn to the buzzing. He focused on it, probing it with his mind. At once, images began to flash inside his head. He saw people and places, some that he recognized and some that he didn't. He saw Brethren and Guard, the presence of both telling him nothing about his own state of being. The images raced through his mind too fast to follow. It was like watching a screen flipping between channels at maximum speed.

Gradually, Jeth forced his mind away from the buzzing. He had to get this thing out. He raised his hand to the implant once more, but again fear stilled him. What if it was a clear one? A Guard implant?

No, it can't be, he thought. From what he'd seen, a clear implant would've rendered him brainless, incapable of the worry he was feeling now. It must be black, one of the Brethren implants. Those allowed for the wearer to retain self-autonomy, at least to a certain extent. But how much? Already Jeth felt like a stranger in his own head.

His fingers closed once more around the stem, but he couldn't muster the courage to pull it out, not without knowing what would happen. It might hurt; he might faint. *I might never be the same again.*

Shuddering, he pushed the idea away before it overtook him.

On shaking legs, he crossed the room to the sealed door. He pounded on it, focusing entirely on getting out and keeping his thoughts away from the implant and what it meant.

Several minutes passed with no response from the other side. His hands began to ache from the constant percussion, and he forced himself to stop and regroup. He turned toward the right of the door where he knew the lock was located behind a hidden panel. He placed his palm against the smooth surface. To his surprise the panel slid open at his touch.

A simple keypad waited beneath. Jeth stared at the numbers, the buzzing in his head close to a roar. There were millions of possibilities for the code to open the door. He had no way of knowing. No way of guessing.

And yet . . .

An image as sharp as a digital photograph appeared in his mind. Except it wasn't an image at all but an actual thought, devoid of precise shape and appearance but absolutely clear to him nevertheless.

Without contemplating his actions, Jeth keyed the number. The lock clicked, and the door slid open with a quiet hiss.

Jeth stared at the opening, his breath quickening by the moment. How had that worked? Where had the information come from? He touched the implant again. It was a black one, it had to be. The black ones were networked, he knew, allowing all the Malleus Brethren to communicate mind-to-mind with one another. He'd seen it before, but had never tried to imagine how it might work. Even now, he couldn't quite imagine it.

Get going, an inner voice prompted him. Jeth stepped out into the corridor, a strange calm coming over him, a sense of rightness he couldn't explain and didn't want to contemplate. All that mattered was he was free. The corridor outside was empty of guards, empty of everything except more sealed doors. He debated which way to go, then turned left on instinct. He had to find the crew, find his ship. And he had to find Daxton Price.

To kill him.

The idea gave Jeth pause. He meant it, and yet he didn't. He was outraged, furious, and yet he wasn't. It was as if something had cleaved his mind and emotions in two. He could sense both but didn't feel truly connected to either, like he was a passenger in his own being.

He broke into a trot and then a run, avoiding the reality of such thoughts by staying focused on the goal. He slowed before the first intersection, hearing voices around the corner. His head buzzed, and another image flashed. He saw two of the Malleus Brethren, easily identifiable by their black implants and black coats trimmed in indigo silk, arguing back and forth. Both carried guns holstered at their sides.

Implicitly trusting the truth of the image, Jeth charged into the corridor. The Brethren gaped in surprise, too slow to react. Jeth took out the first one with a punch to the temple, using his right hand. He didn't hold back, letting the strength in his cybernetic hand do the maximum damage. By the time the first Brethren started to fall he was after the second with another well-aimed punch. A shock pulsed through him, and then a thrill at how easily they fell. He stared at his right hand, wondering how he ever could've despised it so. Never again.

But no, that wasn't right. He did hate it. It was alien and dangerous.

But useful.

Jeth shook off the internal argument and stooped to remove the Brethren's guns. He debated tucking one into the waistband of his pants so as to leave his right hand free, but he resisted the impulse.

He moved on, catching sight of two women in white uniforms, either nurses or perhaps maids or some other kind of employee of the prison. He didn't care. Both of the women fled when they spotted him bearing down on them with a gun in each hand.

Find Daxton. The thought become a mantra, playing on repeat in his head. Once he found him the rest would sort itself out. He knew it instinctively. Jeth barely noticed how all the people he came across fled at the sight of him as he made his way to the exit. When he got there, he realized the structure was hardly a prison at all, but more of a medical facility. Or maybe it was both. A place for the insane.

Find Daxton, the mantra reasserted itself, blocking out all other thoughts and worries.

If his escape was too easy, the knowledge didn't fully register in his mind, but passed through it in a fleeting moment. As soon as he was out of the building, he saw he was on the central level of the spaceport, not far from the main entrance to the governor's estate. He stepped onto the walkway and tucked the guns into his waistband. In this uniform and with the implant, the people passing by wouldn't question his presence.

The need to find Daxton reached fever pitch, and he picked up the pace, soon arriving at the public entrance to the gardens that surrounded the govenor's estate. Not much had changed under Daxton's leadership, at least not on the surface. The place was as decadent as ever, the smell of flowers and plants strong in Jeth's nose as he entered, navigating the flowerbeds, fountains, and hedgerows without conscious thought. Surrounded by all that plant life it was easy to forget this was a spaceport, everything artificially built and maintained.

Jeth reached the gate that led into Daxton's private gardens. It was locked but unguarded. He didn't question why he'd come here when Daxton could be anywhere. The sight of that unguarded door should've pointed him in a new direction, and yet he stepped up to it and entered a code on the keypad. As in the cell, the combination came to him in a flash of thought. The gate opened, and Jeth headed in.

He found Daxton huddled over one of the flowerbeds, spreading peat with his hands. Dirt smears covered the rubber gloves he wore. Sweat coated his brow, dampening his black hair. His face was in profile, giving Jeth a partial view of the brain implant inserted into the back of his skull: a red one, the color of old blood. It was the master implant that controlled all the others. The sight of it filled Jeth with both dread and awe. The back of his skull tingled.

Memories flooded Jeth's mind of all the times he'd seen Hammer wearing the red implant. The strongest memory was of the last time he'd seen him. The crime lord had stood over Jeth with a clear-colored implant in his hand. Jeth was on his knees, held in place by Dax, prone and helpless to stop what was coming. Jeth knew that deep down Dax wanted to stop it, that Hammer was as much his enemy as Jeth's. Jeth pleaded with him, begging. But Dax had been wearing his black Brethren implant, and even though he fought for control of his own mind, Hammer's red implant had held sway over him, up until the very last moment when Dax had finally broken free. So close Jeth had come to being made a Malleus Guard that day.

And what am I now?

Jeth didn't say anything, just stood there watching as Dax labored on, carefully freeing some flowered plant with blue petals from a carton and then burying the roots deep in the loose earth. Without the implant, Dax might have been mistaken for a simple gardener, the kind who took pride and pleasure in such honest work.

When he finished, Dax wiped the sweat from his forehead and spoke without looking up. "Welcome back, Jethro. I've been expecting you."

Jeth went rigid at the sound of Dax's voice. He heard it with his ears and yet somehow felt it as well, a vibration in his mind. *He knew I was here the whole time. He knew I was coming.*

A sick feeling twisted in Jeth's gut as full understanding came to him at last. He hadn't escaped the cell. This wasn't a quest for vengeance. This was obedience. Red implant over black. Dax had beckoned him, and Jeth had answered his master's call.

CHAPTER 10

JETH'S HEAD SPUN, HIS HEART POUNDING. *MASTER, MASTER, master.*

Slave, slave, slave.

No. Jeth forced the spinning to cease as he searched for his voice, buried deep in the layers of shock. "How could you do this to me after . . . after . . ."

Daxton looked up, his caramel-colored eyes bright in the artificial sunlight overhead. A frown curved his lips. "After what?"

Jeth scowled. "You know *what.* You helped me escape this when Hammer tried to force it on me. And now you go and do it anyway?" He motioned to the thing in the back of his head, its presence a dead weight.

False sympathy crossed Daxton's face. "Well, it's not a clear one."

"This is just as bad."

"Oh come on now, Jeth, you know that's not true. If I'd given you a Guard implant you wouldn't be yourself anymore, just a programmable shell, a tool in human form. I would never do that to you. I'm not in the habit of courting waste. I've given you a gift instead."

Jeth glowered, distrusting the sincerity in Dax's words, even as he felt himself warming to the man, the way he'd once warmed to his favorite teachers or family doctor, an automatic trust. He fought the feeling back, willing his anger to the surface. It should've been easy. Anger had been his constant companion in life, a bottomless reservoir inside him.

"A gift?"

Dax rolled his thick shoulders, his neck muscles flexing. He wasn't nearly as large as his predecessor, but he'd bulked up these last few months. "If you don't like it, take it out."

Jeth hesitated. There was nothing he wanted more than to rid himself of this thing attached to him, and yet the idea of actually doing it made dread pound in his temples, as if he were considering cutting off his own hand. "How do I know this isn't a trick?"

Dax frowned, his expression wounded. "Honestly, Jeth, what kind of a man do you think I am?"

"I think you're the type who'll do whatever it takes to get what he wants. Just like Hammer."

Daxton's frown vanished, and he nodded. "I'm afraid that's true of most us. The getting what we want bit."

Jeth couldn't believe the changes in the man before him. He had Dax's face, but in so many ways he was Hammer all over again. He wore his arrogance like royal robes. He had the attitude of man absolutely certain of his power and position.

Daxton sighed. "It's a black implant. Nothing will happen,

I promise. If I wanted to kill you, I wouldn't do it this way. Far too messy. You should've seen what happened when Hammer finally tried to take out his Guard implant."

"Hammer's dead?" The last time Jeth had seen him, the man had been catatonic but still alive, reduced from master to slave after Dax forced the clear-colored implant meant for Jeth into Hammer's architecture instead.

"Very much so. Now go on. Man up and get it over with."

Jeth bit his tongue hard enough to draw blood. The sharp taste helped clear his doubt, and he raised his right hand to the back of his skull, wrapped his fingers around the rubbery tentacles, and pulled.

The implant came out with a wet sucking sound that made him want to vomit. Bile burned the back of his throat as he stared down at the thing in his hand—a flaccid, dead spider. He tossed it into the grass at Daxton's feet. Relief came and went in a single breath, driven off by a powerful urge to retrieve the implant and reinsert it. Jeth felt its absence like a physical pain. As if he'd been full a moment before, and now was empty.

He shook his head. *It's not real, not real, not real.*

Across from him, Daxton watched his struggle with almost clinical interest. Jeth wanted to gouge the look from the man's face. Finally, he remembered the guns sheathed at his waist. How could he have forgotten? Why had he waited so long? He pulled one free and aimed the barrel at Daxton's face.

"I'll kill you for doing this to me."

Dax tilted his head, his expression one of mild surprise. "Do you really want to? Are you sure? Or would you rather pick up that implant and put it back where it belongs?"

Jeth's hand trembled as a phantom ache went through the back of his skull. It was different from the old one. Instead of stabbing pain, it was an ache of emptiness, like being alone in the middle of a crowd, or that deep hunger that has nothing to do with food and everything to do with want.

"Go on," Dax said. "No one will think less of you for giving in. Like I said, it's a gift. You're one of us now."

Jeth closed his eyes and shook his head, trying to fight it off. Then he opened them again and forced his hand to steady on the gun. Sweat coated his body, the muscles in his arm close to spasm. "I'm not one of you."

Dax sighed and waved him off. "Suit yourself. I should've known better than to think anything would be easy when it came to you. Then again, I might've been disappointed if it were." Before he'd even finished speaking, two of the Malleus Brethren appeared as if from nowhere. Jeth barely had time to register their hulking presence before they ripped the guns from him.

Too late, Jeth realized they were the same Brethren he'd taken out earlier. In the fervor of his journey here, he'd forgotten that the implants helped their wearers heal faster. The one on the left voiced his grudge with a fist. The punch landed against Jeth's belly, and he doubled over, stomach muscles cramping.

The moment he regained his breath, Jeth lunged for the man, his right hand all the weapon he needed. The shrill pop of a gunshot froze him midswing, the bullet passing so close to his face it burned. Jeth spun toward the source.

"We both know I never miss by accident," said Dax, a Luke 357 clutched in his hand.

Jeth swallowed, the fight going out of him. Daxton might've changed, but not this part of him. He'd always been a crack shot.

Forcing his hands to his sides as the Brethren stepped back from him, Jeth said, "Where's my crew and my ship?"

Dax pointed at the implant on the ground. "Everything you need to know is right there. And considering how well you followed my guidance to get here, you should have no trouble at all finding what else you're looking for."

That longing came over Jeth again, strong enough that his knees threatened to buckle. All it would take was a couple of steps and he could return the implant to its sheath.

A sympathetic look crossed Dax's face. "Tell you what. Why don't we talk things over for a bit? I won't pressure you to wear the implant and you won't pressure me with having to kill you."

Jeth inhaled and slowly nodded, the struggle in him lessening to something bearable.

"Good choice." Daxton waved to a table nearby, one with a huge umbrella to block out the sunlight.

Jeth walked over to it and sat down, thinking clearly for the first time since he'd woken in that cell. He couldn't trust Dax, but he knew for certain the man didn't want him dead. If he did, he wouldn't have gone to the trouble with the implant. *And with guiding me,* Jeth thought and shuddered. Coming here had seemed like his choice. But it wasn't.

Daxton had manipulated him like a puppet on a cognitive string.

Even now he felt the urge to retrieve the implant from where it lay in the grass. He had to resist. *It'll get easier,* he tried to reassure himself.

"Don't worry," Dax said, brushing dirt from the coveralls he wore before sitting down. "You'll get used to it in time. The implant, I mean. It's always rough when the connection first goes live, but you'll adjust to it soon, I promise."

"I don't want to adjust." Jeth folded his arms over his chest. His sides felt naked without the guns and he spared a quick glance at the two Brethren, who had retreated a respectable distance away. But they were still close enough to stop him if he tried anything. Why hadn't he taken out Dax when he had the chance? It should've been easy. He might even have gotten away with it. All he had to do was take the master implant from Dax and insert it into his own architecture. He could've established leadership over all the Malleus, the same as Dax had done.

And yet, Jeth had a feeling that it wouldn't have been so easy. Dax had been under Hammer's control for years before managing it. And there was too much Jeth didn't understand about the implants. He'd always thought it was simple: clear equaled mindless slave; black equaled connected and empowered; red equaled master of all. But now he didn't know what to think. And the ache, the want, blossomed and grew.

"I don't doubt your repulsion," Dax said, "but you will get past it nevertheless."

"How could you do it?" Jeth said. "You were supposed to be better than Hammer. He forced you into his service, didn't he?"

Dax slowly nodded, but his expression didn't look like one of guilt.

Frustrated by his failure to get a response, Jeth switched tactics. He rapped his knuckles on the table. "How's your brother, Dax? Did you force an implant on him, too?" It was a low blow, Jeth knew. Hammer had used Dax's brother as a pressure point to get him to join the Brethren, to submit to wearing a black implant.

A dark emotion, not quite anger and not quite sadness came and went in Dax's eyes. "My brother is dead."

Jeth shivered at the coldness in his voice. He bit back condolences. This man didn't deserve his sympathy.

"What do you want from me?" Jeth asked, even though the answer was obvious. Daxton wanted possession of him. That's what this was, the business with the implant—his way of laying ownership to Jeth's will. Hatred burned in Jeth's chest, and for a moment he had perfect clarity of mind. He would kill Daxton Price for doing this to him, for making him a slave in his own head.

As if he once again had gleaned Jeth's thoughts, Dax set the gun he'd used earlier on the table in front of him. It was close enough to taunt Jeth, but he knew better than to make a grab for it. Daxton was as fast as he was accurate.

"What I want," Dax said as he began tugging off his soiled gloves, "is your help."

Jeth blinked. "My help?"

"Yes, your help. Don't be so surprised. I've needed it before, haven't I? If you hadn't been there, encouraging me to cast off Hammer's control, I never would've defeated him."

Jeth slowly nodded, recalling the memory once more. He hadn't realized his words had made that much difference. Still, that wasn't the same scenario as this one. Yes, they'd taken down Hammer together in the end, but that had been more like mutual aid. If anything, Jeth had needed Dax's help more than the other way around. But the way Dax spoke, they had been in it together from the start and were now old friends reuniting for another common purpose.

Jeth narrowed his gaze on Dax. "Why do this to me, then, if all you want is help?" He gestured to the back of his head.

Dax sighed, and Jeth couldn't tell if it was theatrical or genuine regret this time. "It was necessary. I have to have your loyalty, and the implant will guarantee that I do."

Jeth seethed, even as a part of him understood the logic. Dax knew that Jeth's first loyalty was to himself and his family and crew. He frowned, realizing that Dax could have used his sisters to ensure his compliance instead of the implant, the same way Hammer had used Dax's brother against him. The fact that he hadn't made Jeth feel both relieved and nervous. He already felt cleaved in two by the implant, but he had a feeling that was just the beginning of its power.

Leaning back in his chair, Jeth assumed a calm posture. It was a far cry from his rising desperation, but appearances mattered. Especially to men like Dax. "What is it you need my help with, exactly?"

Daxton smiled. "I want the coordinates to Empyria."

Jeth went still, the conversation with Lizzie popping up in his head at once. *A code,* she had said. *To Empyria.* But how could Dax know about it? Had Lizzie told him? Did he force it out of her?

"And as your mother is the only living person ever to have found the planet," Dax went on, "I need you to—"

He broke off as a shrill scream filled the air around them. Jeth trembled at the sound of it, his pulse doubling in the space of a second. He knew that sound, the way it had physical presence like a shot from a pulse gun, and he understood the danger it could bring. But why was Cora here?

The scream transformed into words. "How dare you!" The voice was female, but far too old to be Cora.

Jeth turned toward the speaker, his gaze falling on a woman marching down one of the paths that led to the small clearing. Her hair, hanging in a long braid pulled over one shoulder, was an impossible shade of white, as if it had been freshly painted. For a moment, Jeth thought she must be an escaped mental patient; she wore all white, the baggy pants and tunic emphasizing a thinness that bordered on emaciation. She looked familiar to him somehow, like someone he ought to know.

That's when the truth of who she was hit him like a physical blow. All the air rushed out of his lungs, and he would've fallen down if he'd been standing.

A foreign word rose to his lips. He expelled it in a single breath.

"Mom."

CHAPTER 11

JETH'S VISION BLURRED. THE WORLD SPUN AROUND HIM. The colors in the garden, the rich greens and vibrant blues, the yellows and reds, all smeared together in a chaotic vortex.

His mother. Alive. And here.

He started to rise, ready to run to her, but the look on her face froze him in place. Her gaze was pinned on Dax, fury in her eyes. Marian Seagrave strode into the clearing, giving no sign that she knew her long-forgotten son was present.

The two Malleus Brethren nearby raised their guns at her approach, ready to defend their master. Marian waved a hand at them, and a loud crack split the air, making Jeth flinch. A phantom pain arced through his cybernetic hand as the sound triggered a vivid memory of when Cora had used her ability to manipulate metaspace to destroy the gun he'd been holding, taking his fingers with it. She'd done it out of fear, not anger, but Jeth would never be able to hear that sound without thinking about it.

He forced his gaze to the Brethren, expecting to find them maimed or cut down entirely. But only their guns had been affected, sliced clean through by an invisible force. His mother had phased the guns into metaspace and out of existence, leaving only useless handles behind.

Daxton jumped to his feet, hands raised. "Please calm down, Marian. You promised not to do this. And no harm has been done."

Jeth understood his fear completely. Fingers were hardly anything. He'd once seen his mother use her ability to kill a man. With a single thought she had phased a chair leg through the heart of an ITA scientist. The memory of it sent a trickle of fear spilling into his joy at her presence.

"No harm." Marian's mouth twisted into a sneer. "You insert one of your implants into my son and claim no harm? Even after you promised to deliver him safe and whole?"

"He is safe and whole. See for yourself."

Jeth braced, waiting for his mother's gaze to alight on him. *She's here.* The realization pounded through him, impossible to believe despite the evidence before him. For a second he wondered if this was all just a dream. Then again, he didn't think his imagination capable of such a feat. This was not the mother of his childhood, the one he had known and loved. Everything about her was transformed, the old recreated in a new image. Her shock of white hair and her ability to manipulate metaspace were strange enough, but it went deeper than that, a fundamental change in her very presence. He remembered easy smiles and a quick laugh. Nothing at all like this hardness and ice before him.

Still, Marian did not look at him, keeping her gaze fixed on Dax. "You lied."

Dax shook his head, sweat beading his hairline. "I didn't lie. And I didn't harm him. The implant architecture was already there. I just inserted the implant when he arrived."

A tremble racked Marian's body, fury emblazoned on her face. Jeth had never seen her so angry. She raised a hand to the back of her head, tracing a finger along the tentacle of a white implant. It blended so perfectly with her hair, Jeth hadn't even noticed it. Its existence wasn't a revelation. He'd seen the implant in the Aether Project videos. But the sight of it meant something wholly different to him now.

She went through this, too, he realized, his head throbbing. He glanced away from her, his eyes drawn to the sight of the black implant, lying a few meters away.

"Was it your predecessor who installed the architecture?" Marian asked, only slightly less angry than before.

"Yes," Dax said, sounding steadier. "And you never said anything about giving him an implant. Surely you can't blame me for wanting to ensure my investment. I've got everything riding on this."

Jeth wanted to ask what they were talking about, but he was still too dazed to speak.

"Very well," Marian said. "It's too late to take it back anyway."

Dax waved her off. "He'll be fine."

Marian's mouth tightened into a grimace. Finally, slowly, she turned her gaze on Jeth. As her eyes met his, he could barely look away from the white hair, and the crystal glass smoothness of her skin, which made her appear impossibly young, hardly any older than he was himself.

That's when she smiled, and the hardness in her face

drained away. "Hello, Jeth. I'm so glad to see you."

The soft, gentle tone of her voice shattered his reservations. He leaped up, crossed the short distance over to her, and swept her up into a hug. She was so light, he lifted her off her feet easily, hugging her tight enough that she gasped. "Mom . . . you're here . . . you're alive."

"Yes." She cradled the back of his head, her hands gentle and warm against his skull. For a moment he forgot the ache of the absent implant. Tears burned his eyes, more than a couple escaping down his cheeks. He didn't care. He was too caught up in the swell of his emotions. Pain and happiness whirled inside him, as strong as two gale winds. He wanted to laugh and cry. He wanted to scream in rage at those lost years, believing she was dead. And he wanted to scream in relief that it was now over.

Marian was crying too, and he held her for a very long time, before finally setting her on her feet once more.

She patted his back. "It's going to be all right, Jeth."

He nodded then slowly backed away from the embrace, wiping away his tears. He knew giving in to his emotions in front of Dax had been unwise, but there was nothing for it now. He couldn't help it.

"Well, now that the sweet reunion is over," said Dax, a cold smile twisting his mouth, "why don't you sit and we'll discuss the rest of our business."

Marian wrinkled her nose in a gesture that reminded Jeth so much of Lizzie it hurt, and he glanced away, fighting back tears as he sought out his chair again. Marian took the seat opposite him. Her familiar scent, a mixture that defied exact description other than that it was uniquely hers, was all around him.

Daxton sat down as well, looking at ease, but only on the surface. He flashed a too-friendly smile at Jeth. "To answer what I am sure is your most burning question: While you were out there running the ITA back and forth across the galaxy, I have been busy liberating Marian here from their clutches."

Jeth drew a breath, trying to regain his center. But he didn't know how to manage it when his whole world had just been flipped upside down.

"Don't pretend it was some mercy mission, Price," Marian said in a scolding tone Jeth knew well. The sound of it, which used to fill him with dread, brought him sweet comfort now.

Dax laughed. "Always so direct and to the point, you Seagraves." He shifted his gaze to Jeth. "I can see where you learned it."

Jeth nodded, still struggling to find words. "It saves time," he managed at last. He cleared his throat. "So you rescued my mother in the hope that she would tell you how to find Empyria. I'm guessing that plan backfired."

"Too right," Dax said, sighing.

Jeth wanted to point out that Dax should've known that Marian wouldn't spill her secrets for him. The ITA had been trying for years without luck.

"But that's where you come in." Dax raised a finger his direction.

Jeth's brow furrowed. "How?"

"What Dax wants is going to come at a price," Marian said, casting Jeth a warm smile. "You're part one of my demands."

"You made a deal?"

She nodded. "And so far, he's delivered. You and your sisters are here. Our family can be whole again."

Jeth glanced away, still too emotionally fragile to look at her for long. He fixed a stare on Dax. "So what's part two?"

Dax grimaced. "Not as easy as part one, I can tell you."

Jeth grunted. Dax thought that was easy? If Shady hadn't sent that message, he never would've found them. Jeth supposed in the light of being reunited with his mother, he ought to be grateful at Shady's betrayal, but he couldn't forget the buzz still lingering in his head and the insistent desire to retrieve the implant. Not even the shock of his mother's presence had driven it away.

"And part two is completely insane, I might point out," added Dax.

Marian fixed a chilly gaze on him. "You can whine all you want, but completing the mission is the only way you will ever get the coordinates to Empyria."

Jeth frowned, thinking of Lizzie and the hidden code once more. But he stopped himself at once. He didn't think it wise to dwell on that now. If he did have access to the information Dax wanted, it was a secret worth protecting.

"What're you after, Mom?" Jeth asked. "What does Dax have to do?"

Marian looked at him, that alien hardness on her face once more. "We're going to destroy the Harvester on First-Earth."

Jeth blinked back at her, incredulous. The Harvester on First-Earth was the biggest and oldest of them all, ground zero of the discovery of the Pyreans. That was where they first appeared some several hundred years ago, branching out from metaspace for a purpose no one understood. Not that it mattered to the early scientists, who quickly discovered their usefulness in creating a doorway between the physical world and metaspace.

"Destroy?" Jeth said. "Like, blow it up?"

"Blow it up, tear it down. Whatever it takes," Marian said, unflinching.

"Like I was saying." Dax shook his head. "Completely insane."

Jeth nodded. First-Earth was First-Earth. Rescuing Marian would've been hard enough, but this was hard to the tenth power.

"Do you have any idea what you're doing, Marian?" Dax said. "People will die. The Harvester is manned by a crew of hundreds, and if this makes things worse with the metatech, dozens of star systems could be left to die."

Marian turned a glare on Dax. "As if you're concerned about collateral damage. But yes, I know exactly what I'm doing. It has to be done. And if you are set on finding Empyria, you best share my determination. If the Harvester on First-Earth isn't destroyed, there will be no Empyria left for you to find. It's the Harvester that's causing the Pyreans to wither away, and if they perish, so will Empyria. So will everything."

Daxton looked skeptical, but Marian didn't give him a chance to argue.

"The Pyreans aren't sick from some disease, as the ITA believes. It's the harvesting itself that's doing it. The unrelenting rape of their world that's been going on for hundreds of years is finally taking its toll." She fell silent, although her sides heaved. She looked like a woman gone mad, like the woman Jeth had seen in her video journals. What had happened to her when she visited Empyria? He wanted to ask, but held back. She might tell him, but certainly not in front of Dax.

As for Marian's theory, he supposed it made sense. He remembered Sierra's tree metaphor. Maybe it was more accurate than either of them had realized. He didn't know much about trees, but he guessed that if you stripped away its branches, its bark, all the way down to its core, it would die. Same as anything else.

Only, if the harvesting stopped, the consequences would be the same as if the Pyreans died out—the end of interstellar travel, just like Dax had said. The ITA had no way to pass through metaspace without the Pyreans. Their plan had been to clone Cora, creating a human-Pyrean species, a slave race that would take the place of the metadrives. But Jeth would die and take the entire universe with him before he let them have her.

He shook his head as another complication occurred to him. "What's the point in only destroying the one on First-Earth? What about all the others?"

"No, don't go there," Dax said, glaring. "Our deal is for First-Earth only. The other Harvesters don't come into play. Not for this. I've risked enough already."

Marian sighed. "Yes, that's what we agreed on. One galaxy-sized problem at a time, please. But the mission won't be in vain. The Harvester on First-Earth is the largest and most destructive by far. Taking it down will have a massive impact."

Jeth frowned, confused by her dismissal of what seemed so obvious a problem. He glanced from her to Dax, wondering just how extensive their "negotiations" had been.

"Okay, but how do I fit into this?" Jeth asked, remembering Dax's words about ensuring his investment. The growing throb in his head was making it hard to think.

"Sierra has information we need to complete the mission," said Dax. "And I believe you are the only person capable of getting her to cooperate."

Jeth shot him a puzzled look, at first not understanding. Once he did, he snorted. "You must be joking, right? I can't make Sierra do anything she doesn't want to. Nobody can. Besides"—he shifted his gaze to his mother—"Mom, I can see how much this means to you, but . . . you're free of the ITA, finally. Cora, Lizzie, Uncle Milton, everyone else, we're all together again. We can leave now, never look back."

For a moment he feared his mother would turn the same

hard anger on him that she'd shown Dax, but instead her expression softened. "I know, Jeth. I promise you I understand. But we have no choice. We *must* do this."

Jeth clasped his hands together, the idea of the risk involved beyond his ability to contemplate even for a second. "Why?"

"First," Marian said, her expression darkening, "destroying the Harvester will be a devastating blow to the ITA, one they might never recover from. And I trust you see the benefit of that."

Jeth gave a reluctant nod. *Revenge.* That was a motivation he could understand, but it wasn't enough.

"And the second, more important reason, is because of Cora." Marian's voice hitched as she said the name, her eyes glistening with tears. The sight of them made Jeth's breath catch as he remembered that his mother had never seen her youngest daughter at all, had never touched her or kissed her or soothed her fears. The ITA had taken Cora from Marian at birth as part of their cruel experiments in their determination to master the power of metaspace.

"Cora's here, Mom," Jeth said, wanting to comfort her. "She's safe. At least, I think she is." He shot a glare at Dax.

"Of course she's safe. Your whole crew is just fine."

"I know she's here, Jeth," Marian said. "And trust me, it took all of my willpower not to go to her the moment I found out. And Lizzie, too. But seeing you first was more important."

Jeth swallowed, his emotions clawing up his throat again.

"We have to destroy the Harvester," Marian continued,

"because if the Pyreans die, so will Cora. They are connected. Cora is a part of the superorganism. Physically separate in her body, yes, but connected in her mind, in the part of her that allows her to touch metaspace. As the Pyreans deteriorate, so will she."

Jeth's heart lurched as understanding struck him. *It's happening already.* Cora, with the dark bruises beneath her eyes, the sallow skin, and the lethargy that was always present, even after hours of sleep. Then an even more horrible idea occurred to him. "What about you?" he said to his mother. "Aren't you connected to them as well?"

Marian hesitated. "I . . . I don't know. It's not the same for me as it is for Cora."

"But it's possible you might die, too." The world seemed to spin around Jeth for a moment as old memories rose up in his mind as fresh as yesterday. He already knew what it felt like for her to die. He'd been through it once before. It didn't matter that it had been a lie the ITA made up in order to keep her a prisoner. It didn't matter that she stood here now, dispelling any doubt that she still lived. The pain before had been real. He never wanted to experience that again.

Before his mother could reply, Jeth turned to Dax. "All right, I'm in. I can only imagine I'm part of whatever plan you're cooking up for destroying the Harvester. What do you need me to do?"

A wide grin split Dax's face, and he waved behind him to where the implant was lying, a black blemish against the green. "You know what step one is."

Jeth didn't move for several long seconds. It wasn't surprise that held him in place. He'd known from the beginning this was what Dax was after. No, what paralyzed him was how eager he was to comply. And it had little to do with his mother or Cora or anything else. It was pure desire, almost instinctual.

"Why must he wear it?" said Marian, her earlier anger seething beneath the surface once more.

Dax drummed his fingers on the table. "Jeth and I have a complicated history. And we can't afford any complications on this mission."

Marian scowled. "Jeth doesn't have to go on this mission at all. With a couple of your men, I'm more than capable of handling this without risking my son."

"There's no way I'm not going with you," Jeth said, outraged by the idea. They'd been apart for years. He wasn't about to let anything separate them now.

"You see." Dax motioned to Jeth. "I doubt you'll be changing his mind, Marian. Your son is too much like you. Not to mention there's the issue with Sierra. It's not as if I can take her trust on faith. She's already proven herself skilled at betrayal." Dax touched a finger to his chin. "I suppose I could outfit her with an implant too—"

"Don't you dare." Jeth leaned toward him, ready to snatch the gun off the table.

Dax gestured him back. "But I prefer not to. Giving Jeth one was distasteful enough. No matter how necessary."

Jeth's fingers curled into fists. He wanted to hit Dax, to

kill him. All the anger Jeth had been unable to feel earlier burst fresh and hot inside him. For a moment he almost lost control, but he reined it in at the last second. Relief that he was still capable of feeling such anger toward Dax came over him a moment later. The implant had seemed to cut him off from his anger, but it was only temporary. That was good. He could still escape its influence, Dax's control, eventually. He hoped.

"And I also want Lizzie on this mission," Dax continued, oblivious to Jeth's internal battle. "Her skills are invaluable. But both girls are absolutely loyal to Jeth. So it stands to reason that if Jeth is loyal to me—"

"Yeah, I get it," Marian said. She sighed, and Jeth heard the defeat in it. "You must agree to let him go afterward."

"Of course," Dax said, his expression intent. "I'll even take care of the surgery to remove the implant architecture. That is, assuming Jeth wants to be free of it. The choice will be his, of course."

Jeth forced air into his lungs, catching the implication. *If I do this, I might never want to undo it.*

Dax flashed a smile. "You see, Jeth. In the end you'll get everything you've ever wanted. Once I have Empyria, you and your family will be free to go. I'll even send you off with enough money and protection to avoid the ITA forever. It's all in your hands."

Jeth's eyes drifted over to the implant once more, his stomach a hard knot in his center and his mind afire with doubt and possibilities. And want. Yes, there was that, too.

He wanted the freedom Dax promised, the dream come true. But he also wanted the implant. The empty feeling from its absence gnawed at him.

The want scared him more than anything. He knew that Dax could be lying about the whole thing. That he might renege on the entire deal the moment he had the location. Or he might let the others go but force Jeth to stay on as one of the Brethren. Only, if Jeth accepted the implant, would he even care? Or would he gladly choose to follow Dax like the rest of the Brethren, his will distorted by the implant's seductive power?

It was an impossible choice. A devil's deal. And yet it was no choice at all. Not really.

On tremulous legs, Jeth stood and walked over to the implant while his mother and Dax silently watched. He picked it up with both hands, wondering how he could both loathe and desire one object so much at the same time.

The desire is fake. A trick of the mind.

But it didn't matter. If wearing this implant meant freedom for his family, for his crew, he would do it. He would sacrifice anything for them. Even his own soul.

Jeth closed his eyes, and then with an ease that suggested he'd done it a thousand times before, he raised the point of the implant to the base of his skull and drove it home.

CHAPTER 12

A BATTLE RAGED IN JETH'S MIND. HE HATED THE FEEL OF the implant, the knowledge that it was there.

But he loved it, too.

The first few seconds after he inserted it were something close to ecstasy, as if questions he'd had all his life had finally been answered. He knew it was a dangerous feeling, intoxicating and addictive, but he'd made the bargain with Dax and now he just had to hope this would all be over soon and he could get rid of the implant forever.

A few minutes later, he and his mother left the gardens. There was more for them to discuss, plans to be finalized, but Marian wanted to see her daughters. And Jeth needed time to deal with this alien presence in his head, and the irrevocable decision he had made.

They followed behind the two Brethren now serving as escorts back to *Avalon*. Marian walked in silence beside him, not even her footfalls making a sound. A child might think her a ghost, with her white hair and clothes and her uncanny grace, which made it look as if she floated instead of walked. Being next to her was just as distracting as the implant. Jeth was taller than her now, could practically wrap his arms twice around her small frame. The last time he was with her, it had been the opposite.

My mother. She's here. She's here. No matter how many times he thought it, no matter how many glances he stole, he still couldn't believe it.

The buzzing in his head didn't help matters. It had been steadily growing since the moment he'd inserted the implant. Soon it was too loud for him to ignore. But he didn't know what to do about it either. It was too much with him, calling him to tune into it, to focus his thoughts on it. But that was dangerous, he knew. He couldn't give in to it, no matter how desperately he wanted to, how easy it would be. Not if he wanted to be able to walk away from this. And so he had to learn to cope with it. Somehow he must find a way to hold on to all the things that made him who he was.

"Keep up, Brother."

Jeth flinched at the sound of the voice, so gruff and loud, and at the title: *Brother.* He stared at the back of the heads in front of him, both framed with black implants. The one on the left had spoken. *Perry,* the name came to Jeth without effort, transmitted directly to his thoughts through the implant. And that wasn't all. Jeth knew that Perry was twenty-seven years old, the middle child of three, and fond of virtual shooter games.

Jeth frowned, the image of one of the Brethren playing a video game incompatible with his worldview. The Brethren did not do such mundane things as play video games. Did they?

"What do you think we do?" Perry glanced over his shoulder, something like a smile twisting his burly features. "Work round the clock? Switch ourselves off at night and recharge our batteries?"

Jeth narrowed his eyes. The Brethren also didn't have any sense of humor.

"What are you talking about?" Marian asked, but Perry only faced front again. She glanced at Jeth, but he had no words for what was going on inside his head. She reached over and touched his arm, offering him wordless comfort. Maybe she couldn't know what they were saying through the link, but she wore an implant as well. Jeth guessed she knew how this felt.

Drawing strength from her touch, he considered the men in front of him again. At least Perry didn't seem too bad. He shifted his gaze to the other Brethren. At once, the knowledge came into Jeth's head that Eric had killed nearly a dozen people, a score he kept with carefully drawn white lines on the butt of the gun sheathed at his right hip. Some of those deaths had been women, some of them elderly, but all his victims had been guilty of some offense against Hammer. There hadn't been any since Daxton had taken control as far as Jeth could tell.

You liked it, Jeth thought, and when Eric sneered over his shoulder at him, Jeth knew the other man had heard, that somehow his thought had traveled through the link that connected their minds. It had happened involuntarily, as if his brain were an open faucet, thoughts pouring out of him.

And into him, Jeth realized, as images and emotions that weren't his filled his consciousness. For a moment, he felt the pleasure Eric had taken in those killings as if it were his own, as if *he* had done the killing himself. He covered his mouth with his hand, stomach clenching, first from revulsion, then from fear. It was all so intimate, this sharing of knowledge mind to mind.

What will they see in my memories?

An image of Sierra lying naked on his bed, all blond hair and pale skin, flashed unbidden into Jeth's mind. He tried to stop it, tried to take it back, but it was too late. The Brethren in front of him exchanged smirks, and a flush heated Jeth's body from the top of his hairline to his toes. He forced his thoughts to something else, picturing a blank wall, steel gray and as strong as plasinum. Sweat trickled down his neck from the effort of the concentration.

At last, they arrived in Sector 3 where *Avalon* was moored. From the implant, Jeth knew the entire crew was inside, all of them under a temporary lockdown, one that would end as soon as he came on board.

"I've got it from here," he said to the Brethren as he approached the door. He didn't want them around to witness the crew's reactions, not just to Marian, but also to his new status as one of Dax's soldiers.

Eric grunted a good-bye and turned to leave, but Perry remained, his gray-eyed gaze fixed on Jeth. Jeth stared back at him as he tentatively probed the buzzing for some clue as to what the other man was thinking.

"First of all," Perry said, raising a hand, "stop thinking of it as the buzz or buzzing. It's a link, a doorway between your mind and the Axis."

"Axis?" Jeth's brow furrowed. Beside him, Marian listened to the exchange, intently. She looked tense, as if ready to defend Jeth if Perry dared threaten him. Jeth had seen that look often enough on Sierra's face.

Perry shrugged. "That's what we call it, the thing we're plugged into."

Jeth folded his arms over his chest. "Fascinating."

Perry rolled his eyes. "The point is that you need to learn how to filter. Once you let a thought loose on the Axis, we all have access to it. Forever."

Jeth scowled, the image of Sierra leaping to the forefront of his mind again. Then he realized what he was doing and willed that imaginary wall to rise up once more. *What have I done? How do I deal with this?* He didn't know how not to think.

"It doesn't have to be that hard," said Perry, running a finger down the length of his nose. A deep scar crossed the center of it, a remnant from some knife fight long ago, Jeth knew. "All you have to do is think something and the implant will obey—including a command to not release a certain thought or memory."

Jeth shook his head. "I can't even imagine how that's going to work."

"It will, but first you've got to stop fighting it. By trying to ignore the Axis, you're just making its pull on you stronger.

Give in to it instead. Once you've done that, you can establish control over it. You'll be able to access any information you want but stop it from sharing what you don't want. Just like a computer command."

"But I'm already accessing information."

"You're catching glimpses all right, but there's a whole lot more." Perry tapped a finger against his forehead. "Trust me, just let go and everything will fall into place. You'll be able to close the door when you want, and when you open it again, you'll control the view. The rest of us will only see what you want us to see, nothing more."

Jeth didn't reply, doubt robbing him of words. It didn't make sense. It couldn't be that simple. And if he gave in to the seductive pull of the Axis, would he lose himself in the process?

Perry rolled his eyes once more. "Suit yourself. Go crazy if you want. But I'm telling you, if you don't give in, all the Brethren will see everything. Sooner or later." He started to walk away then turned back. "Oh yeah, one more thing. This is probably obvious, but you're safe when the implant is out. The link is completely disconnected."

Jeth frowned, but didn't reply. He waited until Perry was out of sight before raising his hand to his head and removing the implant for a second time. It was easier than before, less like cutting off a limb—but he felt its absence more keenly.

He stared down at the thing, holding it stem up so the tentacles splayed over his hand. He couldn't leave it out forever.

Marian touched his shoulder, making him jump. She'd been so quiet, he'd almost forgotten she was there. He swore, realizing a second too late that his mother was in range to hear it.

"Sorry," he said, his guilt now feeling childish.

"No mind." Marian lowered her hand. "Are you all right?"

He nodded, unable to voice the lie.

"I'm so sorry." Marian pursed her lips. "I didn't know about the architecture. If I had, I would've made Dax swear not to do this. But I'm afraid he doesn't trust me."

"Yeah, well, he's a criminal," Jeth said. "You don't last long in that line of work trusting people like us."

"I suppose." She cupped his face. "Jeth . . . how you've changed. You look so much like your father."

Jeth swallowed, his emotions going into overload. It was hard enough dealing with the implant and the strange, wonderful reality of his mother's presence. He wasn't ready for a discussion of his dead father.

Marian released his face "There will be time to talk of such things later. We have so much to discuss. But first, we need to talk about this." She motioned to the implant in his hand. "I think that man was telling the truth."

Jeth started to dismiss her claim automatically until he caught sight of the barely visible tentacles of her implant. "Are you saying your implant works the same?"

"No, not the same." She paused, thinking it over. "My implant is designed to enhance my ability to perceive metaspace, nothing more. It's not a networked implant like that one. There is no Axis for me to link to, and I can't communicate mind-to-mind with anyone else wearing one. But the way he described the way it works sounds similar to my experience, and I know for certain the core technology is the same in both."

"Right," Jeth said. "All implants are manufactured by the ITA."

Marian grimaced. "Yes, but it's more than that. They all use the same power source—Pyreans."

"What?"

"It's true." Marian reached up and pulled out her implant, the tentacles sliding through her hair like white fingers. She held it out to him, and he could see it was almost identical to his, aside from the color. "The Pyreans have been used for much more than just space travel. It makes sense, doesn't it? Especially when you consider implants like the Brethren's, that allow for communication between minds and over great distances. Only the existence of metaspace makes such things possible."

"And only the Pyreans allow us to access it," Jeth said, making the connection. Now that she had pointed it out, he couldn't understand why he hadn't seen it before. "Does this means Pyreans are used in comm units, too?"

She flashed a proud smile. "It does."

Jeth worried at his lower lip. "But the Pyreans have been dying out for years. Why isn't there a shortage of comm devices, like there is metadrives?"

"Even a dead Pyrean retains its link to metaspace. It's not usually strong enough to transport physical objects, but communication is a different matter. The ITA has been using dead Pyreans in comm devices and implants such as these since they first discovered them."

"That's blowing my mind a little," Jeth said, smiling at the unintentional pun. He considered the implant in his hand, his thoughts on the Pyreans. They were a remarkable life-form, so useful. *And they're dying.* But would saving them matter? Could they be saved? He didn't know.

"Yes, mind-blowing." Marian raised her white implant to her head and slid it in. "But back to the point. When the ITA first forced this implant on me, I fought it as hard as I could. It was as if I'd been given a new set of instincts, but ones that worked against the ones I already had, like the feeling I should put my hand into the fire instead of avoiding the pain of getting burned."

Jeth's pulse quickened, her words a perfect articulation of how it felt to have this alien thing inside him. The urge to embrace its presence was as strong as his instinct to avoid pain, but equally as perverse as craving it. He swallowed. "What happened?"

"The more I fought, the more I lost control of my ability to manipulate metaspace. Eventually it started to manipulate me instead. I was phasing things all the time without meaning to." A pained look crossed her face, and Jeth couldn't help remembering the way she had killed that ITA scientist in one of the video recordings on the Aether Project. The man had been torturing her, yes, but she'd done it so easily and with little sign of regret or hesitation. Had she been in control then? He guessed she must've been. The act had appeared so deliberate.

"Finally," Marian went on, "I gave up fighting it. I held out for a long time, but no one can stand that kind of pressure forever. Once I gave in, though, everything changed. Suddenly I was in full control again, and I have been ever since."

Jeth exhaled, hating the answer. He didn't want it to be true, didn't want to trust it. But he couldn't see any way around it. Already the need to reinsert the implant thrummed through his system, setting his nerve endings on fire.

Marian patted his shoulder again. "It'll be all right. If anyone is strong enough to master this Axis, it's you." She smiled, the gesture lighting up her whole face. For a moment she was so dazzling Jeth couldn't stand the sight of it. It was like trying to look directly into a sun. She squeezed his shoulder. "You *need* to be able to control it, Jeth. You have to be ready for what we'll face on First-Earth, and mastering it is the only way you'll be able to stand up to Dax now. You cannot let him command your loyalty."

No, he couldn't. Dax was dangerous. Jeth needed to be loyal to himself. His thoughts and actions needed to be his alone; he couldn't let Dax hold all the strings, the way Hammer had done for all those years.

Jeth gritted his teeth, wishing there was some other way. But he couldn't reject the implant—Dax had insisted he wear it regularly. Jeth had no choice but to face it and overcome. He sighed and met his mother's gaze. "I'll do it, but not yet. I need a little time to prepare."

And to gather my courage. The implant seemed to vibrate in his hands like something alive. He slid it into his pocket, wanting to hide it from the crew for as long as he could.

Courage. He didn't know if he had enough. Not this time.

CHAPTER 13

"WHENEVER YOU'RE READY," MARIAN SAID, MOTIONING TO the door into *Avalon*. She sounded calm, but Jeth could tell she was as nervous about this homecoming as he was.

"You'll do fine," he said, smoothing the front of his shirt. He wished he had asked Dax for his old clothes back before leaving the gardens. The crew would find out about what happened to him soon enough, but he wanted to put it off as long as possible.

Marian didn't reply as Jeth keyed the code to unlock the door. He led the way through into the cargo bay, expecting to find it empty at such a late hour.

But he was wrong. The entire crew was there. For a second, Jeth couldn't understand why, but then the sound of Cora screaming assaulted his ears. She was standing a short distance away, struggling to free herself from the grip Sierra and Lizzie had on her arms. Her screams were the kind that made his cybernetic hand ache and his mind cloud with memories.

Then the sound shifted to something less shrill and painful, but no less powerful. "Mom!"

Jeth saw every face turn toward him and Marian, their

expressions unified in response—first confusion and then complete and utter incredulity.

Sierra and Lizzie let go of Cora, and the girl catapulted forward. "Mom! I knew you were here. I felt it!"

Marian, who'd been standing just behind Jeth as they entered, stepped around him, arms held out. When Cora leaped into them, Marian caught her, hoisting her up easily. In seconds she was raining kisses down on her face as Cora giggled, both of them crying.

Seconds later Lizzie was there, too, somehow managing to wrap her arms around them both. She was crying as well, the gesture punctuated by a kind of hysterical laughter. The joy of their reunion was painful to watch. Not because Jeth didn't share in it, but because he'd forgotten how to process such an emotion, one he hadn't felt in so long. Witnessing their joy finally made it feel real. She was here. His mother.

But she's different, he thought, examining her too-young face. One moment she was the mother he knew, but in the next she was an alien creature, one who phased the Brethren's guns with a wave of her hand. He had wanted to ask her about the changes when they had been walking, but the incessant pull of the implant on his mind had distracted him too much.

Jeth looked away, his thoughts a whirlwind inside his head. His gaze fell on Milton who was stumbling toward them. For a second, Jeth thought he would fall down, his limbs were shaking so badly. Or maybe his heart would give out. He had twenty years on Marian, an old man by some standards. But he reached them still upright, his age-wrinkled cheeks wet and glistening like glass in the cargo bay lights overhead.

"Marian."

The emotion in his uncle's voice made the tears sting Jeth's eyes more than ever. A couple of them escaped, and he hastily wiped them away. He didn't want to lose control in front of the crew, especially not Shady, who was standing farthest back from the group, in the middle of the makeshift gym area they'd built next to the brig. For the past few months, all of them had been learning military fighting techniques from Vince, skills they would've needed for rescuing Marian. They might need them even more now, Jeth thought, with the Harvester mission before them.

But not Shady. The memory of his betrayal flooded Jeth's mind, and he welcomed it, the anger steadying him. Only now wasn't the time to call him on it. He refused to ruin this reunion with such business.

He turned back to his family, wrapping his arms around as much of them as he could. Marian was busy telling her story of how Daxton had organized her rescue and what she doing here. She could barely speak for the hugging and crying.

Jeth felt hands touch his back and he turned to see Sierra had joined them. She was crying, too, and listening intently to Marian's story. Sierra had nearly as much reason to be moved to tears by her unexpected appearance as Lizzie and Milton did. She had risked her life for Marian, rescuing Cora from the ITA's cruel machinations, in part because Marian had begged her to do it. But mostly because Sierra understood what it was like to live a life she had no control over, the only life Cora had known until that time.

Finally, some of the fervor died down, and Lizzie introduced Marian to the rest of the crew. Jeth was glad she was doing it. He didn't want to address Shady. Or Celeste for that matter. Flynn was all right, but the gnawing ache in the back of Jeth's head was growing steadily worse, and Shady's presence was not making things any easier. His entire body felt coated with lead, his muscles heavy and sore. The implant might speed up healing, but it seemed that part hadn't happened for him yet.

Maybe that's because you haven't yet embraced it, Jeth thought. He supposed it was true, but that didn't make him any less wary of what awaited him.

Sierra leaned in close, her breath warm against his ear. "Come on," she whispered. "You look like you need a break."

Jeth smiled at her, more grateful than he cared to admit. She was so beautiful. His heart wrenched as he remembered that the rest of the Brethren had seen her beauty, too, that he'd exposed her to the Axis. His smile vanished. It was his own fault, but he couldn't help the sting of jealousy it brought.

"Okay," he said. He stepped toward Marian, pushing his way through Milton and Lizzie. "Mom," he said, the word alone still a miracle to him. "I'm going to lie down for a while. Will you be all right?"

A smile brightened her face. "Of course. Absolutely

perfect." Her smile lessened. "Do whatever you need to. I can take care of myself."

He nodded then turned toward Sierra, locking his gaze on hers to avoid looking at the others.

Without discussion, they headed to Jeth's cabin. Sierra closed the door and locked it behind her. Then she faced him. "Are you okay?"

Jeth flinched at the question, his emotions a jumbled mess inside him. "I'm fine. Mom's back."

Sierra pursed her lips. "Yes, it's like a dream. But that's not what I'm talking about and you know it."

Jeth swallowed, the back of his skull aching. The implant felt like a boulder inside his pocket.

Sierra took a slow step toward him, as if he were an animal that might flee at her approach. "Did the implant hurt?" She motioned toward his head.

Jeth took an involuntary step back from her, maintaining the distance. "How did you know?"

Sierra bit her lip. "Educated guess. Why else would Dax take you away from us and return you in those clothes? When we first woke up, he told us that you were okay and that he had business to discuss with you, but I had a feeling there was more to it."

Yes, a lot more. Shame made the muscles in his body clench. *Am I one of the Brethren now?*

Sierra closed the distance between them. He now stood next to the bed with no more room to retreat. She raised her hands to his face, cupping his jaw. "So I'll ask again. Are you okay?"

Slowly, gently, Jeth shook his head. He felt the walls crumbling inside, his joy at having his mother back giving way to the agony of what he now faced—being a prisoner in his own mind, a slave. It was his worst fear come true.

Sierra leaned forward to soothe him with a kiss, but Jeth jerked away from her. The look of hurt that crossed her face only deepened his shame. She lowered her hands, held awkwardly in the air between them.

"I don't want the Brethren to see," he said, searching for a way to explain. "Through the link. That's how it works. What I think and see the Brethren think and see, too. I can't control it . . . I keep showing them things I don't mean to."

"I understand." Sierra held his gaze for several long seconds. "I know a bit about how the implants work. But I understand there's a way to control it. Daxton was able to keep things from Hammer, wasn't he? Maybe he can help."

Jeth grunted. "Sure. That conversation will go well. Hey Dax, would you mind teaching me how I can keep secrets from you even with this brain implant, the same way you deceived the guy you betrayed and then killed?"

"Hammer's dead?"

Jeth nodded and filled her in on what Dax told him about Hammer finally removing his Guard implant, one rigged to explode if separated from the architecture.

Sierra gave a shudder. "Yes, I guess you've got a point." She turned away from him and sat on the chair next to the dresser. "So, Daxton rescued your mother. What does he want in return?"

Jeth grimaced. "What, you don't think he did it out of the kindness of his heart?"

"Ha, ha."

Sighing, Jeth sat on the bed. He pulled the implant out of his pocket and began turning it over in his hand. "He's after the location for Empyria. And Mom's agreed to give it to him—but only after he helps her—helps us—destroy the Harvester on First-Earth. He forced the implant on me to ensure that I don't try to betray him while we're on the mission. And apparently there's something specific *you* need to do as well. Oh, and Mom says that the Pyreans are dying because of the Harvesting and that if it doesn't stop Cora will die too." He drew a breath, his mind abuzz with unanswered questions once more.

Sierra didn't say anything when he finished, her expression inscrutable.

"You don't seem surprised by any of this," he said after a few seconds.

She shook her head. "I'm not. Not really, anyway. I've had my suspicions about Cora, especially with the way she spends all that time in the engine room next to the metadrive. As for your mother, well, it was obvious she's always had an agenda. It was the only way she could've endured all those years in the ITA labs without breaking."

Jeth shivered, trying not to think about it. He could guess that some of the icy hardness in her was because of the suffering she had gone through at the hands of the ITA. The reality of that torture was suddenly more real to him, too.

Revenge. The motivation had its appeal.

"I wonder what it is she needs from me," Sierra said. "I never had anything to do with the Harvesters."

"I don't know." Jeth exhaled. "But Mom was insistent."

Worry clouded Sierra's eyes for a moment, then she shrugged it off. "I'm sure we'll find out soon."

Jeth frowned. "You seem awfully calm about this. Do you think destroying the Harvester isn't going to be as hard as it sounds?"

Sierra ran a tongue over her lower lip. "No, not exactly. But it'll be a helluva lot easier than rescuing your mom would've been, especially with Dax's resources behind us."

Jeth sighed, conceding that point with no hesitation. The difference between having money and power behind a mission and not having it was perfectly clear to him now. Every job they'd worked since escaping Hammer had ended in disaster, or close to it. Look at what had happened with Wainwright. That job had been a failure before they'd even arrived at Nuvali.

"And even though the Harvester is a classified installation," Sierra continued, "it isn't better protected than any other ITA facility. The only difference is it's located out in the middle of the ocean, surrounded by nothing but water and open sky. It's not going to be easy to get in. It's a no-fly zone, and there are ocean patrols, but the only people who know about its existence are those with access to the Aether Project."

"So not many," said Jeth. "That's good to hear." He paused. "But why do you sound doubtful?"

"Because I am." Sierra crossed one leg over the other. "It doesn't make sense."

"How so?"

"All of it. Why target only one Harvester? Yes, the First-Earth one is the largest, but if the harvesting is what's killing them, then all of them need to be destroyed."

"I know. I asked my mom the same thing. But Dax wouldn't commit to helping with anything except the First-Earth mission, and Mom seemed to believe that would be better than nothing."

Sierra shook her head. "Again, no sense. The location to Empyria is priceless. Why would your mother agree to give it up for only a portion of what she wants? She spent *years* guarding that secret and nothing the ITA did, nor anything they offered, was enough to make her give it up."

"Offered?" Jeth couldn't keep the skepticism out of his voice. "What could they have offered her?"

Sierra dropped her gaze. "You and Lizzie."

"What?" Jeth's grip tightened on the implant still clutched in his hands.

"It's true. They offered to let her see you both again, to let you live in the facility with her, to come and go as you all pleased."

Jeth scoffed. "As if she believed them. This is the ITA you're talking about."

Sierra shrugged. "You might be right, but the point is, that your mom refused to even entertain the idea. Keeping it secret meant that much to her."

A pain began to build in Jeth's chest. *She turned down me*

and Lizzie. She could've let us know she was alive, seen us again, but she didn't. He wasn't sure what to think about that, but he couldn't deny the prickle of resentment. Seeing her today had been wonderful, beyond words. To think this could have happened years earlier, that he could have had his suffering put to an end, but his mother had turned it down. Why? What could be so important about the Pyreans? About Empyria?

He took a deep breath, stifling that resentment before it could get in the way. "What's your point?"

Sierra hesitated, aware that the revelation had hurt him. "Why would she give it up now? And to a man like Dax?"

The answer came to Jeth at once, and he didn't like it. "You think she's playing him?"

Sierra met his gaze. "I don't know, but it's possible."

Jeth didn't want to believe she'd willingly put all of them in danger, but he couldn't dismiss the possibility. It made too much sense. Despite how it seemed on the surface, he didn't know his mother at all, not anymore. She might once have been a woman whose word could be trusted, but all bets were off now. He couldn't forget the way she had phased those guns into metaspace, her icy hardness.

"Dax isn't going to let us escape without Marian delivering on her promise," Sierra said. "He's too clever for that."

Jeth grimaced. Even his mother's ability to phase wouldn't keep them safe from Dax. One bullet to the brain and she'd be done. She might take down dozens of his men before one succeeded, but Dax had enough manpower to overwhelm her. Both the Brethren and the Guard would lay down their lives for him. "And even if we managed to get away, he'll just be one more hunter on our trail."

"You're right," Sierra said.

Jeth ran a hand through his hair. This time he avoided the architecture hole, afraid of what he might feel if he touched it. "As soon as things settle down, I'll ask her what she has planned."

"Good idea."

"But even if she does intend to betray him," Jeth said, "we still might have a way out. Lizzie thinks she's found—" He broke off, sweat dampening his skin as he struggled *not* to think about what Lizzie had found on the data crystal. That was the kind of information he couldn't afford to share on the Axis once he put the implant back in. He shook his head. "I'm sorry, but I can't go into that. Not until I learn how to control this." He held up the implant, wishing he had the nerve to just crush it with his cybernetic fingers.

Sierra's nostrils flared, her frustration palpable. "Then you have to ask someone for help."

"I already know what I have to do."

"You do?" Sierra's eyes narrowed. "Then do it already."

Jeth laughed, the sound as rough and raw as his insides felt. "I'm supposed to accept its influence. To *surrender* to it. Once I do I'll be able to control it. Crazy, right?" The solution sounded just as absurd now as it had earlier.

To his surprise, Sierra shook her head. "I remember your mom saying something similar back when she first received hers."

The sound of rushing blood filled Jeth's ears. His mother

had been telling the truth. There was no denying it any-more.

He shook his head. "I can't do it, Sierra. I can't handle this. It's too much." His voice cracked, the sound a pale echo of the way he was breaking on the inside, despair crushing him to dust.

Sierra stood up and crossed the room to him. She knelt before him and cupped his face with her hands. She was so close he could see the flecks of gold in the blue of her irises. "Yes, you can."

Jeth breathed out, then in. "What if it changes me?"

Sierra's lower lip slid in between her teeth. It was all the answer Jeth needed. The implant would change him. It probably already had, he just didn't know it yet.

As if sensing her blunder, she released her lip and leaned toward him, close enough the tips of their noses touched. Her breath warmed his face, sweet and soothing. "We'll make sure it's only temporary. I'll help you hold on to who you are."

Jeth closed his eyes. Once again the memory of his mother killing the ITA scientist swam in his mind. If he hadn't seen it for himself in that video, he never would have believed her capable of such an act, killing a man with a single thought. She'd been cold, remorseless. Wasn't it possible the change in her had something to do with the implant? She said hers was different, that it wasn't networked like the Brethren one . . . but did it still have a similar effect on her mind?

And then there was Dax. He'd been a good person once, a loving son and brother to his family, until Hammer had decided to make him Brethren and force an implant on him. And now Dax was as cruel and twisted as Hammer had ever been.

Nausea burned in Jeth's belly, and he forced his eyes open. Sierra still watched him, her hands warm on his face. He wanted to lean into her touch, wanted to wrap his arms around her, hold her, kiss her. And all at once the idea of not touching her again was too much to bear. He had to master the implant.

He reached up and took hold of her hands, lowering them toward his lap. "Okay, I'll try, but you must promise me something first."

Sierra hesitated. "What?"

Jeth drew a breath and let it out slowly. "If it changes me, if I become a monster, someone like Hammer or Dax, I want you to put me down."

Confusion clouded Sierra's expression but only for a moment. "You won't."

Jeth shook his head. He couldn't phase objects like his mother could, but with his aim, he could be just as deadly with a gun. "I might, and if I do, there's no telling what I might do to you or Lizzie or Cora. I can't risk it. You have to promise you'll stop me, no matter what."

Silence met his words, the seconds slow and weighted between them. Jeth could sense the struggle raging in Sierra's mind, in her heart. He watched it with held breath and a pounding in his chest as fierce as a hammer striking. He watched until he saw her come to her answer at last.

She shifted her hands in his grasp, weaving her fingers through his as if she could braid the two of them together. She slowly nodded. "If you go too far, I'll do whatever it takes to stop you." She paused, the silence loud with dread and possibilities. Her fear was so great he could almost taste it as she breathed in and out. "I promise."

CHAPTER
14

JETH SPENT THE NIGHT ALONE IN HIS CABIN, HIS ONLY companion the strange, unwelcome ghosts in his head. He continued to resist the buzzing, trying to simply pretend it wasn't there. But it kept getting louder and louder until the buzz was all he could hear. It was like trying to ignore an itch on the bottom of his foot trapped inside his shoe, driving him crazy. Finally, he closed his eyes, gave in, and accepted the Axis fully.

At once, the buzzing ceased. Images and ideas flooded his mind, drowning him in the sudden onslaught. He froze, unable to tell where he ended and the Axis began. For a moment he *was* the Axis, a machine reduced to the influx and processing of data. He tried to shut it out again, but he was too paralyzed to respond. Even his body had stopped working.

He was helpless against the chaos, but some of it slowly began to make sense. He felt Eric and Perry through the link, their minds unique to him in a way the others were not, as if the face-to-face interaction had given them a distinguishable tenor among the chorus of thoughts. Seconds later he sensed Dax's presence, his mind stronger than the others, more physically present somehow. Jeth felt his consciousness being pulled toward Dax, but the closer he drew the more his thoughts and memories began to flow out from him as if his mind were a pitcher that had been tipped over: the memory of his first kiss, the time he broke his wrist on the playground, the moment he learned his father had died, the first time he and Sierra— *NO!*

He screamed it through the Axis, the power of his thought resonating like a pulse cannon. It was enough to shake him loose from the Axis's grip, and he raised his hand to his head and yanked the implant out. At once he slumped onto the bed, his muscles letting go. He hadn't realized his entire body had been clenched.

He leaned back and closed his eyes, willing his heartbeat to slow, his breathing to steady. *This is impossible.* He raised the implant before his face, glaring at it. He would never conquer this thing. Never. Jeth closed his eyes and wished for an escape. There was none. Only this brief respite between battles in what would be a long, difficult war.

But I must win.

He let an hour pass, lying there without moving. He waited until the ache in the back of his skull grew unbearable again, then he returned the implant to its sheath. Relief, even greater than all the times before, came over him. And for a few moments, wearing the implant felt right.

But then the buzzing called again. This time he didn't ignore it. Instead, he gently probed it with his mind, approaching it warily, like a cat stepping into a new house.

Images began to appear again, but they came slower, their pace more controlled. He was able to distinguish one thought from another, one mind from another. For a while he was able to be in the flow of the Axis without sharing any of his own thoughts. No memories rose to the surface, no secrets escaped.

It's a doorway, Perry had said, and Jeth thought he was beginning to grasp the concept. A doorway, one with a door he could open and close at will. He tried it, willing the door to close. Resistance met his attempt. He pushed harder. The next moment the Axis's power bowled him over again, and he was swept away in the flow of thoughts and ideas, his own being sucked out of him.

With an effort that left him panting, Jeth pulled away from the Axis once again, jerking the implant out. At least getting away had been a little easier this time.

A few minutes later he tried again. Then again. And so the night went. Each time he came back out feeling like he'd gained another measure of control. It wasn't like Perry had promised—it wasn't easy, but it was working. All it took was concentration and effort.

At some point during the night Jeth drifted off to sleep only to wake up and discover he'd left the implant in. The realization shot terror through him. He couldn't remember dreaming, but what if he had? What had his unconscious mind shared through the night?

Nothing, the familiar voice of Perry reached him. *Stop being so paranoid. The Axis isn't your enemy. Just give in to it.*

I'm trying, Jeth thought back to him. The sensation was bizarre, like having an out-of-body experience.

You're still holding back. Give in all the way. I can help you if you want.

Jeth swallowed. The idea of just relaxing into it, of just accepting this new state of being, made sweat break out on his body once more. He needed a shower.

I bet you do. I can smell you from here.

What?

Kidding. Perry's amusement vibrated through the link. *Just don't stand naked in front of the mirror while you're linked. None of us want to see that, thanks.*

Fuck you, Jeth thought, but to his surprise there was little heat in the response.

Anytime, man, anytime.

The link went quiet. Not dead, just quiet, a gentle hum in the back of Jeth's mind. Maybe he was getting the hang of this after all.

He rolled out of bed and headed for the exit. He paused in the doorway and contemplated leaving the implant behind. He even reached up to remove it from the architecture, but he stopped before going through with it. It felt okay for the moment. He didn't know how long it would last, but wearing it was the only way he was ever going to get used it.

Leaving the implant where it was, Jeth headed out the door into the dim passenger corridor. It was early enough he suspected most of the crew were still asleep, but as he headed for the ladder to the deck below, soft music rose up to greet him. It was familiar music, but not any he'd heard for a very long time. *Mom's music,* he realized. He stepped off the ladder and entered the common room.

A rush of memories came over him as he spotted Marian sitting in one of the armchairs, a reader in her hands. He must have come across her like this hundreds of times in the first ten years of his life—reading and listening to music with a cup of tea set beside her, steam rising up from it in billows. For a second, panic threatened to take hold of Jeth as he realized he was still connected to the Axis. Only, he didn't think he'd shared the memories. The recollection felt different this time, voluntary and private.

Hesitantly, Jeth engaged the Axis, searching for Perry. *Did you see any of that?* Jeth asked once he'd found him.

See what? Perry answered. There was no hint of deception in the reply, at least none that Jeth could sense.

Never mind. Feeling better, he withdrew his thoughts from the link and focused on his mother. She looked up from her reader, her eyes appraising him.

"Good morning, Jeth. How are you feeling?" Marian paused. "How are you *doing*?"

He fidgeted with the hem of his shirt, resisting the impulse to touch the implant tentacles cupped gently around the back of his skull. "Okay. A little better than yesterday."

Marian smiled. "Good, I'm glad to hear it.

"How about you? How does it feel to be ho—to be here?" Jeth gestured around the common room, trying to see the space as his mother was seeing it. *Avalon* had been her second home for years. It was certainly messier than in her day. The furniture was mostly the same, although a good deal shabbier. Most of the decorations would be new to her—the additions made by the crew, including Lizzie's still-life photos and Celeste's tribal masks—all except for the painting of Empyria. That one, positioned directly across from the chair she was sitting in, Marian had hung ages ago. It depicted a vivid, surreal landscape full of trees and plants painted in colors so vibrant they could only be fantasy.

"It's strange being back," she said, glancing around the room. It was a truer statement than she could've realized.

"I know the feeling," said Jeth. Normally every place on *Avalon* felt like home to him. But at the moment it was as if he'd stepped through some metaspace portal into a parallel world, one that resembled this one but that was off-kilter somehow, full of intentional mistakes. *Like my mother being back from the dead.* He shook the feeling off.

"Well, I'm glad you're adjusting to the implant. We'll be leaving soon." Marian stood. "I hope you don't mind, but I already brought the crew up to speed on the mission to First-Earth. They all seemed willing to help."

All of them? "I don't mind," Jeth said, uncertain if he really meant it. He was used to being captain of this crew, but he supposed if anyone were to take charge, his mother would be the best choice.

"Good," Marian said. "Would you like some breakfast?"

"Sure." The reply came out automatically, but astonishment at the idea colored his voice. Breakfast? Homemade by his mother? This had to be a dream. This couldn't be his life.

"Apparently your friend Flynn went to the market," Marian said as she turned toward the galley. "He's got quite the eye for quality ingredients. I like him."

Jeth grinned, remembering Lizzie's words. *Mom will love the crew.* It seemed she was right. About Flynn at least. His thoughts started to turn toward Shady, and he pulled back, unwilling to probe that raw spot this morning.

Jeth followed his mother into the galley, and within minutes he was helping her prepare an elaborate breakfast, the kind that would make Flynn's heart explode from sheer joy. Jeth had never cared much for cooking, but he recalled watching his mother and father prepare meals together, the act a family ritual. They would laugh and talk while they worked, but not about the food and what needed to be done next—the work they accomplished with a kind of silent communication, a dance where one did this while the other did that on instinct.

Jeth found himself falling into the rhythm easily, and for a while, he didn't speak, just listened as his mother talked about days long gone, or gave him pointers about how to mix the best gravy or to dice the onions into the perfect size. At first Jeth was content just to listen and to be near her, savoring the nostalgia and the sweet soft enjoyment of their reunion.

But soon his thoughts turned to the present—and the future. He cleared his throat. "So, you say we'll be leaving soon?"

Marian looked up from the cutting board where she was slicing a tomato. All the food they were using was fresh and not imitation. It had to have come from Dax's personal stock, Jeth knew. Fresh food like this was a luxury most spaceport travelers couldn't afford, and certainly not his crew.

A Brethren perk, he thought, a tremor going through his body. The Axis seemed unnaturally silent.

"Yes, that's right," Marian said. "Another day, maybe two. I'm not sure. Dax is working on the final preparations."

Jeth started to ask what those preparations were, but the realization that he and his mother might not be alone for much longer forced him to get right to the point. His heartbeat began to quicken, and all at once the buzzing grew louder, the Axis suddenly more present than it had been a moment before. Jeth winced and pulled the implant out, stuffing it into his pocket.

Marian cast him a sidelong look, but she didn't ask for an explanation.

Mustering his courage, Jeth said, "Why are we really going to First-Earth, Mom?"

A wry smile curved one side of her mouth, but she didn't stop her slow, methodical slicing of the tomato. "You get your skepticism from me, I hope you know."

Jeth huffed, deciding he would have to take her word for it. He couldn't remember well enough to be certain. "Why, Mom?" he pressed.

She set the knife down and faced him. "For the exact reasons I already gave you—to hit the ITA where it will hurt most, and to free the Pyreans and save Cora."

Jeth sighed. "That's just it. How will destroying one Harvester free them? Won't we need to destroy all of them?"

Marian shook her head.

Jeth's brow furrowed. "Are you saying that destroying the First-Earth Harvester will be enough all by itself?"

"Yes."

He blinked, taken aback by her absolute certainty. "How do you know that? How does that work?"

Marian hesitated for a moment, as if searching for the right words to convince him. "The First-Earth Harvester is the largest, as you know, but it also has the deepest hold on the Pyreans."

"I don't understand."

Marian didn't reply at once, instead letting her gaze wander around the room. Her eyes lingered for a couple of seconds on the wall behind the stove. Bits of dried food and other unidentifiable stains dotted it here and there. Flynn did a lot of the cooking, but tidiness went against his nature.

"Sierra has explained to you the way in which the Pyreans are best thought of as a tree, yes?" Marian finally said.

Jeth nodded.

"Well, imagine it's a tree that can move, like the kind in the fantasy stories I used to read to you when you were a boy."

It took Jeth a moment to recall what she was talking about. But then he remembered—walking, talking trees, the kind that could pull up their roots and go places. Those had been among his favorite make-believe creatures. He started to smile at the memory, but forced it back. Time was ticking.

"The Pyreans are like that," Marian said. "Only instead of moving across the ground, the Pyreans move through metaspace."

"I know that. I mean, I sort of get it."

"All right. Then you might recall from one of the stories in particular that the best way to capture a walking tree is to snag it around the trunk. If you only try and lasso the branches, the tree will either slip free or break free, leaving the leaves and branches behind."

Jeth snorted. "Yeah, I remember that story. It had the best illustrations."

"Yes, it did. Well, like in the story, the First-Earth Harvester has hold of the trunk. The rest only hold the branches. So if we free the trunk, the Pyreans will be able to take care of the rest on their own."

Jeth tilted his head, mulling over the idea. As with everything else connected to the tree symbolism, he supposed it made sense. And if she was right, destroying the First-Earth Harvester would certainly be a critical blow to the ITA. It would be the ultimate revenge, and he suddenly wanted it to be true. Only— "How do you know it's part of the trunk? I've been through the Aether Project and there's no mention of it anywhere."

Marian turned back to the counter and resumed her slicing. "That's because the ITA doesn't understand what exactly they've trapped. Oh, they have theories, some of them are even close, but most fall far from the reality of what the Pyreans actually are."

Jeth folded his arms across his chest. "You've really been there, haven't you?"

Marian shot him a puzzled look. "Of course. Cora and I didn't get this way by magic." As if to emphasize the point, she waved a hand at the discarded tomato bits on the counter and they vanished into metaspace with a loud crack.

Flinching, Jeth returned his attention to the gravy he was supposed to be stirring. A thick crust had coated the bottom of the pan, and he grimaced, hoping like hell he wouldn't get stuck with dish duty afterward. He wanted to ask her what Empyria had been like, but once again he remembered time was short.

"What about Dax?" he said, dread pulsing inside him.

"Excuse me?" Marian looked up.

Jeth sighed at her defensiveness. "Do you really intend to give him the location of Empyria?"

Marian's nostrils flared and she pointed the knife at him. "You have grown entirely too clever and devious for your own good, young man." She set down the knife, picked up the cutting board, and added the tomatoes to the bowl with the onions. "No, I don't intend to give him the coordinates."

"Mom—" Jeth began.

Marian cut him off with a look. "I intend to take him there personally."

Jeth's eyes widened, surprise freezing him in place. "Take him there? What are you talking about?"

"Dax wants Empyria for the same reason the ITA does," Marian said, a coldness creeping into her voice. "He sees it as a way to gain power and wealth and all the things that you'd expect a typical human to want since the dawn of our creation."

"Yes, but won't taking him there give him those things anyway?"

Marian pinned him with her gaze, her expression full of that alien hardness. "No. The Pyreans will change his mind about things."

Jeth closed his mouth, biting off the automatic response. Mystical trees or not, the Pyreans hardly seemed capable of anything other than moving objects through metaspace. *She really has gone mad,* he realized. He didn't know if it was a consistent madness—she seemed so lucid, so normal most of the time—but this, the idea that a trip to Empyria would change Dax's mind about wanting to claim it for his own gain was insanity. Nothing could do that.

"You look doubtful," Marian said.

Jeth slowly nodded.

"Don't be, Jeth. The Pyreans aren't a lower life-form made to fuel these machines the humans have built. They are *sentient*. They have a mind, a consciousness that exceeds even our own."

An alien life-form, Jeth thought. *As smart as humans? Smarter?* He couldn't imagine it. He decided he didn't want to. If it was true, if the Pyreans were sentient, then that meant they had a purpose, a sense of self, and with that came the ability

163

to have moral constructs like good and evil. Who was to say their intent was the former and not the latter? How could he be certain he could trust them? Maybe they had manipulated Marian's mind. Maybe the Pyreans themselves and not the trip to Empyria had altered her DNA. They might have remade her as they wanted her to be. A chill spread across his body, and he shivered.

Marian sighed. "I can tell you don't believe me, but that's all right. All you have to do is trust me."

"Trust you?"

"Yes, Jeth. I'm your mother."

She said it so matter-of-factly that for a second Jeth almost did. But then all the doubt came rushing in. Sudden resentment flared up inside him as he remembered that she had turned down the opportunity to see him and Lizzie. That she had decided her secrets were more important than her family. He might've trusted her before, but he wasn't certain anymore. He couldn't pretend that she hadn't changed, and he couldn't ignore the possibility that she was no longer rational.

"Okay, Mom. Whatever you say," he said, pacifying her. But inwardly he refused to support the plan. Go to Empyria? If the Pyreans could change Dax, they could change all of them. He wasn't about to take her word on it that the Pyreans could be trusted. And he couldn't take the situation on faith either. He was too experienced with how the real world worked—a world without magic trees and the unicorns from the stories she once read him. Faith like that didn't have a place here. Here all that mattered was what you could see and what you could do. And right now, he needed to talk to Lizzie. She had to finish cracking the code. He needed an ace up his sleeve. One he would play if and when his mother's questionable plan went bust.

CHAPTER 15

ALTHOUGH JETH WAS DESPERATE TO TALK TO LIZZIE AND Sierra both, there was still breakfast to attend to. The smells wafting up from the galley had worked like a homing beacon on the crew. Nearly en masse they appeared, first Flynn—naturally—and then Milton, Lizzie, and Cora, followed by Sierra. She cast him a look, asking with her eyes how he was doing. He shrugged. The architecture was itching, impatient to be reconnected with the implant.

Celeste and Shady came in last, both looking bleary eyed. Jeth got the feeling that neither had spent much of the night in their cabins. Honestly, he was surprised to see Celeste at all. He figured she would've opted to spend her time with one of her old boyfriends here at the space station. There were so many, and it had been a while since she'd been able to engage in her favorite pastime. The only reason he could think of why she wouldn't have was because of Vince, his death still fresh for her as it was for him, for all of them. He wondered what Saar had done with Vince's body. But as soon as the thought occurred to him, he shut it down as too painful to contemplate.

He focused on Saar instead. In the overload of the last few

days, he'd almost forgotten the ITA General was still after them. It was a complication he would like to forget forever, but he couldn't. The situation with Dax was tricky enough, but it didn't scare him the way Saar did. *I am the Storm that Rises,* the old man had said. He'd been so certain of himself, that capturing Jeth was just a matter of time—his time, his choice.

Jeth supposed he ought to tell Dax about Saar, especially with the looming First-Earth mission, but that would mean contacting him. He wasn't ready for another face-to-face.

You could use the Axis.

He wasn't ready for that either.

At the thought of the Axis, the ache in the back of his head grew more pronounced. Jeth scanned the faces of the people around him, just tucking into the breakfast feast he and his mother had prepared. For a second it all seemed so normal. Lizzie was talking animatedly to Marian and Milton; Cora was trying to engage all three of them at once. Flynn was eating with the kind of enthusiasm more appropriate for a ravenous feral cat than a grown man, only half listening to the joke Shady was telling next to him.

The sight of Shady telling a joke, acting as if nothing was wrong, made Jeth's stomach clench. Shady had no right to be so normal, not when the back of Jeth's head felt like it was on fire and close to bursting.

I'll show him the new normal.

A vindictive pleasure came over Jeth as he reached inside his pocket and withdrew the implant. He'd planned on waiting until after he'd fully adjusted to it before showing the implant to the crew, but now seemed the better time. Lizzie noticed it first, breaking off mid-sentence. The others followed seconds later. Jeth waited just long enough to have everyone's attention. Then he raised the implant to the back of his skull and slid it home with an ease that scared him nearly as much as it did the others.

"What the hell?" Celeste said, her mouth falling open. Shady had gone unnaturally still, his face bleaching of color.

Sierra spoke first, speaking with a dead calm that was impossible to ignore. "Jeth has been made one of the Brethren. Dax forced the implant on him when we arrived." She paused. "That is, when he captured us in the Belgrave and had us hauled back here."

Silence fell, and Jeth wondered which of them would break it first. But when someone finally spoke, it wasn't the person he would have expected.

"To be more specific," a musical voice intoned, "I hauled you all back here, not Dax."

Jeth turned to see Aileen standing in the doorway— Trouble in the flesh. He hid his surprise with a scowl.

She stepped into the galley, the tail of the long gray coat she wore trailing behind her like folded wings. Her snug black pants only emphasized her birdlike appearance, revealing petite, slender legs. "Sorry, am I intruding?" She reached over Celeste, sitting at the end of the table, and grabbed a blueberry off her plate, popping it into her mouth.

Sierra stood up, her chair scraping the floor with a loud screech. "What are you doing here?" She was considerably taller than Aileen but it didn't make much difference. Aileen seemed to take up the whole room.

"*How* did you get here?" Lizzie added, her fork clutched in her hand as if she intended to use it a weapon.

Aileen flashed a smile. "There are few locks that can keep me out. But my apologies. We haven't been properly introduced. My name is Aileen Stock, and I'm here to welcome you to my crew."

Disbelief pounded in Jeth's ears, making them ring. The Axis buzzed into life, threatening to drag him under. He got to his feet and cleared his throat. "Your crew?"

"Mmmm." Aileen's eyes seemed to twinkle, her smile tightlipped as if she were holding back a laugh. "But we can talk about that as soon as you're done eating. No hurry. I'll be waiting outside."

She swung around, her coat fanning out behind her, and disappeared back through the doorway. Sierra glanced at Jeth, a silent question on her face. Jeth ignored it. He couldn't have answered even if he wanted to. The Axis was roaring inside his head, spurred by his rising anger and the dawning realization of why Aileen was here.

You didn't think I was going to let you lead this mission, did you? The thought thrummed in Jeth's mind, the voice behind it one he had no trouble recognizing.

Dax, he thought back, his hatred a visceral thing inside him.

Now, now, Jeth. Watch yourself.

Jeth raised a hand to the implant at the back of his head, ready to pull it out. But he stopped at the look on Celeste's face. She was watching him with her mouth open, disgust in her expression. Jeth shifted his gaze to the right and saw that Shady wore a similar look.

This is your fault, he thought, wishing that Shady were enslaved to the Axis as well, if only so he could feel Jeth's anger in such an intimate, inescapable way. Laughter seemed to vibrate through the link, the minds of the Axis amused by Jeth's turmoil.

He pulled away from it, trying to close the door on the link without terminating the connection physically—he didn't want Shady to see him struggling.

Dammit, Jeth, just give in, then close the door, Perry spoke through the link.

Steeling himself against the mental invasion, Jeth forced his feet to engage and headed into the common room. Sierra followed right behind, and seconds later the others came as well, breakfast forgotten.

Aileen had made herself comfortable in the same armchair Marian had been in earlier. She sat with one leg crossed over the other, the top one swinging back and forth slightly. She beamed at Jeth as he entered, but he wasn't paying her any attention.

Aileen wasn't alone. A man stood just inside the common room across the way. He was so large he seemed to fill the doorway completely, although he carried not an ounce of fat on his body. Jeth recognized him at once. He'd been with Aileen the first time Jeth had met her, a trusted member of her crew.

And a dangerous one. Jeth hadn't forgotten the way Celeste had looked after a brief confrontation with the man, one that left her bruised and shaken. He glanced at her now, wondering about her reaction. As he had anticipated, she gazed on the man with palpable fear in her eyes.

"Oh, hello again," Aileen said, standing up. "This is Remi, my first mate." She motioned to the man, but he didn't respond, not so much as a finger twitch. He might as well have been a statue carved in human flesh. "Some of you might know him, already," Aileen said, winking.

"Whoa," said Flynn, whistling through his teeth. "Are you a cyborg?"

Remi turned toward Flynn, his face expressionless, but the way he cocked his head sent chills racing down Jeth's spine. Cyborg indeed. A regular Frankenstein's monster in a perfectly chiseled body.

"You will refer to him as Remi and Remi only," said Aileen, her voice suddenly acid and her eyes cutting as she addressed Flynn.

Flynn shifted his weight and withdrew a fresh piece of candy from his pocket, stuffing it into his mouth.

His hackles rising, Jeth glowered at Aileen. "Why are you here?"

"Isn't it obvious?" Aileen said. "No? And here I thought you were supposed to be clever."

"You're awfully brazen for someone outnumbered nine to two," Sierra said, tapping the toe of her boot against the floor.

Aileen arched a slender, angular eyebrow. "Nine? You count the little girl"—she nodded toward Cora—"as a threat?"

A deadly smile turned up the edges of Sierra's lips. "I

should've counted her double."

Aileen grinned back. "Yes, well, don't miscount Remi. He's worth a couple at least, as I believe one of you already knows." She cast Celeste a significant look.

Jeth's hands clenched into fists, and for a second he thought his head would split in two as the Axis leveraged its hold over him, trying to suck him into it.

"I believe," Marian said, her smooth, hard voice commanding the attention of the room, "that you should get on with your business and leave the sniping for a more appropriate time."

If Aileen had been thrown by Marian's words, it didn't register in her expression. "I'm here to discuss crew assignments for the First-Earth mission. As Miss Blondie pointed out, there are nine of you. However, there's only room for five on this job. Obviously, some of the slots are already set. But someone—presumably Jeth here—will need to determine the final roster."

Jeth gritted his teeth, the truth of the situation striking him in the face. He couldn't understand why Dax was making her a part of this, but then Aileen dropped another bomb and the answer came clear. "Oh, and we'll be taking my ship for the mission, *Polaris*."

Now the truth struck Jeth like a blow to the back of the head. The room spun around him, and the Axis roared.

Let go! he heard Perry screaming. *Let go and it'll all be so easy. No.*

Yes. So easy. The Axis is a door, ready to open and shut at your will. Once you surrender to it.

Jeth closed his eyes, on the verge of passing out. *It can't be true. It can't be that easy.* And yet—he sucked in a breath, held it, held it. And then he let go, freeing his hold on the Axis with it.

At once a steady calm spread over him. The change was so alarming he nearly swayed on his feet. The feeling passed a second later, and he was fine. Better than fine. He felt freshly awake and strong, as if he'd spent the last few days hunched over and was finally able to stand tall and straight again. He inhaled then exhaled. The Axis was there, the door open, but nothing was going in or out of it. It was just there, dormant—and a part of him.

"You've got to be kidding," Lizzie was saying, hands on hips. "Why would we take that crappy ship when we have *Avalon*?"

Aileen's lips, usually all fluff and pout, pressed into a thin line as she turned her attention to Lizzie. "Crappy ship? Compared to what?" She glanced around the common room, letting her gaze linger on the run-down furniture and the water stains and bullet holes in the walls. She shrugged. "Never mind. Somehow I imagine you'll survive."

"What's that supposed to mean?" Lizzie said.

Aileen started to respond but froze as a newcomer joined their ranks, this one yellow and hairy. Viggo strode into the common room, tail twitching back and forth, belly close to dragging on the floor. "What is that?" Aileen said, eyeing the cat like some four-legged monster.

"A robot. With hair." Lizzie rolled her eyes. "It's a cat."

Aileen cleared her throat. "I've officially seen it all. Okay then." She ran her gaze over the crew once more. "As I said, we'll be taking *Polaris*."

"Yes, you did," Sierra said. "But you failed to explain why."

"Because *Avalon* is too recognizable with the ITA's Wanted bulletin," Jeth said, the answer coming to him from the Axis. Only this time it wasn't an invasion, just a download of data. Now that he knew the truth, it made sense. At the moment Dax had *Avalon* moored between two of his largest cargo ships, the best cover available to hide her from bounty hunters. But taking her would be an unnecessary complication. They needed a ship for this mission that could get them where they needed to go without drawing attention, and *Polaris* was a Black Devil same as *Avalon*. It would have to do.

"Yes, that's right," Aileen said, some of the smirk leaving her face. "I hope there won't be any problems with us working as a team. So long as you follow my rules, at least while aboard my ship, we'll get along fine."

Jeth bared his teeth in a smile, his anger present but not controlling him for once, just like the Axis. He realized that Aileen was bluffing a bit. They weren't joining her crew; she wasn't leading this mission. They were just using her ship. True, it gave her some rights to make decisions that affected them all, but ultimately Marian would be leading them. He could live with that. "Yes," he said. "Absolutely fine. Sounds like it'll be an interesting mission. Looking forward to it."

Aileen blinked at him, unsure if he was being sincere or not. "How reassuring."

"When do we leave exactly?" Sierra asked. Outwardly she was all calm, but Jeth sensed concern beneath.

Aileen faced Sierra and for once the attitude wasn't present in her voice. "Tomorrow sometime. Not early. I don't do mornings. And we still need a few supplies. But you're welcome to start moving into your cabins today. I'll assign rooms as soon as I get the final list."

Jeth nodded, aware of the way Shady was standing ramrod straight. Again, that vindictive pleasure came over him. The Axis gave a pleasant hum. "I'll send it to you as soon as I've decided who stays and who goes."

"Perfect," Aileen said. "*Polaris* is moored at Dock Nine. Stop by as soon as you're ready." And with that, she swung toward the door, her coat fanning out behind her again. Remi preceded her out the door, but Aileen stopped in the doorway and glanced over her shoulder at them. "Oh, and one more thing. No cats aboard my ship." She paused. "At least, not that one."

The outrage that rose to Lizzie's face was almost comical. She looked as if she might swallow her own tongue.

The second Aileen was gone. Lizzie stomped her foot. "I hate that girl." She marched across the common room and scooped up Viggo. "This sucks. What am I supposed to do with him while we're gone?"

"Calm down, Elizabeth," Marian said. "We will think of an acceptable solution."

Lizzie started to argue, but Celeste cut her off. "So who's staying and who gets to go?" The tremble in her voice gave

Jeth pause, but only for a second.

"Why? Are you volunteering to stay?" He glanced at Shady as he spoke, hoping to find him nervous. He was, but as Jeth turned back to Celeste he saw she was, too. *Serves them both right.*

Celeste shook her head.

Jeth ignored her, addressing the room at large. "I'll have to give this a little thought." He flashed a smile. "But first, I need a shower. Excuse me."

He strode from the room, ignoring the look Sierra gave him as he passed. Normally that look would've made him nervous, but at the moment it had no effect on him. He supposed it had to do with the change in the implant—for the first time since waking up at Peltraz, he felt wholly like himself again.

See, Perry said. *I told you it was easy.*

In answer Jeth closed the door to the Axis. He wasn't ready to think about that, the change too nebulous. He focused on the mission instead. Five slots. He, Lizzie, Sierra, and Marian were a given. But who would be the fifth? He knew for sure who it wouldn't be. But he would wait to make that announcement. Make him sweat. It was only a small portion of what he deserved.

The Axis, its presence still tangible even from behind the closed door, hummed once, and then went silent.

CHAPTER 16

JETH EMERGED FROM THE SHOWER, WEARING JUST A towel—and the implant. He spotted his reflection in the mirror across from the bed. It hadn't occurred to him to take it out. In truth, he'd almost forgotten about it as the need to decide who was going on the mission overtook his thoughts.

He approached the mirror, his eyes raking his reflection. For a second, he looked like a stranger. His hair was the same length it had been, the stubble on his chin a little thicker, but not by much. His eyes were the same shade of green. No, the strangeness came from the implant alone, black tentacles snaked through his hair, lying pressed against his skull as if suctioned to him.

Like a leech.

Disgust at the sight of it went through him, but he squelched it at once, afraid it would break the truce he seemed to have made with the Axis. The implant was here to stay for now. He had to make his peace with it.

Jeth lowered his hand to the towel around his waist, his eyes catching sight of the scar peeking out just above the jut of his right hipbone. The raised dark patch in the shape of a jagged circle was a souvenir from one of the more dangerous jobs he'd ever worked—a gunshot wound that put him in the hospital for six weeks. Jeth considered Perry's scarred nose and the way he'd known the details of how it had happened the moment he saw it, the knowledge available on the link. Perry must've shared that memory. *On purpose,* Jeth decided, recalling the way the memory had felt to him. He thought he understood why. His engagement with the Axis had been limited, but already he'd sensed a sort of hierarchical structure to it, one with Dax residing at the top, of course. But Jeth wondered how the other positions were determined. Could Perry exert more influence over Jeth than Jeth could over him, because he'd been connected to the Axis longer?

A sudden urge to share the information about his own scar—one hard won on a dangerous job—came over him, and he reached for the Axis, opening the door. He let the thought loose. Off it went, catalogued at once. A general sense of appreciation came back to him.

Nice one, Perry said.

Did you like it? Try this. Now Jeth sent the memories of some of his other scars, embellishing the details as he did so. The minds on the Axis reflected approval back to him.

Feeling emboldened, Jeth decided to try something new. With the link still open he thought about his secret tattoo, the one no one but himself, the tattoo artist, and Sierra had ever seen. He pictured it, but then commanded the memory to stay hidden from the Axis, doing it the way Perry had been telling him to all along. He waited for a response from the Axis, but there was no reaction. He probed it, searching to see if it was out there, data waiting to be recalled. But he found no trace of it.

The victory brought a smile to his lips.

"Admiring your new hardware?" a voice spoke from behind him.

Jeth turned to see Sierra standing by the door, leaning against the wall. He couldn't believe he hadn't noticed she was there, even if that part of his cabin was always the darkest. He supposed he'd been too caught up in his own head. It was a sobering thought, and he shut the door to the Axis.

"No," he said, tugging loose the tuck holding the towel in place. It dropped to the floor in a wet heap. He left it there as he turned to the dresser, pulling out fresh clothes. "But I'm glad you're here. I talked to my mom about her plans for Dax and Empyria. She—"

"Wait," Sierra said, cutting him off. "Are you sure you're ready to talk with that thing in?"

"I . . . I think so." He touched the implant, trying to make sure he meant it. He couldn't know for certain, but he felt okay, in control. He supposed it was time to test it. For now, the door was closed, this conversation private, but he would be ready to react at once if that changed.

Sierra surveyed him with a guarded expression. She slowly nodded. "Go ahead."

Pulling on his clothes, Jeth recapped his conversation with his mother that morning.

"She wants to take Dax to Empyria?" Sierra said, eyebrows climbing up her forehead.

"It seems insane to me. I can't figure out why she would want to take any of us there after what happened to her and Cora."

"I don't know," Sierra said, looking lost in thought.

Jeth shrugged. "It doesn't matter. Lizzie found a secret code hidden on my mother's data crystal. She believes it's the coordinates to Empyria. So even if Mom does try to just take Dax there in person instead of giving him the coordinates, we can step in and honor the deal ourselves."

A frown creased Sierra's lips. "Is that what you think we should do?"

"What, you don't?" Jeth said. "Dax has promised us enough money to help us finally disappear for good. Given the choice, I'd rather honor the deal and escape than risk flying off to some dangerous planet we know nothing about."

Sierra pursed her lips, and Jeth waited for her to come to the same conclusion. He suspected the reason she was hesitating was that they couldn't be certain Dax would honor the deal, even if they came through with the coordinates. Supposing she had a point, Jeth realized he might have a way to check. Dax's mind and will were a part of the Axis, easily accessible if Jeth had the nerve.

Summoning his courage, Jeth commanded the conversation to remain private. Then he opened the door to the Axis, forcing all thoughts of Lizzie and the secret code out of his mind, just in case. He searched the Axis for reassurance that Dax would indeed fulfill his end of the bargain. That reassurance came to him a moment later, direct from Dax himself. Relief swept over Jeth. With their minds linked in this way there was no room for deception. He closed the door again and returned his focus to Sierra.

"What do you think, Sierra?" he pressed.

"I—" She hesitated. "I think having the coordinates ourselves is a good idea. It gives us options."

Jeth smiled. "Agreed."

Sierra tilted her head. "Do you think Lizzie has finished decoding it yet?"

"I don't know. I was going to ask her about it as soon as I finished getting dressed."

"Well," Sierra said, crossing the distance between them. "You might want to start over." She tugged the hem of his shirt free of his belt, her fingers grazing his stomach. "You put this on backward."

Laughing, Jeth moved in to kiss her, giddy with the realization that he no longer feared doing so.

But just as his lips met hers the door to the cabin opened.

"Seriously?" Lizzie said. "You're doing this now? With Mom on board? Gross."

Jeth pulled back from the kiss and turned a scowl on his sister. "Did you forget how to knock?"

"Did you forget you can lock the door?" Lizzie stepped in, hands on hips and a determined look on her face.

"I shouldn't have to." Jeth waved. "But come on in, we've got things to discuss."

"Yeah, we do," said Lizzie. "Like about this who's staying and who's going crap."

"I think I'll leave you two alone to argue this one out," Sierra said, heading for the door. Jeth didn't blame her. Lizzie looked fired up and ready to drag them all into the fray.

Once she was gone, Jeth said, "Lock the door, please. I don't want anyone else barging in."

Lizzie did so then turned to face him. To his surprise her temper was gone, an openly wary expression on her face. For a second he couldn't understand it, but then he saw her gaze flick to the side of his head. *The implant.*

He casually traced a finger over one of the tentacles. "Does it really look so awful?"

Lizzie continued to stare, utterly silent.

"I'll take that as a yes." Jeth wrapped his fingers around the base of the implant and pulled it out.

She flinched.

He set the implant on the table beside his bunk. "I know you're afraid, but I really am all right. I promise. And it's going to be worth it in the end. We're going to get everything we ever wanted."

"Even your voice sounds different," Lizzie said, wrapping her arms around herself.

Jeth sighed, understanding her doubt. He would've felt the same in her place. Hell, he did feel the same. Maybe not as much as before, but that doubt was still present. He walked over to her and patted her arm. "It's just me, Lizzie-bear."

"Lizzie-bear?" She snorted. "You haven't called me that in years."

"I know. Not since Mom and Dad left on their last trip." Their mother had given Lizzie the nickname, and the more Jeth came to accept that his parents were gone forever, the more he had drawn back from the things that reminded him of them. Not that this was something he had ever realized on a conscious level before. The implant had brought all those memories and motivations into sharp focus. He was recalling events so old he couldn't believe the memories existed at all.

And yet they did. His oldest newly returned memory was of the time the family cat, Stubbs, had clawed him in the eye after he'd yanked its tail. Jeth was only three years old at the time, and the injury prompted the first of many trips to the hospital for various accidents. Jeth had forgotten how clumsy he had been as a boy, how prone to mischief. He'd forgotten Stubbs, too. The cat had died of old age a few weeks before Lizzie was born, and there'd been no more cats, not until she smuggled Viggo onto *Avalon*.

Jeth shook his head, forcing the memories to the back of his mind where they belonged. "Don't worry. Once we've completed the mission, I'm through with it." He motioned to the implant.

"That's good to hear, Jeth-bow." A smile broke across Lizzie's face.

He grinned, the abandoned nickname bringing fond memories to the forefront again. "I hate it when you call me that."

Lizzie winked. "I know."

"Right. Well, don't make a habit of it." The last thing he wanted was for the Brethren to learn of it. The sobering thought brought his focus back in full force. "So," he said. "The reason I need to talk to you is to find out where you are on decoding the location to Empyria."

Lizzie frowned. "I'm nowhere on it. I haven't even thought

about it in days. Why should I with Mom here?"

"Why, indeed?" Jeth ran his tongue along his teeth, choosing his response carefully. He knew she wouldn't be keen on the idea of going behind Marian's back. He considered a dozen different approaches before deciding on the direct one. "Because Mom has no intention of handing over the location to Dax when we're done." He held off telling her the full truth—that Marian intended to take him there instead. He knew Lizzie well enough to guess that she would be more than willing to trust their mother on faith alone, regardless of what the Pyreans might have done to her.

Lizzie began to shake her head, dismissing the idea, but Jeth cut her off. "She told me herself, Liz. Just this morning. And it makes sense that she wouldn't give it up, right? I mean she sacrificed everything to protect that secret. She wouldn't just give it to Dax."

Lizzie's eyes narrowed on his face, and she put her hands on her hips. "So what if she wants to double-cross Dax? He deserves it. Look what he did to you." She motioned to the implant.

"True," Jeth said, "but we've both been doing this long enough to know how hard it will be to get away from Dax in our current situation. His power is as great as Hammer's ever was."

A surly look crossed Lizzie's face. "Maybe so, but Mom must have some plan we don't know about yet."

Jeth shook his head, the lie coming easily. "I doubt it. All she really cares about is saving the Pyreans." He considered telling her about the deal the ITA offered Marian to see her children again, but he held back, doubting it would go over very well. "She's not exactly in her right mind, I don't think. How could she be, with everything she's been through?"

Lizzie was silent.

"Come on, Liz," Jeth prodded. "Tell me you haven't noticed how different she is. She's got this . . . this coldness about her. . . ." He let his voice trail off, giving Lizzie a chance to fill in the rest.

She gulped. "Yeah, I've noticed. But it's not there all the time. And she's still our mom. Having her back is . . . I wouldn't trade it for anything."

"I know. Me neither." He patted her arm. "But we've got to do what's best for all of us, and we can't trust Mom to know what that is. She's been gone from the real world too long, been through too much." Jeth could tell Lizzie hated hearing it, but she didn't deny it either. "And I'm only talking about insurance here," he pressed. "Mom doesn't understand how hard it's been for us, trying to keep ahead of the ITA. We'll only use the coordinates if we need to. Dax has promised us enough money to ditch the ITA once and for all."

Lizzie paled. "That's just it. *Will* it be enough?"

"Of course."

"But what about Saar?" She shivered. "The way Milton and Sierra described him, he might never give up searching for us."

Jeth exhaled, more surprised by her question than he ought to be. He should have known better than to underestimate Lizzie's perceptiveness.

I am coming for you, Saar had said, determination radiating out from him like some magical force. He could've captured Jeth right then. Instead, Saar had executed Vince for his crimes. He had deemed punishing Vince's desertion the more pressing of his tasks. Jeth had seen a man with infinite patience and determination, a master strategist capable of waiting years before striking if necessary.

But what would happen once they destroyed the First-Earth Harvester? If Marian was right and the Pyreans could break free of all the other Harvesters, that would mean the end of the ITA's power. They would be left with nothing. No Pyreans, no Cora and the cloned race of human-Pyreans to replace their failing metatech, and no Empyria either. But the ITA wouldn't fall in a day. They would die slowly, bleeding out across the galaxy. And the most deadly beast was a wounded one. A beast like Saar.

Then Jeth remembered the Aether Project. He could still upload it to the net, give it away to all of the ITA's enemies. It wasn't as if they would realize the Pyreans were gone, not right away. War would inevitably follow, but at least Jeth would finally be free. Even from Saar. That, he thought, might be worth it.

But Jeth didn't dare express this idea to Lizzie. His little sister was wise beyond her years, but she still clung to her ideals—and starting an interstellar war wasn't one of them.

"We'll worry about Saar later," Jeth said, summoning his most charming smile. "One tyrant at a time, same as always."

Lizzie snorted. "I suppose you're right. First Hammer, then Renford. Now Dax and Saar. The universe owes us a string of benevolent fatherly types, don't you think?"

Jeth grunted. "I surely do. So does this mean you'll keep working on the code?"

"Yeah, and I'll do it discreetly." She stuck out her tongue. "But for the record, I hate deceiving her."

"So do I." He pulled her into a quick hug. "Thanks, Lizzie-bear." As she stepped away from him, he picked up the implant once more. He raised the stem to the back of his skull and slid it home. Lizzie watched him do it, fear etched around the straight line of her mouth.

He ignored it as he felt his mind come alive. He checked the Axis link, automatically commanding the conversation between him and Lizzie to remain hidden.

Satisfied it was safe, he flashed Lizzie another reassuring smile. "Can you get started now? We're running real short on time."

"Okay. Good idea. I have no clue how much longer it'll take me."

"All right," he said. "And in the meantime, I've got a mission roster to finish." He cut off Lizzie's protest. "No need to get upset. I'll make the best decision. The fairest. I mean, don't I always?"

Lizzie cast him a skeptical look. Then she huffed. "Sometimes, I suppose. And it is for just one mission."

Jeth didn't reply. He wasn't sure if that was true or not. Yes, for some of them it would be missing out on only one mission. But he wasn't sure if that would be true for all of them.

CHAPTER
17

JETH CONTEMPLATED THE PROBLEM FOR MORE THAN AN hour, weighing his options. Five slots. Nine on his crew, counting his mother. He, Marian, Lizzie, and Sierra would be coming, that was a given. That left one slot. But who to fill it? Milton was a doctor, a role that was useful only some of the time. When it was needed, however, it became the most important role of all.

There was Flynn, mechanical genius. If anything went wrong with *Avalon—Polaris,* Jeth corrected himself—he would want Flynn there to fix it.

Celeste was invaluable for anything undercover. She was the queen of distracting marks, and she was a skillful pilot, always useful. But he couldn't forget how quickly she had sided with Shady, and the way she had turned on him after Vince's death.

And then there was Shady, of course. He was the best one to have by your side if things turned violent—a skill that might be needed for the Harvester mission. But the idea of trusting him now after the betrayal was impossible.

Rubbing his temple, Jeth knew he needed more information on what exactly the Harvester mission entailed before he could make a decision. With this in mind, he headed for the door, wondering where he could find his mother at the moment. He tried Cora's cabin first. Marian was staying there now, but it was empty. That meant she was probably in the common room. He reached the ladder, then froze as he spotted his mother racing up from the deck below.

"Where's Cora?" Marian said, panic punctuating each word.

"I don't know." Jeth glanced behind him. "She's not in her cabin. Wait, can't you sense her like you did before?"

"The link's gone quiet," Marian said, brushing past him. "She has to be here. I left while she was napping, but it wasn't that long ago. She wouldn't dare go out into the spaceport, would she?"

"I don't think so, but maybe." He followed his mother back down the passenger corridor. "Mom, I said she's not in her cabin." But if not there, then where? The answer came to him at once. "She must be in the engine room," he called.

Marian stopped and swung around, realization lighting her face. "Of course. With the Pyreans."

Jeth turned back, heading up the ladder with his mother hot on his heels. Moments later, Jeth charged into the engine room. Cora was indeed there, but she wasn't playing or watching a video. She was lying sprawled on the floor, face-down in front of the open metadrive compartment.

"Cora!" Jeth raced toward her, rolling over her limp body. Her eyes were open, rolled back in her head, and blood trickled from both nostrils, startlingly red against her white skin.

"Cora!" He scooped her up just as Marian reached them.

She pressed her hands to Cora's face and then her neck, checking for a pulse. But there was no need; Jeth could feel her breathing. She wasn't dead, just . . . gone.

"Let's get her to sick bay," Marian said, standing up. "I'll find Milton."

"Use the comm," Jeth said, struggling to his feet. Cora was just a child, but dead weight made her heavy, the burden compounded by his fear.

"Yes," Marian said, and she darted for the comm unit by the entrance.

Jeth walked past her with Cora clutched to his chest. By the time he reached sick bay on the deck below, Milton was emerging from his cabin. He looked bleary eyed and sluggish, and Jeth prayed he hadn't been drinking.

"Set her down on the table," Milton said. There was gravel in his voice, but not the slowness of alcohol. Savoring momentary relief, Jeth set her down. Then he backed away as both Milton and Marian closed in around Cora.

Hating that he was so useless here, Jeth retreated to the farthest corner, folding his arms over his chest. He listened as well as he could to the conversation between his mother and uncle as they examined Cora, but little of it made any sense to him—stuff about blood pressure numbers, respiratory rate, neural oscillation spikes, and so on. He didn't care what it meant; he just wanted his little sister to come around.

He got his wish moments later, but not in the way he wanted. Cora's body came awake, if not her mind—her muscles jerking uncontrollably. Jeth had never seen a seizure before, but he recognized this as one. After a few moments, the ship walls began to groan around them the way they did whenever Cora was losing control of her ability to manipulate metaspace. With his heartbeat tripling, Jeth braced for the impending destruction. There was no telling what might get phased. It could be the walls, the chair, even the crew. Fear pulsed through him, and the Axis responded. The door opened and it tried to force its way into his mind. Jeth pulled back, but the Axis only tightened its grip.

Relax, he thought, trying to convince the rebelling part of his mind to listen.

Across from him, Marian was yelling, "Hurry up and give her another dose of the Verzipan."

"Are you sure?" Milton said, a tremble in his voice.

"Yes!"

The ship's groaning grew louder, and then a loud pop reverberated through the room. Jeth jumped, forgetting for a moment about his struggle with the Axis. A hole appeared in the floor and part of the door of the cabinet behind Milton. The glass beakers contained inside it cascaded out, shattering across the counter like so many pieces of ice.

Ignoring the crash, Milton rushed forward, carrying a syringe tipped with some bulbous instrument instead of a needle. He slid the instrument up Cora's nose and pressed the end of the syringe.

"What's happening?" Sierra said, appearing in the room with Lizzie beside her.

Jeth shook his head, unable to answer. Sierra joined Marian and Milton around the operating table, offering help, while Lizzie stepped up beside Jeth. She slid her hand into his, fingers squeezing as she sought reassurance. Jeth squeezed back.

Slowly the medicine began to take effect. The ship's groaning quieted as Cora's convulsions first slowed and then disappeared entirely.

"What now?" Sierra said, breaking the silence first. She glanced between Marian and Milton.

"We wait," Marian said, not taking her eyes off her youngest child. "And hope she comes back to us."

Jeth swallowed, afraid he might be sick. Beside him, Lizzie raised a hand to her mouth, stifling a cry. For a moment the Axis threatened to awaken inside Jeth again, but he turned his thoughts away from it, letting his mind go passive to its presence.

The minutes dragged on, each second weighted. Jeth held his silence for as long as he could, then he approached the table and touched his mother's shoulder. "Is this because of the Pyreans?" He knew the answer already, but he needed something to fill the waiting.

"Yes," Marian said, her voice like a fist to his gut. "It is."

Jeth glanced at Sierra, asking for confirmation. She gave it to him in a single slight nod.

"And destroying the Harvester will make it stop?"

"Yes." As before, there was no doubt in his mother at all, no hint that the Pyreans might have manipulated her belief. Jeth still didn't trust them, but he decided he would trust the mission. What choice did he have when his little sister was dying in front of him? It might be a slow death, but there was no doubt she was wasting away, the life draining out of her the same as it did the Pyreans.

Jeth balled his hands into fists, dark emotions pulsing through him—anger at the ITA and hatred for all they'd done to his family. With it came a new determination as strong as any he'd ever had. He would succeed at this mission, one final job to end all the others. Forever.

But first he needed to sort out his crew. The reminder hurt, a sharp sting in his chest. A few days ago he wouldn't have needed to worry about it. There was no one he'd trusted more, no one he'd rather lay down his life with than the people who made up the Malleus Shades. But that certainty was gone—changed forever by Shady's betrayal.

A memory rose up in his mind. It wasn't forced there by the Axis, but came from his own recollection. It was of Hammer telling him that betrayal was like a cancer, that it had to be rooted out before it spread. Jeth hadn't fully understood what Hammer had meant back then.

But he did now.

The desire to get moving pulsed inside Jeth, but he held back. He wouldn't leave until Cora was all right.

Finally, nearly an hour later, Cora began to stir. Marian, who hadn't left her side even for a second, smiled down at Cora as her eyes opened.

"Hello, sweetheart, how are you feeling?"

"Not good," Cora said, tears spilling out from her eyes.

The sound of her pain broke Jeth's heart. He gritted his teeth so hard, his gums ached. The Axis began to stir, and he forced himself to relax.

"I know, sweet Cora, I know." Marian smoothed the sweat-dampened hair from her brow. "Would you like some water?"

Cora nodded, and Sierra came forward, glass at the ready. Cora drank several large gulps then pulled away.

"Good girl," Marian said. "Now Uncle Milton is going to give you something to make you feel better."

"Will it make me sleep?"

"Yes, I hope so."

Cora's lower lip trembled. "I don't want to sleep."

"I know." Marian glanced at Milton, giving him a little nod. "But it's for the best. For now. I promise this will all go away soon. Do you believe me?"

"Yes," Cora said, the word half a sob.

"Good." Marian stepped back, giving Milton room to step in. He placed a jet injector against Cora's arm and pulled the trigger. She flinched at the faint pop, but didn't cry out.

"So brave," Marian said, planting a kiss on her forehead. "I'll stay here with you the whole time. I promise." Then she sat back and waited for Cora to fall asleep—a normal sleep this time, and not like what she'd been under before. It took a while, far longer than it should've, Jeth knew, but that was the price of her high tolerance to the medication.

When she finally did fall asleep, Jeth stood from his hunched position against the wall and said, "We should give Cora some peace." He inclined his head toward Sierra, then Lizzie, indicating the door. They both caught his silent request and headed toward it. Milton had glimpsed the exchange as well and he cast Jeth a discerning look that he ignored.

Once outside, Jeth lowered his voice and said to Lizzie, "I know you just got started, but you've got to work fast on that code. Would it help if Sierra worked with you?"

Lizzie shrugged. "Wouldn't hurt."

Jeth glanced at Sierra. "Do you mind?"

She shook her head. "Whatever we've got to do."

"Good. Thank you." Smiling, he motioned them toward Lizzie's cabin. They both went, not questioning his motives. That was good. He didn't want either of them present when he confronted Shady. Sierra would understand, but he knew that Lizzie wouldn't. She let her heart rule her head far too often.

Once they'd disappeared inside, Jeth checked Shady's cabin. He didn't anticipate him being in there, but it was worth not having to come back up. As he expected it was empty, save for the clothes and various weapons scattered across the bed and floor. Jeth closed the door and moved on, descending the ladder to the common deck. Right away he heard the familiar sound of simulated gunfire and robots in the throes of death. The noise made Jeth's teeth clench from a sudden flare of resentment. The normalcy of the situation offended him on a deep, nearly unfathomable level. His sister lay dying only several meters away, and he was struggling to stay sane while the Axis tried to overtake his mind. And Shady was playing video games.

He strode into the common room, pausing only for a second as he realized Shady wasn't alone. Celeste sat on the sofa next to him, a controller in her hand and eyes fixed on the screen. Her presence didn't matter. She would protest, of course, but she wouldn't stop him.

Celeste noticed him first as Jeth walked up to the gaming table. Her eyes slid toward him then went wide. Her hands stilled on the controller, and she said in a strangely high-pitched voice, "Hi, Jeth."

Shady's head jerked upward. "Oh." He cleared his throat. "Hey. Didn't see you come in." His gaze moved off Jeth's face, homing in on the tentacle curled around Jeth's neck. He visibly paled. "How's Cora?"

"Still alive. Thanks for asking." Jeth braced, preparing his next words. He couldn't believe he was going to say them. They were the kind of words you couldn't take back, damage you couldn't undo. *No different from Shady's betrayal.* He said, "Why are you still here?"

Shady blinked, his mouth open, lower lip jutting out.

"What do you mean?" asked Celeste, sitting up straighter.

Jeth didn't answer but turned toward the table where Viggo was lying sprawled over the small air vent near the center, absorbing all the warmth. The cat didn't so much as twitch a whisker as Jeth reached out and ran a hand over his large belly. In seconds the cat's body began to vibrate with a growing purr. Drawing some small comfort from that, he turned back around.

"You know exactly what I mean." Jeth folded his arms over his chest. "We've been back at Peltraz for days now, and you've been free to go nearly as long."

Shady stiffened, every muscle in his body rigid, knuckles white where they gripped the controller.

"What are you saying, Jeth?" Celeste whispered.

Jeth didn't look at her but kept his gaze fixed on Shady. In the back of his mind, he felt the Axis propping him up once more, lending him strength, "There's no room for traitors on my crew."

Celeste hissed. "You can't do this." She clambered to her feet. "He doesn't deserve it."

Surprisingly calm, Jeth cast a dark look at her. "He contacted Daxton behind my back."

Celeste tossed her hands through the air. "But everything's all right. We're all safe, and your mom is here. We've got a mission, and if we pull it off, we'll finally be free."

Jeth leaned back, crossing one foot over the other. "So you think our situation now justifies his betrayal? You think Shady knew my mother was here before he made that call?"

"No, but . . ." She trailed off, words failing. The veins in her hands and arms popped out as she clenched and unclenched her hands held in front of her like a shield.

Jeth returned his attention to Shady, who hadn't moved, the only change in him the flush of color in his cheeks. "Pack up your personal effects and then get off my ship."

Shady stood up so fast Jeth thought he would overbalance and fall back down again. "This is bullshit."

Still calm, Jeth opened his mouth to repeat the command,

but Celeste cut him off. "Don't do this. You can't make Shady leave."

Jeth turned toward her, giving her his full attention for the first time. There was something wrong here, something off in the way she sounded. She was too emotional, too defensive. Why?

The answer came to him with sudden, cruel clarity—not from intuition, but from the Axis. The information had been there; Jeth just hadn't known to ask for it. Now, it rang out like a gong, vibrating him from his head to his toes. He staggered against the shock. He never would've believed it of her, not after everything they'd been through together.

Jeth breathed in and out, his temper rising, the Axis starting to roar again. He leveled a gaze at Celeste hot enough to cut steel. "It was you. You called Dax."

Fear swept across Celeste's face before her expression hardened into anger. "Yes, I did. But what choice did I have? We were dying out there. Vince *died*. We were all heading that way." She glanced at Shady, searching for support, but not finding any. Not this time.

The world spun around Jeth, her words tearing through him. It was true. She had betrayed him. The Axis quaked inside his head, memories rushing out, a tidal wave dragging him under, drowning him. He fought back, desperate not to lose control now. He wanted to remove the implant but he couldn't move.

Let go! Perry screamed through the Axis. *You were so close but still holding back. Let go and mean it this time.*

Yes, other voices combined with his. *We're here to help you. We're your brothers now. Give in and rise up.*

Jeth closed his eyes.

And let go.

As before, the Axis relaxed the same moment he did. But it was different this time, deeper somehow, more certain. He opened his eyes, strength flooding into him. Something crucial seemed to slip into place inside him. It was liberating, like sloughing off the skin of his past life and all the doubt and despair that came with it.

He cleared his throat, drawing Celeste's attention back to him. His voice was ice as he spoke. "You're both out. I'll give you one hour to gather your things. Starting now."

"But . . ." Celeste sputtered. "But I don't want to leave."

For a second Jeth saw the younger version of her, the way she was when they'd first met. Celeste had been all spit and rage on the outside, but inside she was just a scared kid, abandoned and desperate. The way she appeared now.

For a second, pity threatened to change his mind, but Jeth reached for the surety of the Axis. The way forward was clear. Once again he remembered Hammer: *Betrayal is like a cancer.*

"One hour," Jeth said.

"I'm sorry," Celeste sobbed, her anger shattering into desperation. "I didn't mean to go behind your back, but it turned out for the best. I can help destroy the Harvester. You need me."

Jeth shook his head. "There's nothing you have that I

need." He spoke in little more than a whisper, and yet Celeste recoiled as if he had screamed. As if he had slapped her.

Movement at the doorway drew Jeth's attention and he saw Lizzie entering with Sierra and Flynn close behind. He inwardly cursed. Celeste's shouting must've drawn them.

"What going on here?" Lizzie said. Confusion clouded her expression as she surveyed the room.

Celeste wheeled on her, anger flashing in her eyes that glistened with unshed tears. "Your brother is kicking us off the ship. Me and Shady."

"What?"

All eyes turned on Jeth, waiting for him to explain, expecting him to defend his decision. He wouldn't. This was his ship. His crew. *No traitors.* He pointed to Celeste and Shady. "You two are running out of time to get your things and get out."

This time it was Lizzie who recoiled. "Why? What did they do?"

"Celeste is the one who called Dax," Sierra said, shock coloring her voice as she made the connection.

Celeste turned on her, eyes narrowed. "Yes, I did. And I can't believe you didn't do it first. We needed help. Vince was your brother, and you let Jeth leave him behind!"

Sierra stiffened, sucking in a breath.

Hearing the pain in it, Jeth stood up from his slouched position against the table. "Get out of here, Celeste. Before I carry you out."

She turned toward him, her face livid. "Fine. I don't want

to follow you anymore anyway. You're nothing but Daxton's pawn now, *Brethren*."

Her words fell like hammer strokes, and for a second, doubt rose up in Jeth. But it came and went in an instant. This was the right thing to do. He had to think about Cora, the mission. He had to do what was best, and that meant surrounding himself with a crew he could trust.

Celeste strode for the door, the others parting the way for her. Before she reached it, Jeth turned to Shady. "You go with her." He nodded his head toward the door.

Shady looked ready to argue, to fight, but then he shrugged and followed after Celeste. "I think she has the right of it. You're not the Jeth I knew anymore."

"And you're not the Shady."

Shady didn't reply, but disappeared out of the common room, out of their lives.

Lizzie waited less than a second after their departure before swooping on Jeth. "Why Shady? He didn't do anything wrong!"

"He wanted to," Jeth said, simply. "He planted the idea in Celeste's head, and he didn't deny doing it."

"You never gave him a chance. You just assumed it was him."

Jeth slashed his hand through the air. "I'm done talking about this."

Lizzie's face crumpled, her eyes shiny with tears. Jeth had known the parting would be hard on her. He'd tried to spare her from seeing it go down, but there was nothing he could do about it now. She would just have to accept it.

"I'm sorry, Liz," he said. "But you've got to trust me that it's for the best."

She walked up to the gaming table, glaring at him. "I'm not talking to you right now." She scooped Viggo up and slung him over her shoulder. Then she turned and stormed out of the common room, the cat bearing a resigned look on its face as it suffered the indignity.

"That went well," said Flynn. "Just how you want to kick off a dangerous mission."

Jeth glanced at him, one eyebrow raised. He debated pointing out to Flynn that he didn't have to come, but instinct held him back. His crew was already down by two, three if you counted Vince. That was more than enough to lose at once.

Did I really just kick them off?

Yes, he had. For better or worse the decision had been made. Swallowing back nameless, churning emotions, Jeth headed for the door without comment.

Flynn wasn't wrong, though. It wasn't the best way to start a mission.

CHAPTER 18

THEY WERE READY TO GO LESS THAN TWENTY-FOUR HOURS later. Making the decision about who would fill the fifth slot proved easy once Shady and Celeste were gone, but it wasn't a welcome decision—Flynn would be taking it while Milton and Cora stayed behind at Peltraz in one of Dax's hotels. With the Wanted bulletin, they couldn't risk staying on *Avalon*.

From the start, Jeth had thought Cora would be sharing a cabin with Marian, her presence a given. But Marian disabused him of the idea at once.

"Her health is too unstable," Marian said. "And we can't risk the damage she might do to the ship."

Jeth knew she was right, but he hated the idea. He might have made his peace with the Axis, but that didn't mean he wanted to leave his little sister under the rule and reach of Daxton Price. Milton would be staying with Cora, of course, both to monitor her health and to watch over her, but that was hardly enough to appease Jeth's worry.

Sierra wasn't happy about the decision either, but Marian silenced her protest just as easily.

"We shouldn't bring Cora that close to First-Earth,"

Marian said while the three of them stood on *Avalon*'s bridge, discussing the final arrangements. "If anything goes wrong she could end up back in the ITA's hands, and everything you've sacrificed will have been for nothing."

Sierra paled, and Jeth knew she was thinking about Vince. He wished he had some words of comfort for her, but they did not exist, not in his mind or his heart. No words were deep enough to match what she was feeling.

Jeth touched Sierra's arm. "She's right. Even if we all die on this mission, I'd rather Cora was here, far from the ITA. At least then she'll still have a chance to escape. But if we fail and she's with us, the ITA will have her for sure." For a moment, an old familiar vision of a cloned Cora being plugged into a metadrive like some human fuel cell flashed in Jeth's mind. He'd rather see his little sister dead than have her live in a world where an enslaved race of human-Pyrean clones existed. He knew that the ITA hadn't yet perfected the cloning technology needed to do it—the clones, although born normal enough, often developed physical and mental deficiencies, and none of them were strong enough to survive the advanced aging process the ITA needed to put them through to make them viable alternates to metadrives—but there was no telling when they would succeed. They were certainly determined enough.

"Yes, Jeth's right." A confident expression rose to Marian's face. "And Dax will treat her like a princess while we're gone. He knows full well what will happen if he doesn't."

Helluva choice for insurance, Jeth thought, gritting his teeth.

But at least Cora and Milton staying at Peltraz solved the cat problem. Shortly before they were due to depart, Jeth helped Lizzie force a flailing Viggo inside a carrier Dax had provided. The cat hissed and spat as Jeth slammed the door closed, sealing him in.

"Be gentle, why don't you," Lizzie said, hissing nearly as much as her cat. "You almost shut his paw in the door."

Jeth rolled his eyes, but held back the comment that the stupid cat deserved it for being such a pain in the ass. Lizzie looked too close to tears. She'd barely said two words to him since Celeste and Shady had left.

"He'll be fine, Liz," Jeth said. "Milton will take care of him, and you know that Cora will spoil him with attention."

She scowled. "I don't see why he can't just come along. He does fine on a spaceship."

A dozen retorts to this statement came to Jeth's mind, including all the times that he'd had to rescue the cat from mortal peril when it got stuck in places it never should've been, such as inside one of the engines, under the life support unit, and—Jeth's personal favorite—the latrine piping.

"True," Jeth said at last, "but he'll be happy enough." This might be an understatement. The apartment Dax had set Milton up in was in Sector 1, the nicest the spaceport had to offer. Not to mention the safest and ritziest. "Hell, by the time we get back that belly of his might actually drag on the ground," Jeth said, tapping the top of the carrier. Viggo meowed, a pathetic little sound that made Lizzie mutter under her breath again.

Jeth carried the cat down the ladder to the cargo bay for her and then handed the carrier over. "You have everything you need moved onto *Polaris*?"

Lizzie nodded.

Jeth frowned, remembering that *Polaris* belonged to Aileen, and she couldn't be trusted not to go snooping. He lowered his voice. "You didn't leave the data crystal anywhere discoverable, did you?"

Lizzie made a face. "Of course not. I'm not entirely stupid." She patted her pants pocket. "Come to think of it, I'm pretty much a genius."

"You do all right." Jeth motioned to the carrier. "Sure you don't want me to take him for you?"

"I'm sure." She hoisted the carrier up using both arms and stepped off the ship.

Jeth watched her disappear around a corridor and then closed the door. He headed up to the passenger deck and stopped in his cabin, double-checking he'd packed everything he needed. A duffel bag stuffed with clothes and weapons sat on the bed, waiting for him to take over to *Polaris*. Like Lizzie, the others had already moved their stuff. But Jeth had waited until the last possible moment. Even if it was just for one mission, he hated abandoning *Avalon*.

Sighing, Jeth tossed the bag over his shoulder and left the cabin, shutting the door behind him. He checked the rest of the cabins and sick bay, making sure all the lights were switched off and anything prone to spoil disposed of in a proper manner. He expected to find Shady's cabin still in a state of disarray, but to his surprise, it was utterly spotless. An outsider might find it hard to believe the place had ever been inhabited. Jeth supposed that was the point.

Celeste's cabin was clean too, but not empty. She had left a single item on the bed—a personal comm unit. Jeth picked it up, examining it while the memory of the first time he'd met Celeste played through his mind. They'd gotten in a fight when she tried to steal this very unit from him after he'd just stolen it from one of Hammer's marks. Celeste had even punched him in the face. It was fitting that their relationship had ended in a fight, too, life coming full circle. While Jeth considered it, it almost felt like it had happened to someone else.

He debated tossing the unit into the garbage, but then he tucked it into his pocket. He would dispose of it, he told himself, or maybe he would fence it. It was an old model, but still usable.

Finally he made his way to the bridge. To his surprise, it wasn't empty. Marian sat working at the comm station while Cora was sitting in the pilot's chair, her little hands gripping the control column. She made gunshot sounds, swiveling back and forth in the chair as she took out imaginary targets.

"What are you doing here?" Jeth said.

"Jeth!" Cora said, beaming. She climbed out of the chair and hurried over to him. He was glad to see her looking so much better, although he knew it was only temporary. He picked her up into a hug. She squeezed his neck, completely unalarmed by having her face in such close proximity to the tentacles wrapped around his skull. Of all the crew, Cora was the only one not bothered by the change in his appearance. She accepted him entirely, in the way only a little kid could.

"Cora wanted to say good-bye to *Avalon*," Marian said, not looking up from the comm screen. "I decided to shut down the nonessentials and run a final systems check while she played for a few minutes."

"Oh," Jeth said, setting Cora back on her feet. He ran a hand through his hair. "I was just getting ready to do that."

A knowing smile ghosted across Marian's face. "I'm not surprised."

Disgruntled, Jeth folded his arms and waited for her to offer to let him finish. He wanted to say his own good-byes. When more than a minute passed, he said. "Don't you think you should take Cora to the apartment? You're cutting it close."

"I don't want to go with Uncle Milton," Cora said, tugging on his sleeve. "I want to go with you."

Jeth freed his arm from her grip and smiled down at her. "I know, but you can't, sweetheart."

"Why not? I can help. I know how to fly the ship."

Jeth laughed. "Yes, I saw."

"It's easy. You just move that thing around." She pointed at the control column.

"Yep, it's that simple. You'll have to show me again when we get back."

The delight in Cora's face drained away. "What if you never come back?"

Jeth squatted down, bringing his face on level with hers. He pulled her into his arms. "Don't be silly. We'll be back before you know it."

Cora leaned away far enough to fix a glare on him, the expression comically exaggerated on her face. It almost hid the bags under her bloodshot eyes. "Promise?"

"Promise." He stood up again, ready to force his mother out of the chair if he had to. He walked over to the comm station and peered over her shoulder at the screen. "I thought you were running a systems check."

Marian worried at her lower lip. "I was, but I noticed something off with the nav system. I know Lizzie has made a lot of modifications, but I'm looking at the code now and these particular lines don't feel like her work."

Jeth tilted his head. "What do you mean?" He couldn't understand how something as clinical as computer code could have a "feel" to it.

"This coding . . . it feels more ITA to me."

"What?" Jeth's brow furrowed.

Marian nodded. "Yes, it's definitely ITA. They have a unique structure. Only—" She looked up at him. "How did it get here? Has the ITA been on *Avalon* recently?"

"No, not recently. A couple of months ago when we were trapped on that Strata but I don't—wait. We did have a run-in with the ITA less than a week ago back at Nuvali."

"Were they on the ship?"

"No, not on it, but they planted a tracer on *Avalon*'s door. We found it right away and got rid of it. It was an outdated unit, but Sierra thought it fit the person tracking us."

Marian arched an eyebrow. "How so?"

"It was Admiral Saar. That old war hero." Jeth swallowed, not surprised that no one had told Marian about it. It was a sore subject for all of them. "The ITA enlisted him to capture us. He killed Sierra's brother."

Marian's eyes went wide and she turned her attention back to the screen. "Please tell me you're joking."

"Why?" Jeth said.

"Because you didn't take care of the tracer," Marian said. "Whatever you found was a decoy. Saar imbedded the real tracer in *Avalon*'s code. It's been here, running, the whole time."

Jeth blinked, unable to believe it. "Are you saying Saar knows we're at Peltraz?"

"Yes!" Marian sounded frantic now. Her fingers moved across the screen. "Oh God, if I'd only known . . ."

"Known what?" Jeth gripped the back of the chair.

Marian stood up so fast Jeth nearly tumbled over. "We've got to get out of here!"

He raised his hands, ready to grab her if she bolted. "Why are you panicking?"

Marian pointed at the screen. Jeth glanced down, but it meant nothing to him. It was just a jumble of characters, what he vaguely recognized as computer command statements. All except for the lower right-hand portion of the screen where a red cursor was flashing.

"I didn't know what it was," Marian said. "I already tried to disable it."

"So? Mom, what's going on?" He wanted to shake her. Her fear was getting in the way of her sense.

Marian swallowed. "I triggered an alarm. The ITA knows we found the tracer."

Jeth stared at her, trying to process the consequences of what the alarm meant. If Saar knew they were here all this time, why hadn't he closed in? A dozen reasons sprouted in Jeth's mind at once. Saar might not trust Daxton. He might be worried about trying to grab Cora in such a pub-lic, populated place. He would want to wait until Jeth either left again, or until Saar could insinuate his men into Dax's organization—not an easy or quick task.

But now that he knows we know, he'll— His thought broke off as the door to the Axis swung open. For a second, Jeth worried he was losing control again but then he understood as an alarm began to sound inside his head, vibrating through the Axis link.

The message was simple and terrifying:

Take positions. ITA battleships are closing in.

CHAPTER

19

"WHAT IS IT? *JETH*, WHAT IS IT?"

He pulled away from the Axis and the chaos of thoughts in his head. He looked back at his mother, realizing she must have read the alarm on his face. "The ITA is here. They're putting the spaceport under lockdown." He swung around and headed for the cockpit, adrenaline fueling his focus. "We've got to get out of here."

"What are you doing?" his mother shrieked. "We need to get off this ship."

Jeth looked back at her, mouth agape. "We'll escape on *Avalon*."

"We can't." Marian seized Cora's hand and began dragging her toward the door. "*Polaris* is stocked and fueled. We won't survive on *Avalon*."

"I'm not leaving her behind. The ITA will impound her." Once that happened, he would never get her back. He dove for the pilot's chair, determination blinding him, but he froze halfway as pain lanced through his skull.

He was powerless to stop it as Dax's mind filled his own. *Get out of here on* Polaris. *Finish the job.*

Jeth tried to fight it, but the control of the Axis was too

strong. It wasn't like before—this was not a suggestion, but sheer dominance. Dax was willing him to obey, and he was too strong for Jeth to resist.

The moment he turned away from the cockpit, the pain eased and he regained control of himself. *Lizzie,* he thought through the Axis. By now she would be in a lift on her way to Sector 1. She might even be there already. It would take an eternity for her to get back.

I've got Lizzie and Milton, Dax replied at once. *I'll hide them in the Underground. They'll be fine. Now go!*

Once again, Jeth wanted to protest, but the Axis made it impossible. He gave in, telling himself that Dax would keep his word. The underground network of hidden passages and rooms inside Peltraz were vast, vital as they were to Dax's smuggling operations. The ITA could look for years and never find them.

Clinging to this surety, Jeth raced toward the door after his mother and Cora, stopping only long enough to grab his duffel. He whispered a quick good-bye to *Avalon* as he hurried down the ladder to the cargo bay and out into the spaceport. He didn't bother locking the door behind him. A lock wouldn't keep the ITA out.

No alarm was sounding in the spaceport, but a loud, mechanical voice echoed through the corridor: "By order of the Interstellar Transport Authority, under command of Admiral Saar, all travel to and from Peltraz Spaceport is hereby suspended. Repeat, all travel is suspended. The spaceport is under lockdown. . . ."

Jeth tuned out the voice as he sped down the corridor toward Dock 9, keeping pace with Marian and Cora. Sierra stood waiting for them by the open door into *Polaris*.

"I don't know how they found us," she said as they came on board.

"Saar embedded tracer code in *Avalon*'s nav system while we were on Nuvali," Jeth said between pants.

Already pale, Sierra blanched whiter still. "I should've known."

Jeth touched her arm, all the comfort he had time to give her. Through the Axis, he knew that the ITA was almost in landing range. They would have to fight their way out.

While Sierra sealed and locked the cargo bay door, Jeth headed for the ladder. A wave of vertigo swept over him as he went. This was the first Black Devil he'd ever been inside that wasn't *Avalon*. The similarities were strange, the differences shocking, almost offensive.

There was no denying that *Polaris* was far newer and in better condition than *Avalon*. Even the cargo bay was immaculate. No exposed wires hung from the ceiling, no water stains from busted pipes. The brig, located in the same position as *Avalon*'s, was made of electrified glass instead of old-fashioned plasinum bars. Not that Jeth could see much of it. Barrels and crates, all carefully stacked and aligned, filled most of the bay from floor to ceiling. There were enough supplies in here to last a full crew six months in open space.

He should've been relieved at such a bounty, but all he

could think about was *Avalon*, abandoned and exposed only meters down from them.

Moments later, he arrived on the bridge. Aileen was in the pilot's chair with Remi sitting copilot beside her. There was no sign of Flynn, although Jeth was certain he was on board. Also on board were Perry and Eric, the former at the comm station and the latter at the nav. Jeth's stomach did a hard dip at Eric's presence. He hadn't realized he would be coming, too. He'd thought most of the slots would be Aileen's crew, but it seemed she either didn't have a full crew or they'd been caught away from the ship, same as Lizzie.

Jeth scanned the view beyond the main windows of the cockpit, unsure what to do with himself when he wasn't in charge. A line of ITA battleships hovered in the distance. Most of them were standard cruisers, except for one off to the right. Jeth had never seen a ship of its kind before. It was a massive dark-blue beast easily three times the size of the cruisers, and mounted with enough firepower to level cities. Jeth guessed it was the flagship of this ITA armada. *Saar's ship.*

"We're loose," Perry said. "Get us out of here."

Jeth strode over to the cockpit as Aileen began to pilot them out of the dock. "Shouldn't we be manning the guns? Or does this piece of crap not have any?"

Aileen made a noise deep in her throat. "We don't need guns for this. Just watch."

Jeth gripped the back of her chair. "What are you going to do, sneak in between them?"

"Yep." Aileen reached toward the pilot's control panel and engaged a switch to a system he didn't recognize. Seconds later he realized it was a cloak drive, of the type they'd been trying to buy for months.

"Easy now," Perry said. "If you go too fast they'll see us."

"I know," Aileen said, glancing over her shoulder. "Anybody else want to backseat drive?"

"I'd like to front seat drive," said Jeth.

Aileen scowled back at him. "I've got it, thanks."

"We'll see."

Sierra, who'd arrived a few seconds after Jeth, came to stand beside him. "What if the ITA was watching when you engaged the cloak? They might be monitoring all the ships by now."

Aileen shook her head. "I'm willing to bet they're only concerned with *Avalon* at the moment."

Jeth gritted his teeth, suspecting she was right. He probed the Axis, searching for information. Dax would have a better idea of what was happening. Sure enough, he saw that Saar's flagship was scanning *Avalon* at this very moment, searching for life signs. What would happen when they didn't read any?

"I think we'd better cover the guns," Sierra said.

Aileen snorted. "I find your lack of faith disturbing."

Sierra pointed out the window. "That ship is closing in on our position."

Jeth followed the line of her finger, and sure enough one of the cruisers was flying toward them. It wasn't moving at attack speed, but Jeth couldn't think of a single reason why it would be moving at all, unless someone had spotted their disappearance when Aileen engaged the cloak. And the closer they came to the cloaked the ship, the more likely Polaris's movements would show up on a scanner or radar.

"Slow us down, Aileen," Jeth said.

"No, I've got to stay ahead of it. So long as we're steady it won't matter."

"It's too fast," said Sierra. She turned toward Jeth, a silent communication passing between them.

Aileen began to curse under her breath, the cruiser closing in faster now. "It can't know where we are. It's groping in the dark."

Jeth winced at the way her voice shook—uncertainty not a comforting sign from the person piloting their escape attempt. Jeth considered just booting her out of the chair, but doubted his chances of success. Not with Remi sitting there, silent and hulking.

He turned to Sierra, touching her arm. "Can you jail-break the proximity restrictor on the metadrive like we did at Nuvali?"

"Yeah, of course," Sierra said, coming to the same conclusion that he had—the collateral damage to the ITA ships was worth it. Hell, Jeth thought he would even enjoy it.

"What are you talking about?" Marian said. She and Cora had been standing near the back, watching the scene unfold. "Even if you disable it you can't jump with so many ships in range."

Sierra glanced at her. "Yes, we can. We did it at Nuvali."

Marian's eyes widened then narrowed. "You got lucky then. *Very* lucky. The jump should've torn the ship apart. The only reason why it wouldn't have—" She broke off, her eyes flicking to Cora. She turned back to Jeth. "Let's try to escape with the stealth drive first before we risk it."

Jeth gritted his teeth, wanting to argue, but he recognized that hard look on his mother's face. He glanced at Cora. Marian did know a lot more about Pyreans and metatech. If there was a danger, maybe it was best to make jumping now a last resort.

"I'll take the crow guns," Jeth said, announcing it to the ship at large.

"I've got chase." Sierra turned and headed toward the door while Jeth lowered the ladder to the crow's nest.

"Eric, you get starboard," said Perry. "I'll get port."

Jeth climbed the ladder into the crow's nest and sat down in the single seat. He switched on the guns, drawing comfort from the subtle electronic-mechanical sound as they began to heat up. Inwardly though, he hoped Aileen would keep it together, avoiding detection by the cruiser. A sly getaway would be better. Any fun he might've gleaned in a dog fight was cancelled out by the worries pressing in on him, about Lizzie and Milton, even Shady and Celeste, who had vanished to parts unknown inside Peltraz. If Dax had kept tabs on them, there was no indication on the Axis.

Jeth scanned the radar screen, his heart quickening as he realized there would be nothing sly about this escape. Two more cruisers were closing in on their position, each from a different direction. Between the three of them, they would soon be able to detect *Polaris*'s movements.

"Can't we use that weird blue-beamed weapon you hit us with on *Avalon*?" Jeth said through the comm.

"I wish," said Aileen. "The Disrupter can't be used while cloaked, and it's a single shot. Takes minutes to recharge."

Damn, Jeth thought. *Stupid technology with its stupid limitations.*

Sierra's voice broke in. "Nobody fire anything unless pressed. We'll be harder to follow cloaked if we don't keep giving our location away."

Jeth expected Aileen to countermand the directive, but she didn't. The next second, she dropped *Polaris* into a hard dip, sending them below the current path of the incoming cruisers.

Jeth expelled all the breath in his lungs. The ITA must have detected the movement, the cruisers following after them with too much precision. He wrapped his hands around the crow guns but waited to fire. Sierra was right. The ITA would have a much harder time following them if they had only the scanner to rely on and not their eyes. Gunfire would create a target line.

Any second now, he thought, bracing for the inevitable. But Aileen proved a more skilled pilot than he gave her credit for. She slowed them down hard at the end of the dip, nearly to a complete stop. The drop in speed rendered them invisible to the ITA cruisers again. Aileen held that pace until one of the cruisers was nearly on top of them, and then she wheeled *Polaris* starboard into a hard spin and then up.

Over and over again, she played cat and mouse with the cruisers. She stayed close enough that they couldn't risk firing without hitting one another. It was effective for keeping them safe, but Jeth knew they couldn't keep it up forever or the rest of the fleet would be on them. They had to make a jump, risk be damned.

Do it, Dax's command echoed through the Axis. Jeth winced. He hadn't even realized that he'd had his thoughts open to the Axis. Not that it would've mattered if he hadn't. Perry and Eric had heard the command, too.

Let me handle this, Jeth said to them both through the link. Eric started to protest, but Perry's support held him back.

Jeth switched on the comm, signaling down to the chase guns. "You got me, Sierra?"

"Yes," she came back at once.

"Jailbreak the metadrive. We've got to risk it. Tell my mother."

"All right." Determination hardened her voice.

Jeth switched off the comm and focused out the window once more. But a moment later the video screen on the control panel in front of him flashed into life. He stared down at it, brow furrowing.

The ITA emblem appeared on the screen and then cut to a man's face. Admiral Saar stared back at Jeth with his cold, dark eyes—small and snakelike. Deadly. Saar couldn't really see him, Jeth knew—this was just an incoming message, not a full comm link—but his heart rate ticked higher and higher as fear began to spread through him. Once again, he saw Vince falling, blood blooming over his chest, the light in his eyes vanishing.

Saar began to speak. "This is Admiral David Saar of the Interstellar Transport Authority. We are seeking known fugitive Jethro Seagrave." Saar paused, his expression going colder, if that were even possible. A ghost of a smile haunted his skeletal face. The silver tentacles of his implant only emphasized his thinness. He leaned closer to the screen, dropping the formality. "I know you are listening, Jethro. And I know you have what it is I'm truly after. Give it up now and I will spare your life as I did not spare your friend's."

Hatred, as black as the space beyond the window, unfurled inside Jeth. Saar's speech was as much gloat as threat.

"If you do not surrender," Saar continued, "I will hurt you in all the ways that matter most. Hurt you until you beg me for the mercy of your death."

"Yeah, I'd like to see you try, asshole," Jeth muttered, even as his heart pounded harder still, the faces of Lizzie, Milton, Celeste, and Shady all flashing through his mind. But there was nothing he could do to protect them now. He would have to trust Dax to keep them safe.

Jeth killed the power to the video screen and Saar's face disappeared.

"Are we ready yet, Sierra?" he said through the comm.

"Almost. I— Oh God, Jeth. Saar's ship. It's getting ready to fire missiles."

"At what?" He shifted to the right, locating the flagship

easily. They were close enough to it that he could read the name painted on its side: *Regret*. A chill lanced across Jeth's back, the sensation amplified when he saw Sierra was right. The gun ports on *Regret*'s prow were opened, a red glow building. But it didn't make sense. The ship wasn't facing them at all, but was still pointed toward the spaceport.

Toward *Avalon*.

Jeth saw it at once, following the trajectory. They had scanned *Avalon* and found her empty, their prize not in any danger. No, the only danger was of Jeth and his crew trying to escape the same way they'd done so many times before.

I will hurt you where it matters most . . . until you beg for death.

"No." The word caught in Jet's throat, and afterward, he wasn't sure if he'd spoken at all. But inside, his heart and mind were screaming it.

He tightened his grip on the crow guns, taking aim. He even opened fire, but it didn't matter.

The blast of the flagship's missiles launching flashed red before his eyes. Three of them, all at once. Direct target. Direct hit.

With his heart quivering near his throat like a fish stranded on land, Jeth watched as the missiles struck *Avalon*. For a second, nothing seemed to happen at all, but then fire filled his vision.

He watched his ship burn until she was no more.

CHAPTER 20

THE MOMENTS THAT FOLLOWED AFTER DID NOT EXIST. NOT for Jeth. He was not aware of the metadrive engaging. He did not register the jump as metaspace swallowed them whole while biting through the three cruisers surrounding them.

He didn't know how long he stayed in the gun chair before Sierra finally climbed the ladder up to him. She didn't say anything, just stood there, her body half in and half out of the crow's nest, which didn't have enough room for two.

He waited for her to say something, a dozen responses going through his mind, all of them rage-filled and bitter.

But Sierra didn't say anything. She just reached out and touched his knee. Tears stood in her eyes, making them glisten like wet river rock. He sensed her pain, but he didn't feel it. He couldn't feel it, not through his own. The hurt pulsed inside him like a fever. *Avalon* was gone. She was *gone*. The knowledge spun through his head, over and over, leaving him dizzy and sick.

She'd been so much more than a ship, even more than a home. *Avalon* was everything. She had been for as long as he could remember. Back when both of his parents had been alive, she was a symbol of their homecoming, her appearance a sign that they had returned from whatever weeks- or months-long journey they had taken. Later, she became a symbol of his freedom, his shining white horse that he would ride away on. She was his hope, his purpose. He'd built his life around her.

And now she was gone forever.

Sierra's hand moved on his knee. "Will you be okay?"

It wasn't the question he'd been expecting, and it disarmed his anger, preventing the tirade he'd prepared from exploding out from him. He swallowed, bile and despair burning his throat. When he didn't answer, Sierra squeezed him just once and said, "I'm so sorry." Then she descended the ladder. He heard her tell someone below to leave him be. That he would come down when he was ready.

But he wouldn't be ready. He was never getting over this.

After a while, Jeth felt Perry calling him through the Axis link, insisting he needed to come down. They still had a mission ahead of them; they needed to prepare. Eric seconded him, his mind a stronger force than Perry's, harder to ignore. Eric was higher up on the Axis hierarchy, it seemed.

Jeth yanked the implant out, and for once he didn't regret its absence. In that moment, there was nothing he hated more than this black, rubbery intruder that held so much sway over him. If he hadn't been wearing it he could've ignored Dax's command and taken *Avalon* instead. He would've gotten past the cruisers the same way they had with *Polaris,* even without the stealth drive, and he would've found a way to resupply and refuel. He always did.

Dax will give you a new ship when you finish the job, some distant voice spoke in his head.

I don't want another ship. I want Avalon. *Always.*

Finally, with the loss making him restless, he stowed the implant in his pocket. He felt something else in there and took it out; it was Celeste's personal comm. He climbed down from the crow's nest and hurled it against the wall opposite the bridge.

No one spoke. They all watched him, their expressions wary or curious or indifferent. Jeth ignored them and headed for the door. He'd almost made his escape when his mother called his name.

Jeth froze and closed his eyes, trying to summon the will to leave. To just ignore her. But even after all these years, he couldn't resist his mother's voice. He spun toward her, his lips pressed together as he struggled to keep his anger inside.

Her expression was soft, but her voice cut. "It was just a ship, Jeth."

Her words acted as a catalyst, igniting his fury. Jeth took a step toward her, fists clenched. "Don't you ever say that. Not ever." He raised a hand, index finger extended. "That *ship* was all I had. All you and Dad left when you started this, whatever this shit is you've gotten us caught in. *Avalon* was there when you weren't. You left and never came back, never contacted us, even when you could've. That ship did more for us than you ever did. And now she's gone."

Jeth was trembling all over. He felt his control slipping. He turned, spinning hard enough that the sole of his boot shrieked against the floor. Then he strode off the bridge and down the ladder of this ship that was so familiar and yet so alien. The sensation was acid in an open wound.

Habit urged him to hang right at the bottom of the ladder, toward the captain's cabin, but that wasn't his. Not on this ship. He turned left instead, down the crew corridor. He entered the first cabin on the left, the one Aileen had assigned to him. The smell of Sierra, the unique combination of her soaps and perfumes and just herself, greeted him. But he didn't welcome it. He wanted to be alone. He wanted escape.

Jeth fell onto the bed, which was far narrower than what he was used to, and crushed his face against the single hard pillow. The rough material scraped against the stubble on his chin. *Avalon is gone.* A part of him hoped that if he kept thinking it to himself it would somehow hurt less. The rest of him knew better.

And so he closed his eyes, seeking the darkness of sleep, the only respite from his grief. But he didn't fall asleep, not for hours, the time between a long, bitter mourning.

When he finally slept, that abandoned state came upon him like a thief, striking before he knew it. But the pain followed him into his dreams, cultivating nightmares.

Sierra came in sometime later and lay beside him. He didn't hold her, but the press of her body against his brought a small measure of comfort.

She slept fitfully beside him for several hours, and then

sometime later she left again, whispering to him in the darkness that they were three days away from First-Earth. They had to avoid the ITA-owned metagates, and that meant making smaller jumps with *Polaris*'s metadrive.

First-Earth.

Jeth lay on his back after she left, staring at the ceiling. *Finish the job.* Dax had commanded. The job. They were to destroy the Harvester on First-Earth. Before, the mission had been about saving Cora, and the Pyreans. It was also supposed to be a means to an end, a way out from this life he'd been trying to break free from for so long—the escape hatch to a new life, the one he'd always dreamed about. The dream of that life, though had been wrapped up and bound to *Avalon*.

What was left to hope for now? To survive, he supposed, to succeed. And—

Vengeance.

The idea seemed to pour into him, filling the hole the loss of *Avalon* had left. Or if not filling it, coating it like a salve, numbing it. The motivation was a simple one—and powerful.

Going to First-Earth and destroying the Harvester would bring down the ITA. Even more, Jeth knew it would hurt Saar, the righteous warlord, the hero who'd brought honor and glory to his beloved ITA for so long. And Jeth wanted to hurt him. *I will hurt you where it matters most.* Destroying *Avalon* had been a punishment. Jeth understood that. He would return the favor tenfold.

Jeth's anger simmered inside him in a slow steady burn. Soon it outweighed his despair, or perhaps that despair was just the strong foundation for this renewed focus. It restored in him the will to see this through to the end.

Sitting up, Jeth retrieved the implant from his pocket and slid it into place. The Axis would help focus his anger, keep it under control, point it where it needed to go. As Jeth stood, though, he found there was something wrong with the Axis. It was utterly still and silent, almost as if it didn't exist at all. As he reached out, he felt the connection to Perry and Eric, but no one else. Disoriented by the change, Jeth left the cabin and headed for the deck below.

He found Eric in the common room, cleaning his gun. Jeth stared at the lines drawn on the butt of it, but this time they didn't bother him. He might have to draw a line in his own gun soon—when he put a bullet through Saar's heart.

"What's going on with the Axis?" Jeth said. Eric hadn't looked up as he entered, but Jeth knew he was aware of his arrival, the Axis making stealth impossible.

Eric shrugged. "Nothing to worry your pretty head about."

Jeth glowered, and as he spoke, he put the force of his mind behind it, sending it out through the link. "Tell me what's going on."

Eric looked up, his mouth curling into a snarl, and Jeth felt him pushing back. "Dax has us in isolation mode. Standard protocol for all off-site Brethren in the event Peltraz is compromised."

"But what does that mean?"

"It means," said Eric, dropping his gaze back to the gun, "that we're on our own for now. The three of us will still be able to communicate, but we have no connection to the Axis or to Daxton."

"For how long?" Jeth gritted his teeth. He'd hoped to be in regular contact with Dax. He wanted to know everything that was happening. Not just with Lizzie and Milton, but with Saar. How long would the war admiral stay at Peltraz once he realized his target wasn't there? Even more important, where would Saar go next? If Jeth could just talk to Lizzie she might be able to use Saar's trick against him and plant a tracer in his flagship's code.

Eric grunted. "As long as necessary. But you'll want to keep your implant in. Dax might open the connection at any time to send us updates and instructions. He'll have to be careful about it. The ITA might be monitoring the Axis."

Jeth's stomach wrenched at the thought. "I see," Jeth said. "I'll keep it in." Then having no further comment, he walked past Eric and into the galley.

Just like everything else on this ship, the galley felt sterile. There were no personal touches anywhere, not even of the unintentional variety, like the stains that peppered the wall behind the stove on *Avalon*. Jeth wondered if maybe Flynn was right and Remi was a cyborg with no need to eat.

Jeth helped himself to a bowl of cereal and sat down at the table, eating with a mechanical slowness. The common room beyond began to fill up. First Perry and then Flynn,

Sierra, and Cora. Aileen and Remi followed shortly after and then finally his mother.

Marian didn't stop in the common room but approached the door into the galley, fixing Jeth with an inscrutable stare. For a moment she was all ice and hardness again, but then her expression softened. "I'm sorry for what I said about *Avalon*."

Jeth nodded, teeth clenched.

A few seconds passed between them. Then Marian said, "We need to go over the plan. If you're ready."

She spoke it as if he had the option to decline, but Jeth knew his mother well enough to know that wasn't true. "I'm ready."

Keeping his emotions at bay, he stood up from the table and placed the bowl in the sink, not sparing a moment of guilt at leaving it there. He wasn't captain here, and until someone said otherwise, he wasn't going to take a turn at washing the dishes. Let Aileen figure those problems out.

Marian turned and headed into the common room. Jeth followed after her and sat down in the empty seat beside Sierra. This room, more than any of the others Jeth had seen so far, was the least like *Avalon*. The layout was the same, furniture roughly arranged in a circle around a large table, but there was nothing personal here. Nothing to make it feel like a home. That was all right with him.

Sierra reached over and took his hand. He laced his fingers through hers, his gaze sweeping the others. Flynn sat nearest them, and Jeth could tell at a glance that he hadn't slept well either, if at all. Across from the three of them,

Aileen and Remi had taken the sofa, and to Jeth's dismay, Cora sat in between them. This was a strange, unwelcome development. At least Aileen looked uncomfortable about it, her body turned away from Cora and her head lifted high as if she feared letting the girl into her line of sight.

With no other seats left, Eric and Perry had taken positions behind the sofa, the latter leaning against the wall. He gave Jeth a sad smile, and Jeth turned away at once, shutting down the link before he sensed the man's sympathy. He focused his attention on Marian, who approached the table and slid a data crystal into the main port. A moment later, a 3D image of First-Earth appeared above the table.

"In approximately sixty-seven hours, we will enter the patrolled zone around First-Earth," said Marian, facing the room at large. "From there it might take several more hours to navigate past the patrols, depending on the congestion and security level. We will have to go slow to stay off the radar, but the cloak drive should prove equal to the task this time. Once through, we'll land *Polaris* here, in the Atlantic Ocean, just outside the bay into this city—New Boston." Marian indicated the area on the projection, and the image zoomed in to show the bay and surrounding coastline to the west.

"Why?" Sierra said, a strange tremor in her voice. "That's far from the Hive."

"Hive?" asked Flynn.

Sierra glanced at him. "That's the name of the facility where the Harvester is kept."

"We're landing here," Marian said, "because we have to

secure the means to destroy the Harvester first."

"Wait a minute," Flynn said, rubbing the bridge of his nose. "What about the explosives on board? Aren't those supposed to do the job?"

Marian pursed her lips and swept a glower over the room. "Those are only to be used as a last resort. Conventional tools of destruction could cause as much damage to the Pyreans as the Harvester. We must avoid that at all cost."

"How?" Jeth said, unable to keep skepticism out of his voice. "Is there a bomb smart enough to discriminate between them?"

"As a matter of fact, yes," Marian said. "The Harvester and a good portion of the Hive itself is made of plasinum."

Flynn whistled. "That's one expensive facility."

No kidding, Jeth thought. Plasinum was used primarily in the construction of starships and spaceports, due to its unique properties of being incredibly strong and durable but also extremely lightweight. But usually, only a ship's outer hull would be made from plasinum, to keep the cost down in the someone-can-actually-afford-this range.

Jeth shook his head. "How does its being plasinum matter?"

"It matters," Marian said, glancing at Sierra, "because an ITA bioremediation lab has genetically engineered a microorganism designed to target and destroy plasinum. A microorganism they've since weaponized."

"There's a shocker," muttered Flynn.

"The microorganism will destroy the plasinum that makes

up the Harvester without harming the Pyreans," Marian continued. "Or us."

Sierra gulped. "You're talking about Reinette, aren't you?"

Marian nodded.

"Who's Reinette?" Jeth turned toward Sierra, concerned by the alarm in her voice.

"It's not a who but a what. Only—" Sierra broke off, swallowing. "The Reinette project was one of the biggest to come out of the Hanov Division. *My* division."

"Yes," Marian said. "The very division that held Cora and me captive for so many years." She waved a hand over the map and it zoomed in on their target destination, a skyscraper set among dozens of others in the giant, sprawling city of New Boston.

"We're heading back to Hanov?" Incredulity heightened the pitch of Sierra's voice.

"We have to."

Sierra shook your head. "You've lost your mind. There's no going back there, not for any of us. We'll be caught."

A gentle smile crossed Marian's face. "No we won't. The plan we've devised will see you safely into the lab and out of it again."

"See *me*?" Sierra touched her fingers to her chest, over her heart. "You expect me to go in there?"

Jeth felt his anger stirring. "Is this why you needed Sierra for the job?" No wonder his mother had waited to share the specific details of the mission until they were already on their way.

"Yes," Marian said, her tone apologetic. "The security on all the labs under the Hanov Division is based on biometric tech that identifies people at the DNA level. That means all the methods you've employed in the past for breaking into such places are out. A contact lens isn't going to get you through a retinal scan at Hanov. You'd need the actual eye."

Jeth wrinkled his nose at the gruesome idea. Not that he would be above showing up with a gouged-out eyeball, if it meant taking down the ITA.

Sierra let go of Jeth's hand and folded her arms over her chest. "I hate to put a damper on your plan, but don't you think Hanov security would've removed my biometric clearance when I kidnapped Cora and stole the Aether Project? I think that's what they call 'treason.'"

Marian shook her head. "They merely disable the clearance; they don't remove the record. There's an unintentional redundancy in the software that keeps a permanent record of all biometric signatures. All we have to do is break into the system, reactivate your clearance, and modify your permissions to give you access to the entire building. You'll be able to walk into any lab without issue."

Sierra exhaled, and Jeth braced for the argument. When she didn't say anything, Jeth asked, "How do you know about this redundancy?"

"Dax's people knew about it," Marian answered at once, as if she'd been expecting the question. "I believe it was discovered during Hammer's regime. It seems the moment Hammer learned about the existence of the Aether Project, he did everything in his power to orchestrate its theft. He would've succeeded if Sierra hadn't stolen it first. Much of this break-in plan is indebted to Hammer; you could practically call him a member of the team."

This news didn't surprise Jeth. On the contrary, it made perfect sense, and the explanation relieved the nagging doubts he'd had about the short timeframe. Dax had only rescued Marian some two months ago, and Jeth had enough experience with jobs like this to know you didn't set in motion a plan on this scale that quickly.

Sierra too seemed to be thinking along these lines. Her voice was resigned as she said, "Even so, it's not going to be easy."

"Nothing ever is," Jeth muttered.

"Um, not to add to the complication or anything," said Flynn, raising a hand. "But say we break into the impossibly secure government building and steal this secret demolition project . . . how are we supposed to get anywhere near the Hive? Cloaking won't matter once *Polaris* gets close to the surface of the water; they'll see us coming from kilometers away. And if you say we're swimming, then I quit."

"Yep, swimming. That's the plan." Aileen winked at him, and beside her, Jeth saw Cora mimic the gesture. "And won't you look cute in a wet suit."

Flynn scowled back at her. "At least I'll fit into one, unlike your iron giant over there."

"Be quiet," Marian said. "We will be using *Polaris*'s shuttles for both entering the bay and for approaching the

Hive. Dax had the original shuttles upgraded to make them aquatic capable. We'll be able to move about unseen under the water."

Jeth almost smiled at the news. He'd never piloted a ship under water before, though he'd always wanted to. At least that was something to look forward to.

"Once we have Reinette," Marian continued, "we will approach the Hive to within twenty kilometers and then make the rest of the trip in the shuttles." She manipulated the 3D image with her fingers to show the location. As Sierra had said, the Hive was a couple of thousand kilometers away from New Boston. "At its center, the Hive is an open structure, both above and below. We will pilot the shuttle under the Hive and then come up through the center right into the control room. Once there, we plant the Reinette, and then make our escape the same way we came. Simple."

"Oh sure, simple. And where exactly are we escaping back, too?" Flynn said, tapping his foot. "Peltraz and Saar?"

Jeth's stomach clenched. It was the right question, but not one with any answer. The silence on the Axis only added to his worry.

Perry cleared his throat. "Daxton will contact us sooner or later. He'll let us know how and when to approach Peltraz."

Flynn grunted. "Sure, let's trust the backstabbing crime lord."

Both Perry and Eric glowered back at him, but Flynn ignored them, unconcerned. Jeth frowned, surprised by his bravado. It wasn't like Flynn to be so completely unafraid when faced with two leering Brethren, but he seemed to have adopted an almost fatalistic attitude.

With an effort, Jeth pushed worries about Peltraz and Saar out of his mind. There was nothing he could do about that right now. He focused on the plan instead, well aware of the tension coursing through Sierra's body beside him. He understood her fear. They'd spent many a long night talking about her experiences with the ITA and about her escape with Cora. Her capture would mean her death—or worse. The Hanov Division wasn't above sentencing traitors to serve as test subjects in their many experiments. Sierra had told him about prisoners condemned to genetic manipulation experiments.

Hanov was also the location of the ITA's cloning efforts, he remembered. In some ways, Jeth thought, phase one of this plan was even more dangerous than destroying the Hive, especially since they had been unable to leave Cora on Peltraz.

He faced his mother, his expression hardening. He wanted to know every detail about this mission, find and eliminate every possible hole. "So, going to back to Hanov . . . Sierra is supposed to just march in there bold as anything and snatch this Reinette?"

"She'll be wearing prosthetics and other modifications to disguise her appearance," said Marian. "The outer security protocols on the lab aren't DNA sensitive, only the access doors into the labs themselves. She'll resemble someone named Dr. Praveen closely enough to pass the facial scanner and fool any night security crew."

"Night crew?" said Flynn. "Isn't that a bit obvious? Why would this Dr. Praveen go into the lab at night?"

"A lot of the scientists keep strange hours at Hanov," Sierra said. "It certainly won't be busy at night, but her appearance—my appearance—won't raise any suspicions."

Jeth exhaled. "You're going in by yourself, aren't you?"

"I'll have to." Sierra shifted in her seat. "The security doors into the labs will only allow one person entry, and I'm the only one who'll have clearance."

"She's right," Marian said.

Jeth shot a glare at his mother. "I'm not letting Sierra go into that lab alone."

Sierra made a disgusted noise and tapped him in the shin with the toe of her boot. It wasn't hard, but it got his attention. He gaped at her.

"I can handle myself."

Jeth resisted the urge to reach down and rub his leg, his mind scrambling for the appropriate response. He knew dangerous ground when he was treading it. "Fine," he said. "Sierra goes into the lab alone. But how's it going to work, her getting in there?"

Marian turned back to the table and pressed a couple of buttons on the control panel. The image of the First-Earth map dissolved into a detailed schematic of the Hanov building and surrounding area.

"Dax has secured a hover truck for our use, which we will park wherever we can find room next to the building.

Ideally here, right around the corner." She indicated the spot on the map. "Sierra will head in and approach the guard station first. They will have her step into the body scanner. Fortunately, the scanner sits right next to one of the computer terminals. Sierra will have to place a Mite on the terminal just before she steps into the scanner. The Mite will initiate a remote hack immediately. I'll plug into the security feed first and then reactivate Sierra's clearance remotely from within the truck." Marian glanced at Sierra. "You'll have to burn some time while we wait for the Mite to run the program. I suggest heading into the latrines on the main floor; don't even head up to the labs until we know you're cleared."

"Makes sense," Sierra said. "How long do you think it will take?"

Marian pursed her lips. "I don't know. At least five minutes, maybe ten."

Sierra nodded. "I'll bring makeup with me in the event the guards wonder why I'm taking so long."

Jeth grimaced. "And if anything goes wrong with the Mite, Sierra can just walk out again before getting in too deep, right?"

"Yes, although it won't be necessary. We will succeed." Marian manipulated the display again, turning it so they had an underside view of the building. "Meanwhile, the rest of you will head into the subway. This tunnel runs directly beneath the building. You'll make your way into the alcove here and then use a laser torch to cut a hole into this chamber above." She indicated an odd, sub-ground level that seemed to be appended to the main design of the building.

"What is that?" Jeth asked. "Some kind of secret sub-basement?"

"Not exactly," said Marian. "This city is very old, and most of the buildings that were developed in eighteenth, nineteenth, twentieth, and twenty-first centuries have been preserved rather than torn down and rebuilt. This chamber contained the original heating and cooling systems for the building. They sealed it off when they rebuilt the foundation, but its ventilation shafts will allow us to climb up and then break our way through the foundation into this chamber where the new systems are located."

Flynn raised his hand again. "Here's a crazy question, but why are we bothering with all this if Sierra can just sneak this Reinette thingy out the front door. You know, the easy way."

"Gee," Aileen said, touching a finger to her chin. "Why didn't we think of that before?" Again, Cora mimicked her gesture, and Jeth winced. The last thing he needed was Cora choosing Aileen for a role model.

"The Reinette can't leave through the front door," Sierra said, her voice a calm wave of reason in the tense room. "It can't leave the lab at all without setting off the alarms."

"Yep." Aileen leaned back in her chair, slinging one leg over the other. "Which is why I'll be climbing the ventilation shaft up to the lab. Sierra will hand me the Reinette, and then I'll head down and out through the subway with no one the wiser."

Jeth cocked his head. "Why you?"

"She's the only one small enough to fit inside the shafts,"

said Marian. "And even that will be a challenge, since she'll have to wear scalers to do it."

"Oh, it won't be that tight." Aileen waved a hand through the air. "I'm more limber than I look."

"Wait," Jeth said. "If Aileen can get into the lab through the shaft, why does Sierra have to go in at all?"

"There are motion detectors in each room," Sierra said. "The only time they are disarmed is when a cleared individual is inside. So Aileen can get in, but not without alerting the whole building to her presence the moment she slides out of the shaft."

Jeth stifled a groan, hating every bit of the scenario. Sierra would be trapped like a rat in a maze if anything went sideways. "Can you carry scalers in with you if things go wrong, so you too can escape down the shaft? You're small enough to fit."

Sierra shook her head. "It will set off too many alarms if the guards don't see me exit."

"Of course." Jeth gritted his teeth. It seemed the only way to guarantee Sierra's safety would be for her not to do it at all. But that wasn't an option. This was the only way to destroy the Harvester, to save Cora, and to take down the ITA. Jeth didn't like admitting it, but the importance of what they were doing outweighed the risk.

Jeth reached out and took Sierra's hand once more. She glanced at him and smiled, reassurance in her eyes. A faint flicker of the old hope sparked in him for a minute at the sight of it. *Avalon* was gone, but Sierra was still here.

Guilt at the risk she was being asked to take threatened to rise up in him, but then he remembered that he wasn't the only one who'd suffered loss at Saar's hands. Sierra had buried her grief over Vince deep inside her, but Jeth knew it was there. It haunted her gaze. She wouldn't back out of this now even if he asked her to. She had her own vengeance to exact.

He squeezed her hand. They would do this together, and that made them unstoppable.

CHAPTER 21

THEY SPENT MOST OF THE NEXT TWO DAYS GOING OVER THE plans as well as doing drills in hand-to-hand combat. The drills were Sierra's idea.

"The security in the city is tight," she explained. "You won't be able to carry so much as a pocketknife without setting off the metal detectors at the subway entrance."

Jeth knew she was right, though the idea of a city with that much security seemed hard to imagine. They set up a makeshift ring in the middle of the cargo bay, rearranging the crates and barrels until they'd cleared a rough square. The first day they practiced basic techniques, then moved on to sparring.

By the second day, things turned competitive. Jeth watched from the sidelines, perched atop a crate with his feet dangling, as Perry and Eric's sparring match got more and more intense. Both of the Brethren wore their implants, which gave them insight into how the other would move next. As a result, the fight looked more like a choreographed movie scene than the brawl it actually was. Perry would throw a right cross, which Eric would dodge and then counter with a hook only to have it deflected.

On and on it went, neither man getting tired, their stamina sustained by the implants. Even still, Perry was having the harder time of it. They were matched physically, but the Axis hierarchy was a factor, too. Every now and again Eric would exert his implant power over Perry, trying to get him to make a mistake.

The ploy eventually worked. Perry leaned back to dodge a vicious uppercut, not realizing that Eric was feinting. Eric's true punch, a left hook, caught Perry in the side of the mouth and sent him reeling. He stumbled then fell, blood pouring from a busted lip.

Watching from beside Jeth, Cora let out a gasp, covering her eyes.

"It's all right." Jeth patted her leg, wishing she'd listened when he'd asked her to stay on the bridge with Marian instead of watching the combat lessons. "He's fine, see?"

Cora peered between her fingers to see Perry laughing as he picked himself up off the floor. He and Eric shook hands.

"Congrats, Brother," Perry said, slapping Eric on the back. "This one to you, but not the next one, I promise."

On the other side of the ring, Aileen did a slow, mocking clap, her signature smirk on her lips. "Nicely played. But how about trying Remi next?"

Eric shifted his gaze toward the man in question, appraising him. So far Remi had yet to train, or fight at all. He simply sat there, watching everyone work, silent. *Brainless,* Jeth was beginning to suspect. He'd not yet heard the man utter a single word. It was strange, unsettling.

"Sure, why not?" Eric shrugged.

As Remi stood up to accept this challenge, Jeth could think of a dozen different reasons why not—all of them having to do with the man's size. Eric was big, but Remi was damn near a giant. And yet he didn't possess that lumbering awkwardness Jeth usually associated with someone that size. Remi's movements were easy and smooth, not at all hindered by his muscle mass. Jeth wondered how old he was. He would've guessed late twenties, but the man's eyes suggested someone a lot older. In many ways, Remi's eyes bothered Jeth more than his silence. They weren't empty or dull like somebody slow-witted, but they weren't exactly *present* either, as if he observed the world around him from some far, unknowable distance within his head.

"This is a bad idea," Sierra muttered from Jeth's left. He didn't reply. It wasn't that he disagreed with her, just that curiosity had gotten the best of him—he wanted to see Remi in action. A guy didn't get a physique like that by just lying about all day.

Remi did not disappoint. In seconds he'd landed two punches, one to Eric's face and one to his gut. The sound of them striking made Jeth wince. Through the link, he felt Eric's pain before the implant dulled it, speeding his recovery.

Realizing he needed to stay out of the way of those fists, Eric took a defensive stance, bobbing and weaving to dodge incoming strikes. Nevertheless, Remi landed three more punches. The last one left Eric staggering. Remi raised his fist to follow through with one final punch. Jeth took a shallow breath, fear squeezing his chest, some of it his own, but most of it bleeding through the link from Eric. A powerful urge to leap in and defend him came over Jeth.

"Remi, stop!" Aileen shouted. But it was too late. Remi let go of the punch, his massive, sweat-glistening arm careening through the air like a piston.

At the very last second, though, Remi pivoted his whole body to the left. The punch swung wide of Eric's head, striking the side of a metal barrel that formed one corner of the ring instead. A loud, ear-piercing crunch filled the cargo bay, the sound of a machine chewing through metal. Remi pulled his hand away from the barrel, and Jeth felt his jaw drop. The punch hadn't left a dent—the impact had split the barrel at its seam.

"Whoa," Flynn said. Jeth glanced over at him, and Flynn nodded, knowingly. "Cyborg."

Jeth didn't reply, but looked back at Remi. The man's hand wasn't even bleeding. He might've punched through cardboard instead of metal. *What are you?*

Aileen slid off the crate and into the ring, stopping to examine Remi's hand despite there being no sign of injury. Jeth stared at her, his doubt growing. He'd been so caught up in everything that had happened since *Polaris* first appeared in the Belgrave that he'd forgotten his initial suspicion—that no one simply left the employ of a crime lord. Crime lords didn't let assets go. Not alive, anyway.

Sierra leaned toward him, her words so soft Jeth barely

heard her. "Something's not right about those two. I don't trust them."

He nodded. "I couldn't agree more."

"We should ask her."

Jeth glanced down at her, a smile teasing the edge of his lips. "Somehow I don't think Aileen is going to divulge her darkest secrets to you."

Sierra arched an eyebrow at him. "And you think she'll divulge them to you?"

"Probably not, but at least I'll be able to figure out if she's lying about anything." It was a skill he'd perfected in the years he'd worked for Hammer. "And I doubt she'll try to punch me in the face."

Sierra snorted. "I wouldn't count on it."

The idea was laughable, considering how small Aileen was, but Jeth knew better than to underestimate her. He'd made that mistake the first time they'd met. He'd taken her for some spoiled little rich girl, one of the nobility of the planet Grakkus. It was a mistake that had nearly ended with him imprisoned. Only luck and his brilliant sister had gotten him out of it.

There's no need to doubt her, Perry's voice suddenly intruded in Jeth's mind.

He looked over at the other man, who'd been listening in on Jeth's whispered conversation with Sierra through the link. *Why not?* Jeth thought back.

Perry shrugged. *Dax vetted her thoroughly before signing her on.* Humor filled the link as Perry sent through a memory of

Dax when he'd first met Aileen. He'd been totally smitten with the pretty brunette right from the start.

Perfect, Jeth thought, knowing all too well how dangerous it was to judge Aileen by her looks. He'd made the same mistake.

She's worked dozens of jobs for him already with no issue, Perry continued. *Dax trusts her. The Axis holds the proof.*

Jeth frowned, at once convinced by Perry's certainty but also put off by it. He supposed if the Axis link were live at present, it would be a different story, but this was a little too much to take on faith. *Then what the hell is Remi?*

No idea. The Axis didn't have that information. But Dax trusts him, too.

This news solidified Jeth's resolve to determine the truth for himself. It was one thing for Dax to trust these two from afar, but quite another for Jeth to trust them to have his back on a job like this one.

"There's no damage done," Aileen said, drawing Jeth's attention back to the ring.

He glanced at the ruined barrel and decided her statement was arguable.

Aileen waved at Sierra. "I think it's our turn, don't you?"

Sierra frowned. So far the two girls had seemed content ignoring one another as much as possible, but Aileen's invitation was a challenge. Jeth didn't like it. What if Aileen was harboring superhuman strength like her silent companion? She certainly hadn't possessed it the first time they'd met, but that was a while ago. Maybe she'd been using the Remi Workout Secret or something.

Jeth opened his mouth to tell Sierra not to do it, but then he remembered that she wouldn't listen. Not to mention that he wasn't wearing shin guards either.

His worry, it turned out, was unfounded. Sierra dominated the fight easily. With her longer reach, she kept Aileen on the defensive, the shorter girl having little chance to get in close enough to do much damage. Jeth could also tell that Sierra was pulling her punches.

Pride set him to grinning, and as the fight ended, he flashed Aileen a smirk to rival one of her own. "Nice try." She scowled at him, and he laughed. "No need to get so flustered by your, er, *short*comings."

"Ha ha." She jammed her hands down onto her hips. "I think it's your turn now. Would you like to see how you fare against Remi?"

"Out of the question," Sierra answered for him.

Jeth shot her a look, but she didn't seem the slightest bit guilty about the double standard. Then again, it's not like he was particularly anxious to get into the ring with that monster.

"I'll have a go at him," Eric said, stepping up once more.

The man's smugness reached Jeth through the link, pricking his anger. The last time Jeth had thrown a punch at Eric, he'd knocked him out cold. Jeth sent an image through the link reminding Eric of this fact.

We were under orders not to harm you, Eric answered. *And you weren't fully integrated into the Axis either. You won't get the*

22

drop this time. Emphasizing the point, Eric exerted his power over Jeth as he had Perry.

Jeth bared his teeth in a smile, accepting the challenge. "Let's do it then."

Sierra patted his shoulder and made her way to the seats. As soon as the ring was clear, Eric came at Jeth, fists swinging. For a second, Jeth almost failed to react, his mind a blur of thoughts and images. He managed to block the incoming jabs, but just barely as he wheeled away, on the defensive. Fortunately, the few seconds of respite the move provided proved just enough for him to focus his mind. Soon he was able to see the punches coming, gleaning them straight from Eric's thoughts, both conscious and not.

Not that it mattered. In minutes, Jeth began to experience the same frustration Aileen had as Eric pursued him around the ring, his aggression unrelenting. Eric wasn't much taller than Jeth, but it was enough that he struggled to get inside the man's reach. He threw punch after punch but kept missing by inches. Sooner or later, Eric would wear him down. Jeth knew he ought to just surrender, but he couldn't bring himself to do it. He couldn't lose to Eric. Perry maybe, but not Eric.

Growing desperate, Jeth's punches became sloppy. If he could just land one with his right hand, this would all be over. But he couldn't, no matter how hard he tried. Then finally, he switched his approach. Eric had been consistently using the force of his mind against Jeth, trying to will him into a mistake. Up until now Jeth had simply pushed the force back, concerned only with keeping Eric out. But now Jeth stopped trying to push, and Eric's mind fell forward, committing too much to his next punch. Jeth dodged, and his counter uppercut landed square on Eric's chin. It wasn't hard enough to knock him down, as it was Jeth's left hand, but it was enough that Eric stumbled backward.

Flush with his success, Jeth did it again, this time landing a jab, then a left hook. He sensed Eric's growing anger. It began to affect the link in Jeth's favor. Eric's punches grew clearer until finally Jeth landed the straight right he'd been hoping for. His cybernetic fingers smashed against Eric's face and the man fell backward, hitting the ground with a loud smack.

Victory made Jeth's spirits soar, but it lasted only a second as Eric got to his feet. Through the link Jeth saw murder in the other man's mind. But the force of that mind wasn't as strong as it had been. Eric's position in the hierarchy had shifted.

So had Jeth's.

The realization sent a flood of heady power into him. "Stop!" Jeth screamed, and at the same time, he sent the command through the link with all his might. It struck Eric like a physical blow, and Eric stumbled then fell again, this time slamming to his knees mere inches from Jeth.

He was down physically, but not mentally. Eric pushed back through the link, fury and desperation pulsing through him. *You won't beat me. You won't!* He forced an image of Sierra, naked and vulnerable, into Jeth's mind. It was the same one Jeth had let loose when he first took on the implant. At the sight of it, he almost lost his hold on the link, almost succumbed to Eric's mind once more. Then Eric sent an image of *Avalon* being destroyed, the memory so clear that it almost felt like it had the first time.

But sending it was a mistake. Fury ignited inside Jeth, the rage reaffirming his control rather than undercutting it, as Eric had clearly intended. Jeth raised his right hand, ready to deal a devastating blow, the urge almost instinct inside him. His sides heaved. A look of terror crossed Eric's face, the feeling refracted through the Axis. He couldn't stop what was coming. He couldn't move or defend himself, his will bent completely to Jeth's.

"Jeth, no!" Sierra shrieked, but her voice seemed a long way off, too far to care about. All that mattered was this. The power he had now. He'd been powerless all his life, but not anymore.

Jeth pulled his arm back, fist clenched.

"Stop, Jeth!" This time, Sierra came at him, shoving him hard in the shoulder. Faced with this new threat, Jeth seized her hand on impulse and threw her across the ring. Sierra struck the barrels and then the ground, where she lay unmoving.

Silence descended as loud as thunder in the cargo bay. No one spoke, no one breathed. Jeth stared at Sierra before him, confusion siphoning away the anger that had possessed him so completely. Then finally horror took its place as the realization of what he'd done hit him.

"Sierra." Her name caught in his throat as he rushed over to her.

She sat up, her hands braced against him. "Don't touch me." Fear glistened in her eyes.

"I'm sorry," he said, "I didn't mean—" He broke off as she stood up. Each sign of her pained movement was like a knife to his stomach. He wanted to touch her, wanted to convince her it had been a mistake. He hadn't known what he was doing.

Only he had. Deep down, he knew he'd been aware—he just hadn't been in control. Jeth shoved the realization away and the fear it brought with it.

Sierra didn't respond. She didn't acknowledge him at all as she turned and left the ring, heading for the ladder up to the common deck. Jeth wanted to go after her, but he knew better. She needed time.

And so did he. Time to evaluate what he was doing.

What makes you think you're the one doing it?

Jeth didn't respond to the voice. He didn't have an answer to give.

CHAPTER

SIERRA AVOIDED HIM THE REST OF THE DAY, AND WHEN HE came to bed that night, the cabin they shared was empty. He knew where she was—in the cabin next door, the one Aileen had originally assigned her, not knowing that Sierra and Jeth bunked together.

He sighed at the empty room and sat down on the bed, wrestling with his fear and the constant restless anger. He'd said he was sorry. He didn't know what else to do. He couldn't take it back and he didn't know how to make it right.

He lay back on the bed and closed his eyes, willing sleep to come. They would be arriving at First-Earth sometime in the morning and he would need the rest. But all the things left undone refused to leave him alone.

It wasn't just Sierra. He hadn't managed to confront Aileen yet either. He could've just asked her for a private word after dinner, but he wanted to catch her by surprise. A person caught off their guard was more likely to get hung up on a lie than someone prepared for it.

Figuring Aileen must've turned in, the same as everyone else, Jeth stood from the bed and left the cabin. He started to turn toward the captain's quarters, but a light at the end of the corridor drew his attention. He walked quietly toward sick bay and peered through the door.

Aileen was inside, sitting on the examination table with the back of her pajama top pulled up. Jeth frowned. An unlabeled medicine bottle sat beside her on the table, the lid off.

Jeth had no interest in Aileen's shirt coming off—with his luck the moment Aileen flashed him would be the moment Sierra decided to show up and forgive him, only to change her mind—and so he cleared his throat.

Aileen jumped so hard she nearly slid off the table. The movement made her shirt rise even higher, and for a second, Jeth saw something dark on her back, a scaly patch of black and green, like a rotting bruise. She jerked her shirt down, covering it, then scowled at him.

"What are you doing?" he asked.

She scooted off the table then tugged her shirt down once more, over her pajama pants, a sexy pink ensemble. The sight of it made Jeth regret his choice of cornering her at night.

"Nothing, and none of your business." She picked up the bottle and replaced the lid.

"What was that thing on your back?"

"*Nothing.*" She looked ready to throw the bottle at him. "I've got a skin condition."

Jeth arched an eyebrow. "A condition, huh? It's not contagious, is it?"

"Of course not." Aileen sneered.

Jeth knew she wasn't lying. If she did have something contagious, it would be public knowledge. Bioscanners were set around every dock at Peltraz. Anything dangerous would've set off an alarm.

He smiled, not wanting her to remain on the defensive. "I know. It's just so hard to believe you could be anything less than perfect."

"Yeah, I get that a lot."

He snorted. "So, speaking of your many admirers, what's the story with your silent partner?"

A mock vacant expression appeared on Aileen's face. "Why Mr. Seagrave, whatever do you mean?"

Jeth grunted and crossed his arms over his chest. "Oh, I don't know, maybe the way he superheroed his fist through that barrel?"

Aileen narrowed her eyes at him. "I could ask the same question of you, and the way you knocked Eric down just by shouting at him."

Jeth shook his head. "You wouldn't bother asking questions you already know the answer to." To Jeth's irritation, everyone on board knew what had happened, even his mother. And thanks to Perry, they knew it had something to do with the implant, or the Axis to be more specific. *An adjustment phase,* Perry had called it, although Jeth knew it wasn't anything so simple. Both he and Eric had been absolutely silent through the link; Eric was avoiding him as much as Sierra was.

"True," Aileen said. She turned and placed the bottle in a nearby cabinet. "But no need to worry about Remi. He's just big-boned."

Jeth laughed and stepped all the way into sick bay, closing the door behind him. He knew how well voices could carry down the corridor when the door was open. The knowledge brought an ache to his chest, the loss of *Avalon* as fresh as the moment it had happened.

Aileen eyed the closed door, shifting her weight from one foot to the other as if she feared being shut in the room with him.

"So," she said, "the story with Remi is, I don't really know his story. He's mute, in case you hadn't noticed."

Jeth examined her face for any telltale signs of deception. None so far. "How long have you been together?"

Aileen dropped her gaze and began examining her fingernails, which were painted a bright pink. Noticing this detail for the first time, Jeth wondered if this was why Cora was so enamored with her. What little girl didn't like pink fingernail polish?

"A long time now. I can't remember exactly," Aileen said at last.

"Uh-huh," Jeth said. It wasn't an outright lie, but he could tell she had more to say. "And how did you meet?"

Aileen heaved a huge sigh. "You're not going to go away until you've heard my whole sad story, are you?"

Jeth shook his head. "Nope."

"Very well. Can't say I wasn't expecting it. But this would be a lot less boring with something to drink." She brushed past him and crossed to the door, opening it again. "Care to join me in the galley?"

Jeth frowned, remembering the sterile, cold kitchen. "You're not going to poison me, are you?"

"Darn it, you've gone and ruined the surprise." She winked, the gesture flirtatious instead of antagonistic for once. "Come on, after the day you've had, I'm sure you could use one, too." She disappeared down the corridor.

Jeth followed after her, his gaze lingering on the door to Sierra's cabin as he passed by it. He knew he should stop and check on her, but the need to get to the bottom of Aileen's story drove him toward the kitchen.

Aileen poured them each a scotch from a bottle hidden in one of the pantries, and they sat down across from one another at the table. Jeth took a drink, then fought back a cough as it burned his throat. Despite his efforts, tears stung his eyes.

Aileen openly grinned, taking a drink from her own glass like it was water. "Remi was my bodyguard."

Jeth pounded his chest, forcing a breath. "Excuse me? Your bodyguard?"

"Sounds silly, doesn't it?" She flashed teeth. "But it's true. My father was a very rich, very powerful man."

"What did he do?"

Aileen sighed. "Tricky question. I guess you could call him an arms dealer of a sort."

"Of a sort?" Jeth set his glass down, deciding it best to wait a moment before trying again. He needed his wits about him, if he hoped to catch her in a lie. "So what happened? Where's Daddy now?" The slightest of flinches passed over

Aileen's face at the question, and the sight of it pricked Jeth's curiosity. That had been a genuine reaction, the first of the conversation.

"We had . . . artistic differences. He envisioned my life going one direction, and I envisioned it going another. So I left for a better life, taking Remi with me, because why the hell not? Nobody can say he isn't useful to have around."

"You call this a better life?" Jeth motioned to the ship at large. "Wealthy heiress turned thief?"

"Well, it's a more interesting life at least. I never want for adventure."

"Right." Jeth picked up the glass and took a sip with considerably more finesse than the last time. "Was your father abusive?"

Aileen gaped. "Wow, blunt much?"

"Sorry," Jeth said, "but sometimes the direct approach is best." Cruel maybe, but effective. Her surprise had given him time to read the truth on her face—a resounding, heart-wrenching yes.

Aileen's eyes dropped to the table, and she brushed back strands of hair that had fallen loose from her ponytail. "He wasn't abusive, exactly. More . . . controlling."

Jeth watched the lie on her face as she spoke. *Damn,* he thought, unable to keep his feelings toward her from softening automatically. When he'd started this endeavor, he hadn't expected to end up feeling sorry for her. He preferred regarding her as a rival, not somebody to bother caring about. But he saw too much of the same pain on her face that he sometimes saw in Sierra's. She too had grown up with an abusive, controlling father.

Aileen raised her eyes and met his gaze. "But I'm free of him, and yes, that does make this a better way of life."

"Glad to hear it." He offered her a kind smile. "So you left with bodyguard in tow and then what? Did you join Soleil Marcel's organization right away or did that come later?"

"Later, much later." Aileen tapped a fingernail against the table. "And I never joined her organization. I'm a freelancer, always have been."

Jeth blinked. It wasn't that he didn't know about free-lancers—or mercenaries, to use a more accurate term—he just never pegged Aileen for one. She was too young for one thing, eighteen or nineteen at most. You had to build a reputation for years before anyone would hire you freelance.

"You are such a skeptic," Aileen said, interpreting his silence correctly. "It's why we will never be friends."

"Aw, that breaks my heart." He touched a hand to his chest. "But you've got to understand it, yeah? You were what, fifteen when you left home? No one will hire a kid without any cred."

"I was fourteen actually, but I didn't just start off by myself. Remi and I joined the Dark Stars for a while."

Jeth's mouth fell open. The Dark Stars were mercenar-ies, but they weren't like other gangs. In a lot of ways, the gang functioned like a training unit for criminal organiza-tions. Members came and went without issue among the Dark Stars. No, the leaving wasn't hard, just the joining in the first place. It was highly competitive. Only applicants with exceptional potential ever made it in. Hell, Jeth was pretty sure *he* wouldn't have made it in. Lizzie, maybe, but not him.

"How'd you manage that?"

A gleam shone in Aileen's eyes, and she leaned back in her chair. "I've got a very unique, very valuable skill. The Dark Stars recruited *me*."

Jeth arched an eyebrow. "Oh yeah? What skill?"

Aileen shook her head. "Sorry, Peacock. That's my secret, and I'm not sharing. But just trust me when I say it's a skill that makes me incredibly valuable to anybody in this business, including Dax."

Jeth smirked, wondering how much she was aware of Dax's attraction to her. Probably very aware, he decided. Or maybe her special skill was part of the reason why Dax was so interested in her. But what was it? The Shades all had special skills, too, but none so great that they weren't willing to brag about it to someone else. *Well, not counting Cora.* Her skill, and Marian's, was one that it was best to keep quiet about. Jeth couldn't imagine Aileen possessing anything nearly so extraordinary as that.

He cleared his throat. "And I take it Remi's special skill is punching through steel walls."

Aileen grinned. "Yep. I'm sure you can see the value."

"Uh-huh." He rubbed his chin. "Mercenary. Explains a lot. Can I assume we'll get a demonstration of your special skill on this job?"

Aileen sighed. "Doubtful. There shouldn't be any call for it."

Jeth's brow furrowed. "Then why are you here? If you're a freelancer, why take this job? And why would Dax trust you on something like this?"

Aileen scowled. "I'm trustworthy. When I commit to a job, I do it. No exceptions. And I've proven my loyalty to Dax. Besides, there aren't many people small enough to make it up that air shaft."

"Lizzie could have done it," Jeth said. "If she were here."

Aileen laughed. "Like you would've let her do something so dangerous."

"Good point." Jeth grimaced, worry for Lizzie encroaching on his thoughts again. He'd checked his messages earlier, hoping she'd found a way to send him one, but no luck. "But you still didn't say why you chose this job. It's a lot of risk for someone who doesn't have a personal stake in this fight."

"Oh, but the risk is the point. For me." Aileen met his gaze and held it, unflinching. "That is my only prerequisite for the jobs I take. The bigger the risk, the better."

Jeth tilted his head, his confusion growing. She hadn't been lying, of that he was sure, but her answer didn't make sense. Nobody did jobs just for the thrill of it. Not that he didn't understand the thrill angle—he enjoyed the rush of courting danger too, at least he used to before the stakes had gotten so high, before life had shackled him with so much failure—but without some sort of reward, it just didn't make sense.

"No offense, but I find that hard to believe."

Aileen sighed. "Like I said, skeptic. But it's true. Don't get me wrong, I'll be taking home a nice paycheck once we finish this, but that's not why I'm here. I know it sounds crazy, but this risk, this feeling like we're one mistake away from death, or worse—that's the stuff that makes me feel alive."

"You're right," Jeth said, "that is crazy." He smirked, though in truth he had an easier time understanding it when she put it that way. The high that came after a close call was unlike any other. It was a moment of complete fulfillment, complete elation, as if every fiber of your body and soul was fully engaged in the here and now, fully electrified. Doubts and worries did not exist in that moment. The persistent empty feeling—the daily want for something more, something greater always just out of reach—disappeared.

"But I get it," Jeth said. Envy rose up in him, and he looked away from Aileen, letting his gaze wander over the room. The starkness of it struck him again, and the envy faded as quickly as it had come. Aileen's life had its moments of fun, no doubt, but the in between looked pretty lonely. At least that was one thing Jeth had never struggled with. He'd always had Lizzie and Milton, his crew. Aileen only had this empty ship and a silent, cold bodyguard for company.

"I'm glad to hear it." Aileen smiled, tight-lipped. "Does this mean we're going to set aside our differences and be the best of friends now?"

Jeth laughed. "I wouldn't count on it, but I have decided to trust you enough to let you do your part on the Hanov mission."

Aileen snorted. "Like you have a choice. I'm here on Dax's

orders and you have to follow them." She motioned toward his head. "I know how those implants work."

"Maybe so, but we're not connected to Dax at the moment. His influence isn't so strong out here."

Aileen leaned back in her chair and put her feet on the table. "It's strong enough for Perry and Eric. You have to go along with them."

"I wouldn't be so sure of that," Jeth said, his thoughts returning to the scene in the cargo bay.

"Well, no matter," Aileen said with false bravado. "Like I said, I'm the only one small enough for the job."

Jeth rubbed his chin. He was starting to enjoy teasing her. "I don't know. Flynn is pretty small and limber. And I certainly trust him not to get Sierra caught."

"Don't worry about her." Aileen smirked. "She'll be fine with me, I promise. And definitely a lot safer than she is hanging around you these days."

At once, the lightness between them evaporated, and Jeth's anger flared. He clenched his teeth, fighting it back.

"Oh." Aileen covered her mouth, her eyes wide. "I'm sorry. That was below the belt."

Jeth stared at her, uncertain if she was mocking him or being serious. She always seemed to be doing both at the same time.

"Have you smoothed things over with her yet?" Aileen asked.

Dropping his gaze, Jeth shook his head.

"Well, I wouldn't let it go too long. She's liable to get more pissed as time goes by."

Jeth grimaced, knowing she was right. He just didn't know what to do about it. He'd never done anything so awful. He'd never laid hands on a girl in anger before, not even on Celeste, who'd punched him in the face the first time they met. Not that the attack had anything to do with Sierra being a girl; he would've done the same to anyone who'd stepped in front of him in that moment.

"Here, have another drink." Aileen tipped the bottle over his glass.

Jeth hadn't realized his glass was empty. He should've felt the alcohol, but his head was perfectly clear. He supposed it was a side effect of the implant.

"Then go find her, get on your knees, and beg for forgiveness," Aileen added.

"Like that'll work." He picked up the glass and swallowed half of it down in one gulp.

Aileen rolled her shoulders. "It couldn't hurt. Just tell her you'll do whatever it takes to make her happy again. Girls love that sort of thing."

A grin curled one half of Jeth's mouth and he considered teasing her again, but held back. He polished off his drink then stood to leave.

"Good luck." Aileen raised her glass. "I'll see you in the morning."

Jeth left the galley, heading up to the passenger deck. He stopped in the second cabin on the left and tapped the door. Several seconds passed with no response. Jeth considered tapping again, but decided to try the door instead. To his surprise and encouragement it wasn't locked. He stepped in and closed it behind him.

The room was dark, but he could just make out Sierra's shape on the bed in the faint glow of the safety light on the door handle.

"Are you awake?" he spoke into the darkness.

Sierra didn't reply, but he saw her foot move, just a little. It wasn't much, but he would take any invitation he could get at this point. He stepped up to the bunk and saw she was facing away from him.

He pulled his boots off, trying to be quick but quiet, afraid she would tell him to leave any second. She didn't, and a moment later he slid into the bed behind her, wrapping his arms around her waist. She stiffened at his touch but didn't pull away.

Jeth inhaled, his breath stirring her hair. He let it out slowly. "I'm so sorry, Sierra. I didn't mean to do it. I got caught up in the moment and lost my head."

Sierra made a disgusted sound that was more pain than anger. Jeth flinched, hating it, and hating himself for causing it.

"Is that supposed to be funny?" she said. Her stomach moved beneath his hands as she spoke.

"What do you—" Jeth broke off, catching her meaning. "The implant." He sighed. "No, I wasn't trying to be funny. I just meant I reacted without thinking. I would never do something like that on purpose."

Sierra shifted in his arms, turning to face him. He could just make out her eyes in the darkness. "I know. It's just . . ."

Jeth's heartbeat quickened. He reached out and stroked

the side of her face. "What can I do to make it right?"

Her mouth opened, but she didn't say anything, not for several long, terrible seconds. When she finally did speak, her words struck him like a physical blow. "Take out the implant."

Jeth sucked in a breath, dread at the idea rising inside him. "I . . . I can't."

Sierra sat up, leaning on one arm and looking down at him. "Why not? Dax isn't around to insist that you wear it."

Jeth sat up too, bringing his face on level with hers. "That's just it. Dax might open the link any time. I have to be there when he does."

"No, you don't. Perry or Eric can monitor it."

"But—" Jeth struggled for a response, knowing there wasn't one. Not really. She was right. Dax wouldn't know if he was wearing the implant right now or not. He swallowed, unwilling to admit that he didn't want to take it out. Somehow in the last few days he'd gotten used to its presence. And he knew for certain he didn't want to face that empty, gnawing feeling having it out would bring, not when he'd have to put it in again later. Dealing with the loss of *Avalon* and worry about his loved ones was hard enough without adding that into the mix.

"But what?" Sierra prodded.

"I need to be there when he makes contact. I have to know what's happening at Peltraz." His voice began to shake. "Saar destroyed *Avalon*, he knows we were there, and he could have found Lizzie and Milton by now."

"Oh, Jeth." Sierra cupped the side of his face with her palm. Her skin was as soft as silk against his, but the sympathy in her voice cut him. He didn't want it. He didn't want to break. He wanted to stay angry and focused. He reached for the implant's reassuring presence in the back of his mind, and at once the threat of tears vanished.

"I know you're in pain, but you've got to be careful," Sierra went on. "That implant . . . it scares me, more than I could've guessed. Sometimes when I look at you . . ." Her voice trailed off.

"Sometimes what?" His stubble scraped against her palm as he talked.

"All I can think about is the deal we made, and I get even more scared."

"Don't be. It's going to be fine."

Sierra leaned toward him. "Then take it out."

Jeth closed his eyes, his pulse quickening. *Do whatever it takes to make her happy,* Aileen had said. He reached behind his head and pulled the implant out. At once, a restless feeling came over him. His fingers twitched; his muscles clenched and unclenched. And worst of all, that empty-hole sensation seemed to spread open inside him like a deep hunger, an unquenchable thirst. With an effort, he ignored the inner turmoil and rolled over and set the implant on the table.

Sierra caressed his shoulder. "Thank you."

He nodded and laid his head down on the pillow. She curled up behind him, her arm wrapped around his waist. Jeth closed his eyes and tried to sleep, but in moments the back of his skull began to ache. Began to *itch*. He ignored it, forcing his thoughts on the mission, on Aileen and Remi, on anything besides his desire to insert the implant once more.

He succeeded for half an hour, long enough for Sierra to fall asleep. Then he sat up slowly and retrieved the implant. His guilt at putting it back in was gone in a moment, drowned out by the feeling of all the hollow places inside him filling up once again.

JETH LEFT THE CABIN EARLY THE NEXT MORNING, SNEAK-ing out into the corridor.

"Trying not to get caught spending the night in your girl-friend's room?"

Jeth jumped and swung toward the voice. His mother stood in the doorway to sick bay, an amused expression on her face. He ran a hand through his mussed hair. "Why? Are you going to ground me?"

Marian harrumphed. "If I recall, that never was a very effective punishment for you."

He smiled, and walked down the corridor toward her, noticing the syringe in her hand. "What are you doing?"

All humor vanished from Marian's face. "Cora isn't feeling well again this morning. We're going to try a new medicine."

A tremor of fear went through Jeth's stomach, and he followed his mother into sick bay. Cora was sitting in one of the chairs, her head resting in her hands. A dark flush painted her sunken cheeks as if from a fever. The sallowness of her skin made her eyes look more brown than black. Jeth laid his palm against her forehead and flinched. It was ice-cold.

He glanced at his mother, but she didn't say anything.

There wasn't anything to say.

"Now hold still, Cora," Marian said, holding the syringe at the ready next to Cora's arm. "Just a little sting. But you'll feel a lot better in a few hours."

Cora didn't protest this time, too lethargic for fear. Not that she would be afraid. The poor kid had received more shots in her life than everyone else on this ship combined, probably.

Jeth patted her head. "You're the toughest girl I know."

A weak smile crossed her face. "Tougher than Sierra?"

"Without a doubt."

Marian clucked her tongue. "You're all done, free to run off and play at last."

Cora sat up. "Can I go to the engine room?"

"I don't see why not."

Sliding her legs over the edge, Cora said, "Aileen didn't like it when she saw me there yesterday."

Jeth grunted. "Don't worry about Aileen. If she has a problem I'll deal with it."

Cora jumped down from the table and disappeared through the door. Jeth was just about to follow after her when Marian said, "We'll be arriving at First-Earth soon. Are you ready?"

He pressed his lips together, assuming she was referring to his loss of control yesterday. "I'll be fine."

Marian took a step toward him. She touched his arm, her fingers as light as feathers. "Are you sure?"

"Don't worry, Mom," he said through clenched teeth.

"I'll get it done. We'll free the Pyreans and save Cora."

Marian shook her head. "I'm not worried about the mission. I'm worried about *you*."

Jeth raised his eyebrows. "Why?"

She looked taken aback. "You're my son, and I love you. I know you're struggling right now, and I wish I could do something to make it easier."

He studied her a moment, his eyes lingering on her white implant. So far he'd never seen her without it. "Does it bother you to take your implant out?"

Marian touched one of the tentacles. "Not really. It feels strange, but that's just because I'm so used to wearing it."

Jeth frowned, disliking the answer. The way she made it sound, not wearing it was nothing more significant than forgetting to put on a regular piece of jewelry. "It doesn't make you . . . anxious? I mean, you don't crave putting it back in?"

She shook her head, worry creasing her brow. "No. Why do you ask?"

"No reason." He ran a hand through his hair. "I was just thinking how the implants use Pyreans to work, and I wondered if wearing one is a bit like what Cora's doing with how she wants to be near the metadrive, like if once you experience being connected to them you start to crave the connection." He paused, thinking it through. "Almost as if the Pyreans are influencing that desire. You said they are sentient, yes?"

"Well, yes, but not the dead ones. Trust me, Jeth, you've never encountered a fully alive, fully sentient Pyrean before. Not yet."

"I see," he said. He knew it had been a stretch, but he'd sometimes gotten the impression the implants were living things, what with the way the tentacles would curl up and wrap around the wearer's head when inserted. If they were alive, maybe they could be influencing him, but it seemed unlikely, especially if having it out didn't affect his mother like that.

He sighed. "Anyway, like I said, no need to worry about me. I'm fine. Always am."

Her look told him how well she believed it. Not wanting to give her a chance to call him on it, he headed for the door.

"I really am sorry," Marian said as he reached it. "For what happened to *Avalon*. I know you cared for the ship. So did I. It was awful to see her go like that."

Jeth closed his mouth, distrusting himself to speak. The pain was too fresh. Too strong. He glanced back at her. "Yeah, it was."

"And I'm sorry for dragging you into this," she said, her voice close to a whisper.

Me too, he thought but didn't say.

"But you have to have faith," his mother continued. "It's going to be all right in the end. I know it."

Faith, he thought. Where did hers come from? Surely it wasn't in fate, or some higher power. Their lives had been too dominated by failure and loss for her to believe in that sort of idiotic nonsense. *Maybe her faith is in the Pyreans.* Doubt churned inside him as he nodded and disappeared into the corridor.

They entered First-Earth territory a few hours later. Jeth was on the bridge as the planet came into view, distant, but unmistakable. Yet it didn't seem real. For his whole life, First-Earth had been this object of reverence, the source of all human history, human life. It was the oldest civilization in the universe, a historical monument that every person alive could claim a connection to, a shared past.

It didn't look much different from any other planet.

Except, Jeth realized as he scanned the area of open space before him, for all the traffic. Never before had he seen so many ships in one place at one time aside from during a military operation, and every one of them probably had the ITA on a quick call. Hell, half of them probably were ITA ships.

"This is going to be fun," Flynn said, puffing out his cheeks. He stood to Jeth's right, as interested in seeing First-Earth as Jeth was.

Aileen grinned over her shoulder at them from the pilot's chair. "I'd say so."

Jeth bit his lip. Thrill-seeking was all well and good so long as it wasn't stupid—like breaking the maximum velocity for remaining undetectable with the cloak drive engaged. This was the time for flying with absolute precision, not testing the limits. For a second, Jeth wished Celeste were here. She would be able to do this without question, flawlessly.

Aileen faced front again, her hands steady on the control column. Remi sat in the copilot chair beside her, as still as stone. Jeth stayed where he was for the first twenty minutes before getting tired and sitting down at the comm station. Flynn took the nav, but there was little to do as Aileen piloted them through. The going was slow, uneventful, but not particularly easy. Aileen had to bring them to a complete stop again and again or keep changing directions to avoid a passing ship.

Nevertheless they finally came in range of the planet. Jeth announced it to the bridge at large after Aileen failed to. The old habit felt both familiar and brand new on this ship that wasn't his, but not announcing it would've been bad luck.

Cora came bursting in first, followed by a black-haired woman. Jeth blinked away shock as he realized it was Sierra. He hadn't seen her since breakfast. He had hoped that by leaving the cabin before she woke, she wouldn't know how early he'd reinserted the implant. That optimism hadn't lasted a second as she'd entered the galley this morning. Her eyes had found his for a moment before traveling to the tentacle curled around the base of his neck. Storm clouds had crossed her face, and she'd turned away from him.

Sometime in the intervening hours she had dyed her hair. Jeth had known it was coming, but still the change was startling. It made her already pale face ghost white and nearly unrecognizable. She would be a complete stranger once she put on the facial prosthetics.

With his mouth still open in a gape, Sierra flashed him a smile. It wasn't exactly cold, but distant, inscrutable. He returned it then faced the front once again. Cora walked up to Aileen, leaning against her chair and staring out the window on tiptoes.

"Cora," Jeth called, catching the flustered look on Aileen's face, "you need to leave her be." Cora's expression turned pouty as she turned, but it was good to see her display some energy. Glad the medicine had helped, Jeth motioned her over, and Cora climbed into his lap.

No one spoke as they entered the atmosphere. Jeth kept glancing down at the status screen in front of him, checking that the cloak drive was still engaged. The technology was nearly flawless, but sometimes the stress of passing through the atmosphere could cause a disruption. With broad daylight surrounding them, they would be spotted in an instant if that happened.

But the cloak drive held and Aileen headed for their landing spot in the middle of the Atlantic Ocean.

"Wow, all the water." Cora stood up and approached the front window again. This time Jeth didn't stop her. The scene fascinated him, too. He hadn't seen an ocean this close in years, and he'd never had cause to do a water landing. It was strange, but despite all the wonders of space that he'd seen, the simple, moving grace of an ocean still filled him with awe.

The rocking motion of the ship, however, did not. Jeth hadn't known how much it would bother him, and he wished they'd timed their arrival closer to nightfall to avoid the long wait.

Jeth had a feeling he wasn't the only one plagued with a bit of seasickness. The look on Flynn's face as he and Jeth ran through a systems check on the shuttle several hours later was one of utmost misery.

"Are you going to be all right?" Jeth asked, clapping him on the shoulder. He wished Milton were with them. He would have something to make them both feel better.

Flynn shrugged, not looking up from the screen in front of him. "I wish I was going."

Jeth frowned. "You do?" In all the jobs they'd worked together, Flynn had always been happy to stay behind with the ship. Somebody needed to be there to move *Polaris* out of the way if another ship passed through these waters, and to keep an eye on Cora. It was true someone else could've done it, but of all of them, Flynn was the best choice. Cora needed someone she knew to stay with her, and if anything went wrong with the ship, Flynn was the most qualified to handle it.

Flynn nodded. "Beats the hell out of staying on this thing."

Jeth swallowed, understanding the problem at once. He'd been stupid not to have realized it before.

"It's just so weird, you know?" Flynn peeked over at him. "I wish *Polaris* wasn't a Black Devil. It would be easier to forget about *Avalon*. And there's not a single thing broken on this stupid, shiny ship. I don't know why I bothered bringing all my tools."

"I know," Jeth said, his throat tight. Of course he wasn't the only who cared about *Avalon*. For years, Flynn had been the one who kept her running. How could he not love her?

Flynn sighed. "Everything is changing." He pulled a piece of chocolate from his pocket and began unwrapping it. "I hate change."

"Me too," Jeth said. "Me too." They finished the systems check in silence.

Twenty minutes later, Flynn left to take care of Cora, and the rest of the crew piled into the shuttle. It was a tight fit, cramming seven people in a ship designed for four.

"It's a good thing we're not trying to fly this thing," Aileen noted from the copilot's chair.

"No kidding," Jeth said from beside her in the pilot's seat. He'd been surprised at how easy it was to convince Aileen to let him pilot. It seemed they'd come to an understanding after their late-night conversation. He found himself almost enjoying her company.

"Try not to hit anything until we're close enough to swim to land."

Almost.

"We'll be fine under the water and for such a short distance," Marian said from behind Jeth.

She was right, of course. They navigated through the bay, arriving without issue at an isolated, private dock about thirty kilometers southeast of their destination. Jeth brought the shuttle to the surface, and Remi climbed out through the top hatch, leaping to the dock to tether them.

The hover truck Dax had secured for them was a short walk from the pier. In the distance, a bright haze surrounded the city from so many lights set against the night sky. It was just past nine now, and would be well past ten by the time they arrived, but Jeth had a feeling that a city like that never slept.

"I should drive," Sierra said as they climbed into the truck. The outside was painted a dark green with BOB'S CARPET written on the sides in bright yellow. "I know the city best."

Everyone agreed and piled into the truck. Jeth took the front passenger seat, giving him the clearest view of the city. If he thought the space surrounding First-Earth was congested, it was nothing compared to the traffic in the city itself, both vehicular and pedestrian. The city crawled with life, the sidewalks and streets like undulating surfaces set in between buildings so tall only a fragment of the night sky was visible.

"This place is packed." Jeth glanced at Sierra. "I can't imagine living here."

"It wasn't easy," she said, not looking at him. Tension threaded her voice. It wasn't just fear, but hatred. Of this place, and of the life she thought she'd left behind forever.

He knew why, given her history, but at the moment he was too mesmerized by the view in front of him to dwell on it. He'd never been in a city so ancient. Most of the buildings looked hundreds of years old, some with crumbling facades of gray granite, white marble, or red brick, others with windows that seemed to sag from sinking foundations. And yet everywhere he looked there were new structures as well. Tall steel buildings as sleek and shiny as spaceships and with impeccable facades stretched high overhead. Video advertisements in full 3D rendering covered large expanses of the walls and most of the windows on the storefronts they passed. Nearly all the vehicles were state-of-the-art hovercraft, some with emergency vertical airlift propulsion systems and programmable colored exteriors.

Jeth watched as one such craft, a small, sporty little number, changed color from white to red to cameo-pink all in a matter of seconds. It seemed the craft's owner—or one of its half dozen passengers—couldn't make up her mind about what would look best gliding down the strip. The autopilot system on the craft made such frivolous distractions possible with no danger to the other craft.

But even more startling than the vehicles and buildings were the people. Thousands of them wore brain implants. There were blue ones, red ones, black, brown, pink. Jeth even spotted a zebra print.

"Why are there so many implants?" he asked Sierra.

She glanced at him, her gaze taking in his Brethren implant. She was completely unrecognizable with the facial prostheses in place. To complete the transformation, she wore her black hair pulled back in a severe bun, along with high heels and a dress beneath a white lab coat. She returned her gaze to the road. "People use them for all sorts of things, those that can afford them anyway. Mostly, they're used to interface with computers and other tech. Or to communicate with family members and loved ones far away."

Jeth gaped. Whole families with implants? And they paid for them? He couldn't wrap his mind around it. Nowhere else in the galaxy had he seen implants for personal use like this. The only ones he'd ever seen had been for soldiers or slaves.

"Don't look so surprised," Sierra said. "These implants aren't set up like Dax's. They're not designed to link people together. They're for simple communication and little more."

Jeth considered the idea, especially the way he'd gotten the impression that Hammer's personality—and later Dax's—had influenced the feel of the Axis. He supposed what she was saying made sense. He could see the appeal of being able to communicate so easily with others far away. And it was fitting that they would be used so commonly here, the home of the ITA, the heart of metatech manufacturing. Jeth let out a breath. That was a lot of dead Pyreans.

Thirty minutes later they finally arrived outside the Hanov building. Once they found a place to park—a daunting task that took twenty minutes and multiple trips around the block—they left the truck in staggered formation. Eric went first, followed by Aileen and Remi. Then Jeth and Sierra. Perry would be staying to cover the truck while Marian focused on hacking into the Hanov's security system once Sierra planted the Mite.

Jeth started to pull his jacket hood over his head then decided it wasn't necessary. Not with so many others wearing implants. He sighed in relief. The prosthetic pieces he was wearing to avoid being recognized from the ITA's Most Wanted bulletins were uncomfortable enough.

Jeth had insisted on escorting Sierra as far as he could before joining the others in the subway. They walked in silence, the sidewalks too crowded to carry on a conversation. People of every color, shape, and size filled the streets, bumping into Jeth without so much as a glance of apology. A new and unexpected sense of claustrophobia came over him. If they didn't get there soon, he was going to lose his patience and start bumping back.

As they rounded the corner of the Hanov building toward the entrance, Sierra stopped and faced him. "I've got it from here. Be careful."

"I will." He leaned in and kissed her, hating the distance that still loomed between them.

"Hurry up, Longshot," Aileen's voice spoke through the comm patch affixed to the skin behind his ear. "The train will be coming soon. We only have five minutes to hit the alcove or we go splat."

Jeth made a face at her choice of words. He turned and headed back around the corner toward the subway entrance. The stench as he descended the concrete stairs made him gag, a pungent combination of urine and garbage.

Even though Sierra had warned them that the terminal wouldn't be empty, even at this late hour, Jeth was amazed by the sight of a few dozen people waiting for the next train as he joined the others. Getting into the tunnel without any of them noticing was going to be tough. He didn't quite believe Sierra when she said that no one who lived in this city would look twice at five people hopping down onto the train tracks and making a run for it.

The train arrived a few minutes later, rushing into the station with a hot breath of wind. Like the city above, the subway system was a combination of the very old and new. The mosaics decorating the walls and pillars were faded and indistinguishable, broken and missing tiles dotting the designs. But the train was sleek, shiny, and virtually silent as it hovered over its magnetic tracks. The doors slid open with a quiet hiss, dumping its travelers and taking on more.

Jeth and the others congregated near the edge of the station and waited for the train's departure. The moment the tunnel was clear, they jumped down into it and raced away without a single shout of alarm from anyone on the platform. In seconds, the lights from the terminal faded, the darkness swallowing them until Eric and Remi pulled out flashlights.

Despite the fast pace, they barely made it into the alcove before the next train. Jeth's heart ricocheted in his chest as it swept past the opening, blowing hot air and subway stench in their faces. Splat would've been an understatement.

Once the train had passed, he pulled the portable viewer out of his pocket and switched it on, but there was nothing to see on it. "We're we at, Riptide?" he asked through the comm.

Marian answered a moment later. "Sparrow's in the latrine. She made it through the physical security check without issue and successfully planted the package. The program is running now. You'll have visual as soon as I'm in."

Jeth waited, his gaze fixed on the viewer as the others began to set the plasma charges on the alcove ceiling. The seconds stretched by with no change on the viewer. He resisted the urge to signal Sierra. He didn't want to risk it with guards so near.

Once the plasma charges were set, Eric switched on the frequency device, and ten seconds later there was a loud pop. As the dust cleared, revealing the hole into the room above, Jeth glanced down at the viewer, but there was still no change. *What's taking so long?*

As if she'd heard his thoughts, Marian's voice spoke over the comm. "Almost there. Okay, the vid loop is in place on the guard's screens, and you should have visual control of all cameras in four, three, two . . ." As she reached one, the viewer flicked into life. The picture was blurry at first and then became clear—displaying the camera view of the main entrance to the Hanov building.

"Got it." Jeth ran his finger over the screen to change the view. He oriented it toward the latrines, monitoring for Sierra's return. On the bottom part of the screen he could see a portion of the guard station and one of the guards. The man wore a dark green uniform with a stunner holstered to his right side while an electrified nightstick hung from his belt on the left. Strapped to his back was a Kali shotgun. Jeth quailed at the sight of it. That was some serious firepower. A Kali was capable of shredding a human being into pieces at close range.

"Just another minute, Sparrow, and I'll have the clearance activated," Marian said.

"Good," Sierra whispered. Even still her voice echoed a little off the tiled walls in the latrine.

"Be careful," Jeth said.

He stowed the viewer in his pocket and then walked over to where Remi was hoisting Aileen into the chamber above. Eric followed, and then Jeth. Once up, he bent over the hole to offer Remi a hand, but the man didn't need it, hauling himself up without so much as a grunt of effort.

Thick dust coated the defunct chamber, and Jeth covered his mouth to keep from coughing as their movement stirred it into a cloud. The others were doing the same, all except for Remi, who seemed impervious. The giant headed straight for the main ventilation shaft, grabbed it at the base, and ripped off a two-meter section, exposing the way up.

Jeth whistled through his teeth, unable to help himself. *Big-boned indeed.*

Moments later, Remi headed up the shaft with scalers affixed to his knees, forearms, belly, and back. He would need his hands free to set the plasma charges to blow a hole through the foundation above.

Jeth returned his attention to the viewer, keeping focused on what he could see of the guards. Any sign of restlessness on their part, and he would call for an abort of the mission.

Finally, Marian announced, "The clearance is good. Whenever you're ready, Sparrow."

Jeth held his breath while he watched Sierra emerge from the latrine. She stopped just outside the door and smoothed down her dress. Then she waved to the security guards as she strode to the elevators across the way. One of them waved back, and Jeth inhaled, relief making him momentarily giddy.

He faced the others. "Sierra's heading up. We need to get a move on."

"Already there," Aileen said as she grabbed the rope Remi had just thrown down the shaft toward them.

Jeth blinked, cautiously satisfied at how smoothly things were going. It had been a long time since a job had gone this well for him. He stowed the viewer once more and headed for the rope. He climbed as quickly as he could. He needed to monitor the cameras in case there was anyone heading Sierra's way. Marian would be monitoring, too, but there were a lot of views to cover.

The room Jeth found himself in a moment later was loud enough to make his head ache. The heating and air conditioning units on this building were the size of small tanks, massive steel contraptions that sounded like mechanical dragons feasting on metal bodies. The building might've been renovated, but not recently. The equipment in this room was several decades old, if not older.

Jeth checked the viewer to see Sierra emerge from the elevator onto the fourth floor. The Reinette lab was one of three and the farthest from the elevator. He adjusted the camera view, then looked up from the screen, panic squeezing his chest. It would take time for Aileen to climb the four floors. But to his relief, she had the scalers on and was already on her way up the shaft through the hole Remi had made.

"Angel is on her way up now," Jeth said through the comm, wincing at Aileen's chosen call sign. On the viewer Sierra gave a little nod.

"Now we wait," Eric said as he upturned a waste bin. Trash that looked as ancient as the equipment in the room spilled out from it, and he brushed it aside before sitting down on the bin.

Jeth gritted his teeth, detesting the notion. He hated being idle on a job, stuck watching from afar. Still, he supposed as he returned his attention to the viewer, watching was better than being completely in the dark. He began to fiddle with the camera view, angling it out to get a better look at the place as Sierra walked along.

"Whoever is moving the camera, would you knock it off," Sierra said through the comm. "It's creepy. There are gun turrets attached to those cameras, you know."

He didn't know, but as Jeth adjusted the view one more time, he saw it for himself, the camera he was viewing now pointed at the one at the end of the hallway. Sure, enough, a gun turret hung beneath it. "What the hell are they keeping in these labs?"

"You don't want to know." On the screen, Sierra had just arrived at the main door into the Reinette lab. She pressed her hand palm down and fingers spread against the security panel. Jeth braced, waiting for the alarms to sound. He knew from experience that anything could go wrong with tech ops at any time. And he didn't have the same faith in his mother as he did in Lizzie.

The panel glowed yellow as it processed the request, then flicked to green. The door slid open, and Jeth willed his muscles to unclench.

Sierra stepped through into the decontamination chamber, then came to a stop in front of the interior door as the other closed behind her. The decontamination took a full thirty seconds, the time indicated by a counter above the door.

As it hit one, the interior door opened and Sierra stepped all the way into the lab. She scanned the room, eyeing the equipment set on the exam tables and affixed to the walls. Spotting a handheld laser torch on the nearest wall, she picked it up, then grabbed a chair with her free hand and pulled it over to the air vent in the far corner.

"How far are you, Angel?" Jeth asked through the comm.

"Moving onto the fourth floor now," Aileen answered, breathing heavily from the climb. At least it would be easier now that she was crawling horizontally instead of vertically. She was almost there, the lab vent less than twenty meters from the main shaft.

Sierra ran the laser around the edge of the vent, cutting through the wall itself so as not to set off the alarms on the biofilter covering the vent that was designed to send a signal at any loss of integrity. She pried it off in seconds, dust and debris hitting her face, but she didn't wait for Aileen to arrive, turning instead to face the center of the room where the Reinette tubes were stored inside a sealed glass cabinet.

As with the door into the lab, Sierra pressed her hand against the security panel. It flashed into life, going momentarily red before blinking to yellow, and finally green. Sierra reached through the now-open door and began pulling out small metal tubes, six of them in all, enough to destroy the Harvester.

"Made it," Aileen said.

"Good—" Jeth broke off as he saw Aileen's head poke out from the vent shaft, then her torso, and finally her whole body as she swung herself down onto the chair Sierra had left beneath it. "Angel, what are you doing? You don't need to be in there."

Aileen ignored him as she reached behind her back and withdrew a gun. A dozen questions skidded through Jeth's mind, all of them irrelevant given the evidence before him. Somehow, despite the metal detectors on the subway, Aileen had managed to smuggle in a Luke 40.

"Sparrow, behind you!" Jeth shouted. At the same time, he spun around, heading for the ventilation shaft. He had to get up there. But Remi stood beside the entrance, ready to block the way.

Through the comm, Jeth heard the familiar click of a round entering the chamber of a gun. Then Aileen's smooth, smirking voice filled his ear. "Nobody panic. We're just making a little detour."

CHAPTER

"GET OUT OF MY WAY," JETH SAID, CHARGING AT REMI WITH fists raised. The back of his skull throbbed from the influx of adrenaline—more exhilarating than painful. He was ready to tear his way through the ceiling and up to the fourth floor. Behind him, he sensed the same thing happening to Eric. Whatever Aileen was doing, it was a shock to him as well.

To Jeth's surprise, Remi sidestepped, motioning Jeth on with one hand. He skidded to a stop, first suspecting a trap, but then realizing that Remi had no reason to stop him. It wasn't that Jeth couldn't fit inside the shaft—he could—but there wasn't enough room for him to use his arms for the long climb up. He tried three times without success. He just couldn't get purchase.

"Dammit." He faced Remi, who was standing a mere pace away from Eric, the two men bracing for a fight.

Don't, Jeth said through the link. *He's too strong.* Even if he and Eric ganged up, he doubted they could take him down.

Glowering, Jeth returned his attention to the viewer. His heart struck a frantic rhythm against his breastbone.

"What is this, Angel?" Marian said, her voice like acid.

Aileen ignored her, her attention centered on Sierra. Keeping the Luke aimed at Sierra's chest, Aileen slid the strap of the bag she'd carried up with her off her shoulder and tossed it to the floor at Sierra's feet. "Put the Reinette tubes in there."

A muscle danced in Sierra's jaw as she gritted her teeth, but she didn't argue. She bent and placed all six tubes in the bag, her movements slow and measured. Jeth began to pant, his fury and frustration a wild thing desperate to be uncaged. He couldn't just stand here and let this happen. He couldn't.

Only there was nothing to do. Sierra was trapped. There was no way up there for him, short of bursting through the front door.

Sierra looked up at Aileen, her hands splayed and hovering over the bag. "What now?"

"Set it on the chair. I'll carry them out as promised once we're done with my little side trip."

Sierra did as she said, easing the bag onto the chair. Then she turned to face Aileen once more.

"Head back into the hallway." She motioned Sierra toward the door.

Sierra swallowed, fear creeping into her eyes, but she did as she was told, her steps tense. Aileen followed after her, keeping a safe distance. Sierra's superior reach in the sparring ring didn't matter with the Luke 40 playing host between them.

No decontamination was required to exit the lab, and in seconds Sierra and Aileen entered the hallway. For a moment, Jeth worried the alarms would sound and the gun turrets engage, but then he remembered the security feeds in the building were playing on a loop to anyone outside Marian's hack. Aileen was perfectly safe for the moment. *But there's nowhere to go.*

"That way." Aileen pointed Sierra to the left, back toward the elevators. "Second lab on the right."

Sierra glanced over her shoulder, a question in her gaze.

Aileen scowled. "Just do it."

"You're going to get us caught," Sierra said as she came to a halt in front of the door. The name written across it read simply: STOCK.

Jeth frowned. He switched the view to show the inside of the lab, but it looked hardly different from the Reinette one.

"Stock," Sierra said. Then she swung around, leveling a glower at Aileen. "That's your name."

Aileen Stock, Jeth realized. But she'd said her father was an arms dealer—*of a sort.* He exhaled. *The sort that works for the ITA.*

Aileen smiled, tight-lipped. "The very same. Now use that clearance of yours and open the door."

Sierra put her hands on her hips. "What are you after? The door will only let me through."

Aileen shook her head. "We'll be fine. Just get it open."

"Don't do this," Jeth said through the comm. "If Sierra gets caught, I'll kill you."

Aileen rolled her eyes. "Don't be so dramatic. I promised I'd keep her safe and I will. Now stop worrying." She nudged Sierra on.

Jeth's insides seethed as he watched Sierra face the security panel. But as with the Reinette lab, the door opened smoothly at her touch. Sierra stepped in and Aileen rushed up behind her, following so close she clipped the back of her heels.

"There's no way this will work." Sierra stumbled to a halt as the door sealed and the decontamination process began to run again.

"Yes it will," Aileen said, holding the gun with the barrel pressed to Sierra's back. She didn't sound nearly confident enough for Jeth.

But to his relief, it worked, the inner door opening a few seconds later with no hint of an alarm. Although similar to the Reinette lab, this one was easily twice the size. Nevertheless, Aileen knew right where she was headed. She herded Sierra toward one of the cabinets down on the left, not far from a row of massive biotubes, clouded with smoke that hid their contents.

"That one." Aileen pointed. "Open it."

Sierra hesitated. "What's inside?"

Aileen stomped her foot. "Just open it."

Sierra shook her head and turned to face her, her expression defiant. The sight of her defiance made Jeth's stomach clench. There was no chance Aileen would miss at that range.

"Tell me why first."

"Open it or I'll shoot you."

A cold smile rose to Sierra's lips. "Go ahead. And good luck getting past the security. It doesn't work if there's no pulse." She raised her hand, wiggling her fingers in emphasis. Jeth winced at the gruesome image this conjured in his mind.

"One shot won't kill you right away."

Sierra shrugged. "Maybe so. But you'll have to force me and that means coming in close. Oh, and just be aware my pain threshold is higher than you can imagine."

Red blossomed in Aileen's face. "If you don't open it, I will have Remi rearrange Jeth's body parts."

"Jeth can handle himself," Sierra said. Jeth glanced at Remi, doubting her assertion more than he cared to admit. He thought maybe Sierra doubted it too, as she said, "Tell me what's in there and why you need it first. This lab is where the ITA's cloning research is done. And don't think for a second that I'll help you steal something that will enable Dax to follow through with the ITA's plans to clone Cora."

Dread began to pound in Jeth's ears. A cloning lab. It made far too much sense. He'd been set up all along. He'd—

It wasn't Dax, Eric said through the link. *This wasn't part of the plan.*

"This has nothing to do with Dax or Cora," Aileen said. "This is personal business. *My* business."

Sierra shifted her weight from one foot to the other. "Tell me what it is in this cabinet that you need and why you need it. I'm not letting you take anything to fence it later. There's too much dangerous shit in this place."

"Fine," Aileen huffed. "It's medicine."

"Medicine for who?"

"Me, you idiot. Who else?" Aileen looked ready to explode, her frustration coming off her like ignitable fumes. At once Jeth remembered the odd bruise on her back, the one that looked nothing like a bruise.

Shooting another glare at Remi, Jeth said through the comm, "I think she's telling the truth, Sparrow."

"See," Aileen said, a falsely pleasant smile slipping over her lips. "Even your boyfriend believes me. There's no reason for you not to."

Sierra arched an eyebrow. "No reason? After you pulled a gun on me and attempted to sabotage this mission?"

Aileen blew out a loud breath. "Point taken." She brushed back loose strands of hair from her face. "But I'm not trying to sabotage the mission. I'm just trying to get what I need and then get the hell out of here."

"Why would you need medicine from a . . ." Sierra trailed off, her thoughts overtaking her words.

"Sparrow," Jeth said, picturing the bruise again. "Just do it."

Sierra bit her lip and then exhaled. "All right." She turned toward the security panel. "This better work."

Aileen smirked. "It will. But you've got to enter a passcode with it—five, eight, three, nine, nine, seven."

Sierra nodded as she pressed her finger against the control panel. It flashed red, yellow, then green. But this time a message popped up, prompting for the code. She entered it and the cabinet slid open. True to Aileen's claims, there were several vials of what looked like medicine inside.

"How many do you need?" Sierra asked.

"Just one."

Sierra grabbed two of the nearest vials and pulled them out. "You can put the gun away."

Aileen debated for a moment, but then did as she said, stowing the gun behind her back. "The vial, please."

"Not until we're out of this building safe and alive. All of us."

Aileen grinned. "No problem. Let's go."

They headed for the door, but when Aileen grabbed the handle and yanked, nothing happened. "What the hell?"

Jeth stared down at the viewer and flipped through a couple of camera views. Nothing was happening. The guards at the front desk remained sitting, their conversation idle.

"Try it again," Jeth said. "Maybe it's jammed."

Sierra grabbed the handle, but froze as Marian's voice broke through the comm.

"You've triggered a silent alarm. They've detected my hack. You've got to get out of there. Now!"

"HOW?" SIERRA SPUN AROUND, HER GAZE SWEEPING THE lab.

Jeth didn't answer, his mind racing. "Can't you override the door, Riptide?"

"No, I've got my hands full just trying to stay connected."

"I have a way," Sierra said as she marched to one of the lab tables where another handheld laser torch perched in a holder. She grabbed it and then scanned the ceiling, her gaze stopping on the ventilation shaft.

"What are you doing?" Jeth said as he watched her climb onto a chair and begin cutting another hole as she'd done in the Reinette lab. "There's no way down for you."

"I'll make it. I'm small enough to get leverage to lower myself down."

"It's four stories. That's a long way," said Jeth.

"I've trained. I'll make it."

"But—"

"There's no other way. And I'm not staying here."

Jeth exhaled. She was right. It was the only way out.

"Here, take these," Aileen said before Sierra could climb up. Jeth watched on screen as Aileen removed the scalers from her elbows and handed them over. "I'll manage without them."

With a look of surprise on her face, Sierra accepted the scalers and slipped them on. A welcome surge of relief swept over Jeth. It would still be hard, but she would make it all right.

Sierra climbed up into the shaft first, disappearing from sight as Aileen scrambled up after her.

"How do I get back to the Reinette lab from here?" Sierra said.

"Why?" Jeth began then remembered that they'd left the Reinette canisters in the other lab. "Hold on." He accessed the screen. "I'm pulling up the view now. All right, move down that shaft, make a left, go straight at the first intersection, and then another left. You'll be back where you started."

Sierra didn't respond, but through the comm Jeth could hear the metallic groan of the shaft narrating her movements. "I'm here," she said a few moments later, and Jeth adjusted the camera view in time to see her emerge from the vent shaft into the Reinette lab once more.

"Hurry," Marian said. "Security's heading into the building now. They haven't pushed me out yet, but if they do they'll spot where you are right away."

"I'll be fast."

Jeth watched Sierra sling the bag over her shoulder and climb back onto the chair. She was just pulling into the shaft when the viewer went dark.

"I've lost connection," Marian said.

"We're on our way down now," Sierra said.

"Just don't lose your grip and fall on me," Aileen muttered as she headed down first.

The next few minutes were the worst wait of all. Several times one or both of the girls let out gasps or grunts of effort. Jeth fought back the urge to ask for a progress update every couple of seconds. He would only distract Sierra from the perilous climb down.

Aileen arrived first, flashing Jeth a guilty look. "She's right behind me."

Jeth held his breath until Sierra's legs appeared, soon followed by the rest of her. She was dirt-smeared and sweaty but all right. He pulled her into a quick hug.

Across from them, Eric had fixed a dark look on Aileen. "If this mission fails you will regret it. Dax will make certain."

Aileen waved him off. "Just appreciate the fun of a good challenge, big boy."

Jeth let go of Sierra and spun toward Aileen. Glowering, he held out his hand. "The gun. Now."

She shook her head.

"Now, I said. You got us into this mess."

Sighing, she pulled the Luke from her belt and handed it to him. Relieved to be armed again, Jeth tucked it into his pants. "Let's get out of here."

They headed down the first hole and then the second into the subway alcove.

"We're back at the tunnel," Jeth said through the comm.

"You'll need to wait. The next train is coming through any second," said Marian.

Jeth peeked out into the tunnel, caught a glimpse of bright lights barreling toward him, and pulled back, his heart skipping. The train raced by, sucking the air out of the alcove with the force of its passing.

As soon as the train was gone, they leaped down into the tunnel and took off at a run. This time, several people in the crowd noticed them climbing up off the tracks, but their expressions were only mildly curious. Jeth hurried past them, up the stairs.

"We're almost to the street," he said through the comm. "We'll come to you."

"Be careful. There's ITA everywhere. They've surrounded the building and are setting up a perimeter."

"Are you in danger of being spotted?"

"I don't think so. But getting out of here will be tough. We might have to wait until things die down."

"That's fine," Jeth said, thinking that passing a few hours in the truck would be easy compared to what they'd just been through. "We'll blend in and make our way to you."

Blending in wasn't a problem. Chaos ruled the street as they arrived. The crowds were pressing in around the Hanov building, trying to get a look at the unfolding scene. Lines of local police and ITA agents held them back as they barricaded the sidewalks, setting up perimeter nets. The white, ropy material of the nets was magnetic, stretched taut between the portable metal stands. The nets looked like human-size spiderwebs.

As they stepped out from the subway entrance, the flow of the crowd started to push them toward the barricade. In seconds they were far too close to the ITA agents for Jeth's peace of mind, and he pushed back against the crowd, trying to make a wide berth.

It would take longer, but he decided to go all the way around the back of the building to reach the other side where the hover truck was parked. He guessed most of the focus would remain on the main entrance where the police hovercraft were lined up in a jagged formation, red and blue lights flashing even brighter than the video ads on the buildings surrounding them.

He was right. As they made the first corner around to the back, the crowd thinned to something closer to normal for this wildly packed city. Even so there were still nearly a dozen ITA agents inside the perimeter around Hanov. They were easily recognizable in their gray uniforms with the star and eagle emblem on the sleeves. They had their guns drawn as they surveyed the scene for any sign of the intruder. Several carried the ITA standard-issue .45-caliber Mirage pistol. Others carried high-powered Luke rifles. And two of them, Jeth saw, carried the same Kali shotguns as the security guards inside.

He picked up the pace a little, sticking close to the sidewalk's edge. He glanced behind him, making sure they were all accounted for. He knew Eric was there, his presence inescapable with the link, but he worried Aileen would make a break for it. He spotted her shadowing Sierra's footsteps as if she feared Sierra might suddenly vanish. The medicine—if it really was that—was still inside Sierra's lab coat, which she had removed and slung over her arm, not wanting to draw attention.

They were halfway past the back of the building, when a loud, high-pitched voice suddenly cried out, "It's her!"

Jeth, like every other person in the vicinity, wrenched his head toward the speaker who had screamed so emphatically it reminded Jeth of the hyenas Hammer had kept in his menagerie. He spotted the speaker at once. He stood just inside the police line. He was an old bald man with a rotund belly and sporting a patterned sweater and slacks. Definitely not an ITA agent. He held one hand pointed their direction.

Sierra, he thought, heart pounding.

"Aileen Stock," the man screamed. "That's her! Stop her!"

For a second, shock froze Jeth in place, but then he broke into a run, barreling through the people in front of him. The ITA agents reacted at once, leaping over the perimeter nets and into the crowd. Jeth and the others made it several paces, but the ITA were able to move faster, the crowd parting for them like a human wave. In seconds they were surrounded.

"We've got trouble, Riptide," Jeth said through the link as he came to a halt.

"Stall," Marian said. "We're on our way."

Stall. *Yeah right.* Jeth contemplated drawing the Luke, but there were too many guns pointed his way for such a risky move.

"That's them," the balding man shrieked. He rushed toward the circle of ITA agents surrounding them, his round face flush with excitement.

"Aileen," he said. "Aileen."

"Daddy?"

Jeth turned to see who had spoken. It didn't sound like Aileen at all. That was the voice of a little girl. A scared little girl calling for her—

Daddy.

"Yes, darling," Stock said. "That's right. I'm here. You don't need to run anymore."

"Daddy?" Aileen said again, her voice still strange. Jeth pivoted, bringing her into his line of sight. She was shaking her head, as if trying to dislodge whatever demonic force had taken possession of her voice box. Remi had stepped in front of her, with one hand braced behind his back, as if he worried she would try to run in front of him.

303

"Come now, Aileen. Step away from that man," Stock said. "He's no good for you. Only I'm good for you."

"No," Aileen said, her voice trembling now but once more her own. "No!"

"If that man moves," Stock said, pointing at Remi, "shoot him. Shoot them all."

Oh shit, Jeth thought, racking his mind for some other way to stall.

But a second later, Marian's voice filled his ear through

the comm link. "Get ready," she said.

Jeth turned his gaze toward the edge of the building and saw the hover truck swooping toward them. Its arrival took the ITA agents by surprise and they swung to face this new threat. Perry was driving and he barreled toward them, not slowing down. The agents jumped out of the way, some of them managing to open fire.

Jeth rushed forward as the truck swung hard to the left, bringing the side door into range. He hadn't quite reached it before more gunfire erupted, this time from behind. He ducked, pulling the Luke from his belt. More agents had arrived from around the building and were ringing them in fast.

Jeth let off a couple of rounds, taking down one agent. Then he turned back to the truck as the side door slid open. His mother stood in the doorway with her arms outstretched, as if she were a priestess about to bless the assembled crowd.

"Get down, Mom," he screamed. She was an obvious target, her white clothes a beacon for the ITA agents. She didn't move, and a second later, Jeth understood why as white light began to flash behind him. He glanced back to see the agents' guns disappearing, one after another as Marian phased them into metaspace.

But she couldn't phase them all. Some of the agents managed to open fire before she reached them. Bullets struck the truck, and Jeth flinched at the loud bang from each hit.

"Get down," he screamed again, but his mother was already falling backward.

Jeth sprinted to her. He reached the truck and climbed in to see his mother struggling to get up. A line of blood was spreading across her abdomen.

"Mom!"

She pushed him back, moving toward the door again. She raised her hands and a flash of blinding light erupted behind Jeth. It was a phase stronger than any he'd seen before. One minute there were ITA agents standing by the building, firing on them, and the next they'd been cut down. Bits and pieces of the bodies that remained crumpled to the ground, limbs jerking spasmodically as the life sputtered out of them. Marian had spared no one. ITA agents and bystanders alike had been cut down in the arc of her phase.

But the effort of manipulating that much metaspace had taken its toll. More blood appeared, the wound in her abdomen spurting, and two lines of red trickled from her nose. She slumped back onto the floor, eyes closed and body still. Jeth knelt beside her again as the others piled into the truck around him. Eric hauled the door closed and Perry flew them forward, more bullets striking the hover truck as they passed.

Jeth felt hands press against his back and heard Sierra say, "We need to hold her still." Nodding, Jeth moved to Marian's side. He grasped her arm and hip and did his best to prevent her from sliding as the hover truck rounded a sharp turn. Aileen moved into position by Marian's head, kneeling down to hold her shoulders. Jeth wanted to yell at her to leave his mother alone, that she'd done enough damage, but he couldn't find the will to speak. Fear held his voice prisoner.

Remi, impossibly huge, braced her opposite side. Marian closed her eyes at every bump and rock of the truck, her lips pressed tight as she fought back a scream.

Don't scream, Mom, Jeth thought, staring down at her blood-soaked stomach. *It'll only hurt more.*

Sierra, doing her best to hold Marian's legs still, reached over and began to pull up Marian's shirt, exposing the wound. It wasn't messy, just a neat round hole in her stomach, right above the naval. It wept blood freely.

"We need to stop the bleeding." Sierra grabbed the lab coat on the floor beside her and began to wad it into a compress. When she felt the medicine vials get in the way, she pulled them out and handed them to Jeth. He stuffed them into his pocket, glancing at Aileen, who watched the exchange with an anxious expression.

She turned away, avoiding his gaze.

Sierra placed the lab coat over Marian's wound and pressed down. A soft groan escaped Marian's throat but she didn't struggle or protest.

"We have medicine and supplies on *Polaris,*" Sierra said, her voice a calm, soothing sound against Jeth's nerves. "We just need to get her there and she'll be fine."

Jeth nodded, even though he knew she was lying. Gut wounds were dangerous, and impossible to analyze at a glance. Organs could have been damaged beyond repair. "I'll call Flynn and have him meet us. We need to shave time off this trip."

"Yeah well, we've got to get away first," said Eric as Perry swung the hover truck hard to the right.

Jeth stood up and Sierra moved into his place, keeping pressure on the makeshift bandage. Jeth headed into the cab, switched on the comm, and opened the link to *Polaris*.

"Hey, Boss," Flynn replied. "How's it—"

"I need you to get in the air and head our way. We've got heat and my mom's hurt." Jeth glanced up, spotting at least two ITA helos tracking them in the air. They hadn't opened fire yet, and he guessed that they didn't want to risk destroying the cargo in the truck. Although whether they were concerned with Aileen or if they'd realized who Marian was, he didn't know.

"What hap—never mind," said Flynn. "We're on our way. I'll head toward the city and give them something else to worry about for a while."

"Good. We'll make our way to the shuttle. Then once we're in we'll rendezvous back at sea. I'll let you know when it's safe to cloak again."

"Okay," Flynn said, sounding surprisingly eager. Jeth could only hope the ITA didn't have time to call in anything bigger than the helos.

Perry pressed on, navigating the streets with little concern for anyone who got in the way. They made better time than they had coming in, but the helos stuck with them, along with several ITA trucks following them on the ground.

Soon they were heading out of the city. *Come on Flynn, where are you?* Jeth thought, scanning the sky. They needed to lose the ITA or they would never make it onto the shuttle. Finally, he spotted a flash of light in the darkness overhead and then the familiar predatory shape of a Black Devil starship. The sight of it made his heart both ache and soar.

The moment *Polaris* was in range, Flynn opened fire, taking aim at the trucks first before moving onto the helos. He was limited to the pilot guns, but they were enough for this task. The trucks went down at once, but the helos returned fire. Flynn didn't move to avoid it, knowing the shields could withstand the impact, at least for a little while. He had to block the helos entirely to let them escape. The ploy worked, and soon the truck was pulling ahead and out of sight.

Ten minutes later they made it to the dock. Perry brought them to a stop just as the signal of an incoming call flashed on the comm. Jeth switched it on and Flynn's panicked voice boomed out, "They've sent in reinforcements. I've got to bug out."

"We're at the shuttle. Get out of there." Jeth scanned the sky, no ITA craft in sight. But he knew that could change at any moment. Their flight from the city would've been posted all over the news, and any number of people could be looking for them now.

Jeth climbed into the back to help his mother into the shuttle. He bent down to pick her up, but Remi pushed him out of the way. The giant man slid his arms beneath Marian and raised her up as if she were a small child, his movement gentle but quick. Marian exhaled her pain, tears leaking out from her eyes. Jeth's heart wrenched inside his chest as if an invisible fist were trying to rip it free from the tendons and muscles holding it in place. He knew this feeling, the fear of his mother dying.

Moments later they were all crammed into the shuttle once more. Jeth hauled the door closed and then sat down at the helm. He piloted them beneath the water as Sierra signaled Flynn.

"We're on our way out to sea. Can you meet us soon?"

"Yeah," Flynn said. "I'm tracking you now. I'll land a few kilometers out from you and de-cloak."

When Jeth finally brought the shuttle back to the surface and spotted *Polaris* ahead of them, he took his first full breath since leaving the city. A glance at the clock told him it had only been thirty minutes since they'd left the city, but that was an eternity with a gunshot wound to the gut.

Jeth pushed the thought away, reaching for the reassurance of the implant. Anger bristled inside him, his fury directed at Aileen for bringing this down on them. If they'd stuck to the plan, none of this would've happened. It was their entry into the Stock lab that had triggered the silent alarm. Red clouded his vision. But anger was better than pain, better than fear.

Remi carried Marian onto the ship and down to sick bay. Jeth followed behind. Sierra was already inside, having raced ahead to prep equipment. Remi set Marian on the table and withdrew, as silent as ever but with a dark expression on his face.

As Jeth stepped up to the operating table, Sierra raised her hand. "I need you to leave, Jeth."

He glowered. "No."

"You have to. I need to concentrate, and you'll only distract me."

"I want to help."

She shook her head. "You're no good at this sort of thing. Get me Aileen. She'll be better help."

Jeth's hands clenched into fists. He wanted to hit something, destroy something.

"Please, Jeth." Sierra touched his arm. "You're wasting time."

Her words hit him hard enough to snap him out of his fury. If Sierra needed Aileen, he would make it happen. Whatever it took. Jeth swung around and ran out into the corridor. He could've used the comm to call for her, but he feared she wouldn't come. He was too furious to keep the anger out of his voice.

To his surprise, Aileen appeared at the end of the corridor.

"Sierra needs your help." He swallowed his rage, which was bubbling up like acid. "To save my mother." He expected her to protest, but she only nodded, her face blanching to a sickly white. Then she brushed past him into sick bay and shut the door.

Jeth stared at that closed door for several minutes, unable to make himself move. But when the sound of tiny footsteps reached him from behind, he swung around to find Cora approaching. Fear clouded her face, her eyes red from crying. Jeth had forgotten about the link she shared with their mother. Cora would've sensed Marian's pain as soon as they had arrived. He bent down and scooped her into his arms as she reached him.

"Is she going to be okay?" Cora whispered against his neck.

"I don't know, sweetheart," he said, unable to give her the lie he knew he ought to. Or maybe he knew that she wouldn't believe it. He wished there was a way to disconnect the link she shared with their mother, a link that was no longer so hard to comprehend now that he'd experienced the Axis. Cora's ability was a part of her, not some implant she could just pull out. He wished he could trade places with her and spare her this pain.

He carried her into her cabin and set her on the bed.

"How about a new story," he said, picking up the reader from the end table.

Cora thought it over, her eyes darting to the door and then back to him again several times.

"Come on," Jeth prompted. "It'll help us keep our minds off things."

Cora slowly nodded, and Jeth switched the screen on. He listed off a couple of options, but Cora picked "Cinderella" at once, her favorite.

Jeth sat down to read, taking his time and putting all the effort he could muster into the voices. The distraction helped, allowing him to forget what was happening for a little while.

Sometime later, Sierra opened the door and came inside. Sweat plastered her hair to her face, and there was a smear of blood over her cheek. She looked like she'd been in a battle. Jeth supposed that was close to the truth.

But it was a battle she had lost. He could see the truth in her eyes before she opened her mouth to speak.

"I'm so sorry, Jeth," Sierra said. "I did the best I could, but it's not going to be enough."

"SHE'S ASKING TO SEE YOU." SIERRA SWALLOWED AND looked at the floor, unable to meet his gaze. "I . . . I don't think there's much time. There was too much damage. I removed the bullet and repaired what I could, but there's internal bleeding. Maybe if Milton were here—"

Jeth raised his hand, cutting her off. He didn't mean to be cruel, but he heard Cora's breathing grow rapid. They couldn't risk her losing control. "See to Cora," he said. "She's going to need you now."

Sierra nodded and stepped in. She sat down on the bed beside Cora and wrapped an arm around her shoulders.

Jeth headed out into the corridor, walking slowly toward sick bay. He was unable to make himself walk fast even though he knew each second brought his mother closer to the last. He didn't want to face this. Not again.

If Milton were here . . . There was no point in speculating what might have been. Milton wasn't here. The past couldn't be undone.

The door stood open, and Jeth stepped inside, forcing his eyes up and onto his mother, still lying on the operating table. Sierra had taken the time to make her comfortable with several pillows behind her head and a blanket to keep her warm. A tired smile crossed Marian's face as he entered. He could tell at once that she wasn't in much pain. Whatever drugs Sierra had given her were doing that much at least.

"Come here." Marian motioned him over to her. He went, picking up her hand and holding it in his. He gazed down at his mother. Her eyes were so much like Lizzie's, but he couldn't bear to look at them for long. He shifted his gaze to the left of her face and saw her implant lying on the table beside her pillow. It was the first time he'd seen her without it, and its lifeless form made it feel as if a part of her was already dead.

"Will you take out your implant, please?" Marian said.

The request took him by surprise, and he raised his eyebrows.

"Please, I want us to talk alone. Completely alone."

Jeth gulped, his tears rising fast. These were her final minutes, and he would do whatever he could to make them happy ones. He reached up and pulled out the implant, trying to keep the tremble from his hands. The minute it came out, his fear and sadness threatened to overwhelm him, and he craved the reassuring strength of the implant. But it was his mother's last request, and she squeezed his fingers as he slipped the implant into his pocket.

"I'm sorry," she said.

The tears threatened even harder.

"I never wanted to cause you pain. I didn't plan for any of this to happen." A grimace twisted her mouth.

Jeth inhaled and exhaled, inhaled and exhaled, fighting not to be swept under by the despair rising up inside him.

"I know this is hard," Marian continued, "but you must promise me that you will complete the mission. The Harvesters must be destroyed and the Pyreans set free."

He nodded. There was no question of that. If anything, he was more determined to finish it, loss fueling his need for vengeance.

"Good," she hesitated, squeezing his hand once more. "But there's something else you must promise me."

He cleared his throat. "What is it?"

She held his gaze, her eyes glassy but no less determined. "Once you've destroyed the Harvester, do not give Dax the coordinates to Empyria."

Jeth's brow furrowed, his surprise momentarily staving off his anguish. "You knew what I was planning?"

A smile curled Marian's lips. "Of course. And no, Lizzie didn't tell me. Not directly. But it was easy to guess what she was up to once I realized she had found my data crystal and was studying it. That and the way you questioned my motives concerning Dax."

Dumbfounded, Jeth asked, "Why didn't you call me out on it?"

"There wasn't time before we left Peltraz. And after, well, things were already strained between us. I didn't want to add to it. Not until it was necessary. But it is now, and now you must promise me not to give it to him."

"But—" Jeth began.

"You must honor the deal the way I intended, by taking Dax to Empyria yourself." She paused, running a tongue over her cracked lower lip. "Or don't take him, if you're able to escape. I don't care. Either way, I want *you* to go there. Take Lizzie, Cora, Sierra, anyone else you trust who wants to. But you must go."

A dozen emotions exploded in Jeth at once, too many for a single one to gain dominance—surprise, confusion, and fear, definitely fear. He struggled to keep his voice neutral, but failed. "Why are you so determined?"

"Because I promised the Pyreans I would return and bring others back with me, once I set them free from the Harvester," she said with no hesitation. "But now you must do it in my stead."

"You promised them?"

She nodded. "They truly are sentient, Jeth, as intelligent and alive as you and I. Only more so, in every way."

Doubt pressed in on him. This had to be his mother's delusion speaking, a result of all the trauma she had endured, both from the ITA and whatever she had experienced when she visited Empyria. Still, he couldn't dismiss her claims. Not now. Instead he gently asked, "How do they talk exactly?" The Pyreans he'd seen in metadrives and metagates had nothing resembling a mouth.

"Mind to mind, of course," Marian said, the slightest hint of amusement in her tired voice. "In the same way that the implant allows you to communicate with the others on the Axis. The Pyreans' very nature is what makes it work."

"I see," Jeth said, understanding this aspect at least. "But how did you communicate with them without an implant?"

"You don't need one when you're on Empyria." She shifted her head and picked up the white implant beside her. "Going there changes you. Within days of landing, your father and I were both able to touch metaspace. It was as easy as thinking."

This too Jeth had no choice but to accept. He knew from the Aether Project that Marian's DNA has been altered during her visit to the planet. "But didn't the change . . . hurt?"

Marian shook her head. "Not at all. Not even for a second. You don't have to be afraid of going there, Jeth. It's a planet unlike any other. You won't want to leave, not ever. Everything is new and wondrous. The trees and plants, the animals and water. Even the air is different. Being there, sharing that connection to the Pyreans, it's like coming home after a long time away. Only the feeling doesn't fade. It's like being at peace and elated at the same time. I can't explain it and I can't convince you with words. You must experience it for yourself."

Jeth stared down at her, doubt plaguing him once more. Yet she sounded so sincere, so utterly convinced of what she was saying. He thought about the implant and how it made him feel, that sense of power and rightness. Maybe it did have to do with the Pyreans after all, dead or not. There was no denying they were powerful creatures. Maybe powerful enough to have planted such memories in her mind. The idea chilled him, and he suppressed a shiver. "If it was so great, then why did you ever leave?"

Marian sighed then winced from the pain of moving her abdomen. Jeth looked down, noticing how swollen her stomach was beneath the blanket.

"I left because the Pyreans asked me to. They needed me and your father to set them free."

"But Mom," he said, unable to stop himself. "How could the Pyreans possibly speak to you in a language you understand?"

"They don't need language. They speak in images and emotions, thoughts that need no translation. That's how they told us that they were dying."

"Yeah, the Harvesters, I know."

She shook her head. "It's so much more than that, Jeth. They need *us*. The Harvesting must stop, yes, but they also need *us*."

Fear clouded Jeth's mind, and for a second he questioned the wisdom of indulging her madness. Then again, he didn't have the heart to stop her. "Who exactly do they need?"

Marian focused her gaze on his face, her expression serious and completely lucid. "Humankind. That's why they first appeared on Earth so many centuries ago. They were trying to make contact with us. We have something inside us the Pyreans need in order to live and thrive. They were ailing even before they breached the ocean. Millennia ago, a different humanoid species lived with them, but that race disappeared."

"How?"

"I don't know. The Pyreans refused to tell us anything about that history. All we know is that it was a symbiotic relationship, one they attempted to establish again, with us. We would fulfill their needs even as they fulfilled ours. Needs we didn't even realize we had. They need us still— now more than ever."

Jeth blinked. Another species? Aliens? Needs and fulfillment? It didn't make sense. And yet he couldn't voice those doubts to her, not now. He could tell that this was important to her. Perhaps the most important thing.

Marian squeezed his hand with surprising strength considering how quickly she was fading before his eyes. "That is why you must go back. It will start with you and whoever else you bring with you."

Jeth shook his head. "How can just a few of us make a difference? Why not release the coordinates and let everyone know how to get there?"

"You know why not." Marian coughed, releasing his hand as she wrapped an arm around her stomach, trying to minimize the movement. Sadness squeezed Jeth's chest. He wanted to help her, to take her place, but he could only watch.

Once the fit had passed she continued, "Releasing the coordinates would mean war and destruction. The ITA, the crime lords, anyone with power at all would try to claim the planet for their own, killing one another in the process."

Jeth swallowed, knowing she was right. Only— "If I bring someone like Dax there, the same thing will happen.

He'll try and claim the planet."

"No it won't. No one can claim the planet no matter how hard they try. In their home environment the Pyreans are all-powerful. They can't be captured and harvested on Empyria the way they were on First-Earth. They're too strong there. And Dax will land on the planet with you—and anyone who enters the atmosphere will go through the change—and will understand the truth of what our relationship with the Pyreans can be. As for the rest, I don't know how it will work exactly, how they will bring enough humans to fulfill that need. But I trust the Pyreans to know what they're doing."

"That's an awful lot to take on trust."

"Yes, I know," Marian said. "But I promise you it's the truth, my darling. This is the reason why I didn't reveal these things to the ITA, even when they offered to bring you and me together again. I wanted to save this for you, so that you could live in the world I had witnessed. Please, do this now. For me, for Cora, for Lizzie, and for you."

Jeth held his breath, his heartbeat throbbing in his temples as he wrestled with his desires. He didn't want to lie to his mother on her deathbed, but what choice did he have? Telling her the truth that he had no desire to risk whatever this change was she and Cora had been through when they visited the planet, that he did not believe in this miracle she described, would only hurt her needlessly. One more lie wouldn't matter, not now. The only harm in false hope was living long enough to realize it. But Marian wouldn't.

"Okay, Mom," he said. "I will."

The look of happiness and relief that broke over her face was nearly enough to shatter his resolve along with his heart.

She reached up and cupped his chin. "I know you feel like you're broken, Jeth, but you're not. You've only been bent. But I promise that will change. You will be whole and upright again. Go to Empyria. You will understand."

He nodded, unable to draw breath for another lie. Bent or broken, it didn't matter. All that did matter was destroying the ITA and Saar. That was the only promise he knew he could keep.

Anything beyond it was just smoke and dreams.

Marian lowered her hand. "Be careful of your Brethren implant. It's a powerful tool. Dax will try to use it to force you to tell him the coordinates instead of letting you take him there. You must not let it happen."

"I won't," he said, thinking about the hierarchy and the way he had overcome Eric. The desire to reinsert the implant rose up in him, but he pushed it down out of respect for his mother. This was too private to risk sharing. Eric and Perry wouldn't be able to listen in, but they could still send him thoughts, intruding on these last precious moments.

"And one last thing, before I say good-bye to Cora," Marian said.

Jeth's knees trembled, and he fought back a sob rising in his chest. She was really going. There was nothing he could do about it. "What?"

"You mustn't blame Aileen for what happened, Jeth. This

was beyond her control. She must've had a reason for need-ing that medicine. I imagine once you hear it, you'll realize you would've done the same."

I wouldn't count on it, he thought.

Fortunately, Marian didn't press him to commit to this promise. She closed her eyes, and Jeth waited, unsure of what to do next.

The sound of the door opening drew his attention. He looked behind him and saw Cora stepping inside, her gaze fixed on Marian. No one else existed. Marian waved her forward, and Cora came to the table and attempted to climb up.

Jeth started to tell her no, but stopped at a look from his mother. He picked her up instead and Cora settled down in the crook of Marian's arm. She was careful not to press against Marian's stomach, knowing instinctively that this was where her injury was.

Or maybe it wasn't instinct, Jeth realized as he watched them. He couldn't quite explain how, but he sensed that they were communicating, sharing thoughts and feelings the same way he did with the Brethren, only without the Axis.

After a while, Cora peered over at Jeth. "Will you read me another story?"

He grimaced. "Right now?"

"Yes. Mom will like it too. Won't you?"

Marian smiled and kissed the top of Cora's head. "Yes, I will. I can't imagine anything better."

Jeth tried to swallow, but this time the sob escaped him

and he nearly lost control. Only the motion of forcing himself to turn and walk out into the corridor kept him from it.
He returned to Cora's cabin and fetched the reader. There
was no sign of Sierra.

He came back to sick bay, carrying his heart in his throat.
He didn't think he was going to be able to breathe, let alone
read aloud.

"What would you like to hear, Mom?" Cora asked as Jeth
pulled up a chair and sat down, switching on the reader.

"Have you heard "Sleeping Beauty" yet?" Marian asked.

Cora shook her head.

"Good. That's my favorite."

Giving up the fight against his tears, Jeth searched for the
story. It appeared at the top of the page and he began to read,
his voice shaking and jagged as he wept.

But it grew easier as he went along, the tears tapering off,
the wounds knitting themselves back together. He read and
read, aware of his mother's eyes closing, her breathing slowing. And sometime before he reached the end she slipped
away, silent and at peace, with one child on her arm and
another reading her off into that final, forever sleep.

CHAPTER

It was cold comfort.

When he finished the story, he set down the reader and walked around to the opposite side of the operating table. Cora had closed her eyes, but she wasn't asleep. Her arms were wrapped around Marian's lifeless body, squeezing hard as if to keep Marian from vanishing.

She already has, Jeth thought, but didn't have the heart to say it.

"Come on, Cora." He touched her arm, pulling her gently. "You need to get some sleep."

She shook her head. "I want to stay with Mom. I don't want to leave."

"I know." Jeth stroked the back of her hair. "But you have to."

Cora began to sob. It was soft at first, but quickly grew louder. The power of it made the hairs on Jeth's neck stand up. A vibration went through the ship, the sound of metal shuddering as she began to manipulate metaspace without conscious thought.

"Cora, sweetie . . ." Jeth wrapped his arms around her

body and started to pull her away, but she fought it. She thrashed and screamed, losing control in the onslaught of her despair. He needed to get her calmed down before she ripped a hole in the hull and buried them all at sea.

Jeth opened his mouth to call for Sierra, but there was no need. She was already rushing through the door, the entire ship aware of Cora's distress by now.

"Hold her still a moment," Sierra said, heading for one of the cabinets. A few seconds later, she turned toward them with a loaded jet injector in her hand. When Cora spotted it, she began to fight harder, but Jeth kept hold of her. There was a loud pop as Sierra pulled the trigger. Cora's tolerance was too great for the sedative to work instantly, and she continued to struggle for more than a minute, her screams cutting into Jeth's ear, his whole body aching from the vibration.

Her crying slowly lessened and then died away as her eyes slipped closed. She slumped against Jeth.

Sierra let out a breath and wiped hair from her forehead. "That was close."

Jeth nodded. "How much was in that?" He indicated the jet injector with his head as he scooped Cora into his arms.

"You don't want to know." Sierra set the injector on the counter then crossed the room to Jeth. "I'll take her to her cabin. I know you need some time alone." The look of sympathy on her face brought tears to his eyes again. He didn't reply, just handed Cora over. Sierra was right. He wanted to be alone. If only for a few minutes before he had to deal with the problems awaiting him.

She headed out of sick bay and down the corridor to Cora's cabin. Jeth turned back to his mother's body. He grasped the edge of the blanket and pulled it up over her head. Then he left, switching off the light as he went. He tried to push away the image of her body lying there in the dark but it remained, a ghost haunting the back of his mind.

Even though this wasn't his ship, he went up to the bridge and sat down at the pilot's chair. This had always been his favorite place on *Avalon*. It was where he came to relax or think or reset. He loved to recline behind the control column and stare out at the wide-open view of the main window. The starkness of it, the isolation, often brought clarity to his mind in times of trouble.

But this wasn't *Avalon*. And that wasn't space before him but the sea, bright and glistening in the late afternoon sun.

The weight of his loss crushed down upon him. It was cruel. He'd only just gotten her back, only spent a few precious days with her. Shame at some of the things he'd said burned in his stomach. Regret of the things he hadn't said burned in his heart. And poor Lizzie. She hadn't gotten to say good-bye at all. Or Milton. Jeth dreaded telling them.

But he couldn't dwell on it. Not with so much else that needed to be done. Like preparing for the final stage of the mission, confronting Aileen, *burying my mother*. Sadness sucked the air from his chest, metal clamps tightening around his heart and lungs. For a second he almost reached for the implant, wanting the surety of its presence. But in his current state he didn't know if he could keep his feelings private from Eric and Perry, and he didn't want to share his despair with anyone.

Slowly he forced the emotions away, focusing his mind on the tasks at hand. The hardest decision he faced was what to do with his mother now, the horrible, inelegant task of disposing of her body. If he could have, he would take her back to Therin, to be buried next to his father. But that was impossible. Even if there was time to make the journey, it would take planning and money. It wasn't as if he could just fly in, dig the hole, and leave again. Not with half the galaxy on the lookout for him.

It would have to be the sea then. With her love of history, Jeth didn't think his mother would mind such an ancient burial ceremony. He could empty one of the wooden crates in the cargo bay for a casket. He would need to drill a couple of holes in the bottom to ensure it sank or they could set it on fire, and—

Sudden awareness that he was no longer alone tingled over Jeth's skin, and he stood up and spun around, drawing the Luke 40 still tucked into his belt. Halfway across the bridge, Aileen froze.

She raised her hands to show she wasn't armed. "I didn't mean to startle you."

Jeth grunted. "Is that so? I think startling me was exactly your intention. You just didn't mean for it to happen so soon."

Aileen started to make a face but stopped herself. "I just came up here to talk to you."

"Uh-huh." He adjusted his grip on the gun. "More like you came to steal the medicine in my jacket pocket. Steal it any way possible, I imagine."

For once, Aileen looked ashamed. "I'm serious. I just want to talk." She hesitated, biting her lower lip. "Although I do still need that vial."

Jeth's stare hardened. "Don't I know it."

"I'm sorry about your mother. I didn't mean for that to happen. It shouldn't have happened. If she'd just stayed down and out—"

Jeth dropped a round into the chamber. "Don't you dare put any of the blame on her."

"I'm not. I'm . . ." Aileen inhaled and exhaled loudly. "I'm sorry. It's just I needed that medicine, and I had no idea taking it would trigger a silent alarm."

Realizing he was gritting his teeth, Jeth forced his jaw to relax. He wanted to just shoot her and be done with it. Only, he needed her for the Harvest job—six Reinette canisters, needing six people to arm them. And despite his inclination not to, his mother had asked him to hear her out. He would give her that much.

Jeth lowered the Luke, then returned it to the holster on his hip. "You have exactly one chance to convince me not to kill you."

"What, would you like me to dance for you or something?" It was a pathetic attempt at humor, delivered with a pathetic attempt at a smile.

"No, I want you to play Scheherazade, and convince me

with a story. The true one. About you."

"I think I'd rather dance," Aileen muttered as she turned and sat down at the nav station. "But I suppose you deserve the truth."

Jeth didn't say anything, and soon she began talking.

"What I said before was true. Those vials contain medicine that I need."

Reining in his temper, Jeth said, "What medicine and why did you need to get it from a cloning lab?"

"Because she is one."

Jeth and Aileen both swung their heads toward the door to see that Sierra had arrived. Her face was blotchy and her eyes red from crying. The sight of it brought Jeth's grief bubbling up to the surface. But the impact of Sierra's words drove it off at once.

His mouth fell open, and he turned back to Aileen, who'd flushed crimson. "You're a clone?"

Aileen's blush deepened. "I hate that word."

"But how's that possible?" Jeth said, running his gaze over her. Everything he knew about clones was the opposite of what he saw in Aileen. Clones were born normal but developed severe genetic abnormalities as they grew up. They rarely survived childhood.

"She's an anomaly," Sierra said. "A successful human clone."

Aileen made a face. "Not successful enough it seems."

"Okay," Jeth said, taking in this news. "So you were grown in a science laboratory. But that man at Hanov. He was your father, wasn't he?"

Aileen shrugged, the casual gesture unsuccessful at disguising her discomfort with the subject. "Father, creator, what's the difference?"

Jeth frowned, thinking of at least a dozen, but he was in no mood for a philosophical argument on the subject.

"You're the missing link, aren't you?" Sierra said.

A sneer twisted Aileen's features. "I hate that term even more."

"I don't care," Sierra said, glowering back at her. The venom in her voice made Jeth flinch. "His mother is dead because of you. I suggest you keep your feelings to yourself. Or I will give you something real and present to hate."

Once again, Jeth's despair threatened, and he slid his hand into his pocket, desperate for the assurance of the implant. The pain on Sierra's face stopped him. She hated the implant, and even though he felt its absence like a terrible abyss inside him, he refused to add to her pain by putting it in now.

Jeth waited, wondering how Aileen would react. He could sense the anger rising off Sierra in hot waves. She was spoiling for a fight. He half wished it would happen. He put his hands on his hips. "What do you mean by 'missing link'?"

Sierra turned toward him. "The name itself is a joke, one the scientists at Hanov used to kick around, especially those who specialized in genetics and cloning. They were always searching for the missing piece of the formula that would allow them to successfully clone a human being, one that wouldn't develop genetic abnormalities over time."

"I don't see how that's funny," said Jeth. Across from him, Aileen harrumphed but didn't comment.

"Well, scientists aren't known for their humor," said Sierra, "but it was a riff on the idea of how they were playing god through their work."

Jeth shook his head, still not getting it. Then he decided it was beside the point. "So Aileen is the missing piece of the cloning formula."

Sierra nodded. "Or more like the lost link, if I have the story puzzled out correctly."

"Actually," Aileen said, "the escaped link would be the most accurate."

"Okay." Jeth rubbed the bridge of his nose. "Somebody explain what this means."

Sierra folded her arms. "The rumor at Hanov when I was there was that there had been a breakthrough in the cloning process several years before but that the successful clone had disappeared. Either stolen or misplaced, no two stories were the same."

Aileen laughed. "Misplaced. I like that one. But the truth is *this* successful clone escaped because she wasn't stupid enough to hang around once she realized what she was."

"You didn't know you were a clone?" Jeth felt the need to sit down. He really wished he could put in the implant, but Sierra's pain hadn't faded at all. Even worse, her anger was very near the surface. He didn't want to provoke either.

"Not for the first fourteen years of my life," said Aileen. "Not entirely, anyway. It's all very complicated."

"What isn't these days?" Jeth said, giving in to the urge to sit.

Aileen cleared her throat. "My fath—creator, was the man you saw, Benjamin Stock. Old, wealthy, and wicked smart, he had everything he ever wanted except for a healthy daughter. The real Aileen Stock died when she was nine years old from some rare genetic disorder with a name I can't remember. From the day she was born, her dad knew she was going to die young, and so he set out to find a cure. Instead what he got was a successful clone of his daughter in which the disorder had been eradicated."

"You," Jeth said.

"Me." Aileen swallowed. "I don't recall much of the first nine years of my life. What I do is mostly needles and doctors. I was born in the very lab we just ransacked, but I think I spent most of those early years in a secret lab on Stock's estate. Once he realized that I was a successful clone, he decided to keep me a secret from everyone. He didn't want the ITA to lay claim to me. He had other plans."

"Like taking the place of his dead daughter?" Sierra said.

Aileen flinched, a blush heating her face again. "Precisely."

"Hang on a minute." Jeth raised a hand. "You *replaced* her?"

"Actually, she replaced me." The bitterness in Aileen's voice was a tangible thing, biting like icy air.

"They did a memory transfer?" Sierra said.

Aileen nodded.

"They can do that?" Jeth glanced at Sierra.

"In theory. And only some of the time. It's a very imprecise branch of science. The ITA uses it most often on sleeper agents. The implanted memories allow the spy to exist with complete authenticity. They really believe they are the person their memories tell them they are, until they're activated."

"Well no one ever intended to activate me," Aileen said. "I did that on my own. My old memories started to seep through. Enough that I began to ask questions about it. Of course, Stock just dismissed them and encouraged me to leave it be." Aileen grimaced. "I couldn't. And once I discovered the truth, I left, taking Aileen Stock with me." She forced a weak laugh. "Not that I have a choice about leaving her behind."

Jeth stared at her, remembering the way she had sounded when Stock had called her name. She'd called him "Daddy" in that little-girl voice, one that didn't belong to her. He wondered what it would be like to have your memories replaced by someone else's. To just wake up one day and realize you'd been pushed aside so someone else could take over.

It's like Dax forcing the implant on you, a voice whispered in his head.

Only it wasn't, not really. The implant had given him something, but it hadn't taken anything away. He was still Jeth Seagrave. Still the same person he'd always been, defined by the same memories and life path that had led him to this present.

"I took Remi with me, too," Aileen added after a moment. "He was the first Aileen's bodyguard before me. And I suppose this is obvious, but he's the result of one of Stock's experiments as well. He's not a clone, but his genes have been modified."

Jeth nodded, realizing it was obvious, now that Aileen had connected the dots. "How did he end up like that, if he isn't a clone?"

"He was a convict," Aileen said, her eyes glistening. "It was either volunteer for ITA experimentation or be executed."

Despite his anger, Jeth felt pity rising up in him. In the end, Aileen and Remi were just two more of the ITA's victims. Even worse, Jeth realized that according to interstellar law, Aileen was subhuman and therefore not entitled to even the most basic of human rights. A clone would be treated worse than a convict. She'd taken an awful risk going in to Hanov.

But how had she smuggled in the gun?

"Does being a clone give you . . . superpowers?"

"You mean like fooling the scanners on the subway?" asked Aileen.

"And at Hanov," Sierra added. "Only one of us should've been able to go through those doors."

Aileen shook her head. "I don't know if it's specifically because of the cloning stuff or not, but there's something off about my bioelectricity. It's enough to fool scanners, including metal detectors." She looked at Jeth, a tiny smile passing over her face. "It's that special skill I told you about."

"Oh, it's special all right." Jeth ran his hands through his hair. "So tell us about the medicine. Why do you need it?"

Aileen shifted in her seat, her eyes falling to the floor. "It seems I'm a clone with an expiration date."

"How do you mean?" asked Sierra, and for the first time, the hardness in her voice was absent.

"Cellular degeneration," Aileen said, assuming a mock clinical tone. "My cells are breaking down. Some kind of internal necrosis. I don't know what or why. I just know that whatever is in that canister we stole will cure me. Or at least delay the condition for a while."

"*How* do you know that?" said Sierra.

Aileen rolled her eyes. "Lots of careful, expensive research. As soon as I realized there was something wrong with me, I put everything I could into finding the cure and stealing it."

Sierra scoffed. "Clearly, your efforts weren't good enough. That medicine was obviously a trap meant for you."

Aileen glowered. "Yes, I realize that now. But I swear I didn't know about the silent alarm. The trap was buried even deeper in the ITA's files than I could find, and that's saying something."

"You don't except us to believe that, do you?" Jeth said, his doubt rising up hard. "Sounds to me like you walked into that trap blind and my mother paid the price."

He expected her to respond with anger, but her voice was pleading. "I am sorry about your mother, but I did as much as I could to ensure the plan would work. As much as I could without giving myself away. The truth of my identity is still entirely secret. Or it was. Stock couldn't let the ITA know what he'd done. He wanted me to continue on pretending I was his precious little princess. But I couldn't. Not once I learned the truth."

Jeth felt his resentment toward her ease its grip at the underlying hurt in her voice. He reached into his pocket and withdrew one of the vials. "Just for the record, I'd rather shoot you and be done with it. It's no less than you deserve for what you did."

A look of panic appeared on Aileen's face, her eyes wide and fixed on the vial. "I'm sorry. I was desperate. This was my one shot to get that medicine. The bio clearance in the lab is impenetrable. Sierra was the only way in. It's why I signed on with Dax."

Sierra's eyes narrowed on Aileen's face. "You could've just asked me to get it, you know."

Aileen's mouth fell open. "Are you joking? Like any of you would've agreed to go in there on my behalf. Why would you take that risk just to help me?"

The question gave Jeth pause. She had a point, at least as far as how he would've initially reacted. But the moment Lizzie had gotten wind of this, her bleeding heart sentimentality would've insisted they help, and Jeth would have eventually relented.

Lizzie. Worry over the long silence began to eat away at him. He hadn't checked his messages in hours. He rubbed the back of his neck, trying to ease the ache of the implant's absence.

"We might have," Sierra said. "If you'd just been willing

to work with us instead of playing lone wolf."

Aileen pursed her lips. "Maybe. But it hardly matters now, does it?"

Jeth shook his head. *You would've done the same,* he heard his mother saying. But that wasn't true. His position was so very different from Aileen's. She was alone, friendless aside from Remi, and with no one but herself to depend on; he had help and people he could trust. He'd always had his crew and his sister and uncle. They weren't perfect, but they had his back.

Most of the time. His thoughts turned toward Celeste and Shady, a twinge of regret going through him. Maybe he shouldn't have cast them out, not when they wanted to stay. Celeste had been distraught over Vince's death. Loss and despair could lead one to do terrible things, a fact Jeth knew well.

"You're right," Jeth said. "It doesn't matter now, but this does." He tossed the vial, and Aileen caught it with both hands, mouth agape. "I need you to finish this mission. And you're no good in that capacity if you're dead."

Relief shining on her face, Aileen snorted. She pulled a syringe out of her pocket. Jeth arched an eyebrow at it, and Aileen smiled guiltily. "So maybe I was planning on stealing it back."

He sighed, amused despite himself. Maybe killing her would have been overreacting.

Aileen plunged the needle into the top of the vial, filled the syringe to capacity, and then pulled up her sleeve.

"Here," Sierra said. "Let me do it."

"I'm fine." Aileen took a step back from her. "I remember how to take a shot."

Sierra reached her and grabbed the syringe from her hand. "Giving it is a different set of skills, and you don't want to waste any of the medicine. Now hold out your arm."

Begrudgingly, Aileen did so, and Sierra stuck the needle in, far harder than necessary.

"Ouch," Aileen hissed.

"Just be glad you get to keep feeling pain. That makes you the lucky one."

Aileen bowed her head and didn't utter so much as a sound of complaint as Sierra finished.

"Are you sure this is even going to work?" Jeth asked.

Aileen started to respond but broke off as *Polaris*'s proximity alarm began to sound. Jeth turned toward the window, scanning the horizon for sign of a ship headed their way, but not seeing any.

He stepped up to the pilot's seat and looked down at the scanner. His heart plummeted to his knees. He hadn't spotted the incoming ship because it wasn't at sea level—and it wasn't just one.

Nearly twenty ships were closing in on them from above in a locked formation. ITA cruisers, according to the readout.

Somehow, the ITA had found them.

CHAPTER 28

"IT'S IMPOSSIBLE," JETH SAID, HIS WORDS COMING OUT too high-pitched. "We're still cloaked. We're not moving."

Nevertheless the ITA ships knew exactly where they were. And there was nowhere to go. They were trapped between the sea and the ship-filled sky.

"Oh God," Sierra said. Jeth looked back at her. She was staring down at the medicine vial still in her hand. "I'm so stupid. We're all so stupid." She turned toward to the bridge's garbage port, a small airlock hatch. She tossed the vial inside, closed the lid then pressed the eject button, sending the vial out into the sea.

"What is it?" Jeth said.

"The medicine must've been tagged." Sierra wheeled on Aileen, her eyes alight with her fury. "I guess you overlooked *that* in your research, too."

Aileen took a step back. "I'm sorry."

"Stop saying that." Sierra charged her, fists raised. The punch landed clean against Aileen's jaw with a meaty smack, her head careening to the side. Jeth gaped in surprise. He'd rarely seen Sierra lose it on anyone. The stress and heartache of the last few weeks had taken its toll.

Aileen stumbled, but recovered quickly and made to fight back.

"Stop it, both of you!" Jeth shouted. "We've got bigger problems." He waved at the window in front of him where some of the ships were coming into view.

By now, the others were piling onto the bridge, the sound of the proximity alarm drawing them in. All except Perry and Eric, but Jeth didn't have time to wonder at their absence. All his focus was on the incoming ships.

"What's going on?" said Flynn, hurrying over to the comm station, the easiest within reach. "Whoa, that's bad."

"Thanks for the helpful assessment," Jeth huffed, turning his attention back to the screen in front of him.

"They're broadcasting a general message," Flynn said.

"They know we're here, but they can't see us," said Sierra, coming to stand behind Jeth.

He waved at Flynn. "Put it on the main comm."

Flynn switched it on, and a man's voice echoed through the ship: "Attention, unidentified vessel. We know you are holding a wanted fugitive. Disengage your cloaking device, hand over Aileen Stock, and we will ensure your cooperation is noted on your arrest record."

"Cooperation?" Jeth's eyebrows climbed his forehead.

Flynn snorted. "They don't know us very well."

Then again, Jeth realized, it was only Aileen they were after. Maybe they could push her out the airlock and get away in the confusion. He wasn't entirely serious about the thought, but Sierra quashed it anyway. "If they capture us, it's all over. Everything we've fought for."

"I know." Jeth glared over his shoulder at her, panic igniting his temper. They were already caught.

"No, Jeth, it's worse than you realize." Sierra touched his back as if to steady herself. "Aileen is the key to the cloning formula. If the ITA gets her and Cora both, they've won. They won't need the Pyreans. They'll have clones."

The nightmare image of Cora plugged into a metadrive like a living battery flashed in Jeth's mind again. He shoved it away. "I need solutions right now, not consequences."

A stormy look crossed Sierra's face, and for a moment Jeth thought she might hit him, too.

"Can't we make a metaspace jump?" Aileen said. "Jailbreak the proximity sensors again like we did back at Peltraz?"

"I don't know." Sierra turned and pushed Aileen out of the way as she sat down at the nav station. "We're anchored for a water landing. In that mode, I don't know if I can even bring the metadrive system online. I'll have to turn off the anchor system first, if it'll even work while we're still on the water."

Jeth glanced back at the window, running alternatives through his head in case Sierra couldn't bypass the security. The shuttles were out—the cloak drive wasn't a networked system. As soon as they disconnected from the main ship, they would be visible.

A wild idea occurred to him, and he turned to Flynn. "Can *Polaris* go under the water like the shuttles?"

Flynn gaped then blinked a couple of times. "Not if you

want to fly her ever again. The water could damage the hull integrity and pretty much everything else. We've already been parked on it longer than we're supposed to."

"Do it anyway," Aileen said. "She's tough. She can take it for a little while."

"You might damage your ship permanently," said Flynn.

Aileen shrugged. "So what? I'll get another. And it beats getting caught."

Jeth's anger sparked again. No one who truly loved a ship could be so cavalier about destroying it. He felt sorry for *Polaris*. She deserved better. Even if she wasn't *Avalon*.

Still, if damaging the ship meant escaping, he would take it. He gripped the control column, ready to head down. He would have to do it slowly so as not to disturb the water too much and give away their exit strategy.

"Don't, Jeth," Sierra said as he gripped the control column. "I've almost got this."

He stilled his hands and waited.

The sound of heavy footsteps drew his attention to the bridge entrance, where Perry and Eric had just arrived. Both of them held stunners in their hands. But that wasn't the only thing off about them. There was something wrong with their faces—they stared blankly ahead, as if they were sleepwalking. Their movements were off too, weirdly jerky and mechanical. Jeth only had a second to realize what he was seeing when stunner blasts lit up the bridge. They took out Remi first, then turned the guns on Jeth.

He reached for the Luke, a brief flicker of relief that he

wasn't wearing his implant going through the mind. But he wasn't fast enough. The stunner blasts struck him in the chest and the world went dark.

He woke inside the brig of an unknown spacecraft. The cell walls were electrified glass, allowing him easy view of his surroundings. Sierra was in the cell to his right and Flynn to his left. Remi was in the cell across from him. The giant man had been chained to the floor as an extra precaution. There was no sign of Aileen or Cora.

Or Eric and Perry, Jeth realized with a stab of fury as the memory of their betrayal came swooping down on him. Only it hadn't been betrayal. Not exactly. He'd seen someone move like that before—Dax had looked that way when Hammer had used his master implant to force him to act against his will.

Jeth felt certain the same had happened to Perry and Eric. But he couldn't understand it. Why would Dax betray them to the ITA?

Unless it wasn't Dax. Could someone else have seized the master implant and taken control of the Axis? Jeth searched his pocket for his own black implant, but found it empty. He felt its absence as a physical ache, the loss of a limb, but for once, he was glad of that ache. If he'd been wearing it when the coup took place, he might have been the one betraying his friends.

Jeth stood up from the bench and saw that Sierra was awake as well. Spotting him too, she got up and approached the glass but was careful not to touch it. She began to speak, but Jeth shook his head. He couldn't hear her through the glass. Sierra wrung her hands in frustration. The sight of her at such a loss twisted his gut. They were well and truly caught this time.

He glanced away, focusing on the control panel on the front of his cell. It was so close. Only an inch of glass and a couple of hundred volts of electricity separating it from his reach. It might as well be the entire expanse of time and space.

The minutes crawled by as Jeth sat and paced, sat and paced. The dull throb in his head, the aftereffect of the stunners, lingered on. He supposed the absence of the implant made it worse. The restless need to have it back made him want to climb the walls. If something didn't happen soon, he was going to do something desperate, like try and punch his way out of there. But not even Remi, who was conscious now as well, could do that.

Finally, determined to draw the attention of their unseen guards, Jeth closed his eyes and laid the palm of his cybernetic hand against the glass. The shock was instant and monumental, knocking him back half a meter. He stumbled and almost went down. Starbursts danced across his vision, and the smell of burnt hair filled his nose.

He did it again, and again. The third one nearly knocked him unconscious. Beside him, Sierra was waving at him to stop, but he ignored her, going in for a fourth try. Before he did, an ITA soldier appeared in the doorway to the brig. She saw Jeth about to place his hand against the glass once more and approached his cell.

She pressed a comm button on the control panel. "That's enough. All you're doing is dirtying the glass."

"It passes the time." Jeth flashed his most charming smile. "Unless you'd like to help me pass it."

The woman rolled her eyes, placing a hand on the butt of her standard issue ITA rifle, but Jeth could tell she was listening.

"Mind telling me where we're headed?"

The soldier considered the question then shook her head. "You don't need to know that information."

Jeth widened his smile. "Please. Either that or I can just keep on cleaning the window."

She scoffed. "Do that and you'll end up unconscious."

"At least it might get me out of here," Jeth muttered with more venom than he intended.

The woman seemed to take pity on him. She sighed. "We're headed for the Hive. Should be there any minute."

Jeth's smile faltered as surprise struck him. Why were they heading for the Hive, and not some other ITA facility? "What's the Hive?" he said, keeping up the act.

The soldier shook her head. "You'll see." Then she turned and left without another glance at him.

Jeth exchanged a look with Sierra. There were headed for the Hive, the home of the Harvester. They were captured, but all was not lost. Not yet.

As the soldier had predicted, they arrived at the Hive a

short while later. Jeth felt the ship's engines slowing down and then eventually the telltale bump of the landing. After another long wait the brig filled with soldiers. Two approached each cell, except for Remi's, where four stopped. The soldiers who came for Jeth shoved his wrists into heavy manacles that nipped at his flesh, then dragged him from his cell and out of the brig.

He considered making a break for it, but knew it would be pointless. Even if he could wrench himself free of their grip, there were too many soldiers to get through and the ship's corridors were too small.

The soldiers led their prisoners down to the cargo bay and then out the main door. The dim gray light outside was still strong enough to make Jeth blink. Several seconds later, his vision adjusted and he saw the wide expanse of a flight deck before him, one that stood several stories above sea level. He could just barely see the ocean over the nearest edge. From here the Hive resembled a small spaceport on water. Every surface was sleek, shiny plasinum.

He understood at once why this place was called the Hive. It was shaped like a honeycomb, the landing pads at its top circling around a wide gaping hole in the center. At first Jeth didn't understand the point of the opening, but then he saw the giant beams rising up at even intervals around the perimeter. The Harvester. It was right there, in the middle of the Hive. That made sense. The Pyreans had appeared stretching up from the ocean, reaching out toward the sky. Perhaps they needed the sun and air to live.

He couldn't see the Pyreans, not from here, but he knew they were waiting somewhere down in that hole. For a second, he thought he could even sense them, a faint buzzing in the atmosphere around him. Not electricity but some raw, subtle energy.

With hope stirring inside him, despite the odds, he studied the beams, trying to fix the size and layout of the Hive in his mind as they crossed the flight deck toward the single control tower. Overhead, storm clouds were rolling in, churning the waves. Sea spray struck Jeth's face, and he blinked away the sting of salt water in his eyes.

As they moved nearer, the view across the way opened up, revealing a massive ship. Jeth's heart seized in his chest as he spotted the name painted on its prow:

Regret.

Admiral Saar was waiting for them.

CHAPTER

JETH'S MIND REELED. HOW WAS SAAR HERE ALREADY? HAD he been tracking them the entire time, or had Dax told him where they were headed, how to find them? And the worst thought of all, the one that made his blood crystallize to ice in his veins: Where were Lizzie and Milton?

He had no answers as they entered the control tower and then an elevator. They descended several levels down into the structure, remerging in a long, wide hallway. Most of the doors they passed were sealed, but a few had windows looking in on laboratories or computer rooms. Jeth expected to be taken to another prison cell, but instead he was brought to what was unmistakably an interrogation room. The bland, blank-walled space held a single stark table with two chairs set on either side of it, facing one another.

Jeth didn't have to look up at the corners to know there were live video cameras. He almost smiled at the formality of it, the archaic idea that as a prisoner he still had rights to be treated fairly. *The ITA and their pretenses,* he thought. So long as the appearance of justice was present, the reality didn't matter.

The soldiers forced him into the chair farthest from the

door and then fastened the chain of his manacles to the small metal hoop protruding from the table—its only decoration.

Then they left, leaving him alone in the semidarkness. Jeth didn't expect to wait long, not in this room, but he was mistaken. Hours slipped by. He grew desperate to stand and stretch, returning blood flow to his lower extremities.

Even worse was the oppressive company of his thoughts. Where were the others? What would happen to them with Saar here? Saar, the man who had executed Vince with no remorse or hesitation. A hundred horrible visions of what awaited them came and went in Jeth's mind, leaving him exhausted.

Finally, the torturous wait ended. The door opened, and Saar stepped inside.

Hatred ignited in Jeth's chest, and it was all he could do to sit still and look impassive. His jaw ached from the effort of holding back a scream of rage. Sweat dampened his neck and arms.

Saar carried a blue box in his hands. He approached the table and looked down at Jeth, his expression completely neutral. He was wearing the gray uniform of an ITA soldier, the left breast covered in elaborate rows of insignia. The straight, high collar of the uniform emphasized the gauntness of his face. His cheekbones looked sharp enough to cut glass. The tentacles of his silver brain implant were visible beneath his ear. His eyes were ice—glistening and pale blue. They pierced Jeth, freezing his heart.

"Jethro Seagrave," Saar said, setting the box on the table. His gravel voice sent a jolt of fear through Jeth as he remembered the first time he'd heard it, the moment before Vince died.

He shook the feeling off. He refused to let this man intimidate him. Jeth flashed his cockiest grin. "David Saar. Or should I call you Dave? Can I call you Dave?"

No reaction showed on Saar's face. He might not have heard Jeth speak at all, but Jeth knew better. This was a man who wouldn't provoke easily. His patience made Jeth feel small, inconsequential. He swallowed.

Saar pulled out the chair across from Jeth and sat down, crossing one bony leg over the other. He touched the top of the box with a gnarled finger, the nail thick and yellowed. "Jethro Seagrave, you have been found guilty of treason against the Confederation of Planetary Systems and it is within my authority to bestow on you the punishment of death for your crimes."

"Found guilty?" Jeth said, managing to keep his voice steady. "Funny, but I don't remember a trial."

Saar acknowledged Jeth's response by raising a single eyebrow. "A trial? How quaint that you think one was needed."

"I really didn't." Jeth hesitated, weighing his next words carefully. "Not from your point of view, anyway. Must be nice to feel so justified to commit murder. To be so certain of your authority over every life that crosses your path."

"Certainty," Saar said, "is the only way an entity such as the one I serve can guarantee its authority. There is no room for doubt in the ITA. Not when it comes to criminals and terrorists such as yourself."

Jeth snorted. "Like the average citizen is treated any differently."

Saar bared his teeth in a ghastly smile. "I wouldn't know. I don't deal with the average citizen. But what I do know is that your kind is a cancer and it is my duty to cut you out."

A cancer. Jeth's stomach turned over, guilt churning inside him as he remembered he had thought the same way about Shady and Celeste. How wrong he was—as wrong as Hammer had been. "My kind?" Jeth said, his voice trembling. "You mean free-thinking? Free-willed? Well, then to you all humanity must be a cancer."

Saar ignored the comment. "You have been found guilty, but I am going to give you one opportunity for redemption: a chance to take a more righteous path."

Jeth smacked his lips. "I don't believe any such path exists. Anywhere. But most of all not here."

Saar bowed his head slightly. "Perhaps. Still, it would be something other than immediate execution." Saar bared yellowed teeth in an expression designed to petrify. It very nearly worked.

"I suppose that's something." Jeth leaned back in the chair as far as the manacles would allow. "What would I have to do to earn this chance, then?"

"You will confess all your mother's secrets. Specifically, the location of Empyria."

Jeth glared, the pain of his mother's death an open, seeping wound. He didn't even know what they had done with her body, although he suspected they had collected it like a specimen and sent it back to the Hanov lab to be dissected and studied.

But if Saar wanted the truth, he could have it. "I don't know the location of Empyria."

"Perhaps, but I'm disinclined to believe that your mother died without passing that information on. I've seen the recordings of her time in the ITA labs. That is one secret she would not take to her grave."

Jeth smirked. "That's an interesting conclusion to make. I've seen the recordings too, and it seems to me that taking that secret to the grave was precisely what she was planning to do."

"You're lying." Saar said it so simply that Jeth almost faltered.

Forcing his eyes not to shift off Saar he said again, "I don't know the location of Empyria. Besides, why do you even want it, now that you've got Cora and Aileen Stock?"

"Insurance," Saar said at once. "The cloning project will suffice as an alternative to metadrives for a while, but access to the Pyrean home world will make the ITA's power absolute."

"You mean it'll keep someone else from trying to take your power from you," Jeth said, understanding perfectly.

"There will always be those who try," Saar said. "But none who will succeed. Not while we control the means for interstellar travel." Saar uncrossed his legs and faced the box in front of him. For the first time Jeth wondered at its contents. It was large enough to contain several handguns. A brief fantasy of getting his hands on one went through his mind. He would not hesitate to plant a bullet between this man's eyes.

Saar opened the hinged lid and reached inside the box. Jeth couldn't see anything from his side of the table. He waited, breath shallow as Saar set one of the objects on the table. It took him a second to recognize it. He'd only seen the Reinette canisters briefly during the Hanov mission.

"What did you intend to do with these?" Saar asked.

"You know what it is, right?" said Jeth.

Saar nodded. "Reinette. A microorganism designed to break down plasinum. A highly destructive, though generally nonlethal weapon."

"That's the idea."

"What did you intend to destroy?"

Jeth pressed his lips together. He didn't have a lie to offer, but he refused to speak the truth. If his mother could keep her secrets through years of torture, so could he. The very idea of denying this man something he wanted was enough motivation to seal Jeth's tongue for all eternity.

"I take it you don't wish to convey this information willingly?" Saar said, cocking his head ever so slightly.

"Right again," Jeth said.

"Very well." With a satisfied smile, Saar opened the lid to the box once more. "Then we will try some means of motivation." He set three more objects on the table, each one completely identical—and a thousand times more frightening than the Reinette.

Implants. Three black, Brethren implants. Jeth knew at once that the one in the middle was his. He didn't know how he knew exactly, but he did, without a doubt. He battled down the impulse to reach out and snatch it. He wasn't sure the manacles would be long enough, but he wanted to try. More than anything.

And yet he didn't.

"Who do those belong to?" Jeth asked, eyeing the ones on the right and the left.

"Your companions."

Eric and Perry? Why had Saar collected their implants? Surely whoever was controlling them was working for Saar. "Why do you have their implants?"

Saar sighed, the sound as gravelly as his voice. "They won't be needing them anymore."

"What?" Jeth sat up straighter, his heart rate doubling.

"Yes, they too were found guilty of treason and have already paid for their crimes."

"They're dead? You killed them?"

"I am the Storm that Rises," Saar said. The familiar words made Jeth's gut twist, his hatred and fear a toxic mix inside him.

"I'm not going to tell you anything," Jeth said through gritted teeth.

"We shall see." Saar reached into the box a third time. The object he revealed crushed any hope Jeth had in a single, red-hazed blow. It was another implant, one the color of old blood.

Breathless, Jeth asked, "What did you do to Dax?"

"A cancer must be eradicated wherever it is found." Saar reached a hand to the back of his head and removed his silver implant. He set it on the table next to the others before picking up the red implant once more. He raised it to the back of his skull, and inserted it with quick efficiency.

"This is an amazing device," Saar said, motioning to his new accessory. "Implants with this level of network capability are expensive and hard to come by, even in the ITA. My own is networked, of course." He touched the silver implant. "My men call it the Temple. It's very similar to the Axis—though, to my dismay, not as powerful. The hierarchy structure Hammer introduced with the Axis makes the Temple seem primitive by comparison. It's a fault I have since rectified."

"How do you mean?" Jeth said, his lungs constricting.

"I have combined the two networks, integrating the Axis hierarchy into the Temple. In other words, I have made the Malleus Brethren and the Guard a part of my Temple."

Vomit burned Jeth's throat. Dax was dead, and the Axis now in the control of this man—a man used to wielding power with heartless efficiency.

A moment later, the realization of what Saar intended to do struck Jeth. He leaped up, pulling against the chains. He would cut off his own hands rather than sit here and let it happen.

Saar smiled, and as if the gesture had been a silent command, two ITA soldiers stepped into the room. They weren't the ones who had escorted him here. These men wore silver implants, marking them a part of Saar's army, connected to the Temple. *And now the Axis.*

They walked toward Jeth, who started to flail. In unison, both men pulled clubs from their belts, the short sticks lengthening with the single press of a button.

They rounded on Jeth, swinging. The first blow struck him midthigh, the other in the small of his back. He went down to his knees, his arms wrenching out of their sockets as he reached the end of the manacles' length. Jeth let out a pained cry, and kicked out with his uninjured leg, but it didn't matter. The soldier to his left struck him again and then pressed against him, pinning his body to the table. The soldier to his right grabbed the implant Saar held out to him.

Together the soldiers forced Jeth's head down, neck exposed. The stem of the implant jammed against the back of his skull a couple of times before they managed to find the architecture hole and drive it home.

All the fight went out of Jeth like a light shutting off. He sank to his knees, his head on fire with both relief and a terrible, penetrating fear. He wanted the implant back, wanted its strength and reassurance, but the Axis was gone.

No, not gone. Rather, amplified. It was no longer an inviting hum in the back of his mind, a doorway to information and community. Now it was a tempest, a flood of power barreling over him, bending his will.

You will relent, Saar spoke into his mind. *You will obey.*

Jeth fought against the power, the strength of it seeming to flay his mind. *I will not.*

You will obey.

No.

Obey.

Blood filled Jeth's mouth as he bit down hard on his tongue. He didn't taste it. He felt disconnected from his body. He was all mind and nothing else. And he felt himself bending, surrendering.

Tell me about Empyria, Saar said.

No. But even as he thought it, images rose unbidden in his mind, of Lizzie, and the data crystal. *Hidden code,* Lizzie had said. *Empyria.*

Noooooooo! Jeth screamed. He fought and raged, but it was too late. Once released to the Axis—to the Temple—there was no taking it back. Jeth struggled to shut the door, to turn it off and keep his secrets, but there wasn't any door anymore. There was nothing but Saar. *The Storm that Rises. Storm scourge.*

Destroyer of Minds. Eater of Souls.

The images began to flow freely now, his mind ripped open and spilling out. Saar saw everything. The mission to Hanov, the plan to destroy the Harvesters, even Marian's dying words, her wish for Jeth to go to Empyria, to bring the Pyreans and the humans together, finally.

Jeth didn't know how long it lasted. He didn't know how Saar's mind could handle such an influx of memories all at once, how it didn't destroy him. Except, of course, that Saar was the Temple. His was the strongest mind of any Jeth had felt. Stronger than Dax, stronger than Hammer had been.

And Jeth had no hope against such a mind, such strength. He was a reed, broken in the wind. Saar was the master now.

Forever.

PLEASE JUST LET ME DIE.

It was the only thought Jeth had left, the only one that was truly his. But even this, Saar denied him.

Not yet, Jethro. Your sister will come, your uncle. They will do anything to save you. Your memories are proof enough of that.

Saar didn't have them, Jeth realized. Not yet. Somehow Saar failed to find Lizzie and Milton at Peltraz, even though Jeth knew the Underground had been breached. He saw it all happen, Dax kneeling before Saar, who'd already taken possession of the master implant, and given Dax a black one. Dax had fought, projecting lies and misdirection through the link. He fought so hard the blood vessels in his eyes burst. Blood poured from his nostrils. It didn't matter. The black implant wasn't strong enough; he wasn't strong enough. Saar had emptied his mind of all the information he could glean, and then he had killed him with a single shot through the heart. Elegant, Saar had called the death—and deserved.

But Dax hadn't known about the code. Lizzie had never told him. She had gotten away.

She won't come, Jeth replied. *She's not stupid.*

Saar laughed, the sound a rich, vibrant pressure in Jeth's

mind, full of certainty. Hatred as black and foul as cancer, as death, burned in Jeth's heart. But Saar only laughed harder.

She will come, and once I have the information from her, I will have you kill her.

The image Saar conveyed into Jeth's mind made his stomach wrench, and he vomited over the table.

I won't do it. I won't do it.

But he would. The implant was too powerful. Saar was too powerful. And Jeth was broken.

"Stand him up," Saar said, and Jeth felt hands on his wrists, the soldiers muttering about the stench and the mess. They unlocked the chain from the table and forced him to his feet. Jeth stood on trembling legs. He couldn't fall down. Saar was willing him to stand.

You will keep the implant in at all times, Saar said. *Or your friends will bear the consequences.* This time the image was of Sierra and Flynn subjected to unspeakable torture, the kind that would break them, both in spirit and mind.

They were alive and okay for now, too, Jeth realized, but the thought brought no comfort. He saw the extent of Saar's plan for them. He would keep them alive to keep Jeth in line, until Lizzie and Milton came. Once he had them and the code for Empyria, they would all die. Jeth would kill them all at Saar's bidding before turning the gun on himself.

They took Jeth to a holding cell in the Hive. It was the smallest room he had ever seen, barely tall enough to stand in and only just long enough to lie in. There was no latrine, no sink for washing, not even a place to sit. They shut him inside and he sank to the floor, slumping against the back wall. The closeness of the space pressed against him, setting his nerves on edge. He wanted to scream and rage and beat the walls, but Saar's will remained firm in his mind. He was to sit quietly and obey. He could feel the man's will as clearly as if Saar stood there in the room with him.

And so Jeth sat and obeyed.

He fell asleep sometime later, but Saar's presence greeted him the moment he awoke again.

Time to the bait the hook. You will play your part. Or your friends will endure worse pain than you can imagine.

The image of what Saar wanted him to do flashed in Jeth's mind. The door opened a few minutes later and a pair of Saar's soldiers waved him out of the cell. The silver of their implants gleamed in the lights overhead, mocking Jeth. He went with his eyes downcast and head bowed. No fight. No fuss. Perfect obedience.

They led him to the flight deck once more, then onto the cargo bay ramp of *Regret*. Half a dozen ITA agents carrying cameras were waiting there. Jeth didn't meet their eyes either. Not until they turned the cameras on and gave him the signal.

Manacles were clamped around his wrists again, this time tied behind his back. The moment they were in place Jeth began to struggle. He fought as hard as he could. He screamed and cursed at the soldiers. He played the part of the wanton criminal that Saar wanted the world to see. The soldiers dragged and pushed him across the flight line toward the elevator into the Hive. The cameras panned wide, catching the full stretch of the deck and some of the surrounding ocean, and the distinctive beams of the Harvester, of course. Later, when the ITA journalists described the capture, their voices superimposed over the video, the location would be recognizable to anyone who knew what to look for.

Anyone like Lizzie and Milton.

They returned him to his cell afterward, but only for a little while.

"Time to practice," Saar said as the door swung open. Two soldiers came in and hauled Jeth to his feet. "We must ensure your obedience in every way." As Saar spoke, Jeth saw the image of what Saar intended. Shame flooded him. He tried to hide it from Saar, but it was impossible. The man smiled, his satisfaction flowing through the link.

Shame is good. Through shame, your crimes will be purged.

With Saar leading the way, the soldiers took Jeth to a cell two floors above. The cell was bigger, but still spare. It contained a bench with a thin blanket and an even thinner pillow set atop it. Instead of a toilet, a plastic bucket sat in the corner. The stench assaulted Jeth's nostrils as he walked in.

"Jeth!" Flynn said, standing up from the bench. Jeth didn't respond or even look up. He kept his eyes on the floor, his destination clear as he headed for the bucket, hoisting it up with one hand.

"What are you doing?" said Flynn. "What's wrong with you?"

Jeth wanted to answer, but he couldn't. The harder he

tried, the stronger the pressure in his mind grew. He knew that to Flynn he looked like he was sleepwalking, his movements stiff. Saar watched from outside the door, bearing physical and mental witness to Jeth's punishment.

He carried the bucket out of the cell, the soldiers locking the door behind him. He took it to the nearby latrine and dumped the contents. Then he went to the janitor's closet and rinsed the bucket clean before returning it to the cell. This time, Jeth managed to raise his eyes for a second, long enough to see the look of horror and disgust on Flynn's face. And also of pity. More shame burned in Jeth at the sight of it, and he forced his thoughts to a better memory of Flynn. The taste of chocolate filled his mouth, but it turned bitter as Saar forced the memory out of his mind.

Those memories belong to me now.

Saar led him to Sierra next. She did not react with surprise at the sight of him, as Flynn had, but with action. The moment Jeth stepped through the door, she leaped up from the bench and charged him, her hands rising to his head. Jeth didn't move, didn't look at her. There was no command from Saar.

Sierra's hands closed around the implant in the back of his skull, but just as she began to pull it out, the soldiers stepped in, clubs drawn. They struck her twice and she fell with a strangled cry. Jeth's heart wrenched, and he fought against Saar, against the power binding him in place.

It was no good. All it did was make his limbs tremble and his head ache. A trickle of blood slid from his nose at the effort.

He tasted it as it slipped over his lips and into his mouth.

The soldiers restrained her so Jeth could complete his task. He retrieved the bucket and carried it to the door, Sierra's voice a distant call in his ears.

"Fight it, Jeth," she said. "You can do this. Dax overcame Hammer. Just fight it. It can't end this way."

He dumped and cleaned the bucket and returned it to the cell. Sierra struggled to get at him once more. But the guards restrained her, and still Jeth could not move.

They returned Jeth to his cell where he spent the rest of the day and the night, trapped in his head. Locked in a never-ending nightmare.

Saar came for him again the next morning, still wearing the red implant.

"You have a special task today," Saar said, reinforcing his words with his will through the implant. "You will talk to Cora. You will tell her she must put aside her fears and worries. She is in a better place, a safer place. She must do everything the scientists ask of her without resistance."

For a second, Jeth saw a glimpse of the damage Cora had done to the facility already and a flush of pleasure warmed his body. He summoned what remained of his strength, teeth clenching from the effort. "It won't work," he said.

Saar glowered down at him. "You will not speak out of turn."

Jeth's mouth closed and refused to open.

Saar led the way this time, the two soldiers following behind him, their hands resting on their guns. Cora was not being held in a cell, but in an apartment. Judging by the lavish furniture, Jeth guessed its former occupant had been part of the management team that oversaw the production at the Hive.

As Jeth walked into the living room, Cora looked up from where she sat slumped on the sofa. Exhaustion lined her face. Her eyes were heavy from the sedatives they'd been giving her, drugs that would eventually lose their ability to subdue her entirely, Jeth knew.

He walked toward her, expecting a warm greeting, but Cora recoiled from him, drawing the blanket she'd been using up to her face.

"Go away," she shrieked. "You're not my brother. Go away!"

Jeth frowned, or at least made an attempt at frowning. He tried to speak, tried to convince her that it was really him, but the words came out garbled.

Stop fighting, Saar spoke in his mind. *Give in to my control and you will be able to convince her.*

But Jeth couldn't do it. He hadn't even known he was still fighting. The instinct to protect his sister was so deep beneath the surface of his consciousness he hadn't known it existed. He didn't know how to turn it off.

"There's someone else in your head," Cora shrieked. "You're not supposed to be there! It's not supposed to do that." She began to scream, her voice vibrating the walls. Soon she would tear holes in them. Jeth took another step forward, hoping that she would destroy the place. Maybe she would turn that power against him, killing him, setting him free.

But Saar knew his intention at once, and the soldiers rushed in and hauled Jeth back through the door. He spotted a medic hurrying down the hallway toward them, a jet injector in her hand.

Fight them, Cora, he thought. *Use your gift. Phase them away.* Then he remembered that she could do more. She could save them all the way she'd done once before when they'd been trapped on the Strata starship. *Phase us all!*

But it was no use. She couldn't hear his thoughts, and she couldn't use her abilities when she was sedated.

The soldiers led him back to his cell.

Another day went by, and another night. The morning after, they took him back to Flynn's cell for more cleaning. But this time, he brought in a bucket of hot, soapy water and a couple of rags with him.

"To clean yourself," Jeth said as he set the bucket down. His voice sounded strange to his ears. He'd heard so little of it these last few days, and the words he'd spoken weren't his but Saar's.

Flynn made a pained noise, torn between his desire to be clean and his disgust at Jeth's role as servant. But in the end he stripped off his soiled clothes and washed himself. This time, Jeth did not keep his eyes averted. Saar made him watch. And even though Jeth knew outwardly he looked like some kind of zombie, inwardly he saw everything. Especially the hurt on Flynn's face, along with fear and dread.

Afterward, they took him to Sierra's cell once more, another bucket with fresh water in his hands. This time though, the soldiers went in first, prepared for her reaction. She fought them, but they beat her back quickly. As soon as she was subdued, they stripped off her clothes and then snapped manacles around her wrists and ankles.

Saar appeared in the doorway. Again he'd come to bear witness to Jeth's penance. "Bathe her," he said, sending the command through the Temple.

Every muscle in Jeth's body tensed. He wanted to stand in front of Sierra, use his body to hide her nakedness from Saar.

Bathe her. Saar's command rang in his head.

"Fight it, Jeth," Sierra said. "Fight—" A hand closed over her mouth.

No, he thought through the link. The open defiance was like a ray of light shining through an impenetrable darkness. It filled him with hope, with strength.

Saar crushed it at once. Pain lanced through Jeth's head and he stumbled, dropping to his knees. He raised his hands to his forehead and pressed, desperate for relief. For a second, he pictured himself yanking the implant from his skull. But no matter how hard he tried, his hands wouldn't move to the back of his head.

Spent and beaten, Jeth gave in to the will pressing upon him. He struggled to his feet and picked up one of the rags. He doused it in the warm, soapy water, and then he scrubbed Sierra as Saar had commanded.

Jeth felt the heat of her humiliation as his hands rubbed

the rag over her body. His own shame burned just as hot. She tried over and over again to speak to him, but her captors held her too tightly. He wanted to speak to her, to offer her words of comfort, but he couldn't. The urge to cry rose up in him, but even that Saar denied him.

And Saar watched it all from the doorway, his gaze impassive but his mind filled with intense satisfaction at Jeth's obedience.

Later, Jeth understood why his friends had been cleaned. The three of them were led into a cargo hold somewhere deep inside the Hive. It had been emptied of storage crates and barrels, making room for the large crowd assembled before a makeshift dais.

Jeth, Sierra, and Flynn were led onto the dais at gunpoint, all three of them with their hands shackled behind their backs. None of them struggled or protested. Jeth guessed that Sierra was surveying the scene, searching for an escape. Flynn had withdrawn into himself, unwilling to incur the soldiers' wrath by acting out.

Jeth had been given the command to stay still and silent, properly cowed.

Saar appeared on the dais, and the audience went quiet. The man commanded respect and awe—the truth of it shining in every eye Jeth saw. He wanted to stab them all out. He could tell some of the audience were news reporters, all ITA. This was just another feigned act of legitimacy, a farce as great as the one they'd staged years ago when they claimed Jeth's parents had committed treason and were to be executed. In truth, his father was already dead, and his mother locked up in a lab at Hanov.

Saar cleared his throat, the sound amplified by the small mike affixed to his collar. As always, he was wearing the gray uniform with all the signs of his high rank. He launched into a prepared speech, summarizing Jeth, Sierra, and Flynn's supposed crimes. Some of it was true, but most was not. Jeth tuned the words out, lacking the will to care.

No, he didn't care or listen until Saar came to the end of his speech.

"Four days hence," Saar said, his voice booming, "the guilty will be put to death by firing squad, their threat to the Interstellar Transport Authority and the galaxy at large eliminated."

The crowd broke into applause, and a tremble went through Jeth's knees. He knew Saar would only have gone through this spectacle because he was certain Lizzie was near. The deadline would force her and Milton to act. The bait was hooked, the trap set.

And in less than four days, his family would walk right into it.

CHAPTER
31

ONE DAY CAME AND WENT WITH NO SIGN OF LIZZIE. THEN another. The hours maintained their pattern. Jeth would visit his friends, emptying their buckets, bathing them when necessary.

On the third day, he visited Cora again. This time, he went in without the implant. For the first few minutes with Saar out of his head, Jeth could only stare, the relief rendering him dumb. Then clarity set in and the relief faded to despair. This was worse, this full understanding of how beaten he was. At least the implant barricaded him from his feelings and thoughts. In some ways, that was better.

The sense of utter defeat made his stomach clench. His heart was a stone in his chest. Even with the implant out, he felt the press of Saar's will. *Convince her to trust us.* Saar's words reverberated through his mind. *She is putting herself at risk. She will be better off if she does not resist. She will be spared the pain of punishment.*

Spared the pain. But she'd be an ITA slave.

Was it better?

Jeth weighed the question as he stopped outside the door to the apartment for a moment. Cora was so young, and her life had already been fraught with loss and abuse. He'd wanted to give her something better, but he couldn't.

Or maybe he could. Maybe Saar was right, and her life would be better if she didn't resist, if she just accepted her role in the new order. *Would it have been better for you?* the voice of his consciousness asked. Jeth considered the idea. For years he'd struggled against life under Hammer. But was he better off now that he'd lost everything?

It was a question too painful to answer.

At least for himself. But he could for Cora.

Steeling himself against the pain of what he was about to do, Jeth opened the door and walked inside. Once again, Cora was lying on the sofa with a blanket pulled up to her face. She looked even worse than before, as much of a zombie as he was. The circles beneath her eyes were dark and waxy, her face gaunt and skin pale. She looked like she was dying. *Same as the Pyreans.*

But this time, when her gaze met his, she didn't react in fear. She smiled, the edges of it worn and tired. "Jeth." She sat up and held out her arms.

Jeth went to her, scooping her up and hugging her. Tears stung his eyes, but he didn't fight them back. The emotion hurt but at least he was allowed to feel it. Maybe it was better after all.

"Are you okay?" he asked, planting a kiss on the top of her hair.

She shook her head. "I miss Mom. I miss you. I'm scared."

"I know." *Me too,* he thought, but kept it private. The

fact that he could brought sweet relief. For a moment his mind was completely his own. "But you've got to stop being scared."

Cora leaned back from him far enough to fix a narrowed gaze on his face. He could sense the question in her eyes—*was this the stranger who had come before?*

He forced a smile. "I mean it, Cora. We're going to be here for a while, and you have to be strong and brave. You need to do what these people ask of you without making a fuss. If you do that, they won't hurt you."

She started to protest, but he shushed her. He turned and sat down on the sofa, settling her on his lap. He was too tired to hold her, and the lies came easier without the physical strain.

Cora frowned and reached up to lay a hand against his face. "But they hurt *you*."

Jeth sucked in a breath. "That's different, Cora. And it has nothing to do with you." He paused, searching for the words to convince her. "Isn't there anyone who is nice to you?"

"Aileen," Cora said at once.

"Aileen?" Jeth couldn't keep the surprise from his voice. "They let you see her?"

"Sometimes, for a little bit." Cora cast him a disapproving look. "She's sad, like you."

Jeth nodded. Of course she was. She'd lost everything, too. He tried not to think about how this was her fault. It wasn't, not entirely. The moment Saar claimed Dax's implant, it was all over. It seemed the universe really had been conspiring against him all along.

"Well, you stay close to her whenever you see her,

okay?" Jeth said, patting Cora's back.

"I will. But I'd rather see you. Can I see you more now?"

"I . . . I don't think so, Cora." He took a deep breath, his vision clouding over with tears.

Cora went still, the lack of action so unnatural for her. Like most children, she always seemed to be doing something, fiddling her toes, making noises with her mouth, but in that moment, all the frenetic energy in her had evaporated.

"Are you going away?" Cora said.

"Maybe."

"Like Mom?"

He didn't have the heart to answer. "Just promise me that you'll be a good girl and do what the doctors tell you to, okay?" If she was going to die anyway, he wanted her last days to be as painless as possible.

"If I do good will they let me see you again?"

"I don't know, Cora. Maybe." This time the lie came easier. She needed hope right now, no matter how false.

"But, I want to see you, Jeth. All the time." She wrapped her arms around him and squeezed his neck hard. "I need to know that I'll see you or I can't do what they say. I can't."

Jeth eased her arms around his neck enough to draw a full breath. He racked his brain, searching for words of comfort, a way to motivate her to carry on. Then the answer came to him. "Do you remember the story of the Little Mermaid?"

She nodded.

"Do you remember how it ended? How the Little Mermaid chose not to kill the prince and then jumped into the sea, even though she thought she would die?"

"But she didn't die. She turned into a daughter of the air."

"Yes, but she didn't know that would happen when she jumped in. She did it anyway because it was the right thing to do. Do you understand?"

Cora went silent for a few minutes. "I need to be a good girl and listen to the doctors because it's the right thing to do?"

Jeth clenched his teeth, hating the lie he was letting her believe, even though it was exactly what he'd been hoping for.

But at the same time, there was a deeper truth there.

"You need to be a good girl, because you *are* a daughter of the air. And if you're good, you'll float away someday, just like the Little Mermaid did."

"Float away?" Cora said, skepticism in her voice.

"Sure," Jeth said, an idea forming in his mind. "Just like how you once floated off that big ship and onto *Avalon*. And all of us floated with you. Remember?"

Cora nodded. "I saved you."

"That's right. And you saved yourself. Now you need to learn to do that all the time." Jeth watched her face as he spoke, hoping to see the light of understanding flash in her eyes. But she was only seven, far too young for coded messages about escape attempts.

The frustration built inside him. If only he could communicate with her mind-to-mind like his mother did. It seemed like he ought to be able to, and the fact he couldn't was some flaw in his DNA. Cora could save them all. With her ability to manipulate metaspace, she could get them all out of there. But she didn't know how to control it. Not yet.

But someday, Jeth thought, trying to find comfort in the knowledge. No matter what the ITA had planned for her, they would have a hard time controlling her once she gained full mastery over her powers. He could only hope it would happen before she was old enough to be fitted with an implant. It might be too late for him and the others, but not for her.

"Promise me you'll be good," Jeth pressed, "and that you'll learn how to float again."

This time understanding seemed to flicker in her expression, if only for a moment. "I will, Jeth. I promise."

The fourth day came with no sign of Lizzie and Milton. Jeth mustered the courage to probe the link to Saar's mind, hoping to find doubt there. But as always, Saar was nothing but confidence and power. He was certain that Lizzie would arrive. He was certain that they would catch her.

And so the execution ceremony commenced. They brought Jeth, Sierra, and Flynn onto the flight deck. The soldiers had to drag Sierra and Flynn into place, but Jeth went without much resistance—the implant was too strong, and he was tired from fighting and from losing.

The event wouldn't be broadcast, but the open space would make a rescue attempt more inviting, Jeth knew. The only hindrance was the weather. As when they arrived, a storm was coming in, the wind whipping around them, dousing them with cold water.

There weren't even that many soldiers around, no more

than a dozen, although all of them were Saar's men, easily identifiable by the silver implants. They carried standard-issue rifles and Mirage pistols, but Jeth knew they each had pulse grenades hidden beneath their uniform jackets as well. It would take only a couple of such grenades to disable whatever spacecraft Lizzie and Milton might have commandeered on Peltraz. The scattering of ships on the flight deck looked unoccupied, none of them ready to meet resistance, but again Jeth knew there were whole crews waiting on standby inside. The ships nearest where they stood had pulse cannons hidden beneath their prows, ITA soldiers lying in wait to use them. Everything about this scenario screamed of a setup. Lizzie and Milton wouldn't be so stupid.

But still, Saar's confidence did not waver.

"Get in a line," one of the soldiers shouted at Jeth, shoving him into position. Then the soldier turned and did the same to Sierra. She spat in his face. The soldier backhanded her hard enough to leave an imprint of his fingers on her cheek. Jeth wished she would stop fighting. Watching her get hurt and being powerless to help was the worse kind of torture. If she only knew.

Then again, maybe she did. Her eyes caught his and she gave up the struggle, falling into place beside him. She leaned into his shoulder. He would've slipped his arms around her if he could, but his wrists were bound with manacles again. They weren't behind his back this time, but the binding still limited his movement.

"I love you, Jeth," Sierra whispered. For the first time,

he heard defeat in her voice. She too had given up hope. He thought hearing it would be the end of him, but instead something stirred inside him. Defiance, or the old flicker of hatred, of the desire for vengeance that had driven him here in the first place. Or perhaps it was simply the will to live. He didn't know, but he clung to it. Even now, at the end of all things, he couldn't just let go.

Forcing his lips to move, wrestling for control of his body and mind, if only for a few seconds, he said, "You too."

Sierra choked on a sob, the sound drowned out by the wind around them.

The three of them then waited in silence as Saar paced a couple of times before them, surveying the scene, as if he wanted to make sure every detail was perfect before the execution commenced.

He's buying time, Jeth realized. Despite Saar's confidence, he still wasn't certain of when Lizzie and Milton would attack, or how.

They won't come, Jeth thought, forcing it through the link, pressing Saar with this certainty. For a second he sensed the man's doubt echoing back at him.

But in the next second, a flash of light burst overhead, punctuated by a loud crack—the sound of a ship exiting metaspace. Jeth ducked on instinct as the force of the jump terminating so close rocked the entire Hive, the floor trembling like an earthquake.

Once the shock had passed, Jeth glanced up and saw a familiar ship floating above their heads. The *Citation,* one of

Dax's ships. *Lizzie,* Jeth thought, fear shooting through him. This was too brazen. They would be caught, shot down before they even gained their bearings. Already, an alarm had sounded and the ITA soldiers were heading for cover, pulse grenades and cannons at the ready for when the ship flew into range.

Before they'd gone a couple of meters, a bright blue light burst out from the *Citation.* Everyone froze. The light pulsated outward and downward. People flinched as the light reached them, but it passed over them with little more than a static tingle. A moment later, though, every light and source of power on the Hive died. It didn't affect the rifles and handguns, but every pulse cannon and grenade was rendered useless.

The Disrupter, Jeth realized. Hope blossomed inside him as he sensed Saar's fear through the link. He hadn't anticipated this kind of attack. Jeth spared a moment's regret that the Disrupter didn't work on implants, their Pryean core making them immune to the effect.

But Lizzie and Milton and whatever crew they'd assembled weren't finished yet. They opened fire on the fleeing soldiers, taking out half a dozen of them. Saar fled as well, turning on his heel and racing across the flight deck for cover behind one of the lifeless starships.

Jeth, Sierra, and Flynn stayed where they were, waiting for the path to clear and for their friends to come get them. *The Citation* lowered toward the flight deck, sending up more sea spray and wind in their faces. A couple of soldiers took aim at it with their rifles, but the *Citation*'s crow guns mowed them down easily.

The side hatch on the *Citation* opened. Sierra headed for it first, screaming at Flynn and Jeth to follow. They did, Jeth bringing up the rear.

He couldn't believe it. It couldn't be this easy. He probed the link for Saar's presence but found it empty. Had Saar been caught in the fire? Alarms sounded in his head, but the lure of freedom was too great for him to pay any heed.

They reached the hatch and charged up the ramp. Adrenaline pumped through Jeth's body, making him feel alive for the first time in days.

Then they were on the ship, the hatch closing behind them.

Sierra was screaming ahead of him as they mounted the ladder to the bridge. "Somebody get down here. We need help. Right now."

Milton appeared at the top of the ladder. The sight of his familiar face, so much like Marian's, lifted Jeth's spirits so high he thought he might float away.

Do it now. Saar's voice suddenly flooded Jeth's mind like a dam bursting. Jeth's elation evaporated in a second, his agency following a heartbeat later. Time seemed to stand still as memories surged into his mind, ones he'd forgotten, ones he'd been ordered to forget.

Do it, Saar commanded again, and Jeth was terribly aware of everything now. Saar had ordered him not to act until Lizzie and Milton were in reach, until he was on board the ship with them. He was to lie in wait, a snake lurking in the grass until the perfect moment to strike.

"We need to get that implant out!" Sierra shouted at Milton, incapable of doing it herself with her hands still bound.

Jeth understood her fear. She was right to feel it. He wasn't to be trusted. He reached for the stunner tucked into his pants beneath his flight jacket. He hadn't known it was there. Saar had kept the memory from him. Until now.

Do it, Saar commanded. *Stop them.*

No! Jeth screamed. *No! I won't do it, I won't!* Blood began to fill his nostrils, pool in his eyes.

Do it now, Saar commanded, his mind a powerful, scourging wind.

And like it he had so many times before, Jeth felt himself bending beneath it, breaking.

His finger tightened on the stunner. The first shot struck Sierra, knocking her unconscious in an instant. The next two took down Flynn and Milton. With his limbs shaking and jerking he climbed up the ladder. Before anyone could react, he'd fired three more stunner shots: Lizzie, Celeste, and Shady. The presence of the latter two surprised him. But only for an instant as irony took its place.

Life had come full circle. He was the betrayer now.

CHAPTER

Jeth recoiled from the man's touch, his mind afire with shame and regret, the evidence of his own weakness. If only he'd been able to resist Saar, they would've escaped. But Saar had been conditioning him for this moment for days, weakening his mind and resistance, turning Jeth into an extension of himself.

And it was well and truly over now.

No, fight it, Jeth. Fight it. The thought was weak, barely finding purchase in his mind, a space so infested by the enemy there seemed nowhere to hide. *Fight it, fight it, fight it.*

Jeth closed his eyes, swaying on his feet from the strain. Saar, his back now to Jeth and pacing from one end of the *Citation*'s bridge to the other, was too preoccupied giving orders to notice Jeth's effort. But Saar's inattention wouldn't last long, Jeth knew. And so he buried the thought deep, not extinguishing it, just hiding it as best he could. It was a fleeting hope, but better than the final, inevitable surrender.

"Have you found it yet?" Saar asked the soldier sitting at the comm station.

"No sir. It doesn't appear that she loaded the information

on the ship's computers. It might be on a private unit."

"Very well. Search the passenger quarters," Saar said. "If we haven't found it by the time she wakes up, we'll interrogate her."

Jeth swallowed, dread pounding in his temples. Once Saar had the data crystal with the hidden code . . . but no, he couldn't let himself think about that.

"What would you like us to do with him?" another soldier asked, motioning at Jeth.

Saar turned, momentary surprise on his face. He seemed to have forgotten about Jeth completely. "Take him down with the others. It won't be long before we are ready to start."

The soldiers escorted him out of the ship and back to the flight deck. The oncoming storm seemed to have stalled, but the sky remained dark and ominous, the weather uncertain of its mood. The effects of the Disrupter had also been rectified—the lights back on and the elevators in full working order.

The elevator descended to the detention floors, but then kept going. It appeared Jeth's friends and family were being held somewhere deeper in the facility. He was dumbfounded when the doors opened on a level of the Hive he had come to believe he'd never see—the Reaping Floor, the very heart of the Harvester.

Jeth froze in the doorway, overwhelmed by the sight before him. The floor was at sea level, the vast circular room hardly more than a platform around an area of the sea as wide as a lake. Rising up out of the water like the branches of a giant tree were the Pyreans. They filled all the space in the center and reached nearly to the top of the Hive, twenty levels above them. The coral-like leaves that adorned the branches were all larger than a full grown man, and they came in every shade of every color imaginable—azure blue, moss green, burnt orange, taupe, indigo, magenta. There were colors that didn't have names. All the colors seemed to glow as if from a phosphorescent light. It was as if someone had taken pieces of every metagate Jeth had ever seen and combined them in one majestic organism.

But unlike the gates, these Pyreans were undoubtedly alive. They were moving, only slightly, but deliberately. It might've been the sea moving them about, but Jeth didn't think so. The movement was too independent, too random, as if each branch had its own idea of where it wanted to be.

Alive. Jeth wondered how he ever could've missed it before. Seeing them like this, he could feel the life in them, the energy that made the air vibrate.

And yet, they were dying. The colors, though still vibrant near the bottom where the branches emerged from the sea, were faded to white at the tips and riddled with holes, like brittle, ancient bones. Death had slowly eaten its way through them, sucking them dry. The stench of that death hung in the air, the reek of cancer. Sadness gripped Jeth's throat, cutting off his breath.

He forced his eyes away from the Pyreans to the beams that arched over them. Six in total. Six chains locking the Pyreans into place with some kind of electromagnetic field.

Seeing the Harvester like this, Jeth realized how easily his mother's plan would've worked if they hadn't been captured. If the beams were to be destroyed, there would be nothing preventing the Pyreans from retreating back into the ocean, back into metaspace. The sting of failure heated his skin. Bringing him here was just another of Saar's punishments—rubbing his face in the reality of his failure.

"Move along, Seagrave," one of the soldiers said, prodding Jeth from behind.

He hadn't realized that he'd come to a stop. Then again, he couldn't understand how anyone could pass by the Harvester without care or notice. Reluctantly, Jeth stepped into the chamber. The heavy security doors slid into place behind them, the locks giving a loud click.

A soft hum began to vibrate in the back of Jeth's skull as he drew nearer the Pyreans, following the soldier in front of him. The noise was unsettling at first, as if his mind were being invaded yet again, but after a few moments it brought him a strange sort of comfort, a pleasant distraction from the turmoil in his head.

The soldier led him around the nearest beam, and Jeth came to an involuntary stop once more as he spotted what was waiting on this side. His friends, still unconscious, were lined up in a row on the floor in front of the tank. Each one wore manacles on their wrists whose chains were bound to the safety rail around the tank.

A firing squad, Jeth realized, his stomach churning. It matched the image Saar had projected into his mind again and again nearly perfectly. For a second, Jeth was stunned by Saar's dedication to detail and ceremony. Milton once said he was a man who believed in his own righteousness. This was what that righteousness looked like. An execution staged to the last detail, designed to inflict the most suffering.

"Over there," the soldier said pointing to the open space between Sierra and the beam. A set of manacles waited for him. Jeth stepped up to it, turning his back to the rail and the Pyreans. The soldier clamped the manacles around his wrists, and then left.

Jeth sat down and waited, knowing his friends would recover soon. He wouldn't be able to talk to them—Saar had willed him to be silent—but at least he could savor their presence, no matter how much being near them hurt.

Sierra was the first to wake, slowly stirring a few meters away from Jeth. Her eyes fluttered open and she sat up, taking in the scene with a strangled gasp. She turned her gaze on Jeth, her face livid with fury. But only for a moment before pity rose up to take its place. A part of Jeth wanted to look away from her, to bury his head in his hands and hide from that look. The rest of him didn't dare squander what little time they had left, no matter what it cost him.

Sierra glanced away from him, turning her attention to the others who were also waking up.

"What the hell?" Shady said, pushing himself into a sitting position. Momentary delight went through Jeth at the sound of his voice. It had been too long since he'd heard it. He needed to say he was sorry. That he had been wrong. He should've forgiven, should've given them a second chance. But he couldn't reach the words. Saar's control gripped him.

"What happened?" said Lizzie, rubbing her forehead.

"Jeth shot us," said Celeste. "I'm going to kill him."

"You might be in luck." Shady pointed a thumb in Jeth's direction and every head turned his way.

Celeste's fury evaporated in half a heartbeat. "What's *wrong* with him?"

"The implant," Lizzie said, her voice shaking.

"She's right." Sierra stretched out her arms, testing the manacle's length. Then she explained what Saar had done with Dax's implant. "Jeth's been under his control ever since." Sierra waved her hand at Jeth, as if testing to see if he was paying attention. "He has moments of clarity, but not much."

"Well, isn't that great." Shady balled his hands into fists. "Here we came to save his ass and he went over to the dark side."

Flynn glared. "Lay off him, Shady. You have no idea what he's been through."

Shady started to retort, but then his eyes flicked to Jeth and he swallowed. "I'm sorry. I didn't mean it."

"It's so awful," said Lizzie. "You warned me about the implant, Sierra, but I never expected this."

"Neither did I." Sierra got to her feet, leaning against the rail to steady herself as the stunner's effects lingered. "We couldn't have anticipated Saar."

"Is the damage permanent?" Celeste asked, her voice quiet. "He looks like he's brain-dead."

"I don't know," Sierra answered.

A silent scream sounded in Jeth's mind. He wanted to tell them that it wasn't permanent. He would be okay if he could just break free of Saar's control. But he was trapped, like the Pyreans behind him.

"But we've got bigger problems," Sierra continued.

"Yeah, like getting out of here," added Flynn. "Please tell me you guys have some kind of backup plan."

Lizzie shook her head. "There wasn't time, and like you said, we couldn't anticipate Saar."

Flynn's face contorted. "I hate that son of a bitch."

Me too, Jeth thought, and the hum in his head grew louder. It became rhythmic and strong, like a heartbeat.

"How did you escape Peltraz?" Sierra said. "Saar told us he killed Dax."

Lizzie nodded. "I didn't see it happen, but I'm not surprised. The moment Dax knew that Saar was going to breach the Underground, he sent word to his Brethren to make sure Milton and I got out of there."

Dax saved them. There were probably a hundred other things he could've done in those last moments—he could've offered Jeth's family up in trade to save his own neck—but he'd made sure they were safe instead. A nameless emotion expanded in Jeth's chest.

"What about you two?" Sierra motioned to Shady and Celeste.

"Lizzie found us," Celeste said.

Shady grunted. "She never lost us."

"That's right," Lizzie said, sparing a glance at Jeth. "I kept tabs on them after they left. I knew Jeth would come to his senses sooner or later. At least, I'd hoped so."

"Don't count him out, Lizzie," Milton said. "Jeth's still in there somewhere."

Yes, right here. So close and yet impossibly far away.

"Where are Cora and Marian?" Milton asked.

Sierra pursed her lips, not meeting her gaze. "They've got Cora locked up somewhere around here."

"And Marian?" Milton pressed, emotion already rising in his throat.

Sierra exhaled. "She . . . I'm so sorry, but she died, right before they captured us."

Both Lizzie and Milton stared at her, faces frozen with shock. Milton broke first, tears sparkling in his bloodshot eyes.

"What happened?" Lizzie asked, her voice shaking.

"She was shot by an ITA agent," Sierra said.

Jeth knew she could've said more, a lot more, but he was glad she didn't.

Several moments passed in silence, both Milton and Lizzie choked by grief.

Sometime later, Milton drew a deep breath, reining in his emotions. "We need to figure a way out of here."

"Yes," Sierra said. "And I don't know how much time we have." She turned her gaze on Lizzie. "Saar is looking for the data crystal. He knows about the hidden code. He likely won't kill us until he's found it, but after that . . ."

Lizzie's mouth fell open. "How does he—never mind. If

that's what he's after we're in luck. He'll never find it."

Jeth heard her words and wanted to believe, but he knew at once that she was wrong. Saar's satisfaction was already bleeding through the link. He'd found it. Lizzie had hidden it inside an air vent in her cabin, the same way Marian had hid it on *Avalon* so many years before. The ITA had failed to find it back then.

But Saar hadn't been the one looking—Saar, who had seen all of Jeth's mind and memories.

Jeth tried to force his mouth open to warn them Saar was on his way, but it was hopeless. They weren't paying attention to him anymore, their conversation focused on ways to get out of here. Pointless ways, Jeth knew. And so he tuned them out, withdrawing into his head, finding comfort in that constant heartbeat that filled him up here in the chamber.

Saar arrived a few minutes later with half a dozen of his soldiers following him. *Witnesses,* Jeth thought. Saar was here to pass final judgment.

Jeth's pulse quickened. He took deep, rhythmic breaths, savoring the simple action like he never had before, counting each one until the last.

Saar came to a stop before them, sweeping his gaze over the ragtag crew of teenagers and one grief-riddled old man.

"Hey, you," Lizzie said, drawing Saar's attention. "I know what you're looking for. I'll give it to you if you let us go."

A smile stretched across Saar's lips. "Is that so?"

"Yep," said Lizzie, her whole manner brimming with confidence. "You'll never find it without my help."

Saar reached his hand into his pocket and withdrew a data

crystal. He held it out to her. "Is this the object you would help me find?"

Lizzie paled. "That's impossible."

"No—inevitable." Saar returned the data crystal to his pocket. "But I appreciate your attempt to barter for your lives. I would expect no less."

Lizzie shook her head. "We're not done bartering. You need me to finish decoding it."

This time Saar laughed outright. "That's hardly necessary considering you placed the cipher on the crystal as well. I imagine it won't be too difficult."

Lizzie's face fell.

"But take heart. I'm still impressed nevertheless, especially with the way you coded the crystal to prevent copying of any sort. Very clever. If there were more time I would have to insist you show me how you managed that."

If there were more time. Jeth fought back dizziness.

Tears welled in Lizzie's eyes, and her whole body shook as she fought not to cry.

Saar turned away from her. His cold gaze fell on Jeth. He opened his mouth to speak, but one of the soldiers behind him said, "Excuse me, sir."

Saar paused then turned to face him. "What is it?"

The soldier who spoke came forward and whispered something in Saar's ear.

"This is more important," Saar said when the soldier finished. "Let the others deal with the problem for now."

The soldier nodded and stepped back into the line.

"It's time." Saar motioned to one of the soldiers, who

came forward and released Jeth from his manacles, entering the four-digit code on the lock.

"Come here." Saar beckoned him. Jeth approached, his gaze fixed on Saar's face.

"Don't listen to him, Jeth!" Lizzie screamed. "Help us!" The others echoed her words, but he barely heard them.

Saar pulled a gun from his left side holster. Jeth recognized it at once. It was his very own Triton 9, the first gun he ever purchased for himself. Jeth had left it in the shuttle they'd used for the Hanov mission. Saar wouldn't have had any trouble knowing it was his though—in his vanity and pride, he'd had his initials engraved on the gun's side.

Fitting that his first would be the last he ever used.

Saar held it out to him. Jeth hesitated, fighting the instinct to take it and obey. But his arm rose up and his hand closed around the butt, fingers settling into place. The weight of it in his hands was familiar, almost comforting.

"Eliminate them all," Saar said, folding his arms over his chest.

Jeth swallowed, finding his voice. "Who first?"

Saar considered the question for a moment. "Let's start with the hardest. Your sister, I think."

Jeth nodded, even as Lizzie's cry reached his ears. "Don't listen to him, Jeth. Fight it!"

The others joined in as Jeth stopped in front of his sister, little more than an arm's length away. Tears poured over her face, making her cheeks and eyes glisten. Jeth saw color reflected in the wetness from the glow of the Pyreans overhead.

He raised his eyes to look at them, those swaying, lovely creatures. Sentient beings, his mother had said. And they were. The hum in the back of his skull vibrated harder.

Finish it, Saar's voice spoke through the link, the force of it driving the hum away until it was nothing but a distant echo. *Shoot her.*

No. Jeth put all the will he could into the thought. He wrestled for control, his heart racing, sweat beading his skin. *I won't do it. I won't. I won't. I won't.*

You will.

Jeth's fingers tightened on the gun. *No, no, no.*

YES.

He racked the slide, dropping a bullet into the chamber. *No, no, no.*

NOW.

Jeth raised the gun, barrel pointed at Lizzie's forehead. His arm did not shake; his body did not show any sign of the struggle in his mind. It was all in his head. Just his imagination. Meaningless. Hopeless. Pointless.

"Please, Jeth," Lizzie said, sobs racking her body. "Please."

Do it now. NOW.

"I'm sorry," Jeth whispered.

Then he closed his eyes.

And pulled the trigger.

CHAPTER

AFTERWARD, JETH NEVER FULLY UNDERSTOOD WHAT HAP-
pened. All he knew was that it wasn't him. He didn't do
it. The strength came from somewhere else, *someone* else,
a force working through him, bypassing his tortured mind
and engaging his heart.

Jeth's hand jerked to the right at the last impossible second and the shot went wide. Lizzie screamed and fell, blood
bursting over her cheek as the bullet grazed her.

At the sight of her falling, the sight of her blood, something snapped inside Jeth, and the implant's hold over him
broke. He spun, his mind coming alive, adrenaline fueling
his actions and focusing him into a human weapon.

He fired on Saar, the bullet striking him in the chest.
But before the old man even finished falling, Jeth turned
the Triton on the other ITA soldiers. He got off three shots
before they could even make a move, three soldiers dropping
as surely as their leader.

Jeth ducked to the left as the other three opened fire. One
shot hit his arm, pain lancing up into his shoulder, but it
didn't slow him down. Three more shots and the remaining
soldiers fell.

The silence afterward was even louder than the gunfire had been. It thrummed inside Jeth's skull. He turned his gaze on Saar. The man had fallen backward but landed on his side, his face pressed against the floor. The master implant was in clear view. Jeth still felt its control pressing down on him, the pressure waging a battle inside his own head.

No more.

"What are you doing, Jeth?" Sierra said.

He barely heard her. Her words didn't matter. Not now. Not yet.

Tucking the gun into his belt, Jeth reached up and removed the black Brethren implant. He tossed it aside, savoring the relief of being done with it. Then he stepped over to Saar and bent down. He grabbed the data crystal first, tucking it into his pocket. He would need it later. Then he slid his fingers around the master implant. It came free with a light tug. He stared down at it, his pulse throbbing through his entire body. This was it. This was the key to everything. Once he laid claim to the master implant, he would never be enslaved again. His friends and family would be free forever, and everyone who had threatened them would pay. He would be the master now.

"Stop it, Jeth," Sierra said, her voice much nearer. "Put it down."

With an effort, he turned and looked at her. Somehow she'd managed to free herself from the manacles. She'd even managed to pick up one of the soldiers' guns without his noticing. She held it trained on him now, the barrel a dark, bottomless hole.

Jeth stared at her, unable to understand the threat. Not when the answer was so obvious. He held up the master implant. "This is our way out of here. I'll be able to keep Saar's men at bay."

"No. We'll find another way."

Jeth stared her down. "I have to do this, Sierra."

She shook her head.

"Um, we could use some help, Sierra," said Shady from behind them.

"Eight-five-six-three," she said without looking back. "I watched as the soldier entered it. Let yourselves out. Everybody get a gun. But don't trust Jeth. Not until he's gotten rid of that thing."

His fingers tightened around the implant. "I can't. Don't you see? I can control them with this. We'll be able to walk past those soldiers and onto our ship. I can even make them fight for us."

"It won't work, Jeth." Sierra gulped. "That implant will ruin you. Saar has perverted it. It holds too much power now. Don't do this."

Jeth pressed his lips together, his anger rising. It *was* power. And power meant freedom. It meant everything he ever wanted at last. It was a lesson he'd been learning all his life. Now was time to claim it.

Sierra racked the slide on the gun, her hands steady despite the quiver in her lips and the tears standing in her eyes. "If you put that thing in, I'll kill you."

"What are you saying, Sierra?" Lizzie said. She and the others had finally freed themselves from the manacles. Shady and Celeste were gathering weapons while Flynn, Milton, and Lizzie watched the confrontation.

"He made me promise," Sierra said, sparing Lizzie a quick glance. "If it came to this—this moment, right here—he asked me to stop him, in any way possible."

"I won't be like Hammer," Jeth said, the memory of that distant conversation rising up in his mind. Already his skull ached from the implant's absence. He needed this. Needed it more than anything. Surely she could understand that.

"You don't need it," Sierra said, and Jeth frowned. Had he spoken the last out loud? "You're right, though," she continued. "You won't be like Hammer. You'll be like *Saar*."

Jeth gaped. Fury blurred his vision. "I'll never be like him. I'll use this to help us. For good." He held the implant up, getting it into position.

"Please, Jeth," Sierra said, the tears spilling over now. "Don't do this. Don't make me kill you."

He scoffed. "You won't."

"Yes, I will." Her expression hardened.

Something in it reminded him of his mother. The association sent a chill cascading down his spine. Jeth froze, torn by indecision. It made no sense. The master implant was their only guarantee of getting out of here. And yet, he remembered the way Saar had used it against him, the degradation as he'd forced Jeth to bathe his friends, to watch them suffer, to be the source of it.

The memory turned his stomach, and clarity broke into his thoughts at last. The hum he'd sensed before, the one so much like a heartbeat, began to sound in his head again. He closed his eyes, listening to it.

You don't need it, a voice spoke. It was not one voice, though, but many. *There is a better way.*

Jeth exhaled, and then, against every instinct possible, he squeezed the implant, hard, with his right hand. His cybernetic fingers crushed it, destroying it, and the Axis, forever.

With the others watching, Jeth walked over to the rail, nearer to the Pyreans. He took the ruined remnants of the master implant and tossed them over the side, losing them to the sea.

Before they had even disappeared from sight, arms wrapped around Jeth's waist and Sierra's breath warmed his neck.

"Thank you," she said. "Thank you."

Relief flooded him. For the first time in weeks he felt free, a heavy burden lifted from his shoulders, his mind, his heart. He turned into her embrace. He wrapped his arms around her and hoisted her into the air, kissing her.

"Um, not to break up the beautiful reunion," Lizzie said, tapping him on the arm. "But we need to get out of here."

Jeth set Sierra down then turned to Lizzie, pulling her into a hug. "I'm so sorry, Liz." He raised his gaze, sweeping it over the others. "I'm sorry to all of you."

"We know." Lizzie thumped his back, tears glistening in her eyes. "Come on, we've got to go."

Jeth let go of her. She was right. They needed to get out

of here. The other soldiers who had been connected to the Temple would've sensed Saar dying. They were already on their way. But—

Jeth's gaze swept toward the Pyreans. He was free, but they were still trapped. This was his only chance to free them, to save Cora. But he didn't know how. He had no idea where the Reinette canisters could be.

"Come on, Jeth," Lizzie called after him as she and the others raced for the door.

He turned and followed, defeat pressing down on him.

"There's someone firing out there," Sierra said as Jeth arrived at the door.

"What do you mean?" Jeth stepped up next to her, hearing it for himself. *Why would there be fighting anywhere but in here?*

Unless . . . he waited, listening a few moments longer, until the gunfire died down.

"Open it," he said to Sierra.

She frowned. "Are you sure?"

He nodded. "But everybody get ready to fire, just in case." The others did so, taking cover on either side of the door.

Sierra pressed the lock and the door slid open. Jeth stared a full five seconds at the scene before him, incredulity blocking his thoughts. It couldn't be. It wasn't possible.

Aileen stood in the doorway with Cora beside her. Behind them was Remi. He was bleeding from a graze to his forehead and his arms, but he was alive and as formidable as ever. A one-man war machine, it seemed. Behind him lay a pile of

ITA soldiers, all dead.

"What the hell?" Shady said from somewhere behind Jeth.

Aileen beamed back at them. "I think you're in need of these." She reached her hand into the bag slung over her shoulder and pulled out a small metal canister. Jeth didn't know how she'd managed it, or why. But he didn't care as he reached out and took the Reinette from her.

It seemed that he would fulfill his mother's dying wish after all.

CHAPTER 34

"HOW DID YOU GET HERE?" SIERRA SAID, HER VOICE SHAKING with surprise. She reached for Cora and pulled her into a hug.

Aileen smirked. "Someone killed the power. It was just long enough for Remi here to break free." She motioned to her giant partner. "Cora and I were together when he found us and broke us out."

Jeth couldn't believe it, not just the luck of the Disrupter giving Remi the chance to escape, but that they had taken the risk to fight their way down here. He would have bet anything that Aileen would've made a run for it. Yet, here she was.

"I wanted to just get the hell out of here," Aileen said, hands on hips. "But Cora insisted."

"Yeah," Cora said, pulling out of Sierra's arms. "We need to do what Mom wanted." She fixed a glare on Jeth as if daring him to disagree.

Jeth shook his head, feeling a wild urge to laugh. He handed the Reinette device to Sierra then turned back to Aileen. "Do you have the rest?"

"Sure do." Aileen patted the bag. "What's the plan?"

"Six of us need to stay here long enough to set the devices. Then we get out of here."

"Works for me," said Aileen.

Jeth nodded. "You, Cora, Lizzie, and Remi head up to the flight deck. Get *Polaris* ready to go. The rest of us will set the devices and meet you up there."

For once, no one argued with his command. Aileen pulled the bag off her shoulder and handed it to Jeth. Lizzie checked the safety on the gun she'd snatched off a dead soldier then stepped out into the hallway.

"Hold on, Liz." Jeth reached into his pocket and withdrew the data crystal. He tossed it to her. "Keep it safe."

"Right." She stowed it into her pants pocket.

Jeth turned to Remi. "You go first. And take care of them."

The big man nodded. Then he led the way out, Cora, Lizzie, and Aileen following after him. Pushing away his worry for them, Jeth faced the others. He handed each a Reinette device, keeping one for himself.

"We need to do it in succession," Jeth said. "These things are supposed to work fast. If we're not careful we'll get caught in the destruction as the Harvester collapses." He pointed at Celeste and Sierra. "You two take the farthest beams. Once you've discharged them and are on your way out, Shady and Flynn will discharge theirs next. Then Milton. I'll go last."

Sierra and Celeste turned in unison and took off at a run. Flynn and Shady followed after them. Milton hurried too, moving surprisingly fast in his old age. Jeth took position at the beam nearest where Saar had fallen. Then he waited while the others did their part.

Moving together, Celeste and Sierra opened their canisters and discharged the Reinette right on their assigned beams. The results were nearly instantaneous. The loud groan of metal echoed through the chamber as holes began to form in the beams. The Harvester was disintegrating before their eyes.

Sierra and Celeste were on the move, soon passing Flynn and Shady. They wasted no time discharging their canisters. Next it was Milton's turn. The first two beams were half-way gone, but the Reinette didn't stop there. The floor was plasinum too, and already it was eating away at it, the plat-form that made up the reaping floor disappearing into the sea. Above them, the Pyrean branches were moving more violently. Their sway was nearly a thrashing now, as if they could sense their impending freedom. That strange hum buzzed in Jeth's mind.

As Milton turned and headed for the door, Jeth opened his Reinette and leaned toward the beam.

Something struck him from behind. The canister went sailing to his left, out of his hands. Jeth spun around, ignor-ing the pain in his right side. Horror froze him in place as he stared at Saar. Blood was flowing freely from the man's mouth and from the wound in his chest. His gray uniform was stained brown, but he was still alive. Still fighting.

Hatred exploded inside Jeth, and he leaped at the man. Saar ducked to the right, just barely escaping Jeth's punch.

He wheezed from the effort, but it didn't stop him from throwing another punch. Jeth blocked it, then followed through with a left hook that connected with the old man's face.

Across the way, Jeth saw Milton standing in the doorway. "Go!" he shouted. "I've got this. Right behind you."

Milton hesitated a moment, then disappeared from view. Jeth stifled his relief, focusing on the fight. He needed to get this over with now. The Reinette was more powerful than his mother had anticipated. Jeth had a feeling the whole place would be going down in a matter of moments.

No sooner had he thought it than the floor beneath his feet gave way. He felt himself slip, sliding downward. Saar, a malevolent grin still on his face, looked down at him as he too lost his footing and they both fell into the writhing, chaotic ocean beneath.

Panic grabbed Jeth by the throat and squeezed. He couldn't breathe. He couldn't control his body. He didn't know which way was up or down. The Pyreans were churning the ocean around him, their departure and the destruction of the Hive whipping the water into a vicious whirlpool. It was sucking him down, batting him about like a cat with a toy.

This is it, he realized as his body struck something. Through blurred vision he saw that it was Saar. The man's mouth was open in a sneer, but the light in his eyes had gone out. He disappeared from view, falling deeper into the sea.

One of the Pyrean branches brushed past Jeth, tossing him about again. He tried to swim up, but it was no good. The turbulence was too strong. Already his lungs were screaming for oxygen. Soon he would open his mouth and inhale water, drowning in seconds. Black clouds started to fill his vision.

Help, he thought, his approaching death driving him to madness. There was no one to help him. No way out of this. And yet he thought it again, pleading it with all his mind and heart. *Help. I don't want to die.*

The black kept creeping in, his consciousness slipping.

But then bright, blinding light filled his vision. The light was something alive. It filled the entire ocean, wrapping over all of them, Jeth and the Pyreans both.

They're retreating, Jeth realized, understanding what he was seeing as if the Pyreans themselves were speaking to him. Maybe they were. *Sentient,* his mother had called them.

They were retreating back into metaspace, from where they had first come, set free from the beams of the Harvester that had held them here so long. The familiar sense of being unmade came over Jeth and he disappeared into metaspace with them. Away from the sea, away from First-Earth. Away to somewhere elsewhere.

He woke to the sound of leaves stirring. It was a strange sound, one he hadn't heard for so long that he almost didn't recognize it. He slowly opened his eyes. Tall trees unlike any he'd ever seen stretched far above him. They were moving, swaying back and forth but not from any wind. They looked completely alive, as if at any moment they might pull up their roots and march away like the ones in those old stories he used to know. Light poured down in between the trees from a sky as blue and glistening as sapphires.

Jeth pushed himself into a sitting position, his hands sinking into the cool, soft grass he'd been lying on. The blades were so pleasant against his skin that he ran his hands over the tops of them, petting it.

He looked around, taking in more of the strange landscape. Beneath the trees, near the earth, were hundreds upon thousands of different species of plants. Nearly all of them bore flowers with brightly colored petals in shades Jeth had never seen on any plant before.

Scattered among the plants and trees like a vast network of vines were Pyreans, easily recognizable by their luminescent glow.

Where am I? Jeth thought. He could guess the answer, but it seemed incredible. There was no way he could've traveled so far in a single metaspace jump, unless he hadn't traveled at all, merely passed into the dimension of metaspace.

A musical laughing voice filled his head. *We know no limitations.*

Not *a* voice, Jeth realized, but multiple voices. Millions of them. *The Pyreans.* Jeth drew a deep breath, marveling at how sweet the air tasted. It seemed to fill him up, making his body feel weightless. *Is this Empyria?*

Yes. More voices, more musical laughter. *Welcome, Jethro Seagrave. We thank you.*

Jeth sensed their gratitude. It filled him like light fills glass, both capturing the glow and letting it seep through, magnified. He suddenly wanted to dance and scream and run about like a small child. *You're welcome,* he thought, a grin breaking over his face. He thought he might never stop grinning.

We didn't mean to take you with us. We are sorry.

Sorry? Jeth laughed out loud. He stood up, taking another of those deep breaths. He thought he might make a career out of just breathing. *I never want to leave.*

We know. But you must.

Jeth frowned, remembering his mother's story. *Why?*

We want more of you. All who will come.

Jeth shook his head. *Why? We hurt you, almost killed you. It'll happen again.*

No, they said with absolute certainty. *The past will not repeat. We are stronger here. We will not be captured again. When we came for you the first time you were not ready. You had forgotten how to sense us. But some of you are ready now. Others will follow.*

At once images began to fill his head. He saw hundreds of faces, people of all colors and types from all the worlds. He saw them on spaceships or passing through metagates, and he understood that even dead, the harvested Pyreans had been watching humankind, waiting, evaluating. He saw faces of people like Lizzie, Marian, Sierra, even himself—people ready for the change the Pyreans offered.

How will I find these people? How will I bring them? Jeth said, overwhelmed by the prospect.

We will help you. We have all the time of the universe and infinite reach.

Impossibly, Jeth understood. These were beings of meta-space—they existed outside the dimension of time. And they could transport him anywhere without need of a spaceship.

We will help your race become greater than you are now. We will solve problems you never thought solvable.

Again, images filled his mind—this time, of the future as the Pyreans would make it. Jeth saw a new race of humans, ones evolved like Cora, all bearing the ability to perceive metaspace. The need for metatech would be no longer. Once humans were able to perceive this dimension, they could build new machines for metaspace travel, computers that could simulate the Pyreans' abilities. And in time, some humans would be able to move through metaspace on their own.

But what about right now? Jeth asked. *The metatech is dying. My kind won't survive long without the ability to travel through space. And all this will take time, time that matters to humans.*

Yes, we understand. But have no fear. Our dead will not disintegrate so quickly, not now that you have freed us. Your kind will continue on as they have been, long enough for us to bring about these changes. And now you must return and be the catalyst for this change as your mother was before you.

Jeth felt his heart breaking. He didn't think he could bear to leave this place. There was so much to see and explore. It was as if he'd been dead before and was now alive. He felt whole, complete, free. Gone was the hunger no food or drink or drug could satisfy. This was what he'd always wanted, always needed. He just never knew. Until now. How could he have ever doubted his mother? How could he have ever not trusted in these strange, comforting creatures whose presence seemed to fill his mind, not as an invasion but as a puzzle piece slipping into place, one he'd never before realized had been missing.

I can't go.

You must. But it will be for a short time. You will be back. This we know. And you won't be alone.

Alone. For the first time since his arrival—a time that might have been only minutes and yet seemed like years, Jeth thought about the others. About Lizzie and Sierra, Cora and Milton. They were waiting for him back on First-Earth. How long would they wait? How much time did they have before the ITA came in and captured them?

They will wait forever for you, the Pyreans said.

Jeth swallowed, knowing it was true. Then something new occurred to him. *Did you . . . did you keep me from killing my sister?*

No. The decision to save her was yours. We just lent you the strength to follow through. Your connection to her is very strong. We thrive in those connections.

Jeth wasn't sure what that meant, but it didn't matter. Gratitude filled him. It made the reality of leaving this place hurt even more, although he understood that he had to. But it would be a temporary exodus. No power in the universe would keep him from returning.

Okay, he thought. *Send me back.*

A bright light, an opening into metaspace, filled his vision, and he stepped into it, and through it, traveling millions of light years in a single moment.

He felt himself falling and then wetness swept over him. Salty water filled his mouth and stung his eyes. He was back in the wreckage of the Harvester, but the Pyreans were gone, vanished as if they had never been. Jeth kicked upward, breasting the surface. The Hive was still disintegrating around him. He had to hurry. Swimming as hard as he could, he headed for what remained of the platform, arriving just ahead of the final stages of the Reinettes' destruction.

He pulled himself out and ran. He ran as fast as he could, his breath coming in quick, hard pants. The air felt wrong here, too heavy. Too much effort. There were others running as well, ITA agents and soldiers. But they paid him no mind. They were as desperate for escape as he was.

Moments later Jeth arrived on the flight deck. He scanned the few remaining ships, and his heart leaped in his chest as he spotted *Polaris*. For the first time the sight didn't hurt him. He was glad that she so closely resembled his *Avalon*.

Jeth sprinted across the flight deck toward the open cargo bay. Sierra was waiting for him. He reached it a moment later, flinging himself inside.

"Jeth's on board," Sierra signaled through the comm. "Get us out of here."

CHAPTER 35

"ARE YOU SURE YOU WANT TO DO THIS?"

"ARE YOU SURE YOU WANT TO DO THIS?"

Jeth glanced up from the comm station where he was sitting to see Lizzie staring down at him, brow furrowed.

"Sure you don't want to take some time to think it over?" she pressed.

He froze, hand poised over the screen. Beneath his fingers, the command prompt read:

Are you sure you want to permanently delete all content on this data cell?

"I mean, we just escaped," Lizzie said. "We might still need the Aether Project to barter with later on, don't you think?"

They'd only made it through First-Earth's atmo and out of the region a few hours ago. It had been tricky, with all the incoming cruisers converging on the planet in a futile attempt to stop the destruction of the Hive, but they made it with the help of the cloak drive and some skilled piloting.

Jeth smiled. He understood her fear. He had felt the same for so very long. But not anymore. The truth was, he'd never been more sure of anything. "We won't need it where we're going."

Lizzie shook her head. They were alone on the bridge

of *Polaris* except for Sierra, who sat behind the pilot's seat. Aileen and the others had retreated to their cabins, seeing to personal needs or simply seeking solitude to recover from their harrowing ordeal. "I don't get it. We hardly seem better off now than we were before. Mom's gone, and so's *Avalon*. We've got nothing." Emotion shook her voice and Jeth regretted letting her be a part of this. He should've waited and told her later.

He reached over and took her hand, squeezing it. "It's going to be all right, Liz. We lost a lot, I know, but for the first time we can be sure of where we're going."

"Empyria," Lizzie said, skepticism in her voice.

"Empyria," Jeth repeated, absolutely certain. He hadn't told any of them about what had happened when he'd fallen into the ocean He wasn't entirely sure it had been real. It might've been a dream or vision, but he didn't think so. Not that it mattered. The outcome remained the same—he was determined to take them to Empyria. To fulfill his mother's last dying wish, the one he'd never intended to fulfill. Now, there was nothing else in the world but that.

"But why destroy the Aether Project?" Lizzie said. "It's still valuable."

"That's exactly why," Jeth said. "As long as this data crystal exists, it represents a danger to us and to the Pyreans. Destroying it is the one way to guarantee that never happens. Besides, I'm sure Mom would've wanted us to."

Jeth lowered his hand, selecting the yes button. The next moment it was over. All the data gone. A huge relief came over him. It would lessen the chance of anyone finding out about Cora, especially now as the ITA would begin its slow, inevitable fall. The predators would be moving in soon. Crime lords, Independent Planetary governments, and who knew what else, would converge on the ITA, taking it down, exploiting its secrets.

But they wouldn't get any from Jeth. Especially not the most important one—the pathway to Empyria. *Not until the Pyreans are ready, and only the chosen will be shown the way.*

Lizzie had said she was hours away from decoding the last of it.

"Well," Lizzie said, puffing out her cheeks. "That's that."

"Good riddance," Sierra said.

"Yes," Jeth said, standing up. "And no regrets." He stretched, raising his hands high above him. His back popped in several places and he breathed a sigh of pleasure. He'd just given away millions in potential profit—but he'd never felt better. Even his implant architecture wasn't bothering him. The desire for the implant was gone, erased perhaps, by this new focus, his desire to reach Empyria.

"Only one problem," Lizzie said, sitting down at the comm station. As if on cue, Viggo jumped up into her lap. The cat's presence on the ship was the only thing that had surprised Jeth when he arrived. It seemed Lizzie, against all better judgment, had taken the time to fetch the cat off the *Citation* where the ITA soldiers had left him. "How are we going to get to Empyria? This isn't our ship."

Jeth slid his tongue over his teeth. She wasn't wrong,

but for some reason he couldn't quite make himself worry too much about this detail. A couple of ideas were already bouncing around in his mind. Sooner or later one of them would form into a reasonable plan. "We're spaceship thieves, Liz. I'm sure we'll figure it out."

Someone coughed from behind them. "I might have a way for you to get there."

Lizzie, Jeth, and Sierra all turned toward the newcomer. Aileen smiled at them, the gesture strangely shy. Jeth felt an urge to tease her about it, but he refrained. She seemed too fragile at the moment. Although why she should be feeling that way given their escape, he didn't know.

"How's that?" Sierra asked, arching an eyebrow.

"I'll tell you when we reach Nuvali," Aileen said.

"Nuvali?" Lizzie gaped. "Why would we go back there?"

Aileen smiled. "Because it's the fastest way to get you a new ship."

Jeth opened his mouth to press her for more but then closed it again. He shrugged. "Nuvali sounds as good a destination as any." They weren't out of the ITA's reach yet, but Nuvali was still an Independent spaceport. And this wasn't *Avalon*. As far as Jeth knew, the ITA hadn't put out any Wanted bulletins for *Polaris* yet.

"You think so?" Sierra said, her voice quiet.

Jeth turned to look at her, realizing why the idea of returning there upset her. He nodded, then turned back to Aileen. "I'm not sure Nuvali is the best place for us. That's where Vince died."

"I know," Aileen said, her voice sincere. "But I have some friends in high places at Nuvali. Trust me. It'll be worth it."

Jeth pressed his lips together, thinking it over. He knew he probably shouldn't trust her. But for some reason everyone and everything looked different to him now. Fresh and new. Anything was possible. And this was her ship, like it or not. If Nuvali was where she wanted to make port, then so be it.

"All right," he said. "Nuvali it is."

They arrived a few days later, mooring at one of the overnight docks.

"I'll be back in an hour or so," Aileen announced to Jeth moments after they arrived. "With luck I'll bring back good news."

"With luck," Jeth said, trying to hide his growing skepticism. Sierra had been right—coming back here was painful. It made the loss seem nearer. Not just Vince, but Marian and *Avalon*, too. Even Dax. Jeth had no love for the man, but he'd grown to understand him a little these past few days. In many ways, Hammer had done to Dax what Saar had done to Jeth, forcing him to obey and to serve a man he hated, a monster in human flesh. It wasn't the implant that had changed Dax or Jeth. It was the Axis, and the very human tendency to want to exert power over others, those weaker and more vulnerable. The Pyreans were what made that power possible, but the human element of the Axis and the hierarchy was a perversion of what they were, not a reflection, as Jeth had once feared.

When faced with that power, Dax had given in to the temptation. Jeth would've too, if not for Sierra and his crew. His connection to his family had saved him. *We thrive in these connections,* the Pyreans had said. He was beginning to understand.

While Aileen was away, Jeth took the time to seek out Celeste and Shady. He found them in the common room, playing a video game once more. This time they both stopped as soon as he entered, gazing at him with guarded expressions.

"You left this on *Avalon*," Jeth said, reaching into his pocket. He withdrew the personal comm that he'd retrieved from a crevice in the hallway where he'd hurled it so many days ago. He tossed it to her.

Celeste caught it, surprise registering on her face. "What's this?"

"An apology."

Celeste examined the comm for a few seconds, then stood up and came over to him. She opened her arms as if to hug him, but then she punched him in the face instead. It wasn't hard, not much more than a tap.

He grinned. "You did that a lot harder the first time."

Celeste smirked. "I know. Consider it my apology." Her expression softened, and she pulled him into a hug. "I'm sorry, too."

Jeth nodded and hugged her back.

When they withdrew a few seconds later, Jeth turned his gaze to Shady. He rolled his eyes. "Don't you dare expect a hug from me."

Jeth shook his head. "Never. But are we good?"

Shady considered it a moment, scratching at the stubble on his face. "We're good. I did risk my life to save you, after all."

"So you did. Sorry I shot you with that stunner."

Shady shrugged. "We all go a little crazy from time to time." He returned his attention to the game in front of him.

Relieved at the sense of normalcy, Jeth left the two of them to their competition and headed up the ladder to the passenger deck. He found Sierra in the second cabin on the left. She was lying on the bed, staring up at the ceiling.

Jeth strode in and walked over to her. As she started to sit up, he bent down, cupping her face in her hands. Then before she could speak, he pressed his lips to hers. She resisted the kiss for a second, but only out of surprise. Then she gave in to it, kissing him deeper than she ever had before.

When Jeth pulled away a few moments later, Sierra stared up at him. "What was that for?"

Jeth grinned at the breathlessness in her voice. "For not killing me like you promised you would."

Sierra's mouth twisted into a reluctant smile. "Well, thank you for not doing something really stupid."

Jeth laughed. Then he stood up and went to the door.

"Leaving already?" Sierra said, cocking an eyebrow at him.

In answer, Jeth locked the door. Then he turned and came back to the bed, sliding in beside her. "I'm never leaving," he said, pulling her into his arms. "I might be inclined to do something stupid at any time."

"Good," Sierra said. "Because I'll always be here to stop you." She said it like a challenge, and he answered it with another kiss. And he didn't stop for a long time.

Aileen returned a few hours later carrying two objects with her onto *Polaris*. One was a box tucked under her arm. The other was a data crystal.

"Will you ask everyone to meet me in the common room?" Aileen asked him when he cornered her on the ladder up from the cargo bay. He'd been sitting on the bridge for the last twenty minutes, monitoring for her return.

"Okay," he said, uncertain, but he resisted the urge to press. Such patience was an alien behavior for him, but he kind of liked it.

Minutes later, Jeth settled down in one of the chairs in the common room. He winced at how uncomfortable it was. He scanned the stark room. Before he said good-bye to Aileen, he decided to give her a few tips on personal comfort. A nice armchair wouldn't hurt anybody, and the walls could use a personal touch here and there.

"Um, thanks for coming," Aileen said, glancing nervously about the room. She stood in front of the gaming table, the box and the data crystal she'd brought back with her lying on top of it. "I don't really have a speech or anything. So here you go." She picked up the box and carried it over to Sierra, who was sitting in the chair next to Jeth.

Sierra eyed the box like a snake that might bite her.

"Go on," Aileen prodded. "Open it."

Hesitating a moment longer, Sierra took the box and popped off the lid. A murmur went through the room as she pulled out the object inside. Cylindrical in shape, it was made of glass with decorative frosting around the top and bottom. An ashy substance filled the center of it, completely sealed within the glass.

"Is that a—" Lizzie began.

"Funeral urn," Aileen finished for her. "Yes it is."

Sierra sucked in a breath, tears stinging her eyes. "Vince?"

Aileen nodded. "I just barely got there in time. It's standard spaceport policy. Any unclaimed remains are held for a period of time before being disposed of permanently."

"Thank you," Sierra said, hugging the urn to her chest. Across from her, Celeste repeated the words of gratitude.

"It's the least I could do," Aileen said. She offered Jeth a sad smile. "I'm just sorry that I couldn't do the same for your mother."

Jeth swallowed. He was sorry about that, too, but the victory they'd managed eased the loss. He'd met all of his mother's dying wishes, except for the last one—that he travel to Empyria on his own.

I will, Mom, he thought. *Soon.* This spaceport would be ripe with a likely ship to steal.

"But to make up for it a little bit," Aileen said, "I've decided to give you this as well." She picked up the data crystal and held it out to him.

It was Jeth's turn to stare like he'd been presented with a snake. Unlike Sierra, he didn't accept it. "What is it?"

Aileen shook it at him. "It's papers, you moron."

"Papers?"

Aileen rolled her eyes. "You know, papers, like ownership papers, the title and stuff."

"Title? To what?"

"*Polaris,*" Aileen said.

"Uh, come again?" Shady broke in.

Aileen glanced over her shoulder at him. "I'm giving Jeth *Polaris*, as in the ship we're all sitting in right now." She eyed the group at large. "Honestly, have you all gone stupid or something?"

"Or something," Flynn said, leaning back in his chair.

"Why are you doing this?" Jeth said, even as his hands closed over the data crystal. He couldn't believe it. This had to be some cruel prank.

Aileen shrugged. "You need a ship, and I think she likes you better than me anyhow." Aileen cleared her throat, apparently embarrassed by the disbelief that had met her gesture. She put her hands on her hips. "Look, it's really not that big a deal, you know. I have another ship docked right here at Nuvali."

Shady whistled. "Damn, must be nice to be so rich."

"It's not everything," Aileen muttered, a dark look passing over her face before the usual smirk took its place. "But it doesn't hurt."

Jeth stood up and, against his better judgment, pulled her into a hug and planted a kiss on the top of her head. "Thank you," he said.

She pulled out of the hug, her face pink. "You're welcome. But don't go all sissy on me."

Lizzie started to clap and the rest joined in.

Afterward, they celebrated. Flynn prepared an elaborate

meal. They laughed and told jokes, danced and played games. They all enjoyed themselves and the lives they were still living despite the odds they had faced.

All except for Aileen, Jeth noticed. Not long after the meal ended, she disappeared from the common room. Jeth waited a few minutes to see if she would return. When she didn't, he went to find her.

She was on the bridge, looking out at the stars beyond the spaceport. She glanced over her shoulder as he stepped in.

"Thanks again," Jeth said, coming to stand beside her.

She nodded. "I owed you. Now we're square."

Jeth frowned down at her, his growing suspicions of the last few hours confirmed. Softening his voice, he said, "The medicine didn't work, did it?"

"Nope," Aileen said, her glib attitude at odds with the sorrow in her voice. "It seems I risked your lives and got your mother killed for nothing."

Jeth waited a moment before responding. He didn't want to add to her pain. "How do you know it failed?"

Aileen glanced up at him, tears now standing in her eyes. "They ran some tests at the Hive. But I know they weren't lying. The necrosis hasn't stopped."

Jeth sighed, wishing he had a way to comfort her. "Where will you go now? What will you do?"

"I don't know." She paused, wiping away an escaped tear. "Probably the same thing I always do. Find something new and fun to occupy my time."

Jeth touched her shoulder. "You could come with us, you know. To Empyria."

Aileen frowned as if he'd asked her to marry him. "Why would I want to go there?"

Jeth considered the question for a few moments. Then deciding that it wouldn't hurt anything, he told her about what happened when he fell into the water. He couldn't tell if she believed his story or not, but at least she listened.

When he finished, she turned her gaze back to the window. A couple of minutes passed in silence.

Then she slowly shook her head. "Thanks for the invite, but I think I'll have to pass." She exhaled. "Who's to say these Pyreans will welcome me the way they welcome you? I'm a clone, after all." She flashed a smile but there was no humor in it.

"I don't think what you are will matter one bit," Jeth said, the words coming with no hesitation. "Just because you're a clone doesn't mean you're not human."

"Maybe," Aileen said. "But a place as wonderful as the one you're describing might be awfully boring. And you know how I feel about danger, Peacock."

Jeth sighed. "That I do, Trouble. But if you change your mind, send me a message. If I can, I'll come back to get you."

They said good-bye the following morning. Aileen and Remi had packed up all their personal belongings—enough to fill two duffel bags only—and then everyone gathered in the cargo bay to see them off.

They exchanged a couple of hugs and some last-minute teasing, and then Aileen and Remi departed, disappearing into the station toward whatever ship she had waiting for them.

Jeth headed for the bridge as soon as they were gone. The others soon joined him. Jeth settled down in the pilot's chair while Sierra took copilot. Lizzie assumed her usual place behind the comm and Celeste took nav. Milton, Shady, and Flynn found places at the rest of the stations.

No one spoke as the locks holding *Polaris* in place released and Jeth piloted them forward. No ships intercepted them on the way out. Not a single spaceport security patrol or an ITA cruiser or anything else noticed their passing. They might as well have been cloaked.

"That was weird," Shady said as they passed through the spaceport's patrolled zone and into open space.

"You mean not getting shot at?" said Flynn.

"Yeah, that."

"Makes for a nice change if you ask me," Lizzie said, kicking back in the chair. She raised her feet and dropped them on top of the panel.

"Hey," Jeth said, scowling at her over his shoulder. "Treat my ship with some respect, please."

Lizzie snickered. "I'm not hurting anything." As if to emphasize her point, Viggo appeared, jumping on top of the console and walking across the screen. Lizzie leaned forward and picked him up, setting him on her lap. "Besides," she added, patting the dashboard, "she's a tough old girl."

"Young girl, you mean," Flynn said, sounding disappointed that they'd ended up with a ship in such good shape. Jeth wanted to reassure him that something would break sooner or later, but he didn't know if that was the truth.

They were headed to Empyria. *Polaris* might become nothing but a lawn ornament once they got there. In his heart, he hoped not. He was happy to be going there, but a part of him still wanted to fly free and explore the wonders the universe held for him.

Maybe you will, a voice whispered in his mind.

Yes, maybe he would. Maybe he would do anything.

"Will you rechristen her *Avalon II*?" Milton asked as he lit his pipe.

Jeth shook his head. "There'll never be another *Avalon*. And I kind of like *Polaris*. I looked up the definition. It means the North Star."

"A star to guide us by," Milton said. "Just like those ancient First-Earth seafarers."

"And explorers," Sierra added. "They say those old sailors would never be lost so long as they could find the North Star."

Jeth nodded, liking the story. They would never be lost— never be *trapped*—again. They were finally free. *And on our way home.* He leaned forward and engaged the metadrive. The bright light of metaspace enveloped them and they disappeared into the jump.

ACKNOWLEDGMENTS

WHEN YOU REACH THE END OF A BOOK, ESPECIALLY THE book at the end of a series, it feels a bit like making a meta-space jump—traveling thousands of light years in a single second. It's a process made possible by the dozens of "Pyre-ans" with whom I share a connection.

First, thank you to the readers. You give the books purpose and life. I am eternally grateful to each one of you.

As always, thanks to God and his Son.

Thank you to my editor, Jordan Brown. Without your guidance, inspiration, and generosity this book would not have been possible.

To my agent, Suzie Townsend, who always knows the right thing to say and when to say it.

To the folks at New Leaf Literary & Media for all you do, which is far more than I can ever know, I'm sure.

To the team at Balzer + Bray: Alessandra Balzer, Donna Bray, Viana Siniscalchi, Alison Donalty, Ray Shappell, Renée Cafiero, Caroline Sun, and Emilie Polster for your support of Jeth and his crew.

To my critique partners and first readers: Lori M. Lee, Amanda & Jay Sharritt, and Cat York. When the writing is hard, you make it easier. And better. So much better.

Love and gratitude to my family. Especially to my

husband, Adam, and my two kids, who tolerate the craziness of deadlines and who so happily bear the sacrifices involved in letting me explore this writing dream.

And finally to C. S. Lewis, whose stories and teachings inspired the heart and soul of this book.

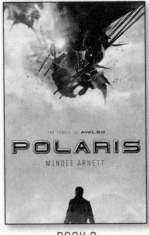